HERS NO LONGER

Caroline went out in the fields to find her son.

"What do you want, Mother? Is anything wrong at the house?"

"Wrong!" she exclaimed. "Yes, there is something wrong. My daughter-in-law has seen fit to relieve me of my authority. Peregrine, who is mistress here?"

That was the most difficult question she could have asked him, the one Peregrine had hoped never to have to answer.

"Well, Father left no will, so the farm must be mine. And since Charity is my wife, then she must be mistress."

Caroline was so shocked that she could not speak ...

Bantam Books by Phyllis Hastings

ALL EARTH TO LOVE
DAY OF THE DANCING SUN

DAY
OF THE
DANCING SUN

Phyllis Hastings

BANTAM BOOKS
TORONTO · NEW YORK · LONDON

DAY OF THE DANCING SUN
A Bantam Book

PRINTING HISTORY
Originally published in Great Britain by Corgi Books, 1971
Bantam edition / July 1976

ISBN 0–553–02352–7

PRINTED IN THE UNITED STATES OF AMERICA

Part One

CHAPTER ONE

HOLY SUNDAY

There was a saying that the sun danced in the sky on the morning of Easter Day, but it was not easy to find anyone who had seen it. In Sussex, where the people were not as silly as some thought them to be, they had an answer to this. They said they had not seen the sun dance because the Devil always put a hill in the way to hide it, and that might be no exaggeration, for everyone knew the Devil was lodged in Sussex, on account of having got stuck in the mud there.

Young Lancelot Dyke proved the saying to be true, to his own satisfaction, for early on Holy Sunday, Peregrine's wedding day, he ran down across the meadows to where the river flowed through the valley bottom, and there, reflected in the sparkling water, was a sun which glittered and twinkled and leaped from side to side.

The man they called John Allen found him standing on the bank of the Rother, lost in a dream.

"Hi, Lancelot!" he shouted, before he had come near him, and the noise sent a reed-bunting exploding and stammering from a riverside bush. "Hi, Lancelot! Is it not time you were putting on your gaudy clothes?"

"I am watching the sun-dance."

"There is better than that to watch today."

Lancelot turned his head away, to hide the sulky,

rebellious expression on his face. "I prefer to watch this."

"And be late for your father's wedding? Why, most young 'uns like nothing better than a wedding, with the food and the dancing to follow."

Lancelot turned his back on the river and walked towards the man who had come to fetch him. In Lancelot's eyes he was mature, almost middle-aged, for he was thirty-eight, but he was still handsome, and strong, though not so strong and heavily-built as Peregrine.

"Do *you* like weddings?" Lancelot asked.

"Certainly I do."

"I would like them better if they could be celebrated without women. Women get in the way. Don't laugh at me, John! And don't call me young 'un. I am thirteen, almost a man."

Sylvanus sighed. It was at times like this that he realized it had grown no easier to deny his son. He wanted to catch him up now, and hold him close, and tell him, "I am your father. I betrayed my brother, and for this, and other things, I am an outcast in my own home." But silence bound him like the web of some monstrous spider, and he could not escape, though the silence was a pain which gnawed at his heart.

Lancelot, watching shrewdly, saw the pain on Sylvanus's face, and itched with twin desires—to assuage that pain, and to satisfy his curiosity. John was his friend, had been for as long as he could remember, from the time when Lancelot's legs were so short and unsteady that he would fall over a hillock of horsedung. John was there eternally, like the sky and the earth and God Almighty, but he was more temperate than the sky, more lively than the earth, and more approachable than God.

"You don't approve of this wedding, do you?" Lancelot asked.

"It's not for me to approve or disapprove. I'm—"

"—only a servant," Lancelot finished for him. "But you are not. No servant is treated as you are. No servant has such an elegant bedchamber. No servant talks to the family as you do. No servant is allowed to beat the master's son."

"You deserved it," Sylvanus said, briefly.

"Perhaps I did," Lancelot allowed, feeling generous. "But I am older now, and I understand things. There is a mystery about you."

"You should respect other folks' mysteries."

"Will you ever tell me?"

"One day, perhaps."

"Grandmama gets confused when I ask her things."

"She is growing old."

"Not as old as that, and she is only confused about certain things. She talks of my uncle Sylvanus, and when I ask where he is, she says he is dead, but she does not speak of him as we speak of dead people. You have violet eyes, John, like mine."

"Why not? Eyes must be some color."

"But violet is rare. Grandmama told me that of all our family only poor Grandpapa and Uncle Sylvanus and I have violet eyes."

"A mean trick on the part of Providence. They should have gone to the young ladies, who need such aids to beauty. And now, come you must, or we'll both go to your father's wedding smelling of the cowyard."

They went back up the meadow, more slowly than Lancelot had come down. Then he had had wings to his feet; now they were transformed into millstones.

"John, I do not want another mother."

His assumed manliness had fallen from him, and he sounded so like a frightened child that, without realizing what he was doing, Sylvanus took his hand. "What a foolish idea! Of course you will not have another mother. A man has but one mother. Even a king cannot claim more."

"Did you know my mother?"

"Yes." The word was out before Sylvanus even thought about it. Perhaps he should have said "No," but he knew he could not have forced his tongue to pronounce the lie.

"Was she beautiful?"

Sylvanus thought of her poor face ruined by the smallpox, and would not insult his son by offering him anything but the truth. "She was beautiful in the only way that matters, from the inside outwards."

"Then my father should not want anyone else."

"A man's needs are various, and your father is still young."

"He is older than you."

Sylvanus smiled. "A year, no more."

"She is eighteen, only five years older than I am."

"Call her by name."

"What can I call her? I won't say mother."

"Consult her wishes in this matter."

They had reached the top of the meadow. Lancelot turned and looked back. His grandmother told him his grandfather had planted those trees, on the near side of the river. When first they came to the farm, she said, the river had wound like a silver snake along the valley, but the trees had been placed to bind the soil and conserve the moisture, and now the snake was dressed in foliage, and only in winter could you catch the gleam of his skin. But those water meadows were as rich as any in Sussex, and though it was only Easter the cattle were already feeding off the lush grass, and giving milk that, even unseparated, slid down your throat like cream.

Sylvanus followed Lancelot's eyes. Under a bare ash-tree the celandines looked as if someone had thrown down a handful of sovereigns.

"Beautiful, isn't it?"

"Father has the farm," Lancelot said, violently. "He shouldn't need another woman as well. He should be thinking of Mother. Mother is in Heaven, and we are told to lay up treasure in Heaven."

"Why, so we do," Sylvanus said, softly, as if talking to himself. "Everything in which I have taken pleasure lays up treasure in Heaven for me."

Lancelot stared at him in horror. "Pleasure! Father has no right to have pleasure with that woman. It is wicked! He mustn't put her where Mother belongs. He can't!" Then, for fear John Allen would see the tears in his eyes, he turned and ran.

At the farm-house there was such a to-do that Lancelot felt as if he were invisible. They would not have noticed, he thought, if he had arrived with horns on his head and a forked tail thrashing behind him, so certainly they would not be aware of a slight redness about the eyes.

Days ago the house had been scrubbed and polished from top to bottom, the fire put out in the hall, the hearth cleaned and decorated with flowers, and all the floors strewn with herbs and rushes. It was an old-fashioned notion, only seen in the country nowadays, for townspeople were civilized and put carpets on their floors. But Caroline was still head of the household, as a grand-parent should be, and she intended to stick to the rustic life she had embraced, and which had brought her enough of happiness to veil her sorrows. She had dressed early for the wedding and now stood like Admiral Nelson on his deck, as much in command of her fleet as the admiral was in command of his. She issued orders, or merely pointed, and servants rushed hither and thither with jugs and bowls and platters and dishes containing mountains and rivers of food and drink. There were turkeys and geese and hams and wild pigeons, to say nothing of a large quantity of mackerel, soles and herrings which had been brought from Brighton in vans drawn by four horses, for speediness and freshness. Of animal flesh there was a whole roast ox and two grass-lambs, and the puddings and pastries represented almost every recipe Caroline had read or heard of or invented.

She was finely dressed for a countrywoman, wearing a striped crape petticoat, and over it a gauze dress in pale green, bright as the new leaves that were unfolding. She wore a cap, as befitted her age, but even to that she had lent a rakish air by affixing to it a plume of feathers.

Marthanna, arriving in good time in case help should be required, exclaimed at the sight of her. "Mother! I do declare I mistook you for the bride."

"You are mocking me," Caroline said, plaintively,

"but I see no reason why I should creep about in black, like an old hag, striving to escape notice."

Marthanna kissed her. "Why, no more do I. You are still a handsome woman. How is Father?"

"As he always is." Caroline spoke sharply. "How could he be any different? Every time you visit us you ask the same question. He lies like a log, as he has done these many years."

"It is sad he cannot attend Peregrine's wedding."

"That is the least of his sadness."

It always made Caroline angry to talk of Will. She tried to feel pity, but invariably the anger broke through. It was anger against her children for not understanding how badly fate had treated her in this matter, and anger against fate, and anger even against Will for allowing himself to be robbed of his health and strength. Her children were sorry for their father, but they should have been sorry for her, she felt. Was she not an unwidowed widow, scarcely past the prime of life, and was not that misfortune enough for a woman?

"Have Rebecca and Richard come?"

"Yes, last evening, with all seven children. Think of it! Seven! It is a blessing I have one daughter who is fertile."

"Are you reproaching me, Mother?"

"Of course not! But if you had married a lusty young farmer instead of a degenerate Frenchman—"

"Mother! How dare you speak so! He saved your son's life."

"Ah! My Sylvanus! Why must we still keep up the pretense that he is a servant?"

"Not for long now. They speak of peace with France, and then Sylvanus cannot be punished as a deserter, nor Gerrance as an alien."

"It is good to have my family around me. If only there were not that emptiness! If little Hal—"

"The time to weep is during the ceremony, Mother, not now."

Caroline took out a fine cambric handkerchief and wiped her eyes. "That is true. I must attend to the servants or they'll make a sorry mess of setting the

tables. Will you go to Rebecca? She is in her room, with
the children. Pretty creatures they are, with delightful
manners, but that is only to be expected. Richard has
such gentlemanly breeding that he is bound to rear his
children gently."

"I will go when I have seen Father."

"What good will that do?" Caroline asked, petulant-
ly. "You talk to him by the hour, but he does not hear
a word."

"We do not know that he cannot hear. I watch his
eyes and it seems to me that he understands what I say.
We do not want him to feel we have abandoned him.
Who will remain with him while we are at church?"

"Most of the servants will be here."

"Perhaps I should stay."

"Don't be foolish, Marthanna! You weave fantasies
round your father, but I know him best, and I know he
is not aware of the season or the time of day or the face
that bends over him. We are shadows to him, and he is
locked in the prison of his body. There! Now you have
made me cry again."

Marthanna spent only a few minutes with her father,
and when she left him her heart was heavy. Not one
word had he spoken since stricken with the apoplexy,
but his eyes had moved, and sometimes they had questioned, sometimes pleaded. Now, however, they were
half-closed, and there was a film over them. Life, it
seemed, was retreating.

When she went downstairs the company was assembled and the carriages waiting outside the doors.
She greeted her sister and her sister's family, but a true
interchange of news would have to wait. This was an
occasion for which they had put on formality with their
formal clothes, and they were almost strangers to each
other. Lancelot, washed and combed and feeling quite
unlike himself, eyed his cousins with suspicion. Most of
them were pale and slim, favoring their father, and he
felt they were not true Dykes, as he was. "Seven Balls!"
he muttered to himself, scornfully. "Seven little Balls!"

That was when someone asked where Peregrine was,
and it appeared no one had seen him for a while. Ser-

vants were sent to search for him in his room and other parts of the house, but without success.

"Fools!" Caroline raged. "You would not see a bear if it bit you. Look again. Bridegrooms do not disappear."

"Perhaps he is afeared," Rebecca suggested, "I have not yet seen the bride. Mayhap she is a monster, a creature of terror."

"Rubbish!" exclaimed her mother. "She is a girl of eighteen years. *She* is the one who should be afeared, not a man of experience like Peregrine."

The search went on, and everyone became disturbed, for it was a serious matter to lose a bridegroom, and a shaming one for the bride to be kept waiting at the church.

Sylvanus said nothing, but presently he went out unobserved and crossed the yard to the stables. He was gone some fifteen minutes, and when he returned he said, "I can put your minds at rest. Peregrine is with Hasty Pun."

"And who or what is Hasty Pun?" Rebecca demanded.

"A mare," Sylvanus told her. "She is in the midst of foaling and is having a difficult time."

Rebecca looked shocked. "He would be late for his wedding, for the sake of a horse?"

"Not a horse, a mare. And not an ordinary mare at that. She is a grand-daughter of Quibbler."

Rebecca sniffed. "Am I expected to be impressed?"

"You might be, if you knew something about horses. Quibbler has rarely been equalled for strength as well as speed. Fourteen years ago he ran twenty-three miles round the course at Newmarket in just over fifty-seven minutes."

"Well, if I were a bride to be jilted for a horse I would expect it to be a flying horse, at the very least."

"He will not be long," Sylvanus assured them. "The head groom is with him, and they are momentarily expecting results. I offered to take Peregrine's place, but he would not trust me."

Rebecca was about to make a sarcastic rejoinder,

but Richard pressed her arm and whispered that she must remember country ways were not the same as town ways.

When Peregrine appeared his hair was dishevelled and his new cloth coat spotted, but no one commented on this, for everyone was too anxious to be off, and finally they entered the carriages and drove to Mayfield.

Saint Dunstan's was a handsome stone church built on the ruins of an earlier one destroyed by fire. It stood a little back from the village street, as though watching over the inhabitants, and its bells were now ringing joyfully, but their peals were almost drowned by other, less joyful sounds. In the porch was a concourse of people, all talking at once, some sitting on the porch seats, which were practically new, the churchwardens having paid five pounds, sixteen shillings and twopence for them, only twenty-three years previously. Other persons were milling around, and the center of them was a young woman who was alternately wringing her hands and stamping her feet, as if two emotions fought an indecisive battle within her.

Peregrine went to her, penitent but not unduly so.

"Ah, Charity! Have I kept you waiting long?"

She turned away from him. "So long that I was nigh on returning home. How could you shame me so?"

"It is no shame," Peregrine assured her. "Those who know me can vouch for me, that I would not break my word."

"My friends from Tunbridge Wells do not know you. They see only a man who has no care to be prompt for his wedding."

"A farmer is never his own master. But, come, the guests are impatient, and the parson's face grows longer and longer. Remember, we are not the only couple to be married on Holy Sunday."

Charity Mewett stared at him in astonishment. It was on the tip of her tongue to say, "It is for you to remember," but she restrained herself. It would not do to sound like a scold, and, besides, Peregrine was so much older than herself that she must respect him. Only gradually and with patience would she win him to better ways, and better ways, she was convinced, he needed. She had heard of his deceased wife, who had been his first cousin. This cousin had had an outlandish name, Philadelphia, and she had come from London, where, Charity understood, there was a great deal more sin than salvation. But she would not be discouraged. A widower was never easy, and was a challenge to a virtuous and dedicated girl. And not only was Peregrine a challenge, thought Charity, as she went up the aisle on her father's arm, but his whole family stood in need of conversion. They were not true country folk, in the manner of the word. Oh, yes, Peregrine's father had been a laborer, she had been told, but his mother had been a lady who had run away with the stable-boy. Rumor even whispered Gretna Green. Charity frowned. Was Gretna Green legal? God forbid that Peregrine should have been born out of wedlock!

Charity passed Caroline. Just look at her, with feathers in her cap! And the men of the family, as bright as kingfishers, when it would have been more to their credit had they worn the traditional smock. Charity herself would not have dreamed of putting on satin or lace. She chose a calamanco dress, because it would be useful later, and because Easter was so often a chilly season.

Rebececa nudged Marthanna who was beside her in the pew. "Did you ever see such a country mouse? That dowdy dress! And a posy of violets and primroses! Think you she will suit Peregrine?"

"Who knows what holds two people together?" Marthanna whispered. "Take Gerrance and myself—"

"Or Richard and me. There is as much difference in our ages as between Peregrine and—what is her name?"

"Charity."

Rebecca raised her eyebrows and turned down her mouth. "Charity! Let us hope she has it, and does not merely set herself up as the greatest of these. But the time has come for me to pray, instead of carping."

Caroline admired Charity's bouquet, for it reminded her of the wild violets she had found in her father's garden, and loved so much more than the planted flowers. That had been her nature always, to embrace the wild and spontaneous, the weeds and the stable-boy, the rough earth rather than the smooth turf. Well, here she was, attending another wedding, and soon it would be the turn of her grand-children. That was how life went on, and you praised God it did. If only poor Will—But she tried not to think of him. Will now was not Will then. It was Will then she had loved, and Will now spoilt her picture of him. Her children could not understand this, and thought her hardhearted, whereas in truth she had a heart like a bed of down. Why, if it were possible she would be willing to stand herself in place of that plain young woman. She felt herself about to giggle, and hastily covered her face with her hand-kerchief. Now they would think she was weeping, and that would be correct, because she was losing a son. But, dang it, she had no intention of losing Pere-grine, or Lancelot either. If she could not manage that chit of a girl—

The ceremony seemed long to Lancelot, and to the Ball children, but it was over at last, and they could stretch stiff legs and scratch itching buttocks. Lancelot beckoned to his cousins to follow him, and they were first out of the church. He led them to a large tub which was filled with wood anemones and violets and primroses and daffodils and celandines.

"They are beautiful," said Alice Ball, "but what are they for?"

Lancelot looked at her pityingly, triumphant that he should know more than these town fashion-plates. "They are for strewing in front of the bride and groom. Have you never been to a wedding?"

"Yes, but we do not have flowers like these. There are not many flowers growing in London."

"They will tread on them and crush them," said Rosemary.

"What does it matter? There are plenty more."

"I would like to save some for myself. May I?"

Lancelot shrugged his shoulders. "If you wish." It was like a girl, he thought, to be timid and begrudge the grand gesture. Himself, he would spread them so thickly that the churchyard path would be a bed of flowers and it would be like walking across a meadow. Joyfully he flung them, and the Ball boys followed suit, trying to out-throw him. This was fun, leading to the still greater fun of stuffing themselves with those mouth-watering foods they had already seen and smelled.

Back to Hastingford they all drove, the horses making excellent speed, as if they too anticipated a banquet in the stables. Late for his wedding Peregrine might have been, but he was not tardy in taking his bride home and leading his guests to the feast. There were hours ahead of them for eating and drinking, for speech-making and pledging each other in wine and ale and cider, for dancing to the fiddler Caroline had engaged, for laughing and forgetting there was anything in the world but laughter.

Only Marthanna remembered her father. She went to him and found that while they had been in church he had slipped away. Peaceful he looked, and strangely innocent, like the simple boy he had always been. Marthanna kissed him and crept quietly from his room. He would have been distressed, she knew, if she had permitted his death to spoil his son's wedding-feast.

CHAPTER TWO

"His corpes was with funerall pompe conveyed to the church and there solemnly entered, nothing omitted which necessitie or custom could claime: a sermon, a banquet and like observations."
Tragique History of the faire Valeria of London, 1598

Caroline lay on her bed, weeping, while downstairs the remains of the wedding-feast still littered the tables. Meat congealed, cups were over-turned, and spilt ale and wine had dried to blots. The servants did not even begin to clear the fragments and wash the dishes, for the master of the house was dead, and the mistress laid low, and so they had every excuse for congregating in the kitchens and shedding a tear, if they could manage to squeeze one. They were excited by the interruption of their dull routine, and it made no difference that the master, from their point of view, had been as good as dead for years. They chose to look upon it as a tragedy, and so a tragedy it was. Just imagine! A wedding and a death on the same day. It was not every family could boast of the twinning of two such events. They must mean something, those happenings, and maybe they boded no good for the new marriage. Oh, yes, happen on the same day they did, though Mistress Marthanna held back the news until the following morning. Some of the servants considered this a kindness to the newly wed couple, but others professed themselves shocked. Death was not something you hid until a convenient time. It took

15

precedence over everything, even the consummation of a marriage. But, then, one must expect Mistress Marthanna to develop strange ways, her having a foreign husband. Why, they'd heard tell that things done on the other side of the Channel were past believing.

Caroline did not think of the wedding, or the coming funeral, or the state of the house. She lay and wept until her goose-down pillow was sodden, and she wished she could die, for suddenly something had ended which had seemed eternal.

She was not grieving for poor old Will lying stiff and cold on his bed. She was grieving for young Will with his simple passion and his passionate simplicity. While old Will still breathed, young Will had somehow not quite gone, and the fact that she had come to care nothing for a paralyzed, bed-ridden man did not alter it. She should feel guilty, she knew. She should have spent more time with her husband, should have talked to the living corpse who could not answer her. But he had been unimportant, except as the shell which housed the last remnants of her youth and Will's youth.

Now she must confess she was old, but inside her was still the changeless, unrepentant Caroline, laughing and mocking at time. She suspected it was so with everyone, that every old woman who dithered over her knitting needles had imprisoned within her grotesque body a young and lovely girl; that every old man who tottered around on a stick was the same swift boy who could cross the village green in seven-league cricket boots and triumphantly catch a ball or a thunderbolt. But they did not dare to own it, those who wore the disguise of old age. They believed the evidence of their bodies, and the lying mirrors of their neighbors' eyes, and they were afraid of being foolish.

Marthanna came and spoke to her. "Don't cry, Mother! Please don't cry! You will make yourself ill."

"Would that matter?" Caroline demanded. "I am old. No one cares what happens to me."

"Now, Mother, you are being foolish. We all care. But you are doing no good, hugging this sorrow. It was a blessing for Father, that he went. It was a release."

Caroline reared up in bed. "How do you know?" she asked, scornfully. "You can say such things, but you have not died. You have not experienced the release. You have not had the blessing."

Marthanna said no more. Her mother was dramatizing the loss, she thought, for it could be no true loss to her. Marthanna had watched her mother visiting her father many times during the past few years, had heard the perfunctory, conventional words, had seen the smoothing of the pillow and the hasty kiss which betrayed its own repugnance. Everything else for her father had been done by servants, and Marthanna blamed and despised her mother for this. She did not realize that Caroline had been clinging desperately to the remains of her love, and that Will's stroke, coming at the end of the considerable wear and tear of their marriage, was more difficult to bear than his death. If he could have spoken, or shown that he recognized her, Caroline would have nursed him, but his silence merely angered her. It was as if he had withdrawn from her deliberately, and so she went away and remembered Will Dyke, not the man on the bed who bore his name.

Marthanna went towards the door, but she could not resist loosing an arrow on her father's account. "I believe," she said, "it is for yourself that you grieve."

If she expected her mother to be wounded she was disappointed. "Who ever grieved in any other way?" Caroline inquired, in quiet contempt.

Peregrine heard the news when he rose in the morning, which was early. It would have been excusable for him to lie abed, following his nuptials, but this being his second marriage he did not consider it fitting. It was all very well for a young man to wallow in passion and sentiment, but for one nearing forty it looked foolish. First love had its own magic, but the actual taking of a woman was no novelty to him, and the deflowering of a virgin was, he considered, an overrated pleasure. Charity behaved as he had expected she would. She cried out with pain, not with rapture, and though practice would no doubt improve her, she was at present as cold and stiff as the fishes brought from Brighton.

So he was not sorry to rise at dawn, remembering himself a farmer first and a husband second.

His father's death was no more than a long-awaited event. With his mind he was regretful, as at any passing, but his heart was not touched, and this applied to the other children, except perhaps Marthanna. To the running of the farm it made not the slightest difference whether Will lay on his bed or in his grave. Peregrine was master, and it was long since his authority had been questioned.

Marthanna went to tell Charity, and found her already up and in her working dress.

"It is sad it should have happened so soon after your wedding. I wish it could have been at any other time."

"Not *after*," Charity corrected her. "He must have died while we were at the church."

"Why, yes, I suppose so."

"You should have announced it immediately."

"And spoil the feast? Oh, no, Charity! My father would not have wanted that. A girl's wedding-day is something sacred, which cannot be repeated."

Charity sniffed. "There is nothing sacred about eating and drinking too much. We could have dispensed with those celebrations."

"But the neighbors expected to drink your health and wish you well, as the labourers did also. As for my sister and her family, we see them so rarely that it is in itself a festive occasion when they visit us."

"Will they be departing soon?"

"Not until after the funeral, of course."

"Yes. Well, I must go down and take up my duties."

"Your duties? Yes, but——" Marthanna hesitated, wondering how not to offend this self-confident young woman. "——but you are still a bride. You must make holiday."

"No, I must take up my position as lady of the house."

Marthanna was shocked, and blurted out, "My mother is still lady of the house."

Charity shook her head. "Not now that she is a widow. Peregrine is master, is he not?"

"Why, yes."

"Then as his wife I must be mistress. I am sure your mother will be pleased to be relieved of some of her tasks."

Marthanna was not equally sure, but she said no more and resolved to instruct Peregrine to warn his new wife against too much enthusiasm for her position.

Will was laid in Mayfield churchyard, and the contrast between this journey and the previous one made them all doubly sad. Flowers there were in plenty, but they lay pure and unsullied over an old body instead of being crushed beneath the feet of the young. Marthanna almost cried out as the coffin was lowered. They shouldn't put him there, especially at this time of the year, for he would not be able to bear it, alone in the dark, with all the sweetness outside, the pear-blossom unspotted as a virgin, and everything full of juice—the grass, the clouds, and the daffodils that bled over your fingers when you snapped the stalk. The parson might talk of Heaven, but surely Heaven was no place for the man who had been a stable-boy, and who preferred the scent of horse-dung to that of the most immaculate lily.

The funeral dinner quite put Peregrine's wedding feast in the shade, for Hastingford was crowded to the doors, and extra trestles were set up in every available space, to provide tables for the mourners.

Charity had expressed the hope that the food left over from the wedding would be sufficient for their guests, but Marthanna, knowing better, had spoken privately to the servants and instructed them to prepare a quantity of pies, and boil hams and dress capons and geese ready for roasting.

"I would not presume to usurp the position of your mistress," she said, "but there is much confusion at present, and I look to see a large company assembled for my father's burial."

"Our mistress?" asked one of the older servants, in pretended innocence. "And which would that be?"

Marthanna found this difficult to answer, and said, at last, "You have an old mistress and a young mistress."

The servant winked. "Her that is old is not so old as to be silly, and two mistresses is worse than none."

Marthanna agreed heartily with this, and prayed there would not be trouble in the house. She sought out Peregrine and asked him to kill a sheep for roasting. "I fear there will be mouths enough to dispose of an ox."

Peregrine nodded. "It is too late for an ox. The meat would be over-fresh."

"Yes." Marthanna hesitated. "Brother, I shall be returning home after the funeral, but I am near enough if you need me."

Peregrine laughed. "Thank you, but why should I need you? I reckon I've women enough, with a wife and a mother."

"And so you have. Are you happy, Peregrine?"

"That's woman's talk. Happiness! They are always on about happiness, which is beyond anyone's power to describe. I'm a lucky man, for I've a good farm that leaves me no time to brood on things like happiness, and I've a new young wife who's strong and hearty and like to provide me with a family. What more could I ask?"

"You asked more, and had more, with Philadelphia."

A shadow crossed Peregrine's face. "No sense in bringing up the past," he said, harshly. "I was young then, and a young man is like a sapling bending with every wind of chance."

"But be faithful to the past. Be good to Mother."

"Haven't I always been a dutiful son?"

"Yes, but don't let her feel you've put her away for a wife. And be good to Lancelot."

"Be good, be good!" he mocked. "You're mighty tiffy today. What do you look for from me? Lancelot is my son."

"You'll have other sons. That is all I meant. Then there's Sylvanus. I think the time is coming when he should take his rightful place as your brother."

"Why, so do I. We have kept him as a servant only for his own protection."

"It may not be necessary much longer. There is talk of peace with France, and peace brings amnesties. Sylvanus will no longer be a deserter, and Gerrance need not fear to own himself a Frenchman."

Peregrine looked alarmed. "Don't say he'll wish to return to France!" Suddenly it had struck him that, however boldly he might talk, he could not bear the thought of losing Marthanna. It was not so much that she was his favorite sister—though she was—as that she was the strongest link in the family, the one who held them together, who seemed to care equally for all of them, who could solve their problems with sound sense and reason, who held the family sacred, and joined it with Hastingford and with Sussex, so that each enhanced the other, and all became the symbol of home. He thought, not for the first time, it was a pity she had not been born a boy, for she might well have been the best farmer of the lot.

Marthanna smiled. "If you mean would he return to live in France—why, you'd be wrong. He would never do that. His heart is at Wivelridge, as mine is. But if it should be possible to visit France, and if Gerrance's health permitted, then we might go. He has an estate there which he could sell. He often talks of it, says he detests living on the charity of the Dykes. He says it jokingly, of course."

"I should hope so!" Peregrine exclaimed. "He knows he has the right to a share of everything we possess. It's not only that he saved Sylvanus's life, and married my sister—"

"Peregrine, dear, I understand your feelings, and I will not take any more of your time. You will not forget the sheep, will you?"

"How could I?" he asked, innocently. "That was what you came to tell me, wasn't it?"

She laughed and left him. Peregrine might appear somewhat stolid, but he was no fool. Though he might lack Sylvanus's sensitivity and subtlety, his directness and simplicity gave him an understanding of people. It was good, she thought, that he was the head of the family, and she hoped Charity would be worthy of him.

Charity stared with amazement, almost with horror, as the crowds of people arrived. Many who had not gone to the church went directly to Hastingford. There were the neighboring farmers, and those from distances who had met Will at market and drunk with him in the inns of Lewes and Heathfield and Mayfield and of every East Sussex village where one could buy and sell stock and then quench one's thirst and seal the bargain in liquor. There were laborers who had worked for and with him, and smugglers who had smuggled with him —but these last wore no badge of their calling. Most of these people had not seen Will since he was afflicted with his stroke, and might be thought to have forgotten him, but death invested him with dignity and also re- minded his acquaintances of the precariousness of their own position. It was just as well to be reminded occa- sionally that humanity was frail, and to say a prayer for an old friend and hope others would do no less for oneself.

"We must have the whole county on our doorstep," Charity said, with distaste. "No doubt they have come for the free food and drink."

"That is not kind," Caroline told her, sharply. "These men do not have to resort to such means to appease their hunger. They have come out of respect and love for my husband."

"Did so many love him?"

"Indeed, yes!" Caroline had forgotten their early struggles, the hard-heartedness of those surrounding them, the times when they had seemed utterly friend- less. This was the day of Will's triumph, even though he was not there to enjoy it. "He was a wonderful man. You will never meet one like him." Her eyes shone. She was proud, remembering Will in his strength. She could think of him that way, now that the poor wreck upstairs had departed.

"Isn't Peregrine to be compared with him?" Charity asked, with a touch of spite. "Is Peregrine inferior?"

"Peregrine is my son," Caroline said, with dignity, "and the son of his father, but a woman must put her husband first."

Charity tossed her head. "I don't agree with you. A woman's children are her blood relations, and her husband is not."

It irked Caroline to let this chit of a girl have the last word, but at that moment she simply could not think of a reply.

On the following morning Richard Ball departed with Rebecca and their family, but before he did so Caroline managed to have a few words with him. She could accept him now as her son-in-law, and chose to forget the time when she had imagined he harbored tender feelings for herself. He looked older, she thought, and worn with the cares of working as a clerk in the City of London. It could not be easy for a man of his age to provide for seven children, especially when he must buy every crumb of food they ate, and every stick of wood and lump of coal for warmth and cooking. That it might be even harder for Rebecca did not occur to Caroline. She loved her daughters dutifully, but, as always, her heart was drawn to male creatures.

"It will be quiet when you have all gone," she said. "I like a house ringing with voices and laughter, but the family has shrunk sadly. How can it ever be the same, without Will?"

Richard smiled secretly. Dear Caroline! She never changed. Unconquerable she was, living in her own reality, seeing her own side of the face of truth. But for her sake it was necessary to shake her out of her dreams. "You will not miss Will," he told her. "You have had no communication with him for years. He died, for you, when he had his stroke."

Caroline looked surprised. "That was not what I meant. I was thinking of the time before."

"Then do not. At least, not too much. It is not for you to dwell in the past. You are strong and intelligent. You have much before you."

"Yes." She drew herself up. "Oh, yes, Richard! You put things so well. I have Hastingford, and I have years ahead. There is much to do."

"You will see another generation born here."

A shadow crossed her face. "What is your opinion of Charity?"

"A worthy young woman, but I scarcely know her."

"I doubt if Peregrine has chosen wisely. There is a certain narrowness about her, a puritanism."

"A man's mother cannot choose for him."

Caroline sighed, then shook her head, as if ridding herself of unpleasant thoughts. "And you, Richard? Is all well with you?"

"Yes. I have the dearest wife, and good children. If it were not for the expense—"

"But you have four sons, and they are less costly than daughters."

"Scarcely so, in town. I have to set them up in professions. It is not like having a farm, where each growing boy saves the hire of a man."

"That is true. Remember, therefore, if one of them should turn towards country, or two, or all, there will always be a place for them here."

"Kind, generous Caroline! I will not forget. But it is possible Charity might not approve."

"Charity?" Caroline demanded. "Dang me! What has Charity to do with it?"

Richard did not tell her, but Caroline soon found out. The Balls left, and then Marthanna and her husband, by which time Caroline was in tears.

"Silly Mother!" Marthanna scolded her, laughing. "One would think I was going to the Continent of America, instead of just across the valley."

"The house is empty," Caroline complained, wiping her eyes.

"You have Lancelot."

"Ah! He is a big boy now, continually out working with the men. A woman loses her babies almost before she has time to learn how they look. Lancelot comes in to eat and sleep, and that is about all."

"Well, there are the servants."

"Oh, they don't count. They are merely a constant anxiety, having to be watched to make sure they work. Turn your head for five seconds and they are lolling about like lords and ladies, to say nothing to helping themselves to the provisions."

"Anyway, there is Charity now."

"Her!" Caroline sniffed.

Marthanna hesitated. She longed to say, "Do not underestimate your new daughter-in-law," but what would be gained by such a warning? So she just kissed her mother and went to find Gerrance.

In the hard early days of her marriage Caroline had learned to rise at dawn, like a true countrywoman, and now that she was prosperous and life easier she saw no reason to change her habits. Servants, like most of nature's creatures, rose with the sun, and they respected a mistress who did likewise. But on the first morning after the departure of the guests Caroline had not finished her toilet when there came a knock at the door.

It was Charity, fully dressed and even less attractive than she had looked at her wedding.

Caroline smiled blandly. "Good morning, my dear!" She thought, "Heavens! Does she imagine a farmer's wife must be less beautiful than his milk-cows? Is there pollution in the air that she must tuck every lock of hair under that most unbecoming cap? And that bodice, buttoned up to a collar so tight that it is like to cut her throat! At least Peregrine will be under no temptation to fondle her breasts during the day. Let us hope she takes it off at night."

Aloud, she said, "There was no need for you to rise so early. You are still a bride."

Charity did not trouble to answer this patently frivolous remark. She simply asked—no, demanded, "Mother-in-law, will you please give me the keys from your chatelaine."

CHAPTER THREE

Trewly some men there be
That lyve alwayes in great horroure,
And say it goth by destenye:
To hang or wed, both hath one houre,
And whether it be, I am well sure,
Hangynge is better of the twayne,
Sooner done, and shorter payne.
> "The Schole Howse." 1542

Caroline stared at Charity. "My keys? and what would you want with my keys?"

"Why, to examine the closets and discover what requires replenishing. It is the season for making syrups and juleps and electuaries."

"That I know well enough," Caroline said, sharply. "You do not need to tell me what month it is, or what day of the week, or what hour of the day."

"So I must not waste time." Charity spoke smoothly, and as she spoke she moved forward, also smoothly, like a cat, Caroline thought, smoothly and swiftly, giving Caroline no chance to guess her intention. On a small table, near to the window, lay Caroline's chatelaine. Will had given it to her, many years before, bought it with the money from an unexpectedly successful sale of cattle. It was silver, worked in delicate filigree patterns, and with quaint figures. But it was not only for its beauty that Caroline treasured it. It was an essential part of her apparel, as useful as her own right hand, for it clasped her waist, and from it dangled chains at the end of which were her scissors,

26

her thimble, her seal, a buttonhook, a small knife, a vinaigrette, and her keys. It seemed to fly of its own accord into Charity's hands.

"Put that down, girl!" Caroline cried.

"I am not harming it."

"You have no right to lay a finger on it."

"Only the keys." Dexterously she unhooked them, talking the while. "I must get me wood sorrel and distil water from it, lest we should have ulcers in the mouth, and lesser celandine, to cure the piles, and wallflowers for freeing the liver from obstructions, and periwinkle—"

"I grieve that you should suffer so many ills, being young," Caroline said, sarcastically.

Charity chose to ignore the tone of voice. "Not for myself alone, but for the whole family I am responsible." She held out the deprived chatelaine, which Caroline took but also made to snatch at the keys. For a few moments the two women stood clasped, eye to eye, and then Charity pushed Caroline away, quite gently. "It would not look well if we should resort to fighting, mother-in-law."

Caroline waited until the sound of Charity's footsteps had faded, then, fuming, went to find Peregrine. He was sowing barley in Broad Field, and was not in the best of tempers, for he considered the field should have been seeded a month earlier, and the fact that it had been hindered by the attentions he paid Charity, and by the preparations for his wedding, did nothing to appease him. He would have been happier could he have found someone other than himself to blame. Therefore he did not endure the interruption graciously, despite his mother's privileged position.

"What do you want? Is anything wrong at the house?"

Caroline was breathless. She had hurried, and she was discovering, as she frequently did, that age carried its penalties. But, as usual, she would quickly forget the discovery, and would again and again be surprised at her lost youth.

"Wrong!" she exclaimed. "Yes, there is something wrong. What kind of a woman have you married?"

Peregrine groaned. "You leave your duties on account of some domestic trouble? I declare, there's no peace when a man is surrounded by stocky females."

"And who added to the females at Hastingford?" Caroline demanded. "But it is about my duties I come, for it seems I no longer have duties. My daughter-in-law has seen fit to take them from me."

Peregrine wiped his forehead. This kind of talk made him sweat more than the seeding did. "She means well, Mother, and is anxious to relieve you of work."

"To relieve me of authority is more like it. She has taken the keys to my cupboards and closets. Peregrine, who is mistress here?"

This was the most difficult question she could have asked him, the one he had hoped never to have to answer. Deep within him was the habit of respect for his mother, yet a wife had the power to transform wedded bliss into wedded misery, and already he could see that Charity did not possess the sweetness and tolerance of his first wife.

"Well?" Caroline urged, impatient. "Who is mistress?"

"Reckon that takes a fairish bit of thinking about," Peregrine said. "Now when Father was alive——"

"It was my farm, paid for with my money."

"Maybe, but according to the law——"

"If there is any law which says this is not my farm," Caroline interrupted, fiercely, "I shall tear it to pieces."

"Folk like us can't go changing the law."

"Folk like us can do anything, if we set our minds to it."

"Well, how I see it is like this. Father left no will——"

"How could he, poor soul, and he not able to say a word or lift a finger?"

"——so the farm must be mine. And since Charity is my wife, then she must be the mistress."

Caroline was so shocked that for a moment or two she could not speak. Her heart hammered in her breast, and she had to fight to get her breath. At last, with less than her usual vigor, she managed to ask, "You would put that—that creature before me?"

Peregrine sighed. "Mother, it is not that way at all. Take the noble families—"

"Noble? *My* family was noble, or as near noble as makes little difference."

"When the head of the house dies, his son inherits, and the son's wife becomes the mistress. The father's widow is then the dowager, and goes to live in another house."

"Are you telling me—"

"Of course I wouldn't turn you out," Peregrine said, quickly. "You are welcome to remain at Hastingford, but naturally Charity will expect to take over the running of the house."

"*I*—am—welcome—to remain—at——Hastingford." Caroline spoke slowly, with equal emphasis on each word. "I am welcome in my own house, that I bought and beautified and loved and cherished. Who are you? Are you my son that I bore? What have you become? Your father and I fought for you and starved for you. We worked when we could have played, were dirty when we longed to be clean, risked our lives. You are the eldest. You must remember when your father took to smuggling."

"Yes. Mother, I do understand—"

"Oh, I am not here to beg for your gratitude or your mercy."

"I am only telling you what is the law."

"I am not interested in your laws. I am interested in justice and honesty, but I see none here."

She turned, and left him feeling guilty and remorseful, for she went slowly and draggingly, and he thought it was the first time he had noticed that she had the walk of an old woman. But he did not see her when she reached the house, for the slow, hopeless steps gradually quickened, and her head lifted, and she put her shoulders back. So Peregrine had failed her. But it was not the first time she had leaned on a staff which had snapped beneath her weight. Those who betray you, she reflected, are the ones who underrate your strength. Did Peregrine really imagine that she would surrender without a fight? Did he think so highly of that mealy-mouthed Sunday-saint that he believed she could vanquish his mother? Before, she would have tolerated the girl, attempted to like her if not to love her. But now Hastingford was involved, and that meant total warfare. "You are welcome to remain at Hastingford." Ha! By the time she entered the door from the yard Caroline's cheeks were pink, and she strode with the determination of a young woman.

Yet she learned that a war is not won by a single battle, but must build up slowly over a space of time, with a gathering of the forces and a husbanding of the strength. At first it seemed that in Peregrine's eyes Charity could do little wrong, and this made Caroline's position the more hazardous, since he was not blinded by infatuation, but assessed his wife with the eyes of maturity.

"She is unaccountable clever for her age," he said, "and like to save me a mint of money."

Caroline, to whom this remark was addressed, did not reply. It was easy enough to save money, she thought, bitterly, if you gave the family bacon and cabbage every day, and used skim milk for the household cheese, making that hard, unappetizing stuff they called Skim Dick, and for breakfast provided Hopping John, which was no more than skim milk poured on bread; and used tallow candles with a rush wick, at which even the servants sniffed, dubbing them "fried straws," and which gave so miserable a light that there was little to do after dark but doze by the fire. Ever since they had come to Hastingford and a modicum of prosperity Caroline had prided herself on their good living. The laborers had eaten as the family did, and were not stinted. Now Caroline felt shamed that her daughter-in-law should lower the standard of the house by her petty economies.

But Peregrine was not heard to complain until Charity gave him speedwell tea, when he demanded, "What is this decoction?"

She was about to reply, but Peregrine went on, "No, don't tell me it is tea, for I shan't believe you."

Charity was angry that Peregrine should find fault with anything she did, and doubly so that he should criticize her in front of the family, but, with her, anger ran cold, not hot, and she spoke more slowly, thus being accorded, and according herself, the virtues of tolerance and long-suffering.

"It is more wholesome than that foreign stuff," she told him, "which is little better than malt liquor, for it excites the system. Speedwell is a good herb, and opens all obstructions."

"Well, I've something better to do than spend the morning having my bowels opened. You do what you like with yours."

"Peregrine! How can you talk so? The drinking of tea is a bad habit, and people are so simple they do not realize how often there are ash, elder or sloe leaves mixed with it. I declare I have no liking to pay tax on herbs which I can gather free. Indeed, I do not care to buy goods on which there is an excise tax."

"Then you should have gone smuggling with my father."

"That is no subject for joking."

"And I am not joking."

Charity quickly began to talk of other things. Old Mr. Dyke was dead, and one could not speak ill of him, so it was better to pretend one did not know he had once gone in for smuggling, for certainly one would be compelled to speak ill of *that*. She was convinced Peregrine was a good man. Had she not been, she would not have married him. But there was a certain moral laxity in the family. In Caroline's closets she had discovered cowslip and primrose washes for the face, little pots of lip salve and such frivolities, of which she swiftly disposed. Worse still, there were brandies of many flavors—cherry, raspberry, apricot and peach, among others—which she took away and destroyed, not even preserving the bottles, for fear some trace of the spirituous liquor might remain.

Also there was, she considered, a sad lack of discipline at Hastingford. Caroline might grumble about the servants, but she did little to restrain them. They were far too happy to be conscientious, and, until Charity put an end to it, they actually went about their work singing. It was the same with Lancelot, whose freedom was such that it made Charity shudder. He appeared to come and go as he pleased, talked to his father as one man to another, and was on terms altogether too familiar with the worker John Allen. Charity resolved to instill some decorum into the boy at the first opportunity.

This came one morning at breakfast. Lancelot had overslept somewhat, and when he descended the stairs the other men had already left the house.

Lancelot looked at his plate. "Oh, swap-my-bob! Hopping John again!"

"Mind your words!" Charity snapped. "Or you'll get nothing."

"Nothing would be better than this." Suddenly he laughed. "Did you hear what I said? Nothing would be better than this. That's a saying with a double meaning. But this is a melancholy mean breakfast for a man."

"You are not a man. You are a little boy."

"I am not. I am thirteen, and I do a man's work."

"Do not contradict me!"

"It would not be so bad if it had some broth poured over it. Otherwise give me honest bread."

"You will eat that or nothing."

"Oh, don't be swolk, Charity!"

"What did you call me?"

"Charity, of course. It's your name."

"How dare you speak to me that way! You are an unmannerly young dog, but I will teach you respect."

"What would you have me call you?"

"Mother."

"No!" Lancelot shook his head decidedly. "My mother is dead, and they tell me she is in Heaven. But wherever she is, she is my mother, and I will have no other. Besides, you are only a girl, five years older than I am."

Charity lifted her arm to strike him, then thought better of it. Disciplined he should be, but she had no desire to anger Peregrine or drive him to taking the boy's part. Lancelot must be made to feel less important, for less important he would surely be when her own children were born.

"Go to your room!" she commanded.

He stared at her. Was she making fun of him? "To my room? Reckon you're mazed, forgetting the time of day. I must off to work."

"To your room, where I shall lock you until you behave properly."

He sprang to his feet. "You cannot treat me like a child. I shall tell my father."

She smiled, slowly, mockingly. "*I* shall tell your father, and it will be the worse for you if you disobey me."

How stupid she was, he thought. As if his father— And then he wondered whether she was stupid, after all. It was a strange thing, this marrying of men and women, and his father had been different when he went a-courting, had washed in a number of unnecessary places, and had brushed his hair until it lay as smooth and flat as a freshly-curried horse's coat. It was just possible his father would believe what this woman told him, and there was no knowing what she *would* tell him. The realization was as bitter in his mouth as an astringent potion.

He swallowed. "I will do as you command—" He hesitated, then added, wryly, "—madam."

Confiding in his grandmother, Lancelot found her a staunch ally. "She forced me to stay in my room all day, and Father was angry, but when I told him it was her fault, he was more angry still, and said I must have done something bad, or my step-mother would not have punished me. It is most unfair."

Caroline ran her fingers through his hair. What a handsome boy he was! This was what her darling Hal would have been, if he had lived. Most of the Dykes were thick-set, portraying Will's peasant blood, but Lancelot bore the more aristocratic Gildridge blood, except for the rare violet of his grandfather's eyes.

"You must be patient," Caroline advised.

"What is the use of that?" Lancelot demanded. "My step-mother is with us for ever. She will set herself against us, ordering us to do this and that, making our lives a burden. Perhaps it would be better if I should go away."

Caroline was alarmed. She clasped Lancelot to her. "Do not say that! Never ever consider such a plan. You must stay, whatever happens. Hastingford is your home, and one day you will possess it. I bought it that my family might have it as an inheritance through many generations, many centuries. Cling to it, my little man."

He wriggled out of her embrace, for she was nearly suffocating him. "I want to, Grandmother, but I have no desire to cling to Charity."

"She is of no account. Ignore her."

"Yet she has pushed you aside and taken your place," Lancelot said, shrewdly.

"Because I am a widow and an old woman. You are a man, and the heir to the farm."

"She'll have children, Father's children," Lancelot muttered, jealously. "Already her belly swells."

"But you are the first-born. If she should have a dozen children you are above them."

"Am I?" Suddenly he felt more cheerful. His grandmother was clever. She must be right, because she knew many things country people did not know. When she was young she had lived at Blackheath, which was very near to London. She had told him stories of those times, and as a little boy he had found them fascinating, especially those about her brother Leighton, who had been a dandy and spent all night playing cards and drinking inordinate amounts of wine, and had dressed in velvet coats and satin breeches instead of cotton round-frocks and gaiters and chummy hats. Sometimes life on a farm seemed extremely dull, but he realized, sensibly, that it was all he was fitted for.

"What shall I call her?" he asked.

"Who," inquired Caroline, whose thoughts had been wandering.

"Charity. She tells me to say 'Mother', but I will not, and she objects that I should address her by her name."

"Step-mother is the correct title. Besides," Caroline added, craftily, "it will remind her that she is not your father's first wife, and that may teach her a little modesty."

Lancelot laughed. "Oh, Grandmother, you are a cunning lady. Step-mother I will say, though it is a mighty mouthful. I must tell John. He will find it a good joke."

"John?"

"Yes. John Allen."

What was the matter with her, Lancelot wondered, that she did not recognize the names of her own workers? Was she become so old that she was losing her memory?

But Caroline was being tempted by an imp of mischief, and was failing to resist the temptation. Why should she not tell the boy, she demanded of her conscience. He was growing up, and he was one of the family. Why should he not know?

"Would it please you to be let into a secret, my little man?"

"Oh, yes, Grandmother!"

"You must not reveal it to anyone, and, in particular, not to Charity."

"If I told, it wouldn't be a secret. Anyway, I don't tell my step-mother anything of importance."

Again she hugged him. "You are grandmother's dearest boy." And almost my only ally, she thought, sadly. "Well, it is this. John Allen is not John Allen. He is your Uncle Sylvanus."

Lancelot frowned. "I was not aware my Uncle Sylvanus was alive."

"Yes, he is, though it was more than his life was worth to say so. Let me tell you a tale, a true tale. It is about a young naval officer and a mutiny for which he might have been held responsible, and a French prisoner who saved his life. The Frenchman is your Uncle Gerrance."

The tale took some time in the telling, but Lancelot listened entranced. When it was finished, his face was serious. "Then they are both deserters. Would they not be in trouble, if they were caught?"

"Your Aunt Marthanna thinks not, as soon as we are at peace with France. But you will not betray them, will you, Lancelot?"

"Never!" he declared, stoutly. "I would rather die. If the soldiers questioned me, I would not speak a word, even though they tortured me. Thank you for the secret, Grandmother. I shall love John—my Uncle Sylvanus—more than ever." Lancelot's eyes glowed. He had a feeling of power, now that he held in his hands the safety of two noble men. "I always knew in my heart that John was no servant," he said. "He has the air of a prince. Oh, how I hope the peace comes soon!"

But though the negotiations between England and the French, the Dutch and the Spanish went on through the winter of eighteen-hundred-and-one, it was not until March of the following year that the Peace of Amiens was signed.

During that time Charity had borne a son and was pregnant again. But these events did not disturb Caroline half as much as one which occurred soon after the peace celebrations had finished. Marthanna came to her one day and announced that she and Gerrance would be leaving for France.

CHAPTER FOUR

Where, and O where, does this little Boney dwell?
His birthplace is in Corsica, but France he loves so
    well;
But it's O the poor French, how they crouch beneath
    his spell.
Yet still he boldly brags with a consequence full
    cramm'd,
On England's happy island his legions he will land;
But it's O in my heart if he does may I be damned.
           Old song to be sung to the tune of
              The Blue Bells of Scotland

Marthanna's departure left a surprising emptiness at Hastingford, and caused Caroline to realize, for the first time in her life, the value of a daughter. Always, before, her sons had taken primary place, but now she saw how much she had relied on Marthanna, in joy, in sorrow, and in the petty irritations of everyday life.

"She was a tower of strength," she complained, to Peregrine, "a tower of strength. How I miss her! The place is not the same. Even the servants do not behave so well."

"They were not the concern of Marthanna," said Peregrine, a little sharply, for he felt this to be a slight on Charity.

"Everything was the concern of Marthanna," Caroline assured him. "It is the first time she has ever been away from home."

"Oh, nonsense, Mother! I be main sorry she's gone, but she's no longer a little girl. Since she's been over

37

to Wivelridge there's been days on end you never saw hoof nor hide of her."

"But I knew she was there," Caroline persisted, "and now I don't know where she is, or if she's safe."

"She'll be safe," Peregrine said, to comfort her. "We're all fine and friendly with France now. There's a new French Ambassador in London, and I've heard tell as they cheered him till they was hoarse, and drew his carriage round the streets in triumph. No, you don't need to fret yourself. Those bad old fearful days are over."

Charity was not so reassuring. It was her nature to look on the dark side of things, but Caroline considered she was being purposely spiteful.

"I hope you are not expecting to see them back," she told her mother-in-law.

"Not see them back? Why, they'll be here almost before we can notice they have gone. Nothing would keep Marthanna from Hastingford."

"A French husband would."

Caroline's heart sank, but she would not let Charity see she was upset. There was a pride in her which could not acknowledge that Charity had the power to hurt her.

"They have gone to settle Gerrance's estate, that is all. In France, I believe, he is a wealthy man."

"Then in France they'll stay. Oh, I've no doubt of that. Every man craves for his homeland, and Gerrance would be a fool to return to this place, where he's a foreigner, a nobody."

"What of Marthanna?"

"She will do as her husband wishes," Charity said, primly. "Isn't that the duty of a wife, to obey her husband?" She paused, and threw Caroline a bright, suspicious glance. "At least, that's the duty of a real woman, though there's some that would think to usurp a man's place."

Caroline moved away, for she could not trust herself to say more. It was how most conversations ended between them, with Charity having a sly dig and Caroline restraining the temptation to precipitate an open quarrel. She had ceased to complain to her son, for it did her no good, and only troubled Peregrine. In any case, Peregrine would not understand, for the enmity between Charity and herself was woman's business, waged with a disdainful look here and a wounding word there. She must simply bite her tongue and endure being relegated to an inferior position, no longer mistress of her farm, or even of her own kitchen and stillroom. It was hard to bear, and even harder for a woman of her masterful disposition. Sometimes she was so angry that the bile would rise to her mouth, and she would long to strike the smug, censorious face of her son's wife.

It would not have been so bad, she thought, if Peregrine had married one of the local farmer's daughters, a girl reared in the same manner as her own had been. But Charity was prudish, pious and puritanical. She had named her first son Stand Fast, and the new baby, a girl, had been baptized Meek. Caroline suspected Charity's parents of being Quakers, though Charity had not owned to it, and she felt bound to speak of the matter to Peregrine.

"I reckon, my son, that your wife is a Quaker."

Peregrine shrugged his shoulders. "What of it?"

"What of it?" Caroline was shocked. "They are a peculiar people, that's what of it."

"Charity is not peculiar. She goes to church, and she has had the children christened."

"But she does not take Holy Communion."

"That is her affair. Mother, why must you be so old-fashioned? Would you burn her, as the papists burnt the martyrs in Lewes and Mayfield? We are living in modern times and are become more tolerant."

"There is a perversity about my children," Caroline grumbled. "One marries a Frenchman and the other a Quakeress."

"It'd be a melancholy dull world if everybody was the same, and you've no reason to call Charity over because of the way she was brought up. It's little disadvantage these days to be a Quaker, unless you join the militia or serve on a jury or pay tithes, and as Charity is unlikely to do any of these things, let her be."

"Such outlandish names for the children!"

Peregrine looked a little shame-faced. "I'm not wondrous taken with them myself, but if it pleases Charity I won't thwart her."

"No, you'd best not," Caroline agreed, in mock innocence, "else she'd give you the length of her tongue."

Peregrine pretended not to hear her last remark. He had enough on his mind with the running of the farm. Certainly things were better than they had been in his father's time, and he looked back almost with horror on the first bungling efforts to stock and till Hastingford. Though he had been only a lad in those days he had realized that his father might have been a good servant but was a poor specimen of a master. Now the farm ran consistently on his own unchanging policy. New ideas of course appeared, with Mr. Arthur Young, Secretary to the Board of Agriculture, hailed as a veritable prophet, and farmers actually going so far as to read his books—at least, those who could read. But Peregrine was cautious and saw no reason to change his methods. What had worked for thirty years could as well work for another thirty, and the farmers had enough to contend with in fighting wind, tempest, drought and other acts of God, to say nothing of murrain, abortion, mildew, smut and various pestilences surely sent by the Devil. However, he was thankful to be where he was and who he was, for from snatches of talk he heard at market it appeared the country was in a sorry state. No one believed the peace with France would last. Napoleon, they said, was using the cessation of hostilities merely as an interim in which to prepare for a still more violent attack on Europe, and of all Europe, it seemed, his covetous gaze was fixed on Britain.

Peregrine did not waste his time or his money on drinking in public-houses; too often he had watched his father doing that, and had seen how little it profited him. It was all very well for farmers to talk of sealing a bargain over a mug of ale. Such practice was an excuse, Peregrine considered, and he prided himself on striking bargains without recourse to such habits. Less popular it might make him; he did not care. And though on account of his lack of sociability he might lose many a morsel of news, he heard as much as he wished to. Conditions were bad in the large towns, with food becoming scarce and dear. Bread was not allowed to be sold until at least twenty-four hours after it was baked, and eventually it was rationed to one quartern loaf a week for each person. Meat was exceptionally dear, beef being one and sixpence a pound, and mutton one and threepence. There were food riots in London and other parts, and crime flourished.

The state of affairs would not have been so deplorable if provisions could have been more easily transported from the agricultural districts, but the condition of the roads made their conveyance slow and hazardous, especially in winter. Sussex, being no great distance from London, could have supplied large quantities of corn, meat and vegetables, but its roads were still among the worst in the kingdom. So most of the farmers were content to feed themselves and their stock, and buy and sell amongst each other. These expedients did not make their fortunes, but at least they kept their stomachs filled, and the stomachs of their families and workers.

Taxes of course fell heavily on all, even country dwellers, and Peregrine was liable for window tax, game duty, the duty on dogs, property tax, hearth tax, and great and small tithes. Being a farmer, he was exempt from a number of levies, including the toll on servants, horses and carts, but for his mother's curricle he had to pay five pounds, eighteen shillings a year.

Charity complained bitterly about this. "Does she imagine she is a great lady, to keep a carriage of her own? And she scarcely uses it. She scarcely moves away from the house and the fields and the garden."

"It is only a two-wheeled vehicle, which saves me money," Peregrine excused it, "and it gives her pleasure to possess it."

"It is a wicked extravagance."

"My father bought it for her, years ago. I cannot rob her of everything. She has little enough. And I manage to evade paying for the horse, by using it for working."

"Little enough?" Charity sneered. "She has more than she has any right to, in her position. She should be glad of her bed and board, an old woman who has almost lived out her days. And such airs she gives herself! The servants take more notice of her than they do of me. It is not right, Peregrine. You should tell her."

"Oh, adone do!" Peregrine said, wearily. "I've had enough of your bumbling."

Charity clasped her hands and raised her eyes to heaven. "There, now! There's a hard thing to say of a wife who thinks of nothing but doing her duty. I wonder I ever married you, you a middle-aged man with millstones ready to hang around my neck. It's my own home and children I was wanting, but I got more than my share, with your mother that's like a bee in my hair. And as for that boy of yours, him that has no respect nor reverence for his betters—"

But Peregrine was gone, away out to the sweeter atmosphere of the barn and the cow-yard.

Lancelot found his step-mother a sore trial, for she used every method she knew to make him feel unwanted and a hindrance, yet there was little he could complain of to Peregrine, and even if there had been, he reflected, sadly, there was small chance that his father would have listened. Charity's ways were too subtle for the honest, unsophisticated mind of a boy. Slowly, drop by drop, her poison fell, and Lancelot came to look upon himself as a clumsy, ignorant hanger-on, merely tolerated by his father and his Uncle Sylvanus. Because of this his work suffered, and Peregrine had to find fault with him, which only ratified, Lancelot thought, the criticisms Charity had made. There was no one on the farm of his own age, and he took to going off alone, across fields, through woods, mile upon mile, long, lonely walks which made him the more melancholy.

"I don't know what has come over young Lancelot,"

Peregrine complained, to his mother. "He's as dumb as a bell without a clapper, and as obstinate as a mule. He's never around when I want him, and when he's around he takes no joy in his work."

"You must make allowances," Caroline said, "He's neither boy nor man. It's a difficult age."

"Well, I disremember that I was full of whims and fancies."

"You did not have a step-mother, or a half-brother and half-sister that only have to bawl in order to be given the moon and the stars and the sun itself."

"Oh, a pest on you, Mother! You are as bad as he is. And I think the less of him for being jealous of those he should love."

"You think the less of him since you brought that woman into the house."

Peregrine cursed and went away, determined to cease confiding in his mother, and so Caroline's championing did Lancelot harm rather than good. The boy continued to brood and to plan how one day he would run away from the farm, and this prospect made him even the more unhappy, for he loved Hastingford dearly, as he loved all the wild countryside of the Sussex Weald. It was his kingdom, and Charity and her brood were the invaders who had moved in and despoiled the land. Charity talked to her son even before he was old enough to understand, and said, "One day, Stand Fast, these acres will be yours. Drink your milk now, that you may grow big and strong and be a real ruler." These things she took pains to say when Lancelot was within earshot.

National news filtered through slowly to the country districts, and so, having missed many of the rumors and alarums which had swept the land almost since the first moment of the signing of the peace, it came as something of a shock to them when the war with France was resumed on May the sixteenth of the following year. Farmers, like everyone else, fumed and grumbled. What was the Government thinking about? Could it not have foreseen that the Treaty of Amiens had done no more than grant Old Boney a breathing-space? Now he would be well prepared, with men and ships and weapons, and already would be licking his lips, preparing to gobble up the island he had always looked upon as a choice morsel.

"England cannot contend long against France," he had said to Lord Whitworth, the Ambassador, and there was scarcely an Englishman, brave though he might be, boldly though he might speak, who did not feel a pang of doubt or fear. What if the Corsican could carry out his threats? He was a big man now, had been made First Consul, which rendered him virtually King of France.

Patriotic feeling ran even higher than in the ordinary course of war, for this danger was the danger of invasion, a blow at the liberty of every Briton. Handbills and leaflets were distributed everywhere, to the most remote districts, urging men to defend their country, but they needed little persuasion.

"I shall join the militia," Peregrine declared.

"That you will not!" Charity cried. "You must stay to protect me and the children."

"If we do not have a care I shall be protecting you on our own threshold."

"I do not believe in war."

"And I always suspected you to be a Quaker," Peregrine told her, angrily. "But you'll sing a different tune, my girl, when the French overrun the farm, raping you and putting the babies to the sword."

Charity burst into tears. "How cruel you are! And all I ask is to be a dutiful wife with my husband near me. Besides, you are too old."

"If I am young enough to farm I am young enough to fight. At least I shall join the reserves."

Sylvanus was against taking impulsive action. "This looks to be a long, bitter conflict. We shall need every blade of corn we can produce, and every beast that can stand on four legs. If the worst happens and we are invaded, then every man will fight as a matter of course, to defend his home."

Lancelot listened enthralled to these conversations. The war had broken up the dreary monotony of his life. It was exciting to him, rather than frightening, an adventure in which even he, young and useless though he was, could participate. He rode down to the coast, to see the martello towers being hastily built, and went to watch the beacon being erected at Crowborough. By day damp straw would be used to raise a fine smoke, but at night there must be tar barrels to flame through the darkness. Nurses might threaten children, "Boney will eat you up!" but Lancelot longed for nothing better than to tackle Boney or any of his army, which he visualized as sub-human, resembling the frogs they were called, and not at all like his Uncle Gerrance.

Caroline's chief anxiety was for Marthanna. "What will happen to her, Peregrine? Will she be allowed home?"

Peregrine did not know, but he too was deeply troubled, and his fears were realized when they heard that Napoleon had made prisoners of war all the English in France and Holland, almost twelve thousand British subjects.

"Yet she is French," Caroline argued, "being the wife of a Frenchman. Surely that will make a difference!"

"It may make a difference to the way she's treated," Peregrine allowed, "but it won't give her the right to leave France."

These were mere speculations, and speculations they remained, for not a word was heard from Marthanna and Gerrance. The Annual Register gave a morsel of news, stating that, "the great Consul, like a politic shepherd, continually removes the pen of his bleating English flock from spot to spot, well knowing that the soil will everywhere be enriched by their temporary residence. How their wool will look when they return from their summer pasture is of little consequence."

In the absence of real information regarding the proposed invasion rumors were rife. A huge flotilla of gun boats was waiting at Boulogne and other ports, it was said, and people within striking distance of the coast all feared it was their part of the country which would be the landing place of the enemy. Some were so terrified that they kept horses harnessed and wagons packed, ready for immediate flight should the ships be sighted. Sudden alarms caused schools to be closed, valuables to be buried, and householders to desert their properties. When the rumor proved to be unfounded, they would creep back, but this happened again and again within that anxious year.

On a frosty morning in January, eighteen-hundred-and-four, Lancelot rode into Mayfield to see the blacksmith about visiting Hastingford to make new queues for the oxen, and found the village in a great turmoil. Someone had returned from the coast and reported he had actually *seen* Napoleon's boats in the Channel.

"On Beachy Head I stood, and there was all manner of ships making furrows in that water, and coming so unaccountable fast that they seemed to be skimming over the sea like mews, 'stead of touching it."

Had the watchman lighted the beacon, the villagers wanted to know, but the man said the sight gave him a grasping feeling in his belly, and he didn't wait to see.

It was not the first time that such rumors had spread, but the result was always the same. The people congregated in the street, as though by close proximity they gained courage. Some thought of their worldly possessions, some wondered how best to escape and where to go, while a few went into the church to pray.

Lancelot rode back to Hastingford, pressing his horse to its greatest speed. He was excited, seeing himself as a bold courier carrying vital news.

The first person he came upon was Charity, and of her he demanded, "Where is my father?"

She eyed him with distaste. He was breathless, dishevelled and sweating. One would never make a gentleman of him, she thought.

"He's to market."

"And my—" He almost said, "Uncle Sylvanus," so natural had the relationship become to him. "—and John Allen?"

"In the woods with the others, felling trees." It was the season for such jobs, the earth being iron-hard and the cattle housed and farm work at a minimum.

Lancelot drew a deep breath. There was no time to be wasted. "I can't stay to fetch them," he said. "Boney's on his way."

"Why do you talk in such a rude fashion? Boney, indeed!"

"It's true. In the village they are full of it, and a man has seen the boats, hundreds of them, off Beachy Head."

"You cannot believe all you hear."

Lancelot beat his hands together. Why were women so twort? Responsibility lay heavily on him, and here was Charity, who'd raise a din about nothing, treating this news as though it were of no account.

"What can I do? People must be warned." Suddenly he remembered. "The beacon at Crowborough Warren!" he cried. "Light that and it'll signal all over the land."

He did not wait for Charity's comment, but mounted his horse once more and set out. The beast was tired and made poor speed, but there was nothing Lancelot could do to remedy that. They plodded on through the wintry, deserted country. It was well past Lancelot's dinner-time and his stomach was roaring with emptiness, but he tried to ignore it by remembering the urgency of his journey.

When he reached the beacon the sun was low. He looked for the watchman, but he was nowhere to be seen. Well, he would have to light it himself, and it would have to be the tar barrels, for soon it would be too dark for smoke to be visible. Fortunately there were flint and tinder ready for emergencies, and Lancelot had no difficulty in setting light to the massive pile of dry wood and straw. He would have waited for the glorious flaming sight, but by now his hunger was painful, and also he was desperately tired, and so he rode away through the dusk. He did not relish the dark journey, for night was a hazardous time, with danger from both human and superhuman causes. Jarvis Brook was said to be haunted by a ghostly bag of soot, which chased the lonely traveler, and he was glad when he had passed through and was walking his horse up the hill towards Rotherbrook.

At Hastingford Sylvanus was waiting for him. "So there you are! Your father is out seeking you, and he's in a fine pother. No, leave the horse to me. I'll rub him down, and he looks as though he needs it. Where have you been?"

"To Crowborough, to light the beacon."

Sylvanus gave a long whistle. "Let us hope it did not catch fire."

"It did!" Lancelot cried, indignantly. "It was beginning to go splendidly when I left."

"Then you are in for trouble, my lad."

"Why should I be? I did my duty. Boney was coming."

"Well, he didn't come."

"Then he should have." Lancelot yawned and rubbed his eyes. "I'm main tired, and I'm famished with hunger."

Sylvanus saw the exhaustion on the boy's face and could barely resist taking him in his arms. During the long years he had forced himself to look upon Lancelot as his brother's son, but it had not been easy, and when the boy was unhappy, or in trouble, Sylvanus would feel tenderness welling up in him, and it was agony to deny his fatherhood.

"Go in and eat, then," he said, kindly, "and you'd best be in bed before your father returns. I fancy he'll have something to say to you."

In the morning Peregrine did have something to say, and, what was more, he had something to do. Charity had urged him to thrash the boy, and he could not help but be convinced that a thrashing was deserved.

"You young fool!" he raged. "How can you be such a bodger? You hear some gossip and your wits take leave of you. If the watchman hadn't found the fire before it got properly alight you'd have had every beacon in Sussex blazing away, and the militia called out and guns firing and dunno what else. As 'twas, they'd a job to put it out."

"Do they know I did it?" Lancelot asked.

"No, and I didn't tell 'em. But I know, and you know, and I'm going to give you a proper pasting."

"I meant no harm."

"But you did harm. You're wild and you're head-strong and you've got to be learned sense and manners."

"I 'spose Charity told you that."

"Leave your step-mother out of this."

"I won't!" Lancelot shouted. "She puts you against me. Since she came, it's like as I hadn't a father. I hate her. She's a rat-faced old witch."

Peregrine was a troubled man. Times had changed. There was no longer peace in his home. He could not blame Charity, for it seemed to him she was a good wife, or as good as they came. But someone must be at fault, and suddenly it appeared that Lancelot was the source of the trouble. Peregrine did not reason about it, for he was too angry. He simply took a stick and beat the boy, and as he beat he found relief. He did not consider the weight of his arm, or reflect on his strength against the untoughened skin of a stripling. He thrashed, and did not believe he was hurting Lancelot unduly.

Sylvanus came into the barn and found them. For an instant he stared, unbelieving, and then he cried, "Stop it!"

Peregrine took no notice, and Sylvanus went forward. "What are you doing? What in God's name do you think you are doing?" He caught Peregrine's arm and held it, while Lancelot sank to the ground weeping, shamed, and attempting to hide his tears.

Peregrine struggled to release his arm. "Leave me alone! The boy has earned a beating."

"A beating! A beating, perhaps. But what are you trying to do, kill him?"

"I shall do what I like," Peregrine declared. "I shall do what I like with my own son."

It was too much. It was the accumulated burden of years. It was a boy crying in the hay, crying not only from pain, but from the more cruel agony of injustice. It was the memory of the boy's mother, of brief love and an eternity of loneliness.

"No," Sylvanus said, quietly. "No, not your son. Lancelot is *my* son."

CHAPTER FIVE

Think upon every word that you will speak before you
utter it, and remember how nature hath rampered up,
as it were, the tongue with teeth, lips, yea, and hair
without the lips, and all betokening reins or bridles
for the loose use of that member.
*Sir Henry Sidney to Philip at school
at Shrewsbury when 21 years of age*

The meaning of Sylvanus's words filtered slowly
through Peregrine's brain. He was still very angry, and
anger acted as a barrier to the penetration of sense.
He simply stood there, bull-strong, bull-stupid, the stick
held in his upraised hand, staring at his brother, at
the face no more than twelve inches from his, the face
he knew so well, the face which somehow had become
distorted into that of a stranger.

"Blame ye!" he cried. "What are you saying?"

"You heard me," Sylvanus told him, grimly.

"Reckon I'm growing thick of hearing, for I thought
you said the boy was—"

"I did."

" 'Tis a lie, and you're merely trying to pick upon
me."

Sylvanus shrugged his shoulders, bent down, lifted
Lancelot and led him towards the door of the barn.

"Leave him be!" Peregrine commanded. "Take your
hands off my son!"

Sylvanus did not pause. His arm was about Lancelot's shoulders, comfortingly, caressingly, and the boy
was softly blubbering.

51

Peregrine moved up behind them. He was scarcely aware of the stick he held. It was a part of his arm, a part of his anger. He was still not sure what Sylvanus had said, or what he claimed, but his arm knew. His arm came down, holding the stick, upon Sylvanus's head, and Sylvanus fell like a slaughtered ox.

Lancelot did not wait, but rushed screaming from the barn. He had no idea what he should do, or where he should go. He only knew that what had happened was beyond his capacity to remedy or control. It was the province of the purely grown up, of the people who were ruthless and unpredictable, who made him a child once more, longing for the knee and the breast of authority.

The first person he met was Original, coming from swilling down the cow-yard. The old man was much troubled with rheumatics these days, but he considered himself the only one able to perform to perfection those menial tasks on which the health and success of a farm was founded, and so he insisted on doing the jobs which belonged to the inexperienced boys.

"Them nippers nuddle about," he used to say, "and don't leave a tack between the cow-pats, so you're up to your arse in shit afore you can say mother."

Now, as every morning, he was leaving the yard "like a piece of church plate," and the sense of virtue in his soul made up for the ache in his back.

Lancelot caught his arm. "Come! Come quickly!" he spluttered. "I think he has killed him. In the barn. Oh, hurry!"

Original stood stock still, his mouth open. "Who has killed who?"

"My father. Please, Original! Please come!"

"Someone has killed your father?"

"No. My father has killed—my father."

It sounded mad when he said it, but Original was not paying attention. The old man was attempting to force his obstinate legs to keep pace with Lancelot's impatience, and all the way was in imminent danger of those same legs shooting out from under him.

When they reached the barn Sylvanus was lying on the ground, with Peregrine standing above him. The stick was nowhere to be seen.

"Ah!" said Peregrine. "I need you. Fetch a hurdle and we will carry him to the house."

Original peered at the motionless figure. "What's with Master Sylvanus?"

"He has lost his senses," Peregrine explained, "and the sooner he's abed the better."

Lancelot took off his jacket and laid it on the hurdle, and the two men placed Sylvanus on top of it and held each an end of the hurdle.

Caroline met them as they crossed the hall, and gave a great cry. "Sylvanus! Oh, God! My boy! What has happened to my boy? Is it the apoplexy? A fit? Gout of the head? Stop! Let me examine him! Thank heaven, he breathes! Take him to his chamber. No, do not tilt the gate that way. You will send the blood to his brains, and then we shall have utter disaster."

Hindered rather than helped by her lamentations and instructions, they succeeded at last in getting Sylvanus to bed, where he lay unconscious.

The shock to Caroline was so sudden that she fell into a state of panic, and her recollection of the proper remedies deserted her. True, there was a cupboard full of nostrums, some of which had been concocted by Charity and some by herself, but how to marry them to the symptoms Sylvanus displayed, she could not think. Salt of hartshorn held under his nose did not stimulate him to consciousness, so she felt about with her hands and discovered a large lump on the back of his head, whereupon she prepared a pitch plaster and applied it to his scalp. Further, she placed cloves of garlic against the soles of his feet, and then attempted to make him swallow an infusion of Chamomile.

She was nearing the end of her efforts when Charity arrived. "Mother-in-law, what do you pretend to be at? And what is that liquid you are pouring into his mouth and over the bed?" She picked up the bottle and read the label. "Chamomile? Is he, then, in childbirth? And this garlic would do more good in the stewpot than on his feet."

"He has an injury to his head," Caroline said, defensively, "and the garlic is to draw it down."

"Head? That on his head, if I mistake it not, is a pitch plaster. Is it the ringworm which has injured him? Leave that on for a few days and it will be a hairless son you have. That is, if he survives your ministrations."

"Geemany!" Caroline exclaimed, exasperated. "Have you treated the ailing for as many years as I have? Have you reared four fine children to middle age?"

"No, but I have not yet disremembered all I learned. Remove that stinking plaster and I will fetch my basilicon ointment."

Caroline grumbled, muttering under her breath, but she gave way, following Charity's instructions, for she mistrusted the treatment she had given. It was not always thus, she reflected, miserably, as she sat watching over her son. Once she had doctored and nursed humans and animals alike, with as complete a confidence as the Lord must have had when creating the earth and the stars and the moon. What had happened to that power? Why had she lost it, and where had it gone? Surely it could not be from any fault of her own, for she knew of no sin she had committed, no error into which she had fallen. The reason must lie in her loss of authority, for when the voice of authority departed, the inner strength of authority went with it. While Will lived, she knew herself to be the mistress of Hastingford, and so she still would be, had Peregrine left her in her proper place. But her son had dragged her down and set the Quaker woman in her position, and now Caroline Dyke did not know who or what she was.

In the evening Sylvanus opened his eyes. For a moment his mother was afraid, wondering whether he had left his wits behind in that deep sleep of so many hours, but then he saw her and smiled, and she understood that he had returned entire.

After milking, Peregrine came to inquire about his brother and was relieved to find him conscious. "I am pleased he suffered no great harm."

"Harm enough," Caroline told him, sharply. "He is weak and his head is sorely bruised. He must lie abed for a day or two and have nourishing foods."

"Has he spoken?" Peregrine asked, cautiously.

"A word or two, but I have not encouraged him. He should remain quiet."

"Ah! Then he has not told you how it happened."

"No. He has not told me. How *did* it happen?"

"He ran into a beam in the barn."

"Mighty careless of him."

"He was not looking where he was going."

Sylvanus opened his eyes and gazed steadfastly at Peregrine. He seemed faintly amused. "That was the trouble," he said. "I did not look where I was going. We always do ourselves an injury when we go without looking."

Caroline leaned over and stroked his forehead. "Quiet, now! I will fetch you some broth, and then you must sleep until morning. Come, Peregrine, you are not to talk to him and excite him."

"I was not talking," Peregrine said, indignant as an unjustly accused small boy. "I was listening."

He followed his mother from the room and down the stairs, but there they separated, she to go to the kitchens and he out into the yard. All day he had not seen Lancelot. The boy had vanished from the moment they took Sylvanus on to the hurdle, and Peregrine had urgent need to find him and speak to him before he went in for supper. The fiction of Sylvanus's injury had been invented by Peregrine and apparently accepted by Sylvanus, and now Lancelot must subscribe to it. It was the only way the event could be glossed over without hurt to anyone.

Round the outbuildings Peregrine went, calling to his son. There was no reply, but he did not place reliance on this. He went into each shed and searched every corner, and in the end he found him in the loft of the new barn. They still called it the new barn, and probably always would, though it was the place where Sylvanus and Gerrance had lain in hiding during the war, and was already old with the joys and griefs of other years.

Lancelot was sitting on a sack of corn. "Did you not hear me shouting?" Peregrine demanded, harshly. He did not mean to be harsh, but the sight of Lancelot roused his former anger and stabbed him with a pain he had not known before.

"I was not listening," Lancelot replied, indifferently.

"Are you not coming in for your meal?"

"I suppose I am."

"And do you not wish to know how your Uncle Sylvanus fares?"

"How is my Uncle Sylvanus?" Lancelot asked, woodenly.

"He has recovered consciousness. I do not think he has much injury. Your Uncle Sylvanus and I have said he hit his head on a beam. I wish you to say the same."

"You mean you want me to lie?"

"It is not a lie when we change the truth a little, in order to avoid causing anxiety to those we love."

"If truth is changed, it's no longer the truth."

"Don't argue, boy! You are too young to understand."

"Who are the ones who'd be anxious?"

"Lancelot! I have warned you—"

"I mean, my step-mother wouldn't be anxious about my Uncle Sylvanus, because she doesn't love him. She mustn't love him, must she, being your wife?"

The only light came from the lantern Peregrine carried, but as he lunged forward Lancelot imagined he saw murder in his eyes, and retreated hastily to the far end of the loft. There was silence for a few moments, and then Peregrine drew a deep breath. "Come!" he commanded, and swung himself over the edge of the trapdoor and on to the ladder.

Sylvanus recovered rapidly and went back to work. He and his brother had no conversation beyond that concerned with matters pertaining to the farm work, but several times Peregrine seemed on the verge of saying something. He would walk up to Sylvanus and open his mouth, only to close it again without a sound coming forth. This Sylvanus endured for several days, but at last he could bear it no longer.

"Peregrine, if something is bubbling up within you, will you not spit it out? I grow tired of seeing you gasping like a hooked fish."

Peregrine swallowed the bitter bile which rose into his mouth. He was afraid to question Sylvanus, because of the answer he might receive, yet a time came when fear of the fear was worse than the fear itself.

" 'Tis about the boy. You were teasing me, weren't you? You were trying to make me swolk, because I'd offended you. You know full well that Lancelot is my lad."

Sylvanus had been cutting hay and straw with the machine, Salmon's chaff-cutter, they had recently bought. He was extremely pleased with it, the more so since he had advocated it and persuaded Peregrine to invest in one, which had required no small effort, for recently Peregrine had become reluctant to spend more on the farm than was absolutely necessary. It was as if miserliness were a contagious disease, Sylvanus thought, which Peregrine was catching from his close-fisted wife.

"I'm putting one-third of straw with two-thirds of hay," Sylvanus said, "as recommended by Mr. Young."

"Mr. Young! Mr. Young!" Peregrine exclaimed. "You make him the god of the fields and the farms, just on account of he's the secretary to the Board of Agriculture. And why do we need a board, I say. Agriculture's been carrying on without a board since the Creation, and I don't see there's much improvement with one."

"There was a time," Sylvanus reminded him, "when you couldn't get enough of modern ways. Father was old-fashioned, you said."

"Why, so he was. But we're not. We changed things."

"Yes, and time has passed since then. What was new-fangled is now out of date. We can't stand still, any more than the seasons can."

"Putting money into a farm is like pouring water into a river," Peregrine grumbled. "You see no difference. But it was about the boy I wanted to talk."

"What about him?" Sylvanus was not sure he wanted to repeat his assertion. Words spoken in heat did not flow so trippingly when they were cold.

"You told me he was not—not mine. But that's all a boffle. You were making a felelou because I thumped the lad."

It was Sylvanus's chance to retract. If he did so, it would mean a more peaceful life for all of them. The whole business lay in the shadows of the past, and he'd managed well enough without claiming his son. But somehow he found he could no longer pretend. Lancelot was all he had of Philadelphia, and he owed it to her to protect the boy. Had Peregrine not married again it would not have mattered so much, but Charity and Charity's children had ousted Lancelot from his place and made of him an orphan.

"I'll have to watch my words," Sylvanus said, half-smiling, "or you'll set upon me again."

Peregrine sighed. "No, I'll not do that. I was properly riled then, and I'm sorry I went for you."

"I reckon you had the right to do it," Sylvanus allowed. "I had no right to Philadelphia. That was why I went away."

Peregrine stared at him, blankly, without expression, as if he could not take this in. "All those years," he said, "you stayed away, all those years, an exile out of Hastingford, and because of a woman?"

"Not just any woman. Philadelphia."

"You didn't need to have done it."

"Not need? Oh, come now, Peregrine! You'd have killed me if you'd found out."

"I was young and chipper then."

"You're no different today. You're just as ready to give me a lamb-pie."

"It was because of the boy," Peregrine protested, "not because of her."

"You mean you don't care about Philadelphia and me?"

"Blood cools," Peregrine admitted, "and women grow to resemble one another as you get older. Why, I can see more difference between my cows than between women. I'd have minded plenty once, but now —Poor Philadelphia, she's been dead a long time."

"Not to me she hasn't, and I've never wanted another woman."

"Ah, you always were romantic, but I'll not hold it against you. About Philadelphia, I mean. The boy, now, that'd be a different matter. Still, you can't be responsible for that. You'd been gone a year when he was born."

"Less. I'd been gone just over eight months."

"You're lying!" Peregrine cried, angrily. "You're trying to provoke me."

"I am telling you something you should have been told years ago. By God, brother, can you so easily accept my adultery with your wife, and refuse to acknowledge that I fathered her child? Why does the one stick so firmly in your gullet, when you can swallow the other?"

"It sticks because I'll not be made a fool of. I'll not allow that I reared your bastard child, and you can't prove that I did."

"Oh, yes, I can. After I returned, Marthanna gave me a letter which Philadelphia entrusted to her, and in it Philadelphia swore the child was mine. She was dying when she wrote it, and dying women do not perjure their immortal souls. Cast back your mind, Peregrine. How often did you lie with Philadelphia, near the time she told you she was with child?"

"She was delicate," Peregrine mumbled, "after her miscarriage. I did not trouble her overmuch. But I do not believe you."

"Will you believe the letter, in Philadelphia's own handwriting?"

Peregrine turned and went, without another word, and as soon as Sylvanus had finished his bout of work he hurried to his chamber to find the letter. It was not in its usual place, and though he searched every corner and cranny, flinging his belongings into wild disarray, it was nowhere to be found.

CHAPTER SIX

THE BODY-SNATCHER

Caroline sat back and watched her unhappiness growing, as though it had been a malignant tumor. In this
point of view there was some error, she felt, for the
high hopes of youth should not so easily die. Remembering the past, she remembered her courage, and wondered that it had vanished. We are born, she thought.
We grow. We grow old. Pain and grief we expect, but
we expect also to keep our faith in life. Where is it now,
that faith? It has crumbled away to dry words. We give
thanks for our daily bread of comfort, for being allowed
to drag our ageing bodies around and watch the grass
grow, and we suffer the whip of guilt because we cannot
give thanks for our daily bitter bread of sorrow and disappointment and fear. In what can we believe, if not
in life? Up there, she thought, among the alien stars,
that is the road to Heaven, or so they tell us. But she
could not bring herself to be on speaking terms with
God. She wanted the violets around her feet.

It was in the daily stint of daily work that her crucifixion lay. Week by week, month by month, Charity
robbed her of her reason for living, Charity who was
a martyr to toil. There was the customary slaughter of
hogs for the household. Nine they killed that winter,
and not a morsel of meat was wasted. First the puddings, that the uncured portions might not rot. The
blood they used, and the chitterlings and the liver and

the skirt-meat. The fat sides of the large animals were
stored in wooden tubs under strong brine, with large
flat stones to keep them down, and the hams and sides
of the smaller animals were for three weeks rubbed
with salt and a little saltpeter, and then hung in the
wide chimney to be smoked. Caroline was doing this
before ever Charity was born, but now she was banished to the parlor to put up her feet upon the sofa.

It was the same with the weekly baking. Charity
took over the brick oven in the chimney corner, burnt
the hazel faggots in it, shovelled them out with the
oven peel, swept the oven with the bundle of wet green
broom twigs, and then with the wooden peel pushed
in the bread and the meat puddings. She performed
these tasks just as Caroline had done. There was no
complaint which could be made. The trouble for Caroline was that she herself was not doing them.

Whenever Charity was in a bad temper, as she often
was, she would say, "Your mother," as soon as Peregrine came into the house.

Peregrine would sigh. "So that's why you're skrow.
What has she done now?"

And Charity would remember she was a Christian.
"I'm not saying anything against her, but she's that
bumblesome an old woman she makes me feel properly
done-over."

Once Peregrine would have been ready to admit that
he did not understand women. Their mystery had been
a part of their charm, and a great portion of his love
for Philadelphia had been founded on her strangeness,
on the fascination of the unknown. He could have chosen one of a score of farmers' daughters, but Philadelphia had had the attraction of a foreign environment, the irresistibility which in myth mated heroes with
goddesses and fairies. But that was behind him. Now he
knew too well that women were flesh and that flesh
decayed. Now the mystery was no more than the bag
of the womb. Charity was pregnant again, he remembered, and so she found fault with his mother, as she
would find fault with anything, with the sun if it blazed

too fiercely, with the wind if it blew from the wrong quarter.

"When should your time be on you?" he asked.

She cast him a glance of exasperation. "The last week in May, and well you should know, if you were a husband that took thought for his wife."

"Do you expect me to write it down," he demanded, "every time I—All right, I'll not say it, for you're so prudish we have to blow out the candle and stay mum while we perform, as though we pretend it never happened. Mind you, I'll grant I should remember the date, for these events happen so rarely they should be placed in the calendar with the highest saints. But I'll leave the remembering to you, for I've enough to do, attending to the bulling of my cows."

Charity made a sound of disgust, but automatically rather than with deep feeling. She had discovered that men were coarse, in their speech, their habits and their taste, and so she expected nothing better. A husband was a cross one must bear, and one accepted it, even hugged it to one's bosom, because the chastisements of the Lord were all milestones on the road to Heaven. Charity was convinced the Lord loved her dearly; therefore it did not matter that Peregrine found her aggravating, and Caroline found her impossible.

Conditions of life on a farm created a sharp division between the sexes. The men worked away from the house; the women worked in the house and around the yards, and their contact was brief except at meal-times. In towns, especially among the prosperous, there were many entertainments and recreations at which men and women mingled, but country life, among the workers, had few amusements, and those few depended on the seasons and the prodigality or stinginess of nature. So at Hastingford Caroline saw little enough of her sons to be unaware of any quarrel or animosity between them, and they saw little enough of her to be ignorant of her true relationship with her daughter-in-law. The two women were left to the mercy of one another, with no relief but that afforded by servants and small children. Caroline no longer had the solace of Lancelot, for he was now considered a proper worker and expected to put in the same hours as the other men. Needlework she was permitted to do, for Charity considered that a proper occupation for an old woman, and mending there certainly was in plenty, Charity refusing to throw away any article of clothing so long as it could be held together by patches and thread.

Weary with leisure Caroline could not sleep, but often paced her room much of the night, pausing to look out of the window, feeling the sharpness of frost or the sting of rain, watching the moon's slow climbing of the sky, making the weather a drama in which the sudden cry of an owl held an urgency to quicken the beating of the heart. As in all farming establishments the family retired early to bed, and in the winter the hours of darkness were intolerably long.

Caroline counted the days of that January, and was thankful when the last one arrived. Soon it would be spring, and each spring was more welcome, more worthy of celebration, for who knew, at her age, but that it might be her last? This had not been a hard winter, except for the violent storm on the nineteenth of January. In Brighton, they said, it had been so wild and the tide so high, that a portion of cliff had fallen on the road to Rottingdean, blocking the road and leaving a dreadful chasm. Here, inland, it had not been so bad, and now the weather, as if in repentance, had become exceptionally mild. In sheltered places primroses bloomed, and in the orchard crocuses offered their gold to mischievous birds.

It would have been a time of hope, Caroline thought, if men were not so wicked and prone to fight, with that arch-devil Napoleon atop of them and darling Marthanna somewhere in the hurly-burly and unable to send even a note to assure her mother that they were safe.

Against the night sky the bare branches of the apple-trees made fantastic shapes which the mind could mold as it wished. She was glad that from the first she had kept this room for her own. From the back of the house she could have reviewed a wide sweep of her lands, down to the river and up the hill beyond it. (Her lands? Oh, what a mockery that was!) But she no longer could afford the wide view, because time was closing in on her. She needed the close comfort of nature, the knowledge that living creatures, some so small the eyes could not focus on them, were all around her, sleeping or working or suffering in their ineffable resignation.

As she sat there in her chair, warmly wrapped against the chill of the open window, she became aware of a sound which was not a part of the accepted procedure of the night, for it was human, and humans did not commonly move at this hour. Someone was coming up the path from the road, running, but unevenly, as though weariness and secrecy fought to muffle the steps. A figure came into view, and passed, going towards the farm buildings.

Caroline should have been afraid, or cautious, or suspicious. She should have roused one of her sons, but she excused herself from this duty by reflecting that they needed their sleep and the intruder might not be of sufficient importance to warrant breaking in on it. The truth was that she was excited, that she welcomed a change from the monotony of those hundreds of nights when nothing happened, and that she had reached an age when if she could not now dispense with fear, she never would.

Covering her nightgown with a thick cloak she opened the door carefully, crept along the passage and down the stairs. There was no conscious memory of those nights, so long ago, when she had done just this, on her truant visits to Will, but deep within her was a sensation of familiarity and of adventure.

From the kitchens she took and lighted a lantern, then went out of the back door and crossed the yard. For a moment or two she stood, uncertain, until a rustling caused her to look towards the stables, where she saw at once that a door was open. Without hesitation she went forward, and as she entered she heard the muffled sound of hooves upon straw, and there in front of her a man was leading out one of their horses.

"Ha!" she cried. "A horse thief!"

There was silence for three or four seconds, and then a voice said, "Stand aside, mistress!"

"I would be a fool if I did," she retorted. "Who are you? And what are you doing with my horse?"

"Do not attempt to hinder me! I am desperate!"

Something in the voice sent a bubble of silent laughter rising in her chest, for its words did not match its tone. The words were fierce, but the tone was fearful and uncertain.

She raised her lantern, that she might see the man's face, and she discovered him to be little more than a boy, perhaps nineteen, perhaps twenty. His clothes were filthy, and his hands and face bore the appearance of having grovelled in the soil. Yet beneath this surface dirt was an expression of appealing innocence. With his dark hair streaked across his brow he looked, Caroline thought, much as Will had looked at the same age.

"However desperate you may be," Caroline told him, sounding as grim as she was able, "you cannot steal my horse. Men are strung up for less than that."

"I'll be hanged anyway," the boy said. "They are after me."

"Who are they?"

"Most of them that live in Rotherbrook."

"And what have you done to bring the wrath of the villagers on you?"

"There's no time to tell you. Put your head out of the door and you'll hear them. They know the way I've come and they'll look for me here."

Caroline stepped outside, and sure enough there was a crowd approaching along the road. Like most crowds they were unable to maintain their objective in silence, but must remain a-hum in order to keep the pot boiling, and the noise of them was as threatening as a swarm of bees.

She turned back, blocking the door, for the boy still seemed determined to lead out the horse. "Take that animal back to his stall."

"I dare not. They'll catch me if I do."

"Looby! They'll catch you anyway. What kind of a

speed can you make in the dark, across the fields? And if you keep to the road there will be plenty to direct the hunters on the way you have taken. Hurry, now! Back with that animal!"

She shooed them before her, the horse and the boy, as though they had been no more than chickens invading her kitchen. The horse was bridled, but not saddled, so it took no more than a few moments to restore the stable to its natural sleepy appearance.

"What shall I do?" the boy wailed. "Where shall I go?"

Caroline put out her lantern. Now the humming was as fierce as that of an invaded hive. The crowd had reached Hastingford and the people were separating into groups, some climbing fences and crossing fields while others continued along the road towards the house.

"Follow me!" she whispered.

"How can I? I cannot see you in the dark."

"De'il take the boy! Have you no sense? Hold the hem of my cloak."

Across the yard they crept, and into the house. Caroline's fear was that the noise of the villagers might awaken her household before she reached her room, and almost it did, for she had not even shut her door when Peregrine rushed out demanding to know who was murdered, and Sylvanus followed him, declaring that a simple murder would cause a small pother, whereas a commotion such as this could only mean that old Boney had finally decided to invade and the countryside was probably bristling with Frenchmen armed with bottles of wine.

"Armed with muskets, you mean," Peregrine growled.

But Sylvanus, having had close contact with French prisoners, insisted that drinking was more to their taste than killing, and if Peregrine feared for his property he had better hide Charity, for even an Englishwoman might tempt a Frenchman if the night should be dark enough.

Fortunately Peregrine was too sleepy and bewildered to comprehend what Sylvanus was saying, and so he did not take offense, but descended barefoot and trod on a nail as he went to find his boots, and was even more indignant at having his peace disturbed.

Softly Caroline closed the door. "You will be safe here."

The boy looked around in a panic, and up and down, like an animal examining its cage. "How do I know?"

"Because I say so, and I am the mistress of this house. But you must get into my clothes press for a time. My sons will come to assure me that I have nothing to fear, that the evil character which is abroad will soon be apprehended and given a well-deserved exodus from this world."

The boy turned to her, quaking. "You will not let that happen to me?"

"It depends, does it not, on the crime you have committed?"

"I am not wicked, mistress. I swear I am not. At least, I am not more wicked than some, and less so than others."

"Well, we shall see. Now into the press with you."

Peregrine knocked on her door. "Mother?"

By that time she was in bed, yawning and rubbing heavy eyes. "Come in! Why Peregrine, what is wrong? Charity is not near her time. Don't tell me she is miscarrying! I reckon her always to be as firmly stuffed as a pincushion."

"No, it is a criminal the villagers are chasing. I wish they could have waited, for there's not a cutthroat or a pick-pocket worth losing a night's sleep for. I'll tell them he's not here."

"Oh, let them search if it puts their minds at rest. Let them search the stables and the barns and the cow-houses, but don't allow them into the house. Tell them all doors were bolted and barred, so no runaway could enter. Let them in and they'd have more of my pies and possets and preserves than I could replace in a month of Sundays. Oh, I know of old how light-fingered some of those Rotherbrook folk can be!"

Peregrine looked surprised. "How did you know they are from Rotherbrook?"

For an instant only was Caroline nonplussed, and that not long enough for Peregrine to notice. "Where else would they be from?" she asked, tartly. "Would they run through the night from as far as Mayfield?"

Peregrine shrugged. "There's only a mile or so in it, but you're right. These are from Rotherbrook, and I'd best go down before they swarm through the house."

Caroline stood by her window listening to the voices as the village people shuttled hither and thither. No doubt they were having a fine time, and looking upon it as an extra, uncalendared festival. Should they find their quarry, it was unlikely they would be willing to hand him over to a justice of the peace. What did it profit a hunt if the hunted were not turned over to the hounds? The fingers of the men itched to be tearing at their victim, and itched the more because of the anonymity of the mob, and because of their sense of virtue. The women, equally bloodthirsty, would have preferred to see him hang, but whether he dangled from a tree or lay spoiled with torn flesh and booted face, there was no danger for the crowd. No single person could be accused of his death, or held responsible. Such summary justice was by no means unknown, and the law was helpless before it. In any case, authority was apt to turn a blind eye, for people could be excused for acting in hot blood when crimes were committed which struck at the foundations of their community and their beliefs.

It seemed a long time before the villagers were satisfied that the wanted man was not lurking somewhere on Hastingford land, and even when they were convinced they stood around in groups discussing whether they should continue their search or return home. The young ones were for going on until daylight, but some of the older farmers and laborers remembered suddenly that it was no more than two hours until milking, hardly time to warm the sheets, and at last they straggled back to the road and more slowly, more quietly, began the walk back to Rotherbrook.

"You can come out now, boy," Caroline said.

He needed no second bidding, but joined her at the window, breathing as deeply as if he would use up all the air the night provided.

"My eye! I was nigh choked in there."

"You'd have been properly choked if those folk had laid their hands on you. What's your name?"

"Dickon."

"Well, that's a plain enough name, and an honest-sounding one. Now tell me, what was your dreadful deed, Dickon?"

"I didn't do nothing, mistress."

"Ah, come now! You'll not make me believe it was a false chase, that they mistook your face for one which bore a likeness to it. Country-folk are not that leather-headed. No, what you did was something bad, something real bad, or else the whole population would not be turning out on a midnight massacre."

"I did nothing," the boy insisted, sulkily. "I was helping, and the others ran away."

"Indeed? And what were you helping to do? A stabbing? A rape? Raising the devil?"

"Certainly not!" he exclaimed, indignant. "I am no villian. I am a resurrectionist."

For a moment she did not understand. "I hope we all believe in the Resurrection."

"From the grave," he explained. "We take them and sell them."

Her first sensation was one of shock. "Body-snatchers!"

"It doesn't hurt nobody," he assured her. "They're dead, and when you're dead you can't be hurt."

"You are a monster!"

"They want them at the hospitals. The doctors want them, and those that are learning to be doctors. They pay well."

"So was Judas paid well."

"I don't know about him, but my friends come from London, and they wanted someone as knows where folks are buried, and where the new graves are, with fresh corpses."

Caroline shuddered. "I shall go find my sons and give you up to them."

"No!" He caught her by the shoulders as she turned. "You said you would hide me."

"But then I did not know what you were. I thought you a young highwayman, an honest thief. But this! Take your hands off me, boy, or would you think to murder me and offer me as a very fresh body to your anatomists?"

"I wouldn't hurt you." He sounded upset, as if he might burst into tears. "I wouldn't hurt nobody." His hands dropped to his sides. "Please don't let them take me! I don't want to die."

In spite of herself she was touched. So young he was, so pathetic, and yet so evil. "Have you no conception of what you have done? They are not the carcases of animals that you maul. They are men and women, buried in sanctified ground, loved and grieved for by those they have left."

"The doctors has to have bodies," he told her, earnestly. "They has to learn what people is like inside, then they can keep them from dying, those that are sick. It was a doctor that said it to me. The fiddler can't play, he said, unless he knows the notes of music, and the farmer can't grow good crops until he knows what to do with the land."

"You make out a case for yourself," she murmured.

"In London they've put watchmen in the churchyards, so it's not easy to get the bodies. Before, you could sometimes bribe the gravediggers. There was one who repented, and betrayed the resurrectionists. They got away, but the crowd found the empty coffins and turned on the gravedigger and threw him into a grave and he'd have been buried alive if the constables hadn't arrived and saved him. The crowd went to his home then, and broke up his furniture, and took his wife and children and dragged them through a stagnant pond. I tell you, there's bad feeling about all this, so the resurrectionists are coming to the country and putting the bodies into sacks and loading them on a wagon and driving them to London."

"It is barbarous!" Caroline raged. "If the doctors must commit such atrocities, let them cut down the felons from the gibbets. Who could mourn them? But, respectable people! What should I feel were my husband torn from his grave and mutilated, so that we were separated for all eternity, and his spirit wandering lost and homeless?"

"Is he newly dead, mistress?"

"No, he has been gone four years and more, and he has a fine granite cross atop of him."

"Then he'll be safe. It's new graves mostly that we like, and my friends from London have a clever way, for they do not dig the grave, but only the earth at the head of it, and then lift the lid with a crowbar. It saves much time."

"I do not wish to hear," Caroline protested. "It sickens me. And you deserve the most severe punishment."

"There's those as wouldn't agree with you. My friends were saved from prison by a surgeon, and a middlingish pile of money it cost him. A partner of theirs that was convicted couldn't be got off, so he's paid five pounds a week while he's in gaol."

"Do not think to excuse yourself or your friends," Caroline snapped. "I am an old woman, with old-fashioned notions, and I cannot believe that any reputable surgeon would so debase his profession. But if you swear this is true, then I must credit there are some who do, and more shame to them. Times are not what they were—"

She broke off. The boy was leaning against the windowjamb, his head fallen on his chest. "Dickon!" she cried, sharply.

He gave a start. "Ooooh! Ah! Where—What—

Why, dang me! I must have fallen asleep, for I'm melancholy tired."

"Then lie you down! Not on the bed, dolt! You can stretch out on the floor, and that's too good for the likes of you."

He glanced sideways at her. "How do I know you'll not turn me in?"

"You don't know, boy, you don't know. But be sure of one thing. If I do, it will be when you are lively and standing on your feet. I'd not betray a sleeping man. Think you women have no honor?"

He was too weary to answer her, or else he had no reply, for he lay down on the floor beside her bed and closed his eyes.

Caroline did not retire, but remained sitting at the window, meditating on the mixture of emotions within her. She was shocked and disgusted, of course. Crimes such as body-snatching struck at the depths of one's religious beliefs, and offended the sense of decency in a way that few other crimes did. Was she not obliged to believe that souls, in Saint Augustine's words, "return to the same bodies in which they had been before time, and then there shall be a sweet harmony between them, concerning the resurrection of the flesh eternally"?

How could they be re-assembled, those parts which had been dispersed beneath the surgeon's knife? Everything was possible to God, of course. All the same—

The poor widows, who had lost their husbands a second time by having their graves robbed! What hope had they? And how would she, Caroline, feel if on dying she did not see Will again?

A picture came to her, of Will, ageing and shambling, his back bent which had once been so straight, and then of Will lying paralyzed and distorted. Did she really want to see him again like that? Will young, now. Ah! The mind had no difficulty in recalling that sweet memory, and a smile crept to her lips. She knew what she desired, what even her withered body desired. But the Church offered the resurrection, not the rejuvenation of the body.

Stiff from sitting, she got with difficulty to her feet, took the candle and went and stood by the bed, looking down at the boy. He was only a couple of years older than Will had been when they took the road to Gretna Green. How could he be expected to see anything sacred in worn-out bodies which had been half-dead long before they died? What need had he of resurrection, who could stand up in his first manhood, with only his feet touching the earth?

CHAPTER SEVEN

SWEETWILLOW SHAW

Without being aware of having come to a decision Caroline knew, as soon as daylight had sluggishly crept in, exactly what she was going to do. She dressed in her working clothes, which she did faithfully each morning, even though she was not permitted sufficient work to dirty herself. A rusty black gown she wore, shining only where use had rubbed the seat and elbows, but its shabbiness was redeemed by a collar and cap of good, snowy lace. With this toilette she took as much trouble as if she donned a ball-dress, brushing the cloth to rid it of any specks of fluff, and fastening the collar with an ivory brooch which Marthanna had given her on her fiftieth birthday. She had known what it was to be poor, to lose hope and sink into sluttish ways, and she would never allow it to happen again, of that she was certain.

When she was ready she awoke the boy, and he sprang to his feet immediately, bewildered, in a panic, not knowing where he was.

"Quiet!" she cautioned him. "Would you have the whole house hear you? If my sons should discover you, I doubt if even I could save you."

His eyes questioned her even before his mouth had formed the words. "Are you going to? To save me?"

"I will try," she promised, "though I doubt me

whether you deserve it. Now, you are to remain in this room until nightfall. I will lock the door, so you will not be disturbed. It is my room, and I have every right to keep it private." As she said this she wondered whom she aimed to reassure, the boy or herself. "But make no sound, else they will become suspicious."

It was not until after noon she remembered he had not eaten that day, and managed to steal (Alas! What mockery! To term it stealing when it came from her own larder!) some bread and cheese, and conceal it in the folds of her skirt, and with it creep upstairs.

"I have brought you food," she said, and restrained the impulse to apologize for its paucity and plainness. Why should she do so, to a creature who merited little better than hanging?

He wolfed it down, and then told her, as if excusing his bad manners, "I was mortal hungry." It was the first time she had seen him smile, and she marvelled at the gentleness of the smile, the complete absence of greed or cruelty. No doubt the angry villagers had imagined themselves chasing something scarcely human, a werewolf, perhaps, with slavering jaws. Would they be surprised if they came upon him now? Or would they still see him as they pictured him? It might be that the virtuous in their desire for revenge never looked with clear eyes at the object of their punishment, but saw him only as a rat swinging at the end of a rope.

"You cannot stay here," Caroline said.

Fear caught him like an ague, with chattering teeth and twitching body. "Please, mistress! Please! I do not want to die."

"Wait! I have not finished. There is a place where you may hide. It is a small farmhouse on our land, half derelict, for we have not used it since we bought the land. No one goes near it. It has the reputation of being haunted. There is the sound of horses' hooves, they say, and two riders go pounding over the water meadows, the woman with streaming hair, and both laughing. These country folk are superstitious fools."

"I cannot stay there!" he cried.

"Why? Are you fearful of ghosts?"

"No, I am afraid of those who are alive."

"I tell you, they will not find you. You may remain until the excitement has died. People forget quickly."

"I would rather go away."

"Where will you go? What will you do? It is not easy to find work. The war with France has made paupers of many, and a number of farmers pay such low wages that their laborers must appeal to the parish for help. What prospect for you, who have no parish and no recommendation from an employer? You would be forced to volunteer for the Army, where now they are not over-particular, so long as a man has two arms with which to hold a gun."

"I am not anxious to be a soldier."

"It seems you are anxious about little, except the saving of your skin."

"I am equally anxious not to kill," he said, with dignity.

"Ah! But you have no scruples about attacking the dead, who cannot fight back. No, boy! Do not try to justify yourself. I have no time or patience to listen to you. Simply do as I say. When it is dark and there is no one around, I shall unlock the door. I shall not speak, and you also must keep silent. Go down the stairs, out of the back door, and across the yard to the nearest gate. Climb it and go down to Low Field, which is the water meadow bordering the river. Cross the bridge at the corner of the meadow. Do not climb the hill on the other side—that leads to Wivelridge, my daughter's house—but turn left along the river bank and the path will bring you to Sweet-willow Shaw. Have you that firmly in your head?"

He seemed to be watching her, rather than listening, but he nodded. "How long do I stay there?"

"How should I know?" she asked, irritated. "As

long as is necessary, I suppose. I will bring you food from time to time."

The contrivance of her plot, and its element of danger, excited her, though she did not like to own it to herself, for it seemed undignified that a woman of her age should indulge in childish conspiracies. All the same, she found the day pleasurable, and the suspense of wondering whether she would succeed filled her with energy. The dreary sensation of uselessness vanished, and she could even tolerate Charity more easily than usual.

The last hour was filled with a tension that set her heart beating fiercely. She began to wish she had not embarked upon so perilous a scheme. For now she felt as if she herself were involved in the risk, that her safety also was at stake, that should she fail it would be not only a rascally body-snatcher who was destroyed, but also Caroline Dyke.

Yet everything went smoothly, as far as she could tell. She did not know what happened to the boy once she had released him from her room, but she heard no cries or commotion or sounds of pursuit, and so she concluded he had got away.

Before supper she washed her face and changed her dress. There was no festival on this dark, damp January evening, but she felt as though there should have been, and privately she celebrated.

She was not aware that she looked in any way different, and was surprised when she found Charity gazing at her with an expression both dubious and disapproving.

"Why are you smiling, mother-in-law?" Charity asked, suspiciously.

Caroline shrugged slightly, an elegant little gesture she had learned in Blackheath, all those years ago, at her deportment classes. "Is it a sin to smile, my dear?"

Charity scowled and did not reply. She was finding it increasingly difficult to treat her mother-in-law with the respect her age and position decreed. Old people were expected to be tiresome, but most of them knew their place, whereas Peregrine's mother veered between acting with the authority of a great lady and the frivolity of a young girl. It seemed she could not or would not realize that she was no more than a farmer's old widow maintained by the charity of her son and her son's wife. What did she mean by it, smiling that way, as if she hugged to herself a secret, probably a disreputable secret, assuredly one which would not be found edifying by her daughter-in-law?

Caroline smiled often during the weeks which followed, and sometimes she sang, snatches of airs she had heard when she was young, of which she had forgotten the words, or odd couplets to which she could put no tune but one she invented.

On the first day she had feared to find the boy gone from Sweetwillow Shaw, but he was there, waiting, and the next day and the next. He chafed at having to remain indoors, but he exercised himself by sweeping the rooms with a broom he made from a bundle of twigs, and Caroline, encouraging him, carried down a bucket of whitewash for painting the walls, and later a hammer and some nails, though she warned him he must be discreet about his repairs.

"Take care you hammer infrequently and a few blows at a time. People will ignore an isolated sound, but one which continues can soon be traced to its source."

"The old place is looking most like home," Dickon said, with pride.

"Indeed it is. You have been inhospitable to the rats and mice and spiders. It is coming to have the sight and smell of a house habitable for humans. I only wish I could provide you with furnishings."

"I do well enough with those blankets you brought, mistress."

"You must be cold without a fire, but we dare not risk smoke up the chimney."

"I'll not freeze. I'd like, though, to mend the window-frames and knock some nails in those old roof-tiles."

"Do not dare to show yourself outside!" she commanded him. "I am fearful you might be discovered when the men pass by. However, I heard my son Sylvanus say they propose to close this meadow for hay, so you'll not be troubled until haysel, and by then I reckon you'll be free."

He gazed at her earnestly. "What will happen to me, when I'm free?"

She was not expecting such a question, and scarcely knew how to reply. "Well, it will happen no doubt that you please yourself what you do."

He shook his head. "I'm not calculating to please myself. If I did I'd likely take up with bad company and go to the mischief. I'd sooner be an honest worker than a piker. You tell me what to do."

"Then you do not intend to desecrate any more graves?"

"You mean dig up corpses? No, mistress! No! By all that's holy I was that afeard I'll never try it again."

"I am glad to hear you have repented," Caroline said, severely. "I promise nothing, but I will give some thought to your future."

Her smile broadened as she left the house. In some manner, which she could not formulate even to herself, the regeneration of the boy was a triumph, and, as such, a victory over Charity. Charity had robbed Caroline of her place in the household, but Caroline, undeterred, was weaving her own fate, and the fact that Charity would have found her actions highly reprehensible, added savour to Caroline's secret.

Certainly it required an inner satisfaction to make bearable life with Charity that year. Never an easy companion, Charity was at her worst when pregnant. When she herself was physically uncomfortable she did all she could to render the servants and her relatives equally distressed. Harder than ever she worked, and more bitterly than ever she complained. Nothing was clean enough to suit her. The house and the dairies and the yards were worse than pig-sties, and the faster they all swept and scrubbed, the thicker the muck the men carried on their boots.

"You shouldn't put yourself in a hoe over a morsel of January-butter," Caroline observed.

"January-butter? And what is that, pray?"

"Why, mud brought into the house in January. If you were Sussex born you'd know it was lucky."

"There is no luck in filth. And half of it is worse than mud."

"Ah, well, shitten luck is good luck, as they say."

It was at that time almost impossible to force Caroline to quarrel, and this made Charity even angrier, so that she found herself seeking little things of which she might complain to Peregrine.

"Your mother is lazy," she would say. "Most of the day I have been in the attics, picking over the feathers, cutting out the quills, sifting them, ready for the new mattresses. I declare my throat is properly clogged up with down. And your mother didn't lift a finger to help me."

"Did you ask her?"

"There should be no need to ask. Anyway, she was not here, but was wandering across the fields down to the river. One day she'll fall in and be drowned. I think her mind is decaying. But her stomach is healthy enough. Oh, yes! She eats sufficient for a brace of harvesters. I call it a waste of good food."

"When I cannot afford to feed my mother I shall be in a bad state," Peregrine said, angrily. "So hold your maw and let me go to sleep!"

Charity sniffed and turned over in bed away from him, as if denying him, but it was no punishment she doled out, for Peregrine was at the age when, after the hard physical labor he did, he more often required sleep than he desired a woman. Besides which, Charity when pregnant grumbled and wriggled and eased herself away from him in a manner not conducive to keeping passion at a red-hot temperature.

Caroline was aware that Charity watched her as she made her way down to the river, and gradually became nervous that she might be seen crossing the bridge and approaching Sweetwillow Shaw. If she carried a parcel it would appear even more suspicious, and so she had of necessity to go out in the dark and conceal food in the hedge on the way. It was not a pleasant task, at her age, during the cold nights of February, when she would have preferred the comfort of the chimney corner, and she set to planning how she might soon release Dickon from his hiding-place and herself from her deceits.

To prepare Peregrine she said, "You'll soon be needing some more workers."

"That is so," he allowed, "but the way things are going I'll be lucky if I can find the wages. This war will be the ruin of us."

"Wars always are ruinous," Caroline told him, easily, "but somehow we live through them. If we were tenants, or the land was mortgaged, you'd have some reason to fear. But land that's our own, and paid for, can never be taken from us. Ah, Peregrine, you cannot remember what your father and I suffered. That was real poverty, and that is behind us. Now you are a king, and this is your kingdom."

"I don't feel like a king," Peregrine grumbled. "It's work, work, work all the time, and what has a man to look forward to but more work?"

"And what is wrong with that? I can't see you as a fire-spannel twiddling your thumbs. But if that's what you want, your sons will spare you later."

"Much later," Peregrine said, gloomily. "The sons a man gets in his middle age are no comfort to him till he's past enjoying it."

"There's Lancelot, almost a man."

Peregrine's face darkened, and he changed the subject. "Why are you concerned with workers all on a sudden?"

"Because I've one coming that wants to be taken on."

"Oh! Who is he?"

Caroline had thought carefully about this and was ready with her explanation. "He's related to Polly Spackman." This sounded safer, since Polly and George were both dead and had no relatives in the district.

Peregrine frowned. "They'd no children."

"I know that as well as you do. This one is a second cousin and a likely lad, from what I've heard tell."

"When is he coming?"

"As soon as you're ready for him. I've but to send word."

"Does he live far off?"

Caroline waved her arm airily. "Oh, somewhere in Essex, I believe."

So Dickon was liberated in March which, according to the poet Spenser, rode upon a ram and from a bag of weeds strewed the earth and filled her womb with nourishment. He came out, rather pale from his confinement, when the river Rother was self-important and brimmed the banks, and the blackbirds and thrushes were busy in the hedges, and the roads were dusty-dry, and the cattle taking an early bite from the first flush of the grass. He left Sweetwillow Shaw and moved to the servants' quarters of Hastingford, where the unmarried living-in laborers lodged. He said what Caroline had told him to say, but apart from that he spoke little, for he was still nervous that someone might recognize him.

No longer need Caroline make the journey across the river, and she could congratulate herself that her plan had succeeded, but one could not spend all one's time congratulating oneself, she reflected, morosely, and once again time hung heavily on her hands. The coming of spring had always made her restless. It was a season of big thoughts and big dreams, but dreams were an ache and a burden when you had to dream alone.

She walked until she was tired, but that was no

solace, for she tired easily and the day still stretched long and empty before her, with the evenings lengthening and postponing bedtime without offering occupation to take its place.

One April morning when she was driven indoors by a sudden shower she sought the room she had grandiosely named the library. It was sadly fallen from grace, for Charity saw no better use for it than to make of it a storeroom. On the floor were piled chicken-crates, and the oak chest was littered with a trug with a hole in the bottom, a leather costrel, a pair of snuffers, a milk skimmer and a couple of old half-high hats with the crowns crushed. On the settle were two preserving pans and a kettle. The panelling and floor were thick with dust, for Charity's housewifely pride did not extend to this room she never used. It was a sad place, compared with what it once had been, but when Caroline opened the cupboard she found the books she had bought for Sylvanus were still there. They were damp and stained, for the room had no heat, and on some of them the worms had been at work.

Idly she took down one or two, carried them to the window, and made room that she might sit on the chest. She had never been a great reader, but now she dipped into the books, here and there, feeling a kind of nostalgia at handling those volumes which had been so dear to Marthanna and from which she had read to her father, with advice upon farming.

Caroline did not wish to read of farming. It was enough to live it, to have it right in the marrow of her bones. Religion also did not interest her. The books seemed very dull. How could Marthanna have been so excited by them?

She was about to put down a dry and solid book on the law of real property when her eye was caught by the word "dower," and then by a heading, "Rights of the wife in the lands of her husband."

She began to read, slowly, being out of practice,

and became engrossed, and so sat until her back ached and her legs were stiff. Then she returned the books to the cupboard, and went softly from the room.

CHAPTER EIGHT

To love and to cherish,
From Battle to Berrish, (Burwash)
And round-about Robertsbridge home.
    Old Sussex matrimonial rhyme

For several weeks Caroline was so quiet and docile that the household scarcely noticed she was there. Peregrine and Sylvanus, in any case, would have watched blindly and placidly had she sprouted wings, for their attention was wholly held by farm matters at this busy time of the year. As soon as the cattle were turned out to grass there was the dung in the yards to be turned and mixed and then carted to the fields. The lucerne and carrots were ready to be harrowed and the early potatoes to be horse-hoed, as well as a later crop to be planted. Hogs were turned into the clover, and the stallion taken to mares not already covered. The irrigation of the water meadows was an urgent job while the river ran high, for the quality and quantity of the hay depended on it. These and a score of other tasks demanded every man, and yet Peregrine must frequently be away to market, selling his fattened beasts and buying calves and heifers. He would willingly have let Sylvanus go in his place, but Sylvanus preferred to remain on the farm, his long years of hiding as a deserter having bred in him a shyness of crowded places.

Work in the dairy was especially demanding at that season, and placed a heavy burden on Charity, whose pregnancy was advancing to the state of rendering her

clumsy and awkward. But nothing would have persuaded her to make her condition an excuse for evading
this responsibility, and it would never have occurred to
Peregrine to inquire whether she felt sufficiently well
for it. Charity was a farmer's wife, and unless the wife
took charge of this section of the industry, the farmer
stood to lose money. The dairy was important, and un-
supervised servants could not be trusted with it. At
four in the morning Charity rose, to make sure the
dairy-maids did likewise. At five the cows were milked,
to be finished by six. Every day the dairy must be
washed and all utensils scalded, and these were but
routine matters compared with the main business of
making butter and the thick cheeses which must be
done in early summer in order to acquire their proper
firmness.

Charity was thankful for any help she could get,
even Caroline's, but she would allow no orders to be
given except by herself. She was the mistress and the
others the assistants. She expected Caroline to rebel at
this, and was surprised when she did not. "The poor
old thing," she thought, "she must be failing. It is not
like her to show such humility," and she determined
to treat her mother-in-law with more kindness. But these
good intentions did not progress further than her own
conscience, for after she had been on her feet for seven
or eight hours, with her ankles swollen and the child
beating a drum-tattoo on the inside of her belly, she
was as ready as ever to snap at Caroline and find fault
with everything she did.

The war with France continued, and on the eigh-
teenth of May the French senate bestowed the title of
emperor on Napoleon. Lancelot talked about joining
the volunteers, and both Peregrine and Sylvanus, separately, spent a deal of time trying to talk him out of it.
Farmers were more necessary than soldiers, they said.

"More necessary?" Lancelot queried. "If Boney in-
vades can we meet him then with hay-rakes and pitchforks?"

Well, *as* necessary, Peregrine and Sylvanus allowed.
And he had better take care because, though the vol-

unteers were at present a reserve army, who could tell whether a law might not be passed to incorporate it into the regular army?

Lancelot listened, and when the lecture continued for too long, he yawned. My eye! What a burden it was, having two fathers! Twice as many blamings, it meant, and twice as many commandments, but only one portion of wages, and those not too generous, he being the son of the house and therefore not to be especially favored. Still, he was not over keen on the idea of a soldier's life. The farm suited him, and he loved every blade of grass that grew on the land. It was only that of late he had become restless. Life was passing so quickly. In a little more than two months he would be seventeen, and what had he done, so far? He rarely met girls, and not often was he with young men of his own age. Almost everyone was old, except Charity's children who were too young to be interesting. There was, of course, the new boy, Dickon, but he scarcely opened his mouth, and if you came up behind him suddenly, he started forward like a hare that hears the hounds.

The twenty-fifth of May was declared a fast day throughout England, for the people to humble themselves before Almighty God and avert those heavy judgments which their manifold provocations had most justly deserved; and for imploring his blessing and assistance on their arms, for the restoration of peace and prosperity.

Charity observed the ordinance meticulously, and made her children do likewise, but the others were not so particular.

"If we don't eat," Peregrine said, "then the animals shouldn't neither, and it'd take more than a day to put on what they lost in a day. And if we're to tend the animals we need our strength, and without food our kites would be so melancholy empty that they'd sound like the rumble of guns across the Channel."

"You've no reverence," Charity sniffed. "It would serve you right if we lost the war."

"And you've no sense. It would serve you right if you lost the child you're carrying, through starving it."

She refused to cook on that day, but the men did well enough sitting on the straw in the barn, with thick hunks of bread, and cheese as thick, and pickled onions near as big as a man's fist. The servants did well enough too, for they stole what food they wanted, and so Charity, though uplifted in soul, was out of pocket.

Lancelot's other grandmother did not forget him. She wrote from time to time, and sometimes sent presents. That month there arrived from her four of the new five shilling dollars stamped at Mr. Bolton's manufactory at Soho, near Birmingham. The old dollars stamped at the tower were to be withdrawn in June.

Lancelot took them to Caroline. "See what Grandmother Betty has sent me! What shall I buy with them?"

"Best save them," Caroline said, automatically.

"Why? What use are they saved? They don't breed, like animals do."

Caroline laughed. "Don't you let Charity hear you, else she'll be praying for your soul! She puts stinginess above godliness."

"I'm sure you shouldn't speak of her that way," Lancelot said, a twinkle in his eye. "Still, it was kind of my grandmother, was it not?"

Usually Caroline was jealous of Betty, and resented that she should have any part of Lancelot, but now she felt he had reached an age when he should be told how matters stood.

"Grandmother Betty is a wealthy woman. At least, your grandfather has money, and with them that's much the same thing. Your mother was their only child, so when they die their money will come to you."

Lancelot thought about this. If he were surprised, he did not show it, but he appeared to find the information slightly difficult to assimilate. "Is it a great deal of money?" he asked, at last.

Caroline shook her head. "I have no idea of the amount, but I would guess it to be a considerable fortune."

Lancelot smiled. "Then I will buy you a satin gown. Not a black one, but red or gold, like queens wear, and it shall be scattered with precious stones. I reckon you would look unaccountable handsome in such a dress."

"Flatterer! What do you want from me?"

"Nothing. I want to give you things, because you are not like other women. The farmers' wives I see, they are just pimpwood, but you are like a great branch of a fir-tree, dancing in the wind."

"That is breeding," Caroline told him, mightily pleased. "There's quality in breeding, with people as with animals. Your poor grandfather didn't have it, but my family did, and in you it is reinforced, because your father married my sister's child."

Not married, Lancelot thought. No, grandmother, you do not know, but still the breeding is there, because my father got me by his cousin. Aloud, he said, "I will not marry until I find someone like you, a lady of breeding, and gay with it."

"Where will you find such a girl in these parts?" Caroline sighed. "You are not high enough to fly with the gentry, and too good for the milestones that sow and reap and mow."

"Then I shall travel, when I have Grandmother Betty's money. Not," he added, hastily, "that I wish her anything but a long life."

Caroline laughed and leaned forward and patted his cheek. Ah, the dear boy! What a comfort he was! She only wished she could see more of him. But he was away from the house most of the time, and no wonder, with Charity forever fault-finding and abuseful, and his step-brother and sister being raised more like images on a monument than ordinary human children. She was too proud to ask for his company, and in any case she was not so frustrated and lonely as she had been, for she had a plan by which she expected to make her old age more bearable, and was only waiting for the right moment at which to put it into operation.

But which was the right moment? Would the perfect moment ever arrive? Life on the farm was little influenced by outside affairs, and she reflected, somewhat cynically, that to startle her sons out of their concern with the daily and seasonal demands of husbandry it would require Napoleon Bonaparte in person to walk into the farmyard.

In the end she held her peace until the hay was safely made and carried, and then sought out Peregrine one evening after milking was done and before his hunger could drive him indoors to supper.

"Where is Sylvanus?" she demanded.

Peregrine shook his head. "Dunno. Maybe in the stables."

"Then fetch him and bring him to the old barn. I wish to speak to both of you."

Peregrine was puzzled as he went. What was wrong with the old lady? It was a blue-go, that she should make a business of speaking to her own sons, and wishing to see them together. It took him back a good many years, and he found himself wondering, like a boy, if he had done anything wrong. Could it be she had heard the story about Sylvanus and Philadelphia? Peregrine had almost persuaded himself that Sylvanus had been unable, or unwilling, to produce the letter he had spoken of. Perhaps it was true that Sylvanus had loved Philadelphia and now in bitterness and jealousy attempted to lay claim to her and to Lancelot. It had taken Peregrine some time to work this out, his mind moving slowly, but he had come to regard his solution as feasible, to say the least of it. He's got nothing, went Peregrine's reasoning, so when I took me another wife and started a family, he grudged me and thought why couldn't he have Lancelot since he'd got nobody else. Phil would never betray me. No, she wouldn't never have done that, and young Lancelot, he's my boy, I'm as sure as I am of my own name.

He was comforted when he had worked it out, even if not quite convinced, but his feeling for Sylvanus was permanently changed. Sylvanus could never again be trusted. He was slippery as a grass-snake, and having lied about one thing he could lie about another. How could he be depended upon to be honest in farm matters? It behoved Peregrine to have his eyes everywhere, and his fist tight upon all monies. It was an added burden upon a busy man, but he accepted it with resignation, and was even sufficiently charitable to excuse Sylvanus on the grounds of his self-imprisonment as a deserter and his long anonymity as a pretended servant instead of Will Dyke's son. Such things warped a man.

Caroline waited for them, sitting upon a sack. It was a fine barn, the old one, of three bays, and the main beams so strong they could almost hold up the sky itself. It would outlast them all, and generations of their descendants, but the boys preferred the new one with the granary, so this was usually half empty, a store for old-fashioned or outworn implements rusting quietly in dark corners, and stiff, unoiled harness hanging creaking in the wind. The rats and mice could have a good time here, racing unhindered through the night, eyes shining red, for even the cats appeared to have deserted the place.

She was so deep in thought when her sons came that they imagined she was asleep.

"Mother! Mother!" They even wondered, for an instant—"Mother!" Peregrine shook her gently by the shoulder.

"Ah! There you are! And long enough it has taken you."

"What do you want?"

"What should I want?" she demanded, angrily. "Just because I have the desire to speak with my own sons, should I be wanting something?"

"You did ask for us both especially," Sylvanus reminded her. "It was a kind of royal command." He laughed to show her that his words were intended to amuse, with affection.

"Yes. Well, I have something to say. As you know, since your father died, and you married, Peregrine, I have had no place in this household, and I—"

"If you've come just to call Charity over," Peregrine interrupted, "I've no wish to hear."

"Mind your manners!" Caroline cried, sharply. "And

let me finish. I am saying nothing against your wife, and I am not seeking your pity. I am merely stating that my present life is not the life to which I am accustomed, and I have no liking for it."

"Mother, you are growing older. You can't expect to carry on the same way."

"Listen to him!" she mocked. "He'd have me in my shroud before I could put off my dancing-dress."

"Now, Mother—"

"What I want is some land of my own."

They stared at her, astounded. "Blame ye! What would you want with land?"

"My money bought these three farms, and while I admit I am a little too elderly to wish to be troubled with so many acres—"

"The law—"

"Ha! The law! So you would quote the law at me, Peregrine. What of you, Sylvanus? Why have you so little to say?"

He scarcely knew how to reply, for he could not tell them that to him they were like two children wrangling over a fistful of marbles. The things he had always wanted were not so easy to lay hands on, for they were mostly words inside his head, like love and liberty and beauty and peace.

"I don't know," he told her, at last. "I've nothing to give, but I reckon there are times when people have to take."

"So do I, Sylvanus," Caroline said, sternly. "So do I."

"I promised I'd look after you," Peregrine muttered. "You know you'll never want."

"Never want! Ha, that's a ripe joke, that is! What else am I doing but wanting? Every moment of the day I want. I want to lift just one handful of earth and say, 'This is mine!' I don't want to wait for death to endow me with the only morsel of land to which I am entitled."

A rattle of wind sang out from Peregrine's stomach, and he became aware that wind was all it contained.

"Well, what can I do?" he asked, peevishly. "My belly tells me it's supper-time, and I've no hankering to stand here all night."

"Very well. I will tell you briefly, for much of what I have studied in the law books would be over your heads. It concerns the dower due to a widow, and is an ancient right by which the woman is entitled to a third of the land, to be enjoyed by her during the remainder of her life."

"A third!" Peregrine exclaimed, aghast. "That'd be above eighty acres. And what would you be doing with eighty acres?"

"That is my business, my dear son. But I am not an avaricious woman, and I well understand you require a sizeable farm in order to support your family, your growing family, which, if I might advise you, you should not allow to grow out of all restraint, for at your age a young, fertile and demanding wife is not only like to make you bankrupt, but like also to suck all your juices from you and send you dried-up to an early grave."

"If I might unravel the part which concerns you from the part which concerns me and Charity—" Peregrine said, aggrieved.

"The part which concerns me is that I require an establishment of my own, and sufficient land to bring me a small income. Thirty acres should suffice, and I am prepared to take Sweetwillow Shaw and make it fit to live in."

"Never!" cried Peregrine, violently. "I'll not have the farm split. It needs to be run all of a piece to render it profitable."

"My son, you were raised in a hovel with no land at all. When I bought Hastingford your father nigh turned to jelly with fear at the size of it, and when I added Wivelridge and Sweetwillow Shaw he thought I was mad. If you are man enough to farm two hundred and forty acres, then you are man enough to farm just over two hundred."

"It would not be for ever," Sylvanus reminded him. "It will come back when Mother dies."

Peregrine shook his head. "I don't like it, and Charity won't like it."

"Charity! The old man's darling," Caroline said, contemptuously, "and none so darling at that. It's her you're afraid of."

"She is my wife."

"Yes, more's the pity! There's vinegar in her veins instead of blood, and it's polluting you. Yes, you've changed, Peregrine, and it's not the yeast of wisdom that's working in you. I remember how you were with Philadelphia. You were human then, and when your spirit was pricked, pain and compassion and love ran out. You didn't abandon Philadelphia because her poor face was scarred with the smallpox. I was proud of you, but now I have no pride in having borne you. When I remember the agonies you caused me, I wish I had put down my hands and strangled you as they dragged you from my womb."

"Mother!" Peregrine cried, shocked. "How can you say such terrible things! Aren't you afraid God will strike you dumb?"

"No, I am not afraid of God, and I am not afraid of you. If you deny me this I shall go to law and it will be shouted throughout the county that Peregrine Dyke will turn his mother from her land, because he is the puppet of a Quaker woman."

"Have you no shame?" Sylvanus asked. He was looking at Peregrine.

"Shame? Who are you to talk of shame?"

"She is our mother. She gave birth to us, worked for us, went hungry for us, and all she is asking is a few acres and a tumbledown farmhouse. Oh, yes, I can talk of shame, because if you refused her, shame would walk beside, your constant companion, for the rest of your days."

"I need time," Peregrine grumbled. "I must think it over."

Caroline raised herself painfully from the sack. Her limbs became stiff now if she sat too long in one place. "I cannot give you time," she said. "You must decide at once. I have my plans to set into motion."

"But that's not fair," Peregrine objected. "I do not like to be rushed."

"And I do not like to be kept waiting. Come now, which is it to be, my small inheritance, or a battle for Hastingford entire? I am not sure that I would win, but it would cause a fine scandal which would be the talk of the taverns and markets for many a day. Your Aunt Betty would give me the money for such a case. She is not over-fond of you since you ceased to be a grieving widow. She sees it as a slur on her daughter that you should marry again."

"Most men do," Peregrine said, angrily, "and for a farmer a wife is necessary."

"Perhaps. I am merely giving you your aunt's opinion. And one more point. Charity would welcome my removal from Hastingford. My presence is as obnoxious to her as a ringle in a pig's snout is to a pig."

Peregrine capitulated, though with a bad grace. "Have it your way," he muttered. "I'll be bodgen in to supper."

"I'll get the papers drawn up by a lawyer," Caroline called after him, "all right and proper."

She laid her hand on Sylvanus's arm. "Thank you, son. There's some births I don't regret, and yours is one of them."

"Where are you off to now?" he asked. "And in such a hurry?"

She did not reply, but turned and winked, and at that moment he caught a flash of a young girl, a picture of one he could never have seen.

She went straight to the cow-yard. It might be too late. Young men were punctual to supper. But Dickon was still there, swilling away the last traces of the dung he had carefully shovelled into one corner. The water ran in miniature rivers between the cobbles, catching the light of the setting sun and sparkling like diamonds. Caroline picked her way across, choosing the driest places, and the boy turned, the empty bucket in his hand, and lifted his hand to his tousled hair in an awkward gesture of respect. His lips parted in a smile, for he could usually look to a kind word from the old mistress, but certainly he was not expecting the words he heard that evening, for what Caroline said was, "Dickon, will you marry me?"

CHAPTER NINE

A little parlour-stove, to hold
A constant fire from winter's cold;
Where you may sit and think, and sing,
Far off from Court — "God Bless the King!"
　　　　　　　　William Bedingfield

That night Charity went into labor, and during the progress of the birth reiterated with some monotony that her mother-in-law was entirely to blame for providing her with a premature child. Caroline, banished from the bedchamber on the grounds that her presence would further inflame the suffering woman, pished and pshawed and when the baby was delivered gave vent to a shout of triumph.

"There! What did I say? That girl would try to make a May-game of me. Premature? Why, the little monster weighs near eight and a half pounds. Had he delayed another week he would have rivalled Patrick O'Brien, the Irish giant, whom you may see in London at this moment if you care for such raree-shows. What! You have not heard of him? Then you do not read your news-sheets. He is eight feet seven inches high, and his shoe is seventeen inches long. Premature, indeed! The fact is she had not calculated her dates, and no wonder, for she keeps poor Peregrine so busy that she is like to produce a regiment of offspring."

Sylvanus, to whom she addressed these remarks, begged her to speak in tones less likely to be overheard, but all the same he was hard put to it to refrain from bursting into laughter.

Peregrine dutifully admired the lusty boy, but Charity's mind was on other things, once her pains had ceased. "Thirty acres! It is ridiculous! It is extortionate. Would you have your children robbed? Is this my reward for walking in the valley of the shadow of death? How can you be so weak as to allow her to persuade you to such a thing?"

"I did it only to humor her," Peregrine said, soothingly. "You will be relieved to have her out of the way, and what use is Sweetwillow Shaw to us?"

"It must be damp," Charity agreed, more cheerfully. "Down in the valley, beside the river, it cannot be healthy, as it is here. No doubt the roof leaks, and there will be flies and vermin coming off the water. But the land—"

"What can she do with it?" Peregrine asked. "Who will work it for her? My men will not go, for she could not afford to pay a fair wage. You mark my words, girl! In a month or two she'll be begging me to take back the thirty acres, for, whatever her faults, my mother is not one to see land go to rack and ruin."

To Charity this sounded reasonable, and it proved that after all the Lord was protecting her and her children, which she had begun to doubt. She said a prayer, admitting that she was a miserable sinner, and she named the new baby Deliverance, which had more than one meaning, but which she kept a secret between herself and her God, for though she might detest the thought of losing, if only temporarily, a part of the land, the prospect of losing her mother-in-law was ample compensation. She had been delivered of a son, and also of the daily sight of Caroline.

On the following morning Caroline went to find Dickon. He was sowing turnips, driving one horse which drew the roller to which the drill-machine was tied. It was a modern and efficient contraption, she thought, with pride, remembering Will had broadcast all his seed, and it showed how farming was progressing to meet the needs of the times. Whatever their faults, her sons were good husbandmen, and she believed she could reckon on Hastingford belonging to the Dykes when a hundred years had passed, or two hundred, or more. That was what reconciled people to old age and death, the knowledge that something of themselves would endure in their descendants, but, try as she might, she could not quite feel it that way. The whole of what constituted herself seemed to be bound up in the mind and body of Caroline Dyke, and the fate of that person was her first consideration.

"Get down, Dickon!" she commanded. "I want to talk to you."

He got down, slowly, and, it seemed to her, with some reluctance. "Have you thought about what I asked you, Dickon?"

"Yes, mistress."

"And what conclusion have you come to?"

He frowned, puzzled. "Conclusion?"

"I asked if you would marry me."

He looked embarrassed, scuffling at the soil with the toe of his boot. "Oh, I couldn't do that, mistress."

"And why not?"

The blood rose hotly to his head. Had the use of words come easily to him, he might have attempted to explain his feelings, might have told her of the change which had been wrought in him since he had been persuaded into the crime of body-snatching. Only the hardened wrongdoer driven by avarice or poverty could contemplate calmly such a crime, it was said, for the mingling of death and darkness was sufficient to arouse the latent superstition in any man. Dickon was not by nature evil, and the sight of those helpless corpses, their decaying bodies and ruined faces lit by the cold and critical moon struck terror to his soul and sickness to his body. Never, he thought, could he again hold a woman in his arms, for beneath her living warmth he would feel the chill of mortality. But such words were too far for him to seek, and he said only, "I do not aim to marry."

"Listen!" Caroline ordered. "And listen carefully, for it seems I myself must explain your own thoughts to you. You are thinking that this proposal comes from a woman who is old enough to be your mother, and you are right. You are also thinking there is some shame in this, but here you are not right. There is no shame, because what I propose is a marriage of convenience. I shall not expect you to perform those duties which would be onerous for you and undignified for me."

"What is oner—as you said, mistress?"

"Unpleasant. Oh, do not blush more, boy! You already resemble a boiled beetroot. I understand that when a woman passes a certain age she is as unlikely to arouse a man as a bramble-bush would be. No, there would be nothing between us except those small courtesies which are necessary when two persons share the same roof. I would take your name —Why, dang me! I don't even know your second name."

He hung his head. "I've no real name, for I'm bastard born, but my mother was called Esther Hide."

"Then Dickon Hide you must be. So I take your name and I provide you with a roof."

"I'm no cadger, mistress. I aim to make my own way in life."

"By digging up corpses? There! Do not look so distressed, boy! I cannot resist a sly dig when you talk so bravely. You *are* to make your own way. Oh, yes! For you will work hard cultivating my thirty acres, and making the Sweetwillow Shaw a pleasant place in which to live. So you and I both give and take, and thus it is a fair bargain. You will no longer be employed by my sons, for we shall be by ourselves, on our own land."

Experience had made Dickon suspicious of people, and had taught him that those who offered gifts were the least to be trusted, for they expected in return something so much greater that the transaction was one-sided and often impossible to complete. Caroline's offer of marriage had roused considerable qualms in him, for a lady like her could not bestow such an honor upon a nonentity like himself unless she required from him some horrific sacrifice. He was not dim-witted, and had already heard much gossip from the servants, and would not have been surprised had Caroline commanded him to murder one or more of the family. Most likely, he thought, she would want her daughter-in-law out of the way, and he had firmly made up his mind to refuse her offer, for if people had been prepared to hang him for disinterring corpses, what would they not do to him should he transform a living creature into a corpse?

It was a relief, therefore, when he heard that nothing more gruesome was expected of him than to till the ground and keep thirty acres under cultivation. No doubt the old woman would work him like a slave, but he would not be at the beck and call of everyone, and he would have a legal right to his bed and board without fear of dismissal. Besides, the old woman had already saved his life, which meant that he had been in her debt from the beginning. Dickon's ideas of justice might be primitive, but as far as they went they were inflexible, and he demanded no more of others than he did of himself.

So he said, "I'll marry you, mistress," with no expressions of gratitude or avowals of respect or admiration, and Caroline liked him the more for it. The boy was honest at heart, whatever life might have taught him, and he was innocent as an animal is innocent, through ignorance of sin, not through the knowledge to combat it.

Before mentioning her forthcoming marriage, she took care to get the papers signed transferring Sweetwillow Shaw and thirty acres to her for the period of her lifetime. She went to a lawyer in Lewes, having her curricle prepared for one of its rare outings. It was a shabby old vehicle by now, and the most vigorous rubbing could not disguise the fact that it desperately required several coats of paint, but Caroline was not in the least discouraged. She was independent once more, with business to attend to, and she felt young and energetic. This was the act of living, which Charity had denied her, and she needed it for the health of her body and soul. Dickon polished the curricle, harnessed the horse, and drove her to town. He did not talk much, but she could sense the pride in him as he sat up straight, handling the modest equipage as though it had been a coach and four.

The lawyer prepared the deeds and himself visited Hastingford for the signing of the contract, knowing full well, in his country practice, that to get a farmer to come to him would be like asking Mount Caburn to step down and walk up Cliffe High Street.

When all was settled Caroline breathed deeply with relief and then went to break the news to her sons of her impending marriage.

That was indeed a signal for hell to break loose in Hastingford. Neither Peregrine nor Sylvanus did further work that day, and after both had argued with their mother for two hours and more, Peregrine, at his wit's end, fetched Charity, only a few days up from her confinement, hoping that a woman might force a little sense into another woman's mind. Charity was only too ready to lend assistance.

"You are senile, mother-in-law," she said, contemptuously. "You are suffering from the delusions of the aged. That is the only excuse I can find for you. Otherwise I must think you utterly depraved. Such a union would be so unnatural that every decent person would sicken at the very idea of it."

"Consider it!" Sylvanus begged. "It can do you nothing but harm. You will lose the respect of your friends and neighbors. They will say you have been coerced by an adventurer, flattered by false, lying promises. They will think Caroline Dyke has lost her wits and become a foolish old woman."

"And what will they say of us?" Peregrine demanded. "Here are we, her two sons, with no desire but to care for her and devote ourselves to her, and she turns to a stranger, a nameless vagrant young enough to be her grandson."

"It is the most crass ingratitude," Charity declared. "And, what is more, it is a malicious, scheming plot, for, look you, what does she do? She waits until she has possession of the land, which by rights should not be hers at all, and then she announces her evil intention. She does not tell us first. Oh, no! She is too cunning for that. If only I had known. If only I had foreseen what would happen I would never have married into such a godless household."

"Now, Charity!" Peregrine exclaimed. "Don't you be calling me out of name! I'll not be blamed for what my mother does."

"Somehow he has got her into his power," said Sylvanus. "Perhaps he is a gypsy. I hear they still can practice the black arts. Better than abuse her we should aim to save her."

"How can you save a woman so willful and chuckle-headed?" Peregrine demanded. "She had her own way with our father, and she reckons to have her way with us."

Throughout the long stint of lecturing, Caroline did not lose her temper, did not even trouble to speak. Most of the time she sat with a slight smile upon her lips, and in the end the enemy retreated, chiefly for lack of ammunition. They had used up all the words in their vocabulary which expressed anger, disgust and disapproval, had, in fact, used them several times over, until they had reached the stage when they felt that repetition would accomplish nothing.

But though that battle might be lost, the war was by no means over, and after they had conferred together and concocted a plan, Peregrine went alone to interview Dickon.

The boy was harrowing the field for the second time after sowing, but when Peregrine found him he was standing still, just looking.

"What are you staring at?" Peregrine asked.

"I'm staring and I'm listening," Dickon replied. "See that clodbird over there?"

"Corn-bunting."

"Yes, but mostly we calls him clodbird, and that's a good name, for he likes nothing better than sitting on clods."

"He's no great singer, so you'd as well be getting on with your work."

"Yes, master."

"No, not this very minute. I've a wish to talk to you. It was my mother that got me to hire you. She gives it in that you'd be unaccountable useful, you being cousin to Polly Spackman."

"I never heard of her."

"Ha! That's what I reckoned on. She grows faddy, does my mother, and dreams the truth into what she wants to believe. Pay no heed to anything she tells you."

The bird flew away and Dickon hitched up his trousers and took hold of the horse's bridle. "It could be I'm related to that-there Polly. I don't know where I belong, for I'm a come-by-chance, and the king of England could be my father for all I'm aware. Gee-up!" he cried to the horse.

"Wait!" Peregrine commanded. "I'm not done." He was offended that Dickon should take it upon himself to close the interview, and he thought. "The peas are getting above the cask." This was what happened when an old woman made a pet of a young man. "She was wrong to persuade me to take you on. I'm the one that does the hiring around here, and I'll not be wanting you longer, so you can cut your stick and go."

Dickon nodded. "That suits me, master. I was about to leave you, anyway. Would you like that I should finish the field?"

"Yes, you can do that. And I'm glad you have the sense to do what's best for yourself."

"Thank you, master. I reckon I shall be grig and cosy down at Sweetwillow Shaw."

"Down at—Dang it, boy! You're not staying on my land. You're getting right off."

" 'Tis not your land, master. 'Tis the old lady's and I'm marrying her."

"Why, you lying rogue, you said you'd go!"

"I said I'd leave your employ, master."

"I'll have you run in as a thieving, gypsy vagabond."

"It's no sin, master, to wed a lady that's willing."

Peregrine raved and swore, commanded and cajoled, but Dickon would neither be coaxed nor intimidated, and at last Peregrine was forced to resort to the plan he and Charity and Sylvanus had evolved.

"Very well. I will make a bargain with you. If you will go away, right away, out of the county, I will pay you ten pounds."

"No, thank you, master."

"No thank you, you say. Then what do you reckon you are worth? Twenty pounds?"

"Not twenty, and not forty."

"You must be half-baptized!" Peregrine declared, contemptuously. "You'll never come by such money honestly in a lifetime, and I'm a looby to offer it to you. But we've need to protect our mother. Say your price."

"I've got no price, for I'd not disappoint a lady. Marry her she wants, and marry her I will."

Defeated, Peregrine went back. "What shall I do? Offer him a hundred pounds?"

"A hundred pounds!" Charity was scandalized. "You'd rob your children of their birthright, higgling over your mother as if she was a bundle of old clothes?"

"You were as anxious as I was," Peregrine reminded her, "to have him out of the way."

"For ten pounds, yes, though I'd begrudge it. A wickedness it seems to me, to reward one that should be hanged, to let him walk away, whistling and rich, laughing behind his teeth at having made fools of us."

Without telling the others, Sylvanus went to Dickon and offered him five hundred pounds. He did not know where he could lay hands on such a sum, and even if Peregrine were willing, it would mean selling some of their livestock, for, like most farmers, they counted their assets in cattle and crops, rather than in sovereigns. But he decided to risk it, for he was curious to know if the reason for the boy's refusal lay in cupidity or, if not, what value he placed upon the step he was about to take.

The mention of five hundred pounds did not alter the expression on Dickon's face. He was polite, bored and resolute.

"Well, what do you want?" Sylvanus asked. "Do you love my mother?"

Dickon laughed, his mouth wide open, displaying strong white teeth. "Love? What's that?"

"How can I tell you? D'you mean, you've never loved anyone?"

"No, I never loved nobody." ·

"But you've wanted women?"

"Well, that's natural, isn't it? I wouldn't like to think my horse, and my bull and my ram could do what I couldn't do. I've got to keep up with them, haven't I?"

"Do you want my mother in that way?"

A shadow, as of distaste, crossed his face. "Oh, no! She's old. That wouldn't be right."

"Then why, in heaven's name, are you so set on marrying her?"

Dickon was tired of being questioned, and especially of being asked about things which belonged inside himself, which were complicated and difficult to understand, and therefore almost impossible to explain. So he said, as he had said to Peregrine, "I wouldn't disappoint a lady." They did not concern other people, the feelings within him, like the longing to see logs burning on the hearth at Sweetwillow Shaw, and the walls plastered and dry, and the windows tight against the gales, and coming in from the mud and rain and smelling onion soup or bacon frying.

Most people, ordinary people, would laugh at these things, so he couldn't mention them. Only one who had never had a home could set such store by the comforts generally taken for granted. Five hundred pounds? What was that but a bag of gold? He was going to have everything—a house, some land, and an old woman who would be his wife but whom he could pretend was his mother.

To Caroline he did not mention the bribes he had been offered, but he told her Peregrine did not wish to employ him any longer.

She nodded, pleased. "Then there is no need to wait. We can be church-called this very Sunday, and in three weeks we'll be wed."

Sweetwillow Shaw would not be repaired in time, but what did it matter? The warm air of July could creep through the crevices and would not trouble them. If the roof leaked they could use the summer rain in which to bathe themselves. New hay was good and sweet-smelling to strew on the floors.

Four times the largest wagon was filled, and took the long way around by the road to remove Caroline's belongings to her new home, while Charity watched jealously to see her mother-in-law did not grab anything to which she was not entitled. There were several arguments, which Caroline won, and she succeeded in taking with her the whole of her bedroom furnishings, including the bed, and several chests and coffers of clothes and personal effects. She herself departed in her curricle, Sylvanus driving her, for, she said, it was not fitting for Dickon to live at Sweetwillow Shaw before they were man and wife.

She cried all the way there, to Sylvanus's annoyance. If it made her so sad to leave, he said, then, deuce take it, why didn't she stay? Nobody was turning her out.

Oh, yes, they were, she contradicted. Charity had made life impossible and treated her like a servant. It would be better if she were in her grave, but, since she was not, she must go and hide where she would cause no trouble to her ungrateful family. Soon enough they would be rid of her, she sobbed, for there was nothing left for her in this unhappy world, and the last sight of Hastingford was too much for her, for there she had left her heart.

"Last sight! My eye!" Sylvanus exploded. "You'll see the house every time you look out of the window or step out of the door. There it will be, staring down at you from the top of the hill. You won't be able to miss it."

Caroline dried her eyes. "It will not be the same," she said, with dignity. "I find it very disturbing that things do not remain the same."

A few days later she was married at St. Dunstan's Church, by the Reverend John Kirby. Her two sons and her daughter-in-law refused to attend the service, but Lancelot, joyous and rebellious, dressed himself in his best suit, combed his hair, saddled his horse and rode over to Mayfield to give the bride away.

CHAPTER TEN

The death of Nelson was felt in England as something more than a public calamity: men started at
the intelligence, and turned pale, as if they had heard
of the loss of a dear friend.

Robert Southey

If Sweetwillow Shaw could look up to Hastingford,
then Hastingford could look down on Sweetwillow
Shaw, which Charity did every time she crossed the
yard behind the house. She would gaze at it, sitting
so snugly as it did, in the valley, but slightly above
the river and away from the shadowing trees, and
she would say, aloud, as if to give validity to her
words, "This will never last. This will never last."

But to Caroline it was as though she had been
presented with a slice of eternity. Now she had
to count the weeks and the months only as they affected the routine of her farm. It was her land, not
herself, on which time was leaning.

From Peregrine she borrowed money, he lending
it surreptitiously for fear of Charity's tongue, and
she went with Dickon to Lewes to purchase livestock at the market. Ten heifers she bought, a score
of South Down sheep, a strong pony to draw her
curricle when it was not otherwise occupied, and a
pair of goats, as well as some geese and hens.

"We shall have something of everything," she told
Dickon, "for the good Lord has made animals, as
well as humans, partial to different kinds of food,

110

and so we shall render productive every inch of
our land. First we shall put out the pony and the
cows, next the sheep, and last of all the geese and
the goats, who are not such dainty feeders."

"What shall we do for fodder, mistress?" Dickon
asked. He still could not force himself to call her by
her given name. "If we leave our fields down to pasture, we'll have nothing for the lean time of the
year."

"Oh, we'll make our own hay, but crops we cannot grow. If we did, there would be no space for
the stock, and what good would ghostly cows do us?
No, I shall buy my fodder from my sons."

This she did. "I shall pay you full market price,"
she told Peregrine, "and the profit will be deducted
from the loan you made me."

Peregrine blinked. "But, mother, I would make a
profit in any case, so you are paying back nothing."

"You never were clever at the mathematics," Caroline said, blandly. "Look at it this way. You would
feel, naturally, that you could not charge your mother the same price you charged a stranger. You would
make a reduction. But I wish to pay the full price,
and the profit will gradually relieve me of my debt to
you. You see, I am a fair-minded woman, and would
not dream of imposing upon you merely because I
am your closest blood-relation."

Peregrine agreed to this arrangement, though he
suffered the nagging suspicion that his mother had
indulged in a morsel of sharp practice.

The haysel of eighteen-hundred-and-four had
been very abundant, and so Peregrine was willing to
sell his mother all she needed for the coming winter.
He also permitted her to rent his bull.

"You see!" Caroline cried joyfully, to Dickon,
"How well we are doing! The heifers are all in calf.
At least, all except that doubtful one. Come spring
we shall have calves for sale, but not lambs. Those I
shall keep. The calves I shall always sell, and the
cows when they are past their first flush. This small
farm cannot carry a large herd. It will be a matter

of shrewd marketing, to make sufficient on our cows and calves to enable us to replace them continually with good maiden heifers. I shall attend the markets myself. Oh, Dickon, you cannot imagine how excited I am! When my husband—my first husband—was alive he naturally went to market. It would not have been fitting for me to do so. But now I am a cantankerous old woman and can please myself."

"How shall we manage this winter, mistress, with no cows in milk and no money coming in?"

"Gracious, Dickon, what a timid child you are! Have you always been so fine a gentleman that you fear poverty? I have been poor, very poor, and the condition has no terrors for me. There is still time to grow some kale and cabbages, if you will dig me a garden. The nanny-goat is soon due to kid, so we shall have goat's milk and cheese. I will fatten some geese to sell for Michaelmas, and one goose I will keep for our Christmas dinner, though likely we shall be invited to Hastingford.

But they were not invited. Peregrine and Sylvanus visited her with gifts on Christmas morning, good, useful gifts like a side of bacon, a large cheese, and several jars of preserves. Peregrine, somewhat shame-faced, made his excuses. "We would have asked you up to the house, but we are not keeping high celebration this year."

"Why?" Caroline asked, bluntly. "What is different about this year? Have you become bankrupt?"

"Oh, no! With a wife like Charity it would be well nigh impossible for a man to suffer bankruptcy," he said, a little wryly. "She is an excellent manager. But she does not go much for festivals. She considers that most of the Christmas celebrations reek of papistry."

"Damned Quaker!"

"What did you say, Mother?"

"If you heard, I stand by it. If not, I won't repeat it. Well, you go back to your skimmed milk and Sussex pudding. But send young Lancelot if you think he might fancy a fine fat goose stuffed with a plump young fowl."

Peregrine sent Lancelot, partly to please the old lady, and partly for the sake of the boy. He well remembered, as Sylvanus did, the joyful Christmas festivities at Hastingford, and still was not sufficiently tamed to accept as normal Charity's idea of a holiday.

Plenty of food there was, but not delicate or expensive. A good fire blazed on the hearth, but no branch was permitted to be singled out as a Yule log. That was a pagan practice, Charity said, as was the custom of decorating the house with evergreens. The place for trees, she insisted, was in the woods, not oozing sap and dropping berries on her wholesome floors. Young Stand Fast went in carrying a sprig of mistletoe, which he had been given by one of the laborers, and his mother snatched it from him and threw it in the fire, rapping his knuckles to make him remember.

"We are not heathens," she shouted, "to indulge in filthy Druid superstitions."

Lancelot was glad to go down to Sweetwillow Shaw, and not only at Christmas. He spent much of his spare time there and became friendly with Dickon.

Watching with pleasure as they worked or sported together, Caroline thought this was how it should have been with all her family. If Sylvanus had married, and if Philadelphia had not died, but had lived to bear a number of children, and if Rebecca and Richard had not gone to live in London, and if Marthanna had married an Englishman and so kept out of the clutches of Napoleon Bonaparte and his followers—The imagining of the grand-children she might have had around her, if fate had decreed differently, brought tears to Caroline's eyes, just as the sight of Hastingford was still liable to do, but most of the time she was too deeply occupied to think of crying.

"You see!" she said, triumphantly, to Dickon,

when she heard the first cuckoo and felt that spring had officially arrived. 'Winter is over and we have not starved. Now we can begin to restore the house, for the days grow longer and soon there will be so much light that you will not find enough to do. Dickon, are you listening? Dickon! Why, drat you, I do declare, you are half asleep."

"I'm sorry, mistress," he yawned, "but I'm hard set to it to keep my eyes open."

"Because you've been up one night with the ewes? The loss of a few hours' sleep should make no difference at your age. Ah, it does me good to see those lambs so gay and frisky."

"Me too, mistress, and I'm ready and willing to be healing that roof whenever you say."

"There's more to be done than a few tiles on the roof, Dickon, but we'll manage very well with Lancelot to help us."

It was not so easy for Lancelot to find time, at that season of the year. He was still under the authority of Peregrine and Sylvanus, expected to obey their orders without question, and the fact that he was a son of the house made no difference. He put in an hour or two when he was able, but the main part of the work devolved on Dickon.

"Don't you ever get time off?" Lancelot asked him one evening when Dickon was found fixing laths between the storey posts on the front of the house.

"Time off for what?" Dickon asked, his mouth full of nails.

"Oh, I dunno. Time off for fishing, I suppose, or rabbiting, or just sitting around."

Dickon shook his head. "I rather to be doing this."

Lancelot laughed. "She can drive hard, can my grandmother. She should be a general or admiral. We'll call her Madame Bonaparte."

He was not prepared for the fury with which Dickon turned on him. "You are not to talk that way! You are not to say such things about my mistress. She is good, and she asks no more from others than she's ready to do herself."

"Why do you call her mistress? She's your wife."

"It seems more respectful."

"But you don't have to respect a wife. She has to respect you. That's the natural order of things. When I marry I shall choose a girl who thinks I am wonderful, like a god. It's satisfying to have someone looking up to you."

"That's all right, if your wife is less than you are, but if she's greater, you look up to her."

"Or if she's older."

"When people are older they know more, so they *are* greater."

Lancelot glanced sideways at Dickon. He felt in the mood for teasing. "Some people are unaccountably bad at matching themselves. There's my father marries a woman five years older than me, and there's you, no more than two years ahead of me, marrying my grandmother. What's it like, with a woman that age? I mean, what kind of a man-trap can she offer you?"

"Mum your dubber!" Dickon cried, fiercely. "I want no more of that talk, and if you can't speak decently of your elders you'd best go away and leave me to my work. I want no help from you."

Lancelot shrugged his shoulders and went. Dickon was mighty touchy, he thought, but then he was a bit of a mum-chance, a poor foreigner without education, unable to read or write. It was not worth spending time with him, which Lancelot had only done because there was no one else around of a like age. Lancelot was fond of his grandmother, but now Dickon was her pet and she needed no other young man.

"We've not seen Lancelot this past week," Caroline said. "What has come to him?"

"I don't know, mistress."

"I'd go to ask, but I'm not setting foot in that house until I'm invited. You'll be missing him."

"Oh, I'm not particular. I can manage the work alone."

"I was not thinking of work, Dickon. I was thinking of company."

"I'm no-ways lonesome, mistress. Lancelot is hardly more than a boy."

"What are you, then?"

"I'm old for my age, because I've had a lamentable hard life. Anyways, I have you, mistress."

Caroline was touched by his loyalty, though she could not believe that the unadulterated companionship of an old woman could prove sufficiently stimulating to a young man. Yet as she came to know him better she realized that it was his mental limitations which gave him contentment and caused him to ask little of life. He was no Lancelot, restless, inquisitive, progressive, and though life had whittled him to a certain sharpness, he was in some ways no more than a child. Caroline attempted to teach him to read and write, but his concentration could get him no further than words of one syllable. He liked Caroline to read to him, which she did frequently, and as she was a regular subscriber to the *Sussex Weekly Advertiser* she provided him with excerpts from that newspaper, to keep him abreast of the times. He liked to hear of the war and of the generals and admirals in command, but his greatest hero was Lord Nelson, and Caroline was coaxed and implored to provide him with every scrap of information concerning that famous man. When a portrait engraving of Nelson was published, Dickon begged to have it as his own, and pinned it to the wall where he could see it whenever he came into the room.

"What do you admire in him?" Caroline asked, but Dickon was unable to express his feelings in this matter. It was not that he revered the admiral as the saviour of his country, for it had never occurred to him that the country was in real danger. He had heard people talk of invasion, and had visualized it as a struggling line of men of weird appearance who would be sent smartly packing, with the sharp end of a pitchfork. And it was not that he harbored any romantic illusions concerning the sea. His life among paupers and criminals had brought him into contact with a number of sailors and they had had nothing good to say of the life on the ocean wave. No, there was nothing rational in his admiration for Lord Nelson. He had picked on a name, some sparse facts, a likeness more or less faithfully drawn, and of these had made a legendary figure.

Caroline's affection for the boy grew with the passing of the months, and she came to appreciate him for himself and not only for the convenience of having him working for her. Her manner towards him grew less domineering and peremptory, for, strong and intelligent as she was, she had a weakness for simplicity. It was Will's simplicity, as well as his physical attraction, which had from the first appealed to her, and in Dickon she saw something of the nature of the young Will.

It was therefore with tact and gentleness that on a gloomy day early in November she broke some news at which she knew Dickon would be upset. It was evening, and he returned damp and muddy from the fields to find a good hot meal awaiting him. It was a corner of bacon boiled in cider, then covered with sugar and breadcrumbs, stuck with cloves, and baked.

She waited until he had eaten, then said, "The newspaper has come today."

He moved to his chair by the fire and put his stockinged feet on the hearth. "Will you read to me? Is Nelson still in Spain? Has he beaten the enemy?"

"Yes, there has been a big battle, off Cape Trafalgar, and a great victory."

"Have we won the war, then?"

"I cannot say, but I would think we have shown our strength, and Napoleon will never again dare to contemplate invading us."

"Tell me about Nelson. Will he come home? Will they pin more medals on him?"

"No, Dickon. That is the sad part of the affair. You see, battles are not won without sacrifice. Twenty ships have been captured. Imagine it! We are masters of the sea."

"Why will not Nelson come home?"

"He has been killed."

At sight of Dickon's stricken face she was struck by a pang of guilt. Had she spoken too abruptly? Could she have given him the news in a kinder way? But however she had put it, he would have to know. Even children must learn to face facts.

He stumbled from his chair, fell on his knees and buried his face in her lap, crying bitterly. Tenderly she stroked his hair and murmured words intended to console, though perhaps only the tone of her voice would penetrate his desolation.

"Those who protect their country risk their lives, whether they be admirals or common sailors. To fight a war is to expect to die young. But that does not matter, Dickon, if you die bravely and gloriously. Most of us live long and leave no trace, but Nelson will be immortal. He will live for ever on the lips of every man, woman and child. Hundreds of years will pass, and there will not be anyone who has not heard of him. That is a cause for joy, not for grief."

The sobs became less violent, and further apart, and suddenly Dickon reached up and tore open the front of her bodice. With his hand he reached and drew out one of her breasts, the down-drooping, flabby-soft, old woman's breast. He held it to his cheek, and then his lips crept round, nuzzling at it and sucking.

She thought, poor soul! He is a child wanting his mother, and she intended to disregard the matter, ignoring it as a harmless gesture. But her sensations were far from maternal, for her nipples hardened and her breast thrust forward as if it would rise up into the proudness of youth.

She snatched it away from him. "Stop, Dickon! That is not nice behavior."

But he would not be put off. He tore her bodice from her shoulders and caught both breasts, two handfuls, pulling at them, tormenting her. "You are my wife."

And as he said the words, it was so. The pitiful crucifixion of the flesh by death was forgotten, as was the mutilation of the flesh by age. Caroline ceased to be an old body and became the vehicle of affection and protection. She was the goodness of life to which he must draw as near as possible in order to become a part of it.

"You are my wife," he repeated.

Pride would not allow her to persuade him, would not allow her to speak. From the beginning she had sensed in him a shyness towards women, and had concluded that some disaster or evil experience had locked his manhood within him. Because of this he had felt safe with an older woman who would make no demands on him. He had not known, and she had not foreseen, the pressures which nature could exert when man and woman, however ill-assorted, lived together. But still she would not speak, in spite of her longing, for it was the prerogative of the male to give and the female to receive. If he came to her he must come of his own initiative, willing and irresistible.

"You are my wife."

"In name only. I made that quite clear. Don't you understand? There can be nothing else between us. It would be unnatural, beastly. Go away from me!" Now she was imploring. "We are friends. If we were more, you would come to despise me, and I want your respect, Dickon. Be as my son. Be as my grandson. Oh, use your wits, boy! Try to understand the shame I should feel. Old women are ugly. They carry upon them the deformity of age. Once I was beautiful, and so no man shall know me as I am now."

"You are my wife."

"My God, must you keep repeating that for ever?"

He laughed up at her. "Caroline!"

"Have you no mercy? Must you destroy me, because your precious Lord Nelson is dead?"

"Be quiet! Don't say his name! We're alive, aren't we?"

His hand dived under her skirt. She pushed at it feebly. He was so strong. Well, why should he not be strong, at his age? It really was useless to fight him. Her acknowledgement of defeat was an intolerable pang of joy. She moaned, and thrust herself at him. Then she slid to the floor, and there by their own hearth-stone, the light and shadow of the flames flickering over them, Caroline went back in time to the rhythm which was ageless and took no count of years.

CHAPTER ELEVEN

Asses' milk, half a pint, take at seven, or before,
Then sleep for an hour or two, and no more,
At nine stretch your arms, and oh! think when alone
There's no pleasure in bed. —— Mary, bring me my
*   gown:*
Slip on that ere you rise; let your caution be such;
Keep all cold from your breast, there's already too
*   much.*

*   Philip Stanhope, Earl of Chesterfield*

On a cold day of February, eighteen-hundred-and-six, Caroline received a letter from her sister Betty. It was, to her way of thinking, a long and tedious epistle, too full of flowery passages and of affectionate sentiments which compared unnaturally with the difference in the natures of the two sisters and the lack of communion between them. There was, however, one piece of concrete news.

"Poor Wacey has passed away," Betty wrote. "He has gone to that reward he richly deserves, for no woman could have enjoyed the benison of more noble and considerate a husband."

(Or one more amenable to his wife's commands, Caroline thought.)

"By a strange coincidence his demise occurred no more than twenty-four hours after the death of Mr. Pitt. I dread to think how we shall fare without him, for never have we boasted so great a statesman and one so punctual to succor England in her darkest hour. I speak of Mr. Pitt, of course. He died these three weeks past, and with his last breath, I hear, he murmured, 'Alas, my country!' "

("Who does she suppose she mourns?" Caroline muttered. "Wacey or William Pitt?")

"He has left me well provided for, but what is money compared with the companionship of a beloved spouse? I have also inherited our father's estate. What a pity, poor Caroline, that you did not make your peace with him! I fear, however, that nothing you could have done would have persuaded him to forgive you. Your runaway marriage was the tragedy of his life, and I am sure you must often have regretted it, for passion is one of the most fleeting of human emotions. I was the only child who could inherit, Leighton being no more. Did you, I wonder, receive news of our brother's death? He went some years ago, at a comparatively young age, ruined by debauchery and gout of the stomach.

"I think of you frequently, dear sister, for, though wealthy, I am the loneliest of mortals, and I think of my dear grandson, whom you have so cruelly appropriated."

(Ah! Here we come to the heart of the matter, Caroline reflected, grimly.)

"It is my desire to pay you a visit, and I trust you will be as agreeable to see me as I shall be overjoyed to see you. I trust also that the end of next week will be convenient. I can suffer the cold, provided good fires are maintained, and at least we are near the end of winter, so that I may look forward to spring, when even Sussex is tolerable."

Caroline went immmediately to tell Peregrine of the impending visit. "I shall give her hospitality," she said, "even though I warrant she'll consider Sweetwillow Shaw no superior to the stews of Seven Dials. But for her retinue I have no room, except perhaps for her personal maid. Her coachman and footmen and whatever hangers-on she finds it necessary to bring will have to lodge with you."

Peregrine pursed his mouth. "Charity will not like that."

"Then she will have to lump it," Caroline said, flatly.

"Betty is your aunt, and has as great a call on you as she has on me. Besides, she has already spoken of making Lancelot her heir. Indeed, she can scarcely do otherwise, for he is her legal next-of-kin. Does it not please you to have your son inherit a fortune?"

"Reckon it does," Peregrine said, slowly, "though I'll need to give it some thought. It would be melancholy beneficial for the farm."

"It would," Caroline agreed, and knew she would have no further trouble in obtaining lodging for Betty's servants.

Betty had excused herself from attending Will's funeral, it being so soon after Peregrine's marriage, of which she heartily disapproved, and so the sisters had not met for a number of years. When last Caroline saw Betty she had put on considerable weight, but now she was enormous. It required two footmen to ease her from her carriage, which did not trouble Betty at all, for she called out gaily, "If they would but invent a shoe-horn large enough I would find it mightily useful."

"I am sorry," Caroline apologized, "that our road is so poor, but this house was built before ever turnpikes were thought of."

"A road do you call it?" Betty asked. "I would be surprised if it had not broken every spring in my carriage. But what matter? They can be mended. No doubt there is a coach-builder in Lewes, and I am not thinking of being here today and gone tomorrow."

Caroline led her into the parlor where Dickon had made a fine fire of some of his choicest logs which he had been saving for weeks. "We shall be cosy, Betty. There is not a chink where the cold winds can force themselves through and blow upon us."

Betty looked round. "How dark it is!"

"It is a dismal day."

"No, it is not the weather. When they built these cots for laborers they must have imagined they were building for moles."

Caroline felt the old sisterly irritation rising in her. "This is no worker's cottage. It is a farmhouse."

"Ah! We in the towns do not appreciate the privations of the rural life. But do not think I blame you, Caroline. I admire you. What you did was right."

Caroline blinked. "For what do you admire me?"

"Why, for refusing to live in the same house as that woman. When I heard Peregrine was to re-marry I was cut to the heart. That he should so easily forget my darling Philadelphia! And I had looked upon them always as the perfect lovers. To me they were a legend, like Dante and Beatrice. I grieved for him, for poor Peregrine, almost as much as I grieved for myself. To marry again was to besmirch her memory."

"Most widowers marry," Caroline said, reasonably.

"Yes, but they were not the husbands of Philadelphia. To know her was to have known the very peak of womanhood. But that was not the worst. The worst was to choose a wife so unsuitable, a girl young enough to be his daughter. Oh, that disgusted me. After all, I am a woman of the world. Had he married a decent matron, to solace his loneliness.—But, a chit of a girl! One does not have to stretch one's imagination too far to guess what he wanted from *her*. Shameful, it is, and you were wise to leave them. But you were foolish, Caroline, to let them fob you off with this. You should have turned them out, Peregrine and his woman and their brood, and kept Hastingford for yourself and for Lancelot."

Patiently Caroline explained the difficulties of her legal position. "I could not defy Peregrine, for he is now the master, and I could not live with Charity, for less charitable a young woman I have not met. I had no alternative but to make a new home for myself."

Betty was not listening. "Where is he? Where is my handsome young grandson? Why was he not here to greet me?"

"He was working," Caroline told her. "He now does a full day's work on the farm, as all the other men. He would not expect Peregrine and Sylvanus to favor him unduly and give him time off."

"But now it is evening."

"Then he will be at home eating an enormous meal."

"He lives at Hastingford?"

"Where else should he live but with his father?"

"It is unfair," Betty grumbled. "Lancelot should be with you. Peregrine does not need him, for that woman has presented him with a quiverful. Lancelot would be good company for you. You must be lonely, Caroline dear. I know I am. Yes, now I know what loneliness is."

Betty began to cry softly. It was two hours or more since she had reached Sweetwillow Shaw, and she had not shed a tear. So she cried into an expensive and veritable cobweb of a lace handkerchief, for if Betty did not know the proper and fitting thing to do, who did?

For supper Caroline gave her roasted woodcocks, followed by hogs pudding, which was concerned with hogs only regarding the guts into which it was stuffed, and was a delicious mixture of suet, sugar, eggs, cream and spices. After this they partook of a mature cheese which Caroline had been saving for a special occasion. For drink she had taken the trouble to make a syllabub under the cow.

Betty ate heartily, though she kept glancing meaningly at Dickon, and when they had finished she expressed a desire to go to her chamber.

"I have much to unpack, and I do not trust my maid particularly. Will you come with me?"

"I shall be glad. There is a fire piled high and rushing to the top of the chimney, and the bedwagon has been airing your bed these twelve hours."

"Thank you, Caroline, I am sure you do your best. My! How narrow are these stairs! I believe this house must have been built for the fairies."

Caroline had provided her guest with the largest room, but Betty, true to her nature, professed to find it amusingly small. "Why, I declare it is like an ample powder-closet, but so simple and charming." To her maid she said, "Do not stare, girl! Go away! My sister and I wish to be alone."

"What is your name?" Caroline asked.

"Esther, mistress."

"Then go downstairs and serve yourself with supper, Esther."

"The girl is a fool," Betty said, almost before her maid was out of earshot, "but only fools now are willing to serve the gentry. Servants are become so high and mighty. It was different when we were young, was it not? Mamma and Papa always had the most excellent servants. I'll warrant the girl has already broken half of my jars and bottles. Heavens! There is scarcely room to move here."

"You have so much luggage."

"Oh, do not be angry with me, Caroline! I require to bring a few small articles, for I know well how primitive is country life. This is my hysterical water. I have an apothecary who makes it especially for me, of mistletoe and millepedes and Lord knows what else. Then there is my cordial for sleep, and my fever water, and my toothache cure. I have also brought a few delicacies. Here is a delicious marmalade of cherries and a conserve of violets, as well as of roses and water lilies. You shall share them with me, Caroline."

"Shall I store them in my larder for you?"

"Well—well, I thank you, but I think not." Betty stood with a jar held to her bosom, as if she feared it might be wrested from her. "There are times I have a hunger in the long hours of the night."

"Please yourself. I was thinking merely to give you space in your chamber."

"You shall have charge of my bohea tea," Betty said, generously, "but I will keep the key to the caddy, for I know how dishonest servants can be. It is somewhat inconvenient that mine must lodge at Hastingford. How will they know when I require them?"

"You can ask them to report to you each morning."

"Yes, or yours can go to fetch them. Caroline, do you keep but the one servant?"

"I have no servants living in. The wife of one of my old laborers comes to sweep and scour the house."

"What of him who sat at table with us?"

The moment had arrived. Caroline composed her face, for she was suddenly stricken with a great desire to laugh. "That was no servant. He is my husband."

The result was even more dramatic than she had foreseen. Betty swooned and required not only the smelling-salts but the hysterical water as well.

"How could you?" she demanded, as soon as she could speak. "How could you so shock me? You might have caused my death. Bad news should be broken gently."

"I was not aware that it was bad news," Caroline observed, mildly. "To me it appears like good news."

"You are out of your mind. Yes, that is the explanation. Thank God our mother and father are not alive! Yes, thank God for that!"

"If they were, I hardly think any actions of mine would disturb them. Long ago they considered I had done my worst."

"And so you had. Oh, Caroline, what is this perverted facet of your nature which causes you to act so wickedly and extravagantly?"

Caroline could not say, because she did not know, and Betty continued to speculate and lament for another hour or so, fortified by nips of raspberry brandy, orange brandy and lemon brandy, which she discovered miraculously in the bottom of her trunk, and at the sight of which she professed to be amazed.

"Why, how did this find its way into my baggage? I declare I never put it there. That girl must have included it thoughtlessly. It is a wonder she did not pack my bronze statue of Apollo, or my black marble table inset with medallions representing the kings of England."

Caroline repressed her yawns, but at last announced that as a farming woman she must rise early and could not lose further sleep.

"I have so much more to say," Betty complained.

"And you have ample time in which to say it."

"I do not know. I really do not know that I should remain here."

"Such a question is for you to decide."

"I have been an upholder of virtue, and so was poor Wacey. He would not permit Leighton to set foot in our house. 'He may be your brother,' Wacey said to me, 'But I grind my heel on the serpent wherever it raises its head.' Wacey was a god-fearing man."

"He was also a poet once. Do you remember?"

Betty sighed. "I still have that cherished sheet of paper. I inspired him."

"I never believed he composed it," Caroline said, bluntly. "Somehow it had a familiar ring, and it is strange he wrote nothing more."

"Oh, Caroline, how can you be so cruel? And of someone who is dead! You have always lacked reverence and respect. Really I should not countenance your latest escapade, but I am fond of you, and, oh dear, I am so lonely."

She began to cry again, then took a swig of raspberry brandy, which caused her to hic-cup. "One thing I must make clear, Caroline. If I stay, do not expect me to have any communication with your—with that—"

"Dickon will not grieve excessively if you do not speak to him."

"Dickon! It is like the name of a horse."

"You are thinking of Dobbin. And now, goodnight!"

"Goodnight, sister! Tell me, where will he, where does he sleep?"

"In a bed, as you and I do."

"Now you are mocking me. I mean—"

"I know well what you mean, Betty. The virtuous are most inquisitive concerning what they hold to be vice. Perhaps their virtue chafes somewhat, like a hair shirt. Dickon is a man, and my husband. He shares my chamber and my bed. What else should he do?"

"I merely wondered—" Betty faltered.

"Yes, and now you have the answer to your question."

Gently Caroline closed the door behind her, and smiled, for suddenly it seemed that *her* question had been answered, as well as Betty's. It was all perfectly simple, nothing for which she should feel shame. Dickon was with her, and where else should he be?

There was no denying that Betty's visit was a tiring one, chiefly to Caroline, but also to anyone else who

happened to cross her path. Continually she demanded
Lancelot's company, and Lancelot was hard put to it to
be polite to her and at the same time to avert the anger
of Peregrine and Charity.

"Now my coach-springs are repaired you must drive
with me and show me the countryside."

"Grandmother, I have work to do."

"Pooh! Leave that to someone else. You are the
young master, and one day you will be a man of wealth.
Do not allow yourself to be ruled by these country
clods."

"Would you have me defy my father and step-
mother?"

"Step-mother! Oh, what a hateful word that is! My
poor orphan boy! If only you had known your mother!"
And Betty would proceed to regale him with a highly
romanticized account of Philadelphia, of her beauty and
her almost incredible accomplishments.

"La! You are a handsome lad, Lancelot. And why
should you not be? You favor your mother."

"But I have violet eyes, like my—like Uncle Sylvanus."

"You have the look of your mother," Betty insisted.
"And if we could but get the dirt out from under your
finger-nails you could be as fine a dandy as any of
them. When you come to town to stay with me I shall
get you fitted out, else I shall be ashamed to own you
as my grandson. I shall have Weston tailor you or perhaps Stultz, and your boots shall be made by Mac-
Laughlin."

"Fashionable clothes would be wasted here," Lancelot said, practically.

"Why remain here? Your little Quaker steps will be
admirably suited to run the farm. Oh, I have scarcely
patience to wait until I can see you in your fitted coat
and your wide pantaloons. You will not need starched
stays, for your figure is divine, like an Adonis. But a
patch at the corner of your mouth will be monstrous
inviting, for it draws attention to the lips, and when
you lift your quizzing glass on its gold chain and gaze
at the young ladies they'll be swooning faster than you

can catch 'em. That is, if we do not forget to replace your perfume of the farm-yard with a smell less bovine."

Lancelot became fired with enthusiasm. It was true, he decided, that life at Hastingford was monotonous. Farming he liked, but it was spoilt by lack of companionship. Laughter he wanted, foolish laughter, and the running and jumping and kissing and slapping and pushing of young things who attach no meaning to such games, except the explosion of energy. He wanted to measure himself by others of his age, measure his strength, his charm, his virility.

These were the prospects described by his grandmother Betty, and as she talked to him he realized she offered a great deal more. When she died and he inherited her fortune his whole way of life could change. He would be a gentleman, owner of his grandmother's town house, and there would be no necessity for him to work again. Never need he wield a scythe or grasp the teats of a cow. It was strange to think about it, almost overwhelming, and sometimes he would stand before a mirror and study himself, as though assessing a new acquaintance.

Betty was highly delighted, and talked so incessantly of him that Caroline became bored.

"Yes, yes, Betty! He is a good boy, and I am devoted to him, but if you do not have a care he will become puffed up with vanity."

Betty would have none of this. "Nonsense! He has too much sense for vanity. In fact, he is the only one of our descendants who has inherited the qualities of a gentleman. He is pure Gildridge all through."

"Since you have left no children," Caroline observed, drily, "it must be my children you malign."

"I am satisfied with my one and only grandchild."

"Well, you will be able to compare him with Peregrine's other offspring, for Charity has invited us to dinner at Hastingford tomorrow, and I hope, Betty, that you will restrain yourself, for Charity has narrow views."

"I know how to behave in any society," Betty said,

offended, but all the same she found the new ménage at Hastingford a challenge to her. The house, it seemed, was not as she remembered it, for the rooms were bare and spartan, furnished only with necessities, and those as plain as possible. Charity's hair was scraped back from her pale, stern face. Charity's serge dress was the color of mud. Charity's eldest, Stand Fast, in his fifth year, and the little girl, Meek, a year younger, scarcely opened their mouths, and even the baby crawling the floor did not laugh or cry. It seemed to Betty as she ploughed her way through the grey meal—grey stewed mutton, grey suet pudding—that if she did not talk, the whole visit would pass in dumbness. So talk she did, and to whom could she talk better than to Lancelot, and of whom could she talk but of Lancelot?

"How gladsome it has been to make once more the acquaintance of my grandson! Oh, we are birds of a feather, I assure you. Lancelot is cut out for a gay life, but the poor sweet has had no opportunity to indulge his desires."

"Young people should have no desires apart from their duty to their elders," Charity said, severely.

"You are to be pitied, my dear," Betty told her, sympathetically. "Had you known my son-in-law in the first flush of his youth you would have found him very different. Did he come to you in the orchard at the full of the moon?"

"Aunt Betty!" Peregrine exclaimed.

"I am only pointing out," Betty said, innocently, "the differences between old and young. In youth the blood runs hot. I am sure Caroline will not object to my saying that, if she had not hankered after Will Dyke, you would not be sitting here at table, Peregrine, nor Sylvanus, nor Lancelot. And, come to that, even the three young ones would be missing, for they stem from that same desire, though doubtless it ran thin by that time."

"You are not to talk so, Aunt!" Peregrine commanded, angrily.

"If an old woman cannot say what she thinks, then I do not know who can. But I will not offend you further, for I have eaten sufficiently and wish to leave the table. I would walk around the farm to discover whether it is comparable in any way with the prosperous and worthy place it was when my sister was mistress. Will you attend me, Lancelot?"

Caroline scolded Betty, but with a mixture of annoyance and amusement. "What a mill-clapper it is, that tongue of yours! One of these days you will cut yourself on it, it is so sharp. I would think you have offended Charity beyond redemption."

"I shall weep no tears over that, for nothing could redeem my opinion of the young woman. Her face is as long as the long man on the Downs at Wilmington, and her happiest expression is a frown as black as Newgate. I cannot help but feel Peregrine has met his just deserts."

"You are unkind, Betty."

"And so was he, unkind to the wonderful memory of Philadelphia."

It was, Caroline expected, the only meeting there would be between Charity and Betty, and she was therefore surprised when no more than three days later Betty's carriage appeared outside of Sweetwillow Shaw and a footman came to the door with the message that Mistress Dyke would like to see Mistress Dunham, as soon as Mistress Dunham could conveniently set out for Hastingford.

Charity received Betty in the parlor, and after they had exchanged courtesies for a few minutes Betty asked, frankly, "Why do you wish to speak with me, Mistress Charity? I vow it is not merely a social chit-chat."

"You are right," Charity agreed. "It is a matter of conscience."

"Ah, yes!" Betty murmured, sympathetically. "It is said you Quakers are sorely troubled by conscience."

"I am not a Quaker, as you term it. My parents were members of the Society of Friends, but I believe a wife should go with her husband, and so I attend the established Church. It is solely as a Christian that my conscience is troubled, and as the mother of my husband's former wife, it is wrong that you should be deceived and misled."

"It would take a clever one to deceive me," Betty said, placidly. "We in the cities have cut our eye-teeth, and one would have to rise early to find us sleeping."

"All the same, you have been deceived. What do you know of your daughter's marriage?"

"That it was a great and beautiful romance," Betty replied, promptly.

"Then I would ask you to read this letter which has come into my hands."

She passed a sheet of paper to Betty, and Betty, glancing at it, was puzzled. "How did you come upon this?"

"Do you recognize the handwriting?"

"Of course! It is Philadelphia's. Oh, my poor darling!" Betty began to cry softly. "It is as if she has risen from the grave."

"Read it!" Charity commanded, impatiently. "Read it!"

Betty read, and as her eyes travelled down the page it was as though, for all her size, she shrank and became small and lost and desperate.

"This is not true!"

"You said you recognized her hand."

"It is a mistake, a trick."

"When she wrote that, she knew she was dying. Would she confess less than the truth?"

"She was loyal and virtuous," Betty declared, angrily. "She held her marriage vows sacred. What did she suffer from Peregrine, to bring her to such a pass?"

"Better question what Sylvanus did," Charity observed, shrewdly. "I found the letter in his room. It is not my habit to pry into the affairs of others, but this concerns my children. Now that I know Lancelot to be chance-born——"

Betty got up and began to pace the room. "It is intolerable! My innocent girl to be betrayed by one whom marriage had made her brother! Thank God she is in her grave! Yes, I can say it now. Thank God she was saved further guilt and suffering! Oh, I know where the

blame lies. It is all too evident. This is the bad blood of
Will Dyke which will come out unto the third and
fourth generation. This is the sin of the father, to which
my poor sister was a party. If she had not willfully run
off with that low-born stable-boy—How right my parents were to disown her!"

"Judge not that ye be not judged," Charity said,
primly.

Betty tossed her head. "The proof of the pudding is
in the eating. And you had better have a care with your
children."

"I shall bring them up in the fear of the Lord."

"Yes, and see they have a right and proper fear of
Him, for when the Dyke blood gets to boiling in their
veins then hell will break loose. Go tell my coachman I
am ready to leave."

When she reached Sweetwillow Shaw she announced
to Caroline that she would be departing early the following morning, and nothing Caroline could say would
persuade her to divulge her reason. Alternately Caroline pleaded and bullied, but for once Betty's easy
mouth was tightly buttoned.

"You were happy here," Caroline insisted. "You intended to stay through the spring. What has happened?
Oh, I realize it is Charity's doing. What did she say to
you? Why did she wish to see you?"

Betty would not discuss the matter, but she was willing to give Caroline a warning. "Sister, I do not presume to criticize your way of life. What you do is
strange and eccentric, as it has always been, though
perhaps nothing is quite so odd as that you should marry a farm-boy the age of your grandson. I fear you do
but lay up trouble for yourself, and I must inform you
that a few days ago I caught your husband with his
hand down my maid's bodice."

To her amazement Caroline burst out laughing. "If
that is all he does, I have no complaint."

"You can jest about it? Really, I do not understand
you."

"Betty, I live in a real world, not in the fantasies of
the world of fashion. When I look in my glass, what

do I see? An old carcase almost ready for making bone-manure. Dickon is young, and he is human. Why should I fret? He is kind to me."

She meant what she said. Life with Dickon was good, better than the life most ageing women could boast, for usually their husbands were dead or impotent or fancied something meatier. What did trouble her was Betty's hasty departure, and not least was Betty's remark when Caroline said, "Lancelot will be sorry to have had no opportunity to bid you farewell."

Betty was getting into her carriage at the time, and spoke over her shoulder. "I hope I never again set eyes on the—" The horses stamped and fretted at that moment, and the harness jingled, but Caroline could have sworn that the word Betty used was "bastard."

CHAPTER TWELVE

'Tis gone, with its thorns and its roses,
With the dust of dead ages to mix;
Time's charnel for ever encloses
The year eighteen hundred and six!
                    Hon. William R. Spencer

Years there were which passed over with a touch as
light as a feather, and others which pressed heavily,
leaving a scar. To Lancelot the year eighteen-hundred-
and-six was armed with a whip, and later he looked
back on it as a signpost which altered the direction of
his life. That it also contained public events of some
moment did not impress him. Napoleon might vanquish the Prussians and enter Berlin in triumph; he
might issue his Berlin Decree, declaring the British Isles
in a state of blockade, but Lancelot's stomach was well
filled. Two great statesmen might die—William Pitt and
Charles James Fox—but Lancelot lived and breathed.
He took his measure of the times from other
angles.

The departure of his grandmother Betty left him in a
mild intoxication of euphoria. So flattering had she
been, so insistent on his future as a gentleman of fortune, that he came to see himself through her eyes. He
was a special kind of person, a prince disguised in the
round-frock of a farmer, and whatever restrictions or
indignities he might now suffer were purely temporary.
Charity's hostility could be shrugged off, and the authority of his two fathers accepted in no more than a

normal manner. For Peregrine he felt a slightly contemptuous pity. The poor man, to be made a cuckold by his first wife and a slave by his second! And though Lancelot had not entirely lost his affection for Sylvanus, he did not hold himself bound to obey either of the two men. They were tillers of the soil, trapped in the furrows made by their ploughs, and their rare and reluctant innovations made no more noise than the squeak of a fieldmouse. When he inherited his estate, Lancelot decided, he would sweep everything aside and start afresh. New methods, new machinery and the appointment of a land steward such as the gentry employed would enable the two men—elderly in Lancelot's eyes—to retire and take their ease. Oh, yes, he would be generous to his relations, though he was not sure how generous he could bring himself to be towards Charity and her children.

"What a puffed-up wretch it is!" Charity raged. "Why are you so weak, husband? Do you spare the rod through laziness or fear?"

"He is a man," Peregrine protested, "nineteen years old. Would you have me exchange blows with him, and perhaps end up with a broken head?"

"That is a fair illustration of his black and heathen heart, that he should dare to raise his hand against his elders and betters."

"I'll grant he is prickly and contrary," Peregrine was forced to agree. "He's like a young bull that feels its strength and doesn't know what to do with it. Reckon he'll grow out of it. Male creatures are all the same, rams, boars, stallions, till they find a female and can rid themselves of the swelling, pushing seed."

"Do not be bawdy, Peregrine! And do not compare a man with soulless animals."

"There's not all the difference, as far as I can see. I only meant that Lancelot would benefit from a wife."

"A wife? Is he thinking of taking a wife?"

"Not that I know. But it is the natural thing."

"Well, he had better not calculate on bringing her here, for I'll not tolerate another woman in the house. I suffered sorely while your mother lived with us."

"Why, where else should he take her?"

"To your mother, who makes such a pet of him. Or to Wivelridge which has been standing empty for so long."

"Wivelridge belongs to Marthanna and Gerrance."

"Belongs? How does it belong? Did they buy it?"

"Why should they? Marthanna is my sister. She does not need to buy her home."

"You are altogether too lax," Charity said, severely. "But what does it matter? They will never return."

Charity always had the last word, because however long Peregrine chose to argue, she would find a retort, and so he ended most of their conversations by turning and going away, her voice following him so clearly and persistently that sometimes he fancied he could hear it echoing round the fields, though when he looked up he would find it was only a rook flying over and cussing as it flew.

Still he granted there was justice in her opinion of Lancelot, who was getting too big for his boots. Maybe he should speak to him.

It was not easy to find an opportunity. Peregrine knew himself to be no diplomat, and was sure he would be abrupt and clumsy, which he was.

"Are you courting, son?"

Lancelot stared at him. "What gives you that notion?"

"Nothing. You've been that whole lately that you don't mind any of us. Young men get above themselves and it takes a woman to bring them down."

"So I've noticed," Lancelot said, sarcastically.

"You're old enough to marry."

"Perhaps. But I'm not eager enough. The marriages I've seen don't tempt me. I don't like being womenated."

"Marriage is the proper state for a man."

"I'd rather have my freedom. Besides, a woman is a risky throw. If she's ugly she's no good to you, and if she's pretty she's too good to others. There's not a woman round here that I'd push up against a hay-cock, let alone marry. No, I'll wait till I get to London and then I'll look around."

"London? What makes you think you'll get to London?"

"Grandmother Betty will be sending for me. I'm waiting to hear."

But the weeks passed, and then months, and the summons from Betty did not arrive. Lancelot was not troubled. So confident was he of being his grandmother's heir that he was content to let matters take their course. It would be exciting to go to London, but less exciting as the guest of an old woman than on his own. When Betty died he would be, not a guest in the town house, but the owner of it. Naturally he did not wish her any harm; indeed, anticipated gratitude decreed that he must pray she would enjoy a long and healthy life. In the end, of course, nature would not be thwarted, and for that he would be patient.

It came sooner than he expected. On a day in late autumn a messenger arrived to give Caroline news of her sister's death. He came from Betty's lawyer, and brought with him a copy of her will.

Betty had suffered no illness, but had been found dead in her bed one morning. This necessitated an inquest, where, for lack of more concrete evidence, the doctor pronounced that she had died by "the visitation of God."

More likely from too lavish a supper, Caroline thought, and looked down in approval at her own figure still unencumbered by a superfluity of flesh. How could a woman expect to attain to a great age when she stuffed like a michaelmas goose? Caroline was sorry her sister was dead, and had no difficulty in shedding the appropriate tears, but deep within her, deeper than the tears went, flickered a spark of triumph that she, the elder, was still alive, that the sun still shone for her, though not for poor Betty, that her eyes could feed on the picture of grass and daylight and Hastingford and Sussex, while Betty's were closed for ever, or until Judgement Day, if that was what you believed. Betty had had so much, and yet so little, but, much or little, it was over now and would leave not a ripple in the sea of eternity.

Caroline dried her eyes and unfolded the copy of the will. This was her chief concern now, not for herself but for Lancelot. Lancelot would be compensated for the injustice he had suffered at the hands of Charity and his father, and Caroline was determined to make herself his champion and have good care he was not defrauded.

The will was quite short, but it seemed to take Caroline a fair time to read it, for at first she could not believe her eyes. Betty's estate was large, far larger than Caroline had imagined. It came to more than seventy thousand pounds, and the whole of it was to be used for the foundation of a home for fallen women.

"From sad experience," Betty wrote, "I have discovered that even the most respectable female may be led astray by the wiles and subterfuges of a man, and how much more easily must an unprotected, simple and ignorant creature be deceived. Therefore do I desire that the Dunham Home be rendered a sanctuary for those unfortunate ones who have borne children out of wedlock, and that they be treated with kindness and led to understand and abandon the evil of their ways."

Caroline snorted, and was furiously angry with Betty. This was no broadside at Lancelot, but was intended for the sister who had dared to flout convention and find love in an unlikely place. Why else should Betty change her plans, and after such a profession of devotion to her grandson? It was puzzling that she should harbor a grudge for so long, but Caroline could think of no other reason for such a mean trick. It was Lancelot who, in shock and grief, betrayed the secret of his paternity to the only remaining adult member of his family who had not learned it.

Caroline showed him the copy of the will, and was surprised at the effect it had upon him. Disappointed she had expected him to be, but not devastated. Though there had been a time when her poverty had been so great that only money, it seemed, could save the sanity of herself and Will and the lives of their children, she had never accorded wealth an excessive importance. Had she done so, she would have regretted a thousand times her elopement with a penniless stable-lad. But she had known with an intuitive knowledge which was with her even in youth, that life could offer a colorful variety of rewards. There was adventure for those who had the courage to seek it; there was love of people and places; there was the rhythm of living which was in itself a constant joy, binding together all things on earth and in the sky in a relationship which could not be destroyed.

Strange it seemed, therefore, that Lancelot should throw down the document, and beat the table with his fist, and pace the room on heavy, dragging feet, and then fling himself down and weep like a child.

She went to him and lifted his head against her breast.

"My boy! My darling boy! What ails you?"

"Can you ask?" he spluttered.

"Well, it was unkind of your grandmother. But, then, she could be unkind. No doubt she wished to hurt me through you, for, it seems, she never could forgive me that I had so much and she had so little."

"Little?" Lancelot gulped. "You call it little?"

"Yes, I do. And if you had known Wacey Dunham you would have called it little, too, for if ever there was a stuffed imitation of a man, Wacey Dunham was that. And she had small pleasure in her daughter, for your mother, poor soul, was smitten with the smallpox before ever Betty could realize the ambitions she harbored. There was your mother with her beauty ruined, and only a farmer willing to marry her, and your grandmother had to make the best of it. But you have no reason to fret, for you will have all the prosperity any man could reasonably desire."

Lancelot wriggled from Caroline's embrace, almost pushing her over as he stood up. "I have nothing!" he declared, violently. "I was depending on this fortune to give me freedom and self-respect. For the past six years life here has been well-nigh intolerable to me."

Caroline stared. "How can you say such a thing? It is not true."

"Oh, Grandmother, you are old. You do not notice things. But even you were aware of the hell created by my step-mother. You escaped. Why shouldn't I?"

"Escape? Surely you have never contemplated leaving Hastingford?"

"Contemplated?" He laughed. "I have stood at the window of my room night after night, and the trees against the dark sky took on the form of prison bars. I have watched the line of the fields against the horizon, and my feet have itched to run and break through that line."

Caroline was so dumbfounded that for a few moments she could find no words, but at last she said, "It was my belief you loved Hastingford."

He knelt down beside her and took her hand. "And so I do, so I do. Do you think I would have stayed otherwise? I would have run away and hired myself as a ploughboy or performed any sort of labor. But Hastingford held me. It was a tug-of-war between my step-mother and Hastingford, with sometimes one on the top, and sometimes the other."

Caroline sighed. "The young are so impatient, and why not? Patience is for the old, and by the time they acquire it they no longer need it. But remember, Lancelot, Hastingford is yours. It is waiting like a peach on a wall, and when it is ripe it will drop into your hand."

This upset him once more, and he sprang to his feet, drawing himself to his full height and shouting. "Old people are deaf and blind. Do you think Charity would trouble me if I were to be master of Hastingford? By God, I would suffer her! I would say 'Yes, ma'am,' and 'No, ma'am,' and kiss her behind. She would be no more to me than a piece of thistledown or a burr on my coat. But Hastingford will never be mine."

"Nonsense, boy! You are the eldest son."

"I am no son. Oh, Grandmother, why didn't they tell you? You have a right to know. You bore them and reared them. They were a part of you. I think men set too small a store on their mother."

"You think that because you are an orphan. Your mother is to you someone distant and miraculous, an angel."

"No, I do not think her an angel."

"But had she lived she would have suffered the tarnish of every day and become commonplace."

"I do not know what I would have thought of her. I might have pitied her. I might have blamed her. You see, Grandmother, I am not my father's son. I am Uncle Sylvanus's bastard."

For a minute or two he was afraid. Had he done wrong to tell her? Was she too old to endure such a shock? Would she faint, or, perhaps, die? But Caroline did not so much as change color. At first she did not believe him, and then she commanded him to tell her everything he knew, which was little enough, and then she asked him to leave her, as she wished to think things over.

And there was much to think about, though no way in which she could reverse the results of those events of long ago. Now she could understand Betty's motive in changing her will. Someone must have told Betty of Philadelphia and Sylvanus. Poor Betty! Her pride would be deeply hurt by the knowledge that her daughter had not only married a common farmer, but had betrayed him with another. Philadelphia was her failure, the blot on her otherwise successful life. To catch smallpox, to marry beneath her, and then to commit adultery! Oh, what a list of misfortunes! And how like Betty to bequeath her estate to prostitutes! Outraged respectability must redeem itself, and how better than to help those who, in her heart, Betty ranged beside her daughter? Now Caroline understood the last word Betty had spoken to her, the word half heard. "Bastard" it had been, and with that word Betty had disinherited her grandson.

To Caroline the knowledge of the old, sad love of Sylvanus and Philadelphia held something of remoteness. It had happened twenty years ago, and the passions which then flamed were long since dead. She could see it as a thread running through the tapestry of her family's life, revealing the pattern more clearly. Now she understood why Sylvanus had left home. His long exile had been his penance, and he had paid dearly for the flaring of that brief flame which had burnt out and left him nothing but a son he dared not acknowledge. Of her two elder sons he had always been her favorite, and it seemed to her she had known, with some sense beyond that of every day, that he was destined for sorrow.

But while she might dream over these involvements as over a story that is told, to Lancelot they were the forerunners of a present and real disaster. More than ever he saw himself as an intruder in his own home. He was intensely unhappy, and the prospect of remaining at Hastingford while Charity's children grew up to become the owners of the farm was unbearable.

He spoke of his problems to Caroline, for he felt her to be his nearest relative, and only at Sweetwillow Shaw was he really at ease.

"Grandmother, I do not feel I can go on year after year, living as I am. For what am I? I am nothing. I have two fathers, and so none. There is not one blade of grass on this farm which is mine, nor ever will be. I am a servant."

"You have the air and speech of a gentleman, and, believe me, boy, I have knowledge of such things."

"Yes, because I cared to read books and spent much time with my Uncle Sylvanus."

"That is true. Sylvanus learnt the ways of the world, while Peregrine, who stayed at home, still carries some of the Sussex talk."

"Perhaps I also should travel."

"No!" Caroline exclaimed, clutching at his arm. "Do not leave me, dear boy!"

"You have Dickon."

"Yes, and he is a good lad, but does that prevent me from wanting you as well? Have I such a small heart that it can hold only one love at a time? While you have me you are not unwanted or desolate. Remember," she added, with dignity, "I am still head of the family."

"But—"

"Oh, I know what you wish to say, but I intend to live for many years yet. The blood in my veins is not so dried up that they can put me underground."

"Of course you will live! And as long as you are here, Hastingford will draw me back. Yet I cannot see how I can stay. Perhaps I shall join the Army."

Alarmed, Caroline sent for Sylvanus.

"Do you know what that boy of yours is planning to do?" she asked, abruptly.

His mouth dropped. "That boy of—"

"Oh, do not try to look so innocent! Lancelot has told me."

"He should not have done," Sylvanus muttered, annoyed. "Must a man's private life be chewed over by all?"

"Whose is the fault?" Caroline demanded. "You were brave enough to tell Peregrine, and by that you cost the boy my sister's fortune."

"For which I am deeply sorry, but I could not stand by and allow Peregrine to ill-treat him so brutally."

"Peregrine is no brute, and the boy deserved to be punished. But that is another matter, and I must point out that you do stand by now and allow him to regard himself as an outcast."

"What can I do? I am the younger son. Peregrine is the master."

"You are too meek, Sylvanus. You grew too realistically into the part you played of a servant. But I believe you should do something, for Lancelot talks of joining the Army."

Sylvanus thought about it before speaking to Lancelot. There were things which could be said for the plan, and also things against it. He realized the boy was restless and discontented, but also he knew from experience that there were worse fates than being an unimportant member of a farming family. He therefore took the opportunity of finding Lancelot alone.

"Your grandmother tells me you are talking once more of becoming a soldier."

Lancelot shrugged his shoulders. "That, or something."

"I think it would be a mistake."

"You have no right to command me," Lancelot said, cruelly.

"I don't try to command. I merely want you to understand what it would mean. Your father and I—"

"How can you call him my father?"

"—Peregrine and I have been paying to insure you against being recruited."

"Then if I volunteer you need no longer pay."

Sylvanus sighed deeply. "What it is to be young and impetuous! The Army, you say. As if the Army were some kind of heroic paradise."

"At least my country needs me, which is more than Hastingford does."

"Yes, and how will your country reward you? I tell you, when a man enlists in the Army, his friends and relations consider him as lost. It is second only to being dead. When you have served fourteen years your pension is three shillings and sixpence a week. When you have served twenty-one years it is seven shillings."

"Money is not everything," Lancelot told him, loftily.

"Perhaps not. But consider the life, the cruel discipline. Boy, I've seen you grow up. I know what you are for freedom, and I believe the Army would kill you."

"Think you I am so soft?"

Sylvanus took him by the shoulders and sat him down. "Listen, Lancelot! You know I have never lied to you. You have no idea of the life you contemplate entering. Let us take punishment, and this is given for comparatively light offenses. You can be sentenced to receive a thousand lashes, and a surgeon stands by to see that the victim is not killed outright. When no more can be endured the wound is dressed and the offender kept in prison until it is sufficiently healed for the flogging to be repeated, and this is continued until the thousand lashes have been inflicted. Is it any wonder that our country is insufficiently defended, and that

Napoleon sneers at us from across the Channel?"

"You are trying to frighten me," Lancelot said, stoutly.

"What if I am? I would rather have you alive and afraid than brave and dead."

"What does life hold for me?" Lancelot asked.

"What does life hold for any of us? It's as well we don't know, but time brings its own solutions. Stay, boy! I have no one but you. Stay for my sake. That is, if you can forgive me for being your father."

Touched, Lancelot clasped Sylvanus's hand. "I would rather have you than Peregrine."

"Not a noble expression," Sylvanus said, wryly. "Peregrine is the innocent one. It was I who wronged him."

"He wronged me, by marrying Charity. Do you remember their wedding day, when I went to see the sun dancing on the river? I knew then that no good would come of it."

Sylvanus grinned. "Oh, yes! You knew everything. You were a wise youngster."

"Now you are mocking me." An idea struck him and his face lighted up. "Geemany! I have just had the most wondrous notion. Why do we not go away together, the two of us?"

"Well," Sylvanus replied, slowly, "that would require some thinking about."

"How much thinking?"

"I don't know. A year or so."

"A year!" Lancelot exclaimed, dismayed. "A year is practically for ever."

"Tell you what," Sylvanus offered, "I'll strike a bargain with you. Give your troubles a little time to resolve themselves, and if they do not, then together we will go to seek a new life."

"You promise?" Lancelot asked.

"I promise."

"Done!" Lancelot cried. "Let us shake on it." They gazed at one another, father and son, with hope and laughter in their eyes, and then they solemnly shook hands.

their agents which made for a civilized life. Their houses
were sparsely and crudely furnished. Their clothes were
coarse and ill-made, to say nothing of being destitute
of any tackle she had seen in London. As far as she
knew, no urban housewife would have obeyed with
unconcern to her servants. No owners of spirits appeared

Part Two

CHAPTER ONE

In one dread night our city saw and sighed,
Bowed to the dust, the Drama's tower of pride;
In one short hour beheld the blazing fane,
Apollo sink, and Shakespeare cease to reign.
                                        Lord Byron

It was inevitable that Charity's reputation for stinginess should become common gossip. Servants carried news as birds carried seed, often unaware they were doing it, for it seemed, as with birds, that it clung to their feathers or passed unadulterated through their bodies. "Charity?" they laughed. "Charity begins at home? Oh, no! Our Lady Charity ends before she begins."

"Poor Peregrine!" sighed his friends and neighbors, but within the breasts of some of the women a tiny imp sniggered, and they felt a certain satisfaction, for it was as if their sex had won an indirect victory over the men. It served him right, they thought. If he must marry twice, he should not expect to be lucky both times, any more than a player could hope to win with every throw of the dice. Men had the advantage of being forever eligible husbands, whereas they, the women, would be so marked and raddled if they attained to the position of widows that they would need a fortune in four figures before so much as a blind beggar would look at them. Let Peregrine suffer his stale bread and watered ale, but a pity it was that the other Dykes were not equally bent on marriage. Sylvanus still walked upright and handsome, and why he had no wife was past understanding. It was to be hoped young Lancelot was not stepping in his uncle's footprints. More than one farmer's young daughter made the lane to Hastingford a regular rendezvous with her friends on a summer's evening, but the Dykes were seldom to be seen. They remained within the confines of their estate as if they inhabited a principality with frontiers close guarded.

Small wonder then that the emergence of Charity's children and their attendance at a newly opened private school caused a mild sensation. The school-house was a modest dwelling some two miles from Rotherbrook, and the master was a Mr. Cottenham.

Peregrine was at first surprised at his wife's decision. "What is wrong with the school at Mayfield? It was good enough for Sylvanus and for me." But when he made enquiries he learned that Mr. Cottenham was a member of the Society of Friends.

"Your damned Quakers again! Are you some kind of a missionary, that you would try to convert my children?"

"I am concerned with giving them only the best," Charity replied, with dignity.

"The best!" Peregrine exclaimed. "I have not noticed that you are overmuch troubled as to the quality of their food and drink."

"Their victuals are wholesome enough, but food for the mind is of greater moment. Moreover, these damned Quakers, as you call them, have more progressive ideas of education than the drunken village schoolmasters who would be better employed mucking out a stable. Mr. Cottenham has trained with Mr. Joseph Lancaster at his school in the borough of Southwark."

"He can be trained at Eton, for all I care."

"That is just it! You do not care. At Mr. Lancaster's school the children make progress beyond belief, and so economical is the system that a thousand boys may be educated at a cost of only three hundred pounds a year."

"Ah, economy!" Peregrine sneered. "That is what appeals to you. But how do I know he's a fit man for

rearing young 'uns? Will he teach them proper respect,
and give 'em a good bannicking when they deserve it?"

"No, he does not believe in inflicting pain. He rewards merit, and causes the disobedient to feel shame."

"Ha! What I would expect. You're countable sly,
missus, but I'll not have my bairns turned into little
Quakers. One in a house is enough."

"They will be taught no religion but the general
principles of Christianity."

Peregrine continued to argue and complain, and
Charity finally suggested he should visit Mr. Cottenham and judge for himself the character of the man.
But this Peregrine declined to do. It was long since he
had mixed with any of the professional classes, long
since he had read a book, and he felt he would be put
at a disadvantage. Schoolmasters had a way of tying
simple ideas in a web of words, and he had no desire to
be patronized by a poor scholar. So the children went
to Mr. Cottenham's school, and Charity declared herself more than satisfied, though Peregrine pointedly
took no interest in their progress, and when from time
to time they arrived home proudly carrying a toy, he
would ask sarcastically whether they went to school to
learn or to play.

"It is a prize," Stand Fast explained, solemnly.
"When we do well we are given a ticket. For two
tickets we win a paper kite, for three a ball, and for
four a wooden horse."

"It has the sound of a lottery, more than an honest
reward," Peregrine said. "If it is for kites I pay the
fees, it would be cheaper to buy the kites myself."

"Have you heard their reading?" Charity demanded.
"Or asked them to spell? Even Deliverance knows his
alphabet and can count on his fingers."

"I'm aiming to rear farmers, not clerks."

"Oh, adone-do! If folk could hear you they'd set up
a horn-fair for us."

"Not in Sussex. Those are your Kentish ways."

"Maybe, but in Sussex it would be apt enough. Kent
is not the only county where married couples fall out."

"No, and not the only county where a man will put his hand twice in the same fire."

Charity glared at him. "Fools are found everywhere."

She was well aware that their marriage did not improve with the years, but she was not a woman who demanded a great deal of life. She had been brought up to reverence duty and mistrust happiness, and her own experience had ratified her early teaching. Like most women she would have preferred to be the first wife of a man younger than Peregrine, but only Peregrine had come courting her, and a woman would be a fool to throw away what might be her sole chance of marriage. Her children were her pride, but she wanted a larger family and considered Peregrine lax in his marital obligations. Not for anything would she have mentioned it to him, that would have been immodest, but now and again she would drop hints.

"Have you heard about Farmer Woodham's wife? You know them. Over at Hollycombe."

"What of her? Is she dead?"

"God forbid!" Charity cried, piously. "She has had a child, her seventh."

"Then it's nothing out of the ordinary."

"It makes a fine family."

"And a melancholy lot of mouths to feed."

"No more than your sister has. I'm surprised you let her surpass you."

"Rebecca lives in London."

"What difference does that make?"

"There are many professions for her sons and many husbands for her daughters."

Charity tossed her head. "A farmer has a profession ready-made for his sons, and every son means a laborer less to employ, though I hope for better things for my children."

Peregrine nodded absently, and Charity wondered whether he had even heard what she said. But what more could she do or say? At intervals Peregrine still lay with her, but so perfunctory was his love-making that she longed to urge him to put his heart into it, since apparently the organ designed by nature was not enough.

There was little communication between Hastingford and Sweetwillow Shaw, and this contented Charity. Now she was undisputed mistress of her own home, and she intended to preserve these conditions. Too large the house might be for her moderate family, especially since she employed less servants than Caroline had done, but she was under no obligation to use all of the rooms. In any case it was more economical to warm only one room in the winter, the bedrooms of course being unheated. Officially Lancelot still resided at Hastingford, but so rarely did he sit with the family after work was finished that Charity did not exchange more than a score of words with him from one week to another. How he occupied himself she did not ask. He was no concern of hers—or of Peregrine's either, she would think, glancing sideways at her husband. She suffered no remorse at having betrayed Lancelot's illegitimacy to Betty, for she believed she had done no more than her duty. Sometimes she longed to question Peregrine, to discover what he knew, but this even she dared not do. Peregrine was unpredictable. Normally a mild man, he was capable of being roused to violent temper. So she wondered, and bided her time, and promised herself that one day, at the right moment, she would show him the letter his wife had written to his brother.

Not many surprises interrupted the even passage of their days, ordered as their life was by the exigencies of the seasons. Every week the carrier drove out from Lewes, and would stop at Hastingford if he had a parcel to deliver, and sometimes even if he had nothing, for he realized his importance as the line of communication between the country people and the outside world. News of national events filtered slowly through the rural areas, and a carrier was a welcome guest at any of the farms and cottages. But on a day early in October of that year, 1808, he brought more than indirect news to Hastingford, for he set down a passenger, and drove on.

Charity was in the dairy, which was cool and dimly lighted, and she did not recognize the woman standing in the doorway, a strange and eccentric figure unnaturally emaciated, in a cloak which hung so straight to the ground that it surely could not cover a proper or decent gown.

"What do you want?" she asked, abruptly. She did not welcome strangers and was always suspicious that they might be seeking employment or desirous of selling her something.

"Is my mother here?"

"Your mother?"

"Do you not recognize me? I am Rebecca."

"Oh!" Charity moved forward, belatedly aware that some kind of a welcome was expected of her. "I could not see you well, against the light. No, your mother is not here."

"Is she—" There was a note of alarm in the voice. "Is she well?"

Charity shrugged her shoulders. "As far as I know. We see little of her, for she has made Sweetwillow Shaw her home. Surely," she added, with a touch of spite, "she conveyed the news to you?"

"No, my mother is not over-fond of letter-writing." There was silence, and Rebecca still stood in the doorway without moving. "Like a dummy," Charity thought, scornfully. "Has she lost her wits?" Aloud she asked, "Are you from London?"

"Yes, I am from London."

"Well—" Charity was growing tired of this unproductive conversation, and walked purposefully to the door, so that Rebecca was forced to move aside. "You had better come into the house."

Rebecca shook her head. "I will go to my mother."

Charity looked full at her then, and was shocked, for Rebecca had changed beyond belief. Slim and fair she had been. Now she was gaunt and angular, with hollow cheeks. "Are you ill?" Charity asked, impulsively.

"No, I am not ill." Rebecca spoke mechanically, as if in a dream. "I will go to my mother."

"Now?"

"It is not far through the fields."

She turned as she spoke and walked stiffly across the yard and through the gate of Dun Boggs Close, and again to Charity she had the appearance of a puppet. Something had happened, and for a moment Charity contemplated accompanying her sister-in-law, for fear she would not be safe alone, but a certain resentment held her back. If Rebecca did not wish to confide, then she could not expect sympathy and help. If Rebecca wished to see her mother, and treated Charity merely as a signpost, then Charity in her turn would mind her own business. It is the way with these Dykes, she reflected, angrily. They cling together, and not even by marriage can one join their select society.

It was a windless day of yellows and golds and browns, when the rustle of a single falling leaf was a disturbance of the peace. Rebecca went down past the spot where the stallion had trampled little brother Hal, and did not think of it. She crossed Low Field to the bridge over the Rother, now stout and firm. The river flowed as lazily as oil, its only ripples caused by the obstruction of a reed. For a while she stood on the bridge, gazing down at the water, as though time had stopped and haste was something she would never know again. There she might have remained until darkness fell, had she not heard a familiar voice.

"Drat the boy!" it cried. "There's a clump of doddle-grass you've left standing as if it was a bridal bouquet. I'll not have that coming up smack in the middle of my herbs."

Caroline was sitting like a grand lady in a chair before her doorway, directing Dickon as he dug her vegetable patch. Dickon was bare to the waist, and his back was deeply bronzed. He was sweating even on this October day, but as he paused and straightened up, brushing the hair out of his eyes, Rebecca could see that he was laughing.

"Cease twitting me, Caroline! I think I'll go buy you some spectacles to make your eyesight less sharp."

But as Rebecca went forward, Caroline did not seem

to trust her eyes, for she peered and peered and hesitated to speak.

It was not until Rebecca said, "Mother!" that she was sure, and started to get to her feet, though before she could do so Rebecca had rushed to her and fallen upon her knees and buried her face in Caroline's lap.

There was no speaking then, for Rebecca came out of her dream and burst into a torrent of weeping and sobbing. Bewildered, Caroline patted her daughter's shoulder, loosened her bonnet-strings, removed the bonnet, stroked her head, while Dickon leaned upon his spade and stared.

"What is it, child?" Caroline asked. "What has happened? What ails you?" The questions were unanswered. The pitiful sobs went on and on.

"Have you turned to a pillar of salt?" Caroline demanded of Dickon. "Go fetch a cordial. The child will exhaust herself."

At last Rebecca raised her head and drank the cordial, and suddenly, it seemed, there was a chill in the air.

"We will go inside," Caroline said. "Dickon, bring my chair." They moved at a snail's pace, for Rebecca leaned heavily, and scarcely lifted her feet, and when they were indoors Caroline assumed command.

"Well, my child, you had better tell me. Whatever it is, it will have to come out sometime."

Rebecca pressed a handkerchief to her ravaged face. "They have gone," she said. "They have all gone."

"Who have gone?"

Rebecca twisted her handkerchief in her fingers. "I had to come and tell you. I could not write. There was no way of putting it into writing. Did you hear of it?"

"My dear, I do not know of what you speak."

"No. I suppose not," Rebecca said, without expression. "So little news comes to you. The news does not come, and so it is as if nothing happens. You are suspended between heaven and hell. If I had been here, I might have pretended—" Tears rolled down her cheeks. "It was near three weeks ago, on the twentieth day of last month, Alice's birthday. She was twenty, a real woman. Well, you have not seen her since Father's funeral. I was troubled she was not married, and it was no reflection on her, for a prettier girl you could not imagine, but Richard, you understand, was not a wealthy man, and the eligible young men in town expect a dowry. Still, there was time, and on her birthday Richard took her to Covent Garden Theatre. Oh, it was a real treat, I can tell you. He took Thomas and Nicolas and Rosemary as well, and I stayed at home with the younger children. It was not that Richard did not want me, but the expense was more than we could manage. Living in London is a sorry business, I can tell you, what with the taxes and the high prices. Richard's position was one of trust, but to raise seven children costs a great deal."

She fell silent and stared ahead, lost in a dream once more, and Caroline had to prompt her.

"Rebecca, I am no longer young, and my heart plays tricks. Let us have the truth. Why do you speak of Richard and the children as if in the past? Why is it 'was', instead of 'is'?"

Twice Rebecca attempted to speak before she managed it, for to put her tragedy into words was, it seemed to her, to repeat it, to make the fact doubly certain. "That was the night when Covent Garden Theatre burnt down."

"Not—not all of them?" Caroline whispered.

"All but Rosemary. Rosemary was hurt, but she will live."

From the shelter of her old age Caroline sought for words, but there were none. There was no comfort for Rebecca, no comfort for anyone until they had passed through the torment and emerged on the other side. A night's entertainment had cut a family in half and robbed it of its head. If Alice's birthday had fallen on any other date—Caroline almost ascribed the happening to fate, and then derided herself for weakness. The easy way, she thought. The way of acceptance, of passivity. No, let us at least accept the responsibility of our actions. It was Richard's decision, not fate's, that took them to the theater on that evening. Or it may have been Rebecca's suggestion. Whichever it was, they chose their destiny, and there is no more to say on that score. So she put Rebecca to bed, and in the morning it was another day, and that was easier, because it was no longer the day on which Rebecca had to travel into Sussex to break the news to her mother.

"I have to think of my other children now," she said. "They are so young and helpless to lack a father. Rosemary is sixteen years old, Bridget thirteen, Arthur eleven and Edward ten."

"Where are they?" Caroline inquired.

"A neighbor had the kindness to offer to care for them while I was away, but I cannot stay long. I should leave tomorrow."

"And what will you do?"

"That was what I intended to ask. I need your advice, Mother. We shall be so poor."

"Poor?" Caroline was surprised.

"Yes, poor. Do you imagine that Richard was able to save money? War has been the ruin of such as ourselves, and for several years we have had to practice economies. We no longer entertained, for we could not afford the food and wine. We sold the carriage and dismissed the coachman. Lately we have used hackney coaches. We had windows blocked up at the back of the house, to save the window tax, and a few months ago we felt ourselves compelled to have the same done at the house front, for which I was bitterly ashamed, for everyone could see, and thus we advertised our poverty."

"My poor child! We must find an answer to your problems."

"An answer? Oh, what answer is there? Life poses the questions, and the answers are beyond our power. We just shuffle along from day to day. But what can you know of such things, mother? You have had an easy life."

"I?" Caroline was astonished. "An easy life? Is that how it seems to you?"

"What else?"

"Well, I think that dealing with life is like lifting a

hedgehog which has curled itself into a ball. There are prickles wherever you place your fingers. But you are my child, and somehow I must help you."

"I have thought of a way," Rebecca confessed. "If I sell the house I shall have sufficient money for the purchase of a small shop. It is perhaps degrading to enter trade, but I have no talents."

"Degrading?" Caroline asked. "How can you be degraded by making an honest livelihood?"

"Ah, you do not understand the social strata of the towns. There are rigid barriers between one class and another, and when I become a shopkeeper, many of my acquaintances will not call upon me."

"Lud! Then I would say to them 'Your nose up my arse!' "

"Mother! How can you be so vulgar?"

"Why, easily. I find it quite natural."

In spite of herself Rebecca laughed, then, shocked at what she had done, put her hand over her mouth.

"Easy, child!" Caroline counseled. "Laughter never yet hurt the dead, and if you're to remember Richard and the children with a long face you'll look like a blanket-pudding before you're an old woman. So you will buy you a shop, but not of necessity. You can come and live here."

"All of us?"

"Why not? It is your home."

"In this small house?"

"No, no! I was speaking of Hastingford."

"Thank you, Mother! But I cannot be dependent on you. I must make my own way. Besides, the boys are at a good school, and I am trusting that the profits from the shop will enable them to complete their education. I should be grateful, however, if the girls might come for a time. Rosemary is a young lady, and our descent in the social scale would be detrimental to her."

"Detrimental or not, they shall have a good home at Hastingford."

"They can make themselves useful."

"Of course! You know that no one is idle on a farm, and the education they will get in practical matters is worth more than all the book-learning, especially for a girl."

"Oh, mother, you cannot imagine the relief this is to me. When may they come?"

"Why, as soon as you can pack them off on the coach. I'll speak to Peregrine this very day."

She spoke to him, and that evening Peregrine announced to Charity the imminent arrival of the two new members of their household, first relating the tragic destruction of the theater. "A melancholy grievous thing it was, and I'm fair mazed to think about it. That great theater to be burnt to the ground. A quarter of a million pounds lost, they say, though that's nothing compared with the destruction of so many lives."

"It is sad," Charity agreed, "and I hope it will be a lesson to people and teach them not to frequent such places of iniquity. They and other wanton entertainments are the works of Satan!"

"Why, fegs! There was nothing wrong with Covent Garden Theatre. They performed the plays of William Shakespeare."

"Call it what you will," Charity sniffed. "It is only another name for Satan."

"Oh, you and your Satan! You seem wondrous well acquainted with him."

"Now, husband! Do not blaspheme!"

"I wasn't aware it was blasphemy to find fault with the devil. But I've no time to argue religion with you. I'm just telling you that Rebecca's two girls will be coming."

"Here? For how long?"

"For as long as they care to live with us."

Charity stared at him. "Have you taken leave of your senses? Here? Two girls? Two strangers? Two more mouths to feed? Who will pay for them, pray?"

"They will live off the farm, as we do."

"Two idle town-bred females? Two more burdens for whom I must slave? Oh no! I won't have them. Let them go to Sweetwillow Shaw."

"There is more space here. There are rooms we never enter."

"Yes, because this sprawling great house should have been a manor rather than an honest farm. I say I will not have them."

"And I say you will. Furthermore, I say you will treat them with courtesy and consideration. My eye! Am I no longer master in my own house?"

"I doubt if you are fit to be."

"What do you mean by that?"

"It seems you have never known what goes on in your own house."

Peregrine raised his arm threateningly. "I have been a mild man. I've not been abuseful to you. But 'tis time for you to obey me and not to make rough music when I ask a small thing, like to give a home to a couple of mawks."

"I give a home to too many strangers."

"And who are they?"

"Your brother Sylvanus, who should have an establishment of his own and take Lancelot with him."

"Lancelot?"

Charity smiled. "Wait there, husband! I will show you something."

She ran across the room and lightfootedly up the stairs, to return with a paper which she handed to him, watching him closely as he read it. Her heart beat fast from her hasty errand and also from a certain fearful apprehension. She was not sure what he would say or do, but he was a strong man and violence could be his reply.

"Where did you find this?" he asked.

"In Sylvanus's room."

"So for all your piety you are a meddlesome thief."

"I had a right," she retorted, hotly. "It is my house. I have a right to examine what is in it. And I have a right to learn those things which pertain to you. But what does it matter where I found it? Are you not more concerned with what it tells you?"

"That I knew."

"How could you?"

"I had it from my brother."

"Oh, no, Peregrine! I watched your face as you read.

This was something which struck at you, not something with which you were familiar."

"I knew," he persisted, "but I had no proof, and perhaps I did not wish to be certain. Now you have given me assurance."

"Ah! So you are grateful to me."

"Grateful?" He spun round. "I think you are a mealy-mouthed sow! I think you are the devil's whore, which is lower than any honest whore. My first wife betrayed me, but you never would."

"That is true," she agreed, complacently.

"You never would, because no man would want your sour lips and your clapper tongue and your besom-stick body. I'm satisfied your children are mine, but God grant they don't follow your nature. Were I a hard man I'd turn you from my house."

She went a little pale. "You wouldn't do that. I've done my duty by you."

"No, I won't do it, so long as you care for my sister's orphan girls. I married you, though you're no lumping pennyworth, and I'll stand by my part of the bargain. A home you shall have and my wife you shall be, but a wife of my board, not of my bed."

"You have no right to deny me," she cried. "I want more children."

"Then you must needs want, for you'll not get them from me."

He turned and went towards the door, and she noticed he moved like an old man. Perhaps, she thought, he blamed her as an excuse, because he was too proud to acknowledge the waning of his own desires. For what had she done, after all, that was not virtuous and sensible?

At the door he looked back over his shoulder. "When I want it," he said, "there's the fields, and you'll see, I'll give many a dairymaid a green gown."

CHAPTER TWO

"Pay well, and in good things you'll dine,
With good bread, white or brown;
Good beer, good mutton, and good wine,
And famous fish — from Town."
"Brighton! A Comic Sketch"

Not by the progress of war is measured the life of a
human being. War can become as much a part of ordinary living as the acts of eating and sleeping and loving.
Was there not once a war which lasted a hundred
years? The war with France endured for twenty-two
years, with two brief respites, time enough for a child
to be born and attain maturity, so that it became less
a crisis than a background to the routine of every day.

The consequences of the condition of war made
themselves felt keenly, but even these were more apparent to those who remembered other times, than to
the young, and had greater effect upon certain classes,
certain districts, certain individuals. The depredations
of the Luddites, for instance, were unknown in Sussex,
where their name struck no fear in the heart of the
people.

"Who is Ludd?" Stand Fast asked his schoolmaster.
"Is he the good lud to whom we pray?"

"He is nobody," the schoolmaster replied. "General
Ludd, they call him, or Ned Ludd, a poor creature
whose name they have taken in vain."

For farmers such as Peregrine there was the constant
irritation of increased taxation, but actually this did

not make a great deal of difference to him. Rents of farms increased by as much as sixfold, but his farm was his freehold. Land values rose phenomenally, but did not concern him, since he had no intention of selling. Indeed he was no worse off than formerly, even if no better, for unemployment had so risen that labor was cheap and plentiful. In Sussex the wages of an agricultural worker were sevenpence a day if he were single, or, if married, one and sixpence a day or sevenpence and a gallon loaf for each of his family. Many farmers took advantage of the forced prosperity to modernize their methods and introduce a number of improvements, but Peregrine had reached a static stage and had no intention of altering his way of working. Ambition had frozen in him and he saw no purpose in embarking on undertakings which might involve effort and anxiety. Convinced at last that the son on whom he had set his hopes was no son of his, he could not bring himself to put either of Charity's boys in Lancelot's place. They were the children of his middle age, and he might well be dead before they were old enough to replace him. Also they were the children of the woman for whom he could no longer profess anything but bare tolerance. The days passed well enough in their unadventurous calendar, and for enjoyment, since he was no drinking man, he had the occasional company of a widow who lived in the village of Burwash, whom he had made his mistress. He did not, as he had threatened Charity, seduce the dairymaids, for he considered it improper to foul his own nest, but the weekly or fortnightly embraces of a warm, undemanding woman were of considerable comfort to him.

It was Peregrine's apathy, as much as Lancelot's entreaties, which finally persuaded Sylvanus to leave the farm. For months Lancelot had kept at him.

"You said we would seek a new life together."

"Yes, if you did not get over your troubles."

"Well, I haven't."

"And what is wrong now? Your step-mother doesn't bother you."

"No, she scarcely opens her mouth. She has gone quiet, quiet and sour."

Sylvanus laughed. "She has her hands full with Rebecca's girls."

"They are well-mannered," Lancelot said, defending them.

"Think you that satisfies Charity? She is contending with creatures of a different breed. They would be no stranger to her were they Hottentots."

"What are Hottentots?" Lancelot asked, with interest.

"A race of Africans, and you should know it, for they are now under British rule."

"How can I know anything, imprisoned here? I don't even know who I am. I pay Peregrine the respect due to a father, and cannot rid myself of the habit of calling him Father, any more than I can accustom myself to calling you my father. I work and sweat on a farm to which I have no more right than that of any laborer. What is my future here? And what will happen when Peregrine dies? Oh, then I'm safe to be sent packing without a half-farthing. And what about you? What is your rank? Have you an agreement with Peregrine?"

"No. Since Father left no testimony of his wishes I have only the agreement of those who are kin. My brother would not wrong me."

"Do not be too sure!" Lancelot said, scornfully. "Didn't you wrong him? Ah, do not glare at me so! I have a right to say this, for I have suffered from it. But you know I do not hold it against you, and you know that I love you. Even when you posed as a servant I was aware of some bond between us. So let us go away and search for that freedom for which men are said to be prepared to die."

"You'll not get me in the Army or the Navy," Sylvanus warned. "I am too old. Besides, no freedom is to be found there."

"I will do anything you wish," Lancelot promised.

"What can we do? We are trained to be nothing but farmers, and we both know how feeble are the prospects of prosperity if we hire ourselves to another farmer."

"We have courage and good muscles, and you are a traveled man."

"That was a while ago," Sylvanus laughed, "and a man does not see much of the world from the bowels of a British warship."

"You can ask Peregrine to pay you your share of the farm."

"Are you mazed?" Sylvanus asked, in astonishment. "I told you I have no legal right to a share of the farm, and Peregrine has little enough in ready money."

"Still he will not allow you to go empty-handed," Lancelot insisted. "Ask him for a half-dozen cattle to sell. He will not refuse, if you make your request in the right manner. He has a conscience."

"And you are a cunning lad," Sylvanus said, with a certain admiration.

"I am no lad, Father. I am a man of twenty-two, and the years will not wait for me."

Though he would not own it, there was gladness in Sylvanus's heart at Lancelot's decision. Looking back over his life he saw it as a series of broken promises, of appointments he had kept too late. The land which he loved had never been wholly his, nor ever could be. The woman he loved had belonged to his brother before ever he set eyes on her. His years of exile had been his punishment for one brief act of loving, and his return had been an exile of the spirit which prohibited him from claiming the son of his flesh.

But to Peregrine he went apologetically, not in gloating or in wishing to give the appearance of so doing.

"Lancelot has asked me to take him away."

Peregrine frowned, as if he had been presented with a conundrum difficult to solve. "Take him from here? Where would he go?"

"I do not think he has a preference."

Fleetingly Peregrine remembered the restlessness of his youth and his journey to London. "How long would you be gone?"

"Of that he has not thought. It could be a few months, or it could be a lifetime."

"For what is he in badskin?" Peregrine demanded. "Has his step-mother been at him?"

"It is not a question of temper," Sylvanus assured him, "and he has not lost his affection for you."

"What affection? Reckon he's middling choice over where he gives his love."

"Peregrine, he's like any other lad, ready to care for his nearest, but he's been confused, and between you and me it's like he was torn in two."

"So you would rob me?"

"Rob? I am taking nothing you've not already lost."

"How shall I manage with the farm?"

"Easy. Labor's cheap and plentiful these days."

"Yes, and I need as many eyes as in a peacock's tail, to watch what they're doing. You I can trust."

"Ah, but not enough, brother. You won't trust me to bring over this farm to new ways, so that every clod can yield up its treasure. You don't realize what prosperity there could be for you and your children and your children's children. Why, you insist on harrowing with a dredge, to break up the dung."

"Why not? Bushes come free."

"There! Now I think it's Charity talking."

"And I think it not fitting you should call her over. For good or bad, she's my wife." For a few moments they were both silent, and then Peregrine asked, "When will you be going?"

"As soon as maybe. Now we've made up our minds there's no sense in waiting."

"You'll be off to Americky, like, or some such place."

Sylvanus burst out laughing. "Now what would make you imagine that? I've too good a headpiece to go traipsing to the ends of the earth. Dirt is dirt everywhere, and it's in Sussex dirt that I was bred. No, I've a mind to give the lad a change of occupation, and I reckoned we'll get us down to Brighton for the fishing."

In Peregrine's face relief struggled with amazement. It would not be so bad, with Sylvanus and Lancelot no further away than Brighton. There would not be that sense of loss and emptiness, as there had been the other time when Sylvanus went away. Then there had been no knowledge of his whereabouts and the separation had seemed as final as if he were dead. All the same—fishing!

"It's hem little we knows about the sea."

"You, perhaps. But me, I've made an acquaintance with it."

"Oh, well—"

Peregrine was turning away when Sylvanus caught at his arm. "You'll be wanting to know what you can do to help."

"Help? Why should I help? I've not asked you to go away."

"All the same, you wouldn't want your brother and nephew to start their new life as beggars."

"Nephew?"

"That's what Lancelot is, your brother's son."

The last effort at possession pulsed and then died. No longer was it any use pretending. Lancelot was not his son. Philadelphia in her own handwriting had declared the fact. The time had come for relinquishing his claim. But in Peregrine the anger and regret still lingered. Lancelot had been the expression of his love for Philadelphia, and his only precious relic. Beyond the bounds of commonsense he had clung to belief in his fatherhood, but now it was no more. Publicly it was no more, and he had nothing to put in its place. His children by Charity were not in the same category, even though they indisputably were his.

"You've no right to ask anything of me," he declared, angrily. "Besides, I haven't any money to spare."

"I ask only sufficient to buy a small boat," Sylvanus said, "and a few guineas in my pocket for food and lodgings."

Peregrine affected not to hear, but three days later he put a leather bag in Sylvanus's hand. "There's fifty pounds," he said, "and all in good golden sovereigns.

None of your paper money." For an instant he hesitated, but before Sylvanus could begin to thank him, he added, "You've no call to mention this to Charity. And be good to the boy."

It was April when Sylvanus and Lancelot packed their belongings into two portemanteaux and mounted the carrier's cart for Brighton. They had little beside their working clothes and a suit for Sundays and other holy days. Their life had not bred in them a craving for possessions, for it had seemed to them that they, as much as anyone else, owned Hastingford. The fields, the river, the three houses, all were Dyke land, and who could want more than the reach to the horizon? It was the same with the stock. There they were, Dyke animals grazing off Dyke grass. Who could covet more, when the land and the cattle already demanded every hour of a man's day, every ounce of his strength?

With no sense of deprivation therefore they set out, and it was Peregrine who felt shame and guilt as he watched them go.

"It's not fitting," he growled. "My brother and my . . . Riding a public cart like any laborer. You should have taken horses as I offered."

"We're much obliged," Sylvanus replied, cheerfully, "but they'd be of little use. I've never yet heard tell of any that fished from horseback."

"There'll be times you're not fishing."

"Maybe, but we'd need to pay for stabling, and that would not be cheap in a town like Brighton."

"Reckon you should go somewhere else. There's sea all along the south end of Sussex."

"Yes, but Lancelot needs educating, else he'll be a hodge for ever. And for myself I've a fancy for the sight of a fashionable town."

The drive to Lewes was familiar to both of them, and was a leisurely one, with the carrier stopping now and again to take up parcels or deliver them. Down the hill into Cliffe they went, over the river Ouse, then up the steep hill to the Town Hall, all three walking to save the horse.

"Your grandmother has told me of her visit to

Lewes," said Sylvanus. "Here's where the London Coach put them down, at the White Hart, and a sad time they had, poor young things, without a penny to their name."

"Why were they so poor?"

"Oh, it's a long story, and I disremember most of it. Or perhaps your grandmother left some out. There was something about your grandfather being robbed in London, but it happened a long time ago. Must be getting on for fifty years."

"It's not easy to imagine old people when they were young," Lancelot said. "There must be a glimmer left of what they were, but it's not easy to see. In fact, it's not easy to imagine something you don't know. I try to make a picture of what the sea is like, but I can't do it properly. Is it like the Rother, only bigger? Like the Rother when it floods the water meadows?"

Sylvanus shook his head. "I wouldn't say so. It's different in the look of it and the feel of it. River water is dead compared with the sea."

"How big is Brighton? Bigger than Lewes?"

The carrier answered him. "They took a census of Brighton about eight years ago, and the population was over seven thousand then. They say it's growing fast, and no wonder, for the Prince spends a lot of time there, and his gay friends crowd around him."

"There you are!" Sylvanus exclaimed, pleased. "Plenty of customers for good fresh fish, and with plenty of money to pay for it. We should make a fine living."

"Yes," agreed the carrier, "so long as you don't let Brighton take it all back. They call the town a shark that lives on gold. Why, in the season there's landladies asking fourteen guineas a week for lodgings."

"You're poking fun at us."

"No, it's God's truth, that's what it is."

"Then how the pest are we to find a roof to our heads? It'll be the beach for a bed, I can see."

"Oh, it's not so bad yet, for the season hasn't properly started."

Lancelot scarcely heard what they were saying, for

he was as excited as a child, and his attention was fully occupied with looking about him. So circumscribed had been his travels that this seemed a fantastic foreign journey. To Lewes he had been many times, on market days, and to Heathfield and Tunbridge Wells. He had walked or ridden to the villages in his district, to Mayfield and Rotherbrook, to Crowborough and Burwash, to Wadhurst and Ticehurst. But Brighton he had never visited, Brighton which boasted a prince, Brighton of which he had heard such fantastic tales that he half expected to see it hung with cloth-of-gold and blazing with artificial moons.

So busy had the carrier's day been that it was dark by the time they reached their destination, and all Lancelot could see was the bulk of buildings with lamplight teasingly showing through the chinks in drawn curtains.

"What has happened?" he demanded, disappointed. "Where are the lights?"

"Oh, you can't expect to see the Steyne illuminated yet," the carrier replied. "I told you the season hasn't started."

"Well, what about the sea?"

"The sea he must see," Sylvanus chuckled, "or I'll get no peace. Can we meet with you later?"

"Yes, I'll take the luggage and book you a room at the Dog and Fishcart, in the old Town. It's where I stay myself, for folk like ourselves can't expect to lie at an inn like the Old Ship, which has a hundred beds and sleeps such rank and fashion that we could be thrown out as vagrants."

Sylvanus said he was willing to take the carrier's recommendation, and he and Lancelot got down from the cart. It was a moonless night, and Lancelot could make out little of the sea. To him it was a black emptiness stretching into endless distance, fringed with a lace of white foam which pounded upon the beach and pulled at the pebbles with such a scraping and grinding that it seemed to be eating the land away.

For ten minutes or so he stood listening and straining his eyes, and then he said, "I reckon it's a lonely place, the sea. You can't plough it and you can't seed it."

"Maybe not, but you can harvest it."

For a little longer Lancelot listened, and then he turned away. "It's like a live thing. I'd be right scared if my fields growled and heaved at me that way."

But in the morning he took a more cheerful view. On a day of sunny breezes they walked down from the Old Town and stood on the Steyne, from which Lancelot gaped unbelievingly at the Pavilion.

"Does anybody really live there?"

"Yes. It's the Prince Regent's house. Inside, they say, it's so splendid and magnificent it's like a dream."

"I didn't know they built such places." There was a lump in his throat, so that he could scarcely speak, for the Pavilion, with its domes and spires and minarets and pillars, all shining in the sun, seemed of such an unearthly loveliness that he felt he had never seen beauty before. Country houses and churches were earthy and stood heavily in the soil, whereas this place looked as though it might spread its wings and rise lightly into the sky, towards that heaven where surely it belonged. Suddenly anger shook him. If Grandmother Betty had bequeathed him her money, he would have built such a house. If Sylvanus had not betrayed his mother and made of him a bastard—

His face was so twisted with fury that Sylvanus asked, anxiously, "What is wrong with you?"

"Why, nothing. I thought—" The anger went as quickly as it had come. Did he expect things to happen to him as they did in old romances? What would he do with such a house? Carry dung on his boots, most like, to soil its delicate floors. "Nothing," he repeated. "It was just a pang in my guts."

They went on down the Steyne to the Marine Parade, and there Sylvanus nudged Lancelot. "Look, boy, if you're wishful to see persons of celebrity. The Prince himself is hardly more famous than that one."

Lancelot saw an old woman sitting with a basket of pincushions and toys. "Who is she?" Certainly she was not his idea of a celebrity.

"That's Phoebe Hessel. She joined the Army disguised as a man, when her lover was sent to the West Indies. No one guessed her sex and she fought and was wounded. Later she confessed, I hear, and when they retired and were given a pension, they married. She was twice a widow and was in the poorhouse until last year, when the Prince gave her an annuity and allows her to sell her wares here. They say she was born in 1713, so she must be ninety-six years old."

Lancelot glanced at the frilled cap topped by its old-fashioned bonnet, the knitted cape and the long mittens. "She looks it," he said, heartlessly, and hastened across to the sea.

It was very different this morning. Blue sky was reflected in the water, the waves were short and choppy instead of long and sinister, and the sound they made was one of laughter, not threats. In wonder, Lancelot thought, "Why, here also the sun is dancing," and he turned eagerly to Sylvanus, "I want to be a fisherman. I think I shall love the sea."

"Don't use the word love too lightly," Sylvanus warned him. "There's no mistress more fickle than the sea. In one breath she'll kiss you, and in another she'll kill you."

On the beach an auction of fish was being held. In gleaming heaps they lay, chiefly mackerel, scarcely yet dead, and the bidding was brisk. Those intended for Billingsgate were packed in baskets and carried to where light carts, carrying about thirty baskets each, were waiting to take them to London.

"Let us go and buy a boat!" Lancelot urged. "Let us buy one this day."

Sylvanus laughed. "Think you I have money for the purchase of a boat?"

"You told Father—I mean, Uncle Peregrine."

"Yes, I told him, or, rather, asked him, but I'd no hope he could or would spare me such a sum. And, in any case, the two of us couldn't manage a craft, ignorant as we are. Our hope is to join a crew, if we can persuade them we are useful men, and perhaps now is as good a time as any, with shotnett fare just started."

"What's shotnett fare?"

"The mackerel fishery, and it goes on from this month until June. The shotters are the boats, carrying between eight and twelve men."

"You know everything," Lancelot said, admiringly. "To me it's a foreign language."

"And to me, but I'm keeping my ears open, lad."

"Then let's go find the captain of a boat."

"It's a hard life. Have you thought of that?"

"Hard? What's hard?"

"Out all night, when a young man likes to be sleeping."

"I feel as if I never want to sleep again."

"Hands blistered by the ropes."

"They're softer than the handles of a plough."

"Waves as high as the roof of that Pavilion you were staring at, when the sea's out of temper."

"I love her whatever her temper may be," Lancelot said, and was not aware he spoke of her as of a woman, but in his eyes was the light which shines from a boy who has suddenly, unreasonably, fallen in love.

CHAPTER THREE

Always pull a peach
When it is within your reach.
Jonathan Swift

The memory of the fire at Covent Garden Theatre was mercifully vague to Rosemary. There was a bewilderment of screaming and the pressure of bodies, the relief of her father lifting her above the clawing hands and stabbing elbows, and then his voice in her ear telling her he must go back for Alice and the boys. She had no choice but to allow herself to be carried on the human wave towards the doors until a blazing segment of wood fell from the balcony, missing her by inches, spitting out sparks in her face. The force of the crowd carried her over it. There was an agony in her leg and she realized her clothes were burning, but by then came an opening into the air, and though she dropped unconscious she was not left to die.

Her first awareness was of her mother's voice, and her mother was saying, "Thank God her face is not scarred." That seemed an amusing observation, when every inch of her body throbbed with pain. She tried to laugh, and drifted away again into welcome oblivion.

It was not until she was out of danger that they dared tell her of the death of her father, sister and brothers, afraid that grief might prove too much for her. But she did not cry or make any other manifestation of grief.

"She's got no feeling," said the woman who was

177

nursing her. "That's how they are, some of these young 'uns. Family means nothing to them."

But Rosemary's lack of mourning was not on account of any lack of love or regret. It was simply that she scarcely yet felt herself to be alive, and was still nearer to the dead than to the living. They were so close to her that she could not believe them to be gone, and by the time she believed it, the first shock had passed.

In those days her mother's eyes were perpetually red and wet, and Rosemary pitied and envied her at one and the same time. To grieve, she thought, was to accept an event, but she herself could not accept it. Life had so changed for her that when she emerged from the injuries caused by the fire she was convinced she was a different person, and a different person cannot feel the same as the one who existed before. This helped her, though her reasoning was wrong, for it was the essence of her personality that she should probe her mind in such a way. Unloving she certainly was not. Her brothers she had admired and waited upon tirelessly. Alice, four years older, had been more mother to her than Rebecca herself. As for Richard, who was so much older than the fathers of her friends, he was from the beginning of memory her hero. To her he was infinitely wise, gentle and gentlemanly, and when she was old enough to read and understand the romances of ancient times, she compared him with King Arthur, with Charlemagne, with Amadis de Gaul.

When she was able to look to the future she decided that as the eldest remaining of the family she must take the place of those who had gone, and must care for her mother and Bridget and the two little boys. That they would be poor she realized, and she attempted to devise some way in which she might earn money. From the devotion with which she had pursued her studies, and from the breadth of her reading, she could no doubt obtain a post as governess, but this she despised. Only recently had she read Mr. Broadhurst's *Advice to Young Ladies on the Improvement of the Mind,* and had heartily agreed with every word of it. What she desired was to find a private school run by a lady of advanced views, and to assist in teaching. "It is not easy to imagine," said Mr. Broadhurst, "that there can be any just cause why a woman of forty should be more ignorant than a boy of twelve years of age." And, in another place, he asked could anything be more absurd than to suppose that a mother's care for her children depended upon her ignorance of Greek and Mathematics. "And that she would desert an infant for a quadratic equation?" Education, thought Rosemary, dreamily, oh, the solace of education.

It was with amazement and horror that she heard her mother's decision to send her with Bridget to Hastingford.

"Why must I go away?" she demanded. "I wish to remain and help you."

"You will help me most by obeying my wishes. I shall sell this house."

"Then if Bridget and I must leave, let us all go. Let us not be separated, now that we are—we are so small a family."

"Arthur and Edward must continue their education."

"And what of Bridget's education?"

"Pray be sensible, Rosemary! Bridget is thirteen. A girl of that age requires no further schooling. She can persevere with her needlework, and you can help her with her painting."

"A girl! That is the unfair situation. Why should a boy be better educated than a girl?"

Rebecca sighed. "You have such strange ideas. A normal young lady would not ask so odd a question."

"What can I do in the country?" Rosemary inquired, plaintively.

"You can make yourself useful on the farm, and no doubt you will meet some respectable young man. In our changed circumstances I fear I can offer you little opportunity of finding a suitable husband."

"A husband!" Rosemary exclaimed, disdainfully. "I have no intention of getting married," then, seeing her mother's shocked face, she added, hastily, "for a long time."

Hastingford was quite as foreign as she had expected,

and Charity and her children were even more so. That people who were the possessors of what seemed to her a vast estate should live in so frugal a manner was beyond her understanding. They enjoyed none of the refinements which made for a civilized life. Their rooms were sparsely and crudely furnished. Their clothes were coarse and ill-made, to say nothing of being designed in no fashion she had seen in London. As for their food, an urban housewife would not have offered such fare to her servants. No oysters or sprats appeared on the table in November.

Sprats, she informed Charity, came into season on Lord Mayor's day, to be told coldly that she was living with farmers, not fishermen. So, she supposed, it would be useless in March to expect the turbots which would be brought alive in the wells of the boats of Dutch fishermen, or the smelts fished from the Thames, which had the delicious smell of fresh cucumbers and for which her mother paid only six shillings a hundred, and served fried with melted butter and a Seville orange. Obviously there would not be the luxury of sturgeon, which at five shillings a pound her mother bought rarely, as a treat. But surely there was no reason why they should not eat brawn such as that sent up from Canterbury and Oxfordshire, made from half-wild boars specially fattened by having straps fastened tightly round various parts of their anatomy. And what of quails and ortolans and herons, to say nothing of venison and plovers' eggs?

"We live simply," Charity said, severely.

"But you have everything around you," Rosemary pointed out, bewildered. "You have animals wild and tame, and numberless birds, and sufficient land to produce every variety of fruit and vegetable."

"Our land is for earning our living, not for indulging ourselves. We hold abstemiousness a virtue, and do not sit by the flesh-pots. It seems you have had little religious instruction."

"We go to church."

"Some go with deaf ears and come out as they went

in. You should follow the example of your cousins. They are not greedy."

"They are hateful prigs," Bridget said later, to Rosemary. "I cannot abide them."

"Hush!" Rosemary whispered, though at heart she completely agreed with her sister. "We should not find fault with them. They are younger than we are."

"That is the trouble," Bridget sighed. "Everyone here is younger or older than we are. There is no one to play with."

"You are no longer a child. You should not need to play."

"I like to play. But, then, I also like to work," Bridget said, cheerfully.

It was true, Rosemary thought, ruefully. Bridget was settling down to her new life, and accepted without complaint the many tasks Charity imposed on her. She was indeed becoming useful and competent, and might almost have been born on a farm, whereas Rosemary found herself growing no less strange as the months passed. There were few books to read and few persons with whom she could converse on the subjects which interested her. The exception was her cousin Lancelot. Though six years older than herself, his country upbringing made him appear unsophisticated and boyish. Yet she found him quick and intelligent and a veritable mine of information on rustic lore.

"This is Saint Clement's," he said, in November, "and day after tomorrow is Saint Catherine's. Saint Clement is the patron of blacksmiths, and the children make a figure of him which they call Old Clun. They go from house to house singing 'Cattern and Clemen be here, here, here. Give us your apples and give us your beer.' " And he would tell her Sussex sayings, like the time between dark and dawn was "turn-of-the-world," and Saint Valentine's Day was known as birds' wedding-day, and a toad was Charley Frog. Or he would declare that a scythe kept its edge best if it was left hanging in a holly-tree, and that if a robin's nest was taken, the thief or one of his family would die within twelve months.

At some of these things Rosemary would laugh, dubbing them superstitions, but always she was ready to listen to Lancelot, and when she was out walking or doing an errand she would take the long way round if it would bring her through or past a field where he was working.

When Lancelot and Sylvanus left for Brighton it was as if she had lost still another of her family. She missed him more than she would have thought possible, considering she had known him for only a few months, and, lonely and moping, she began to look upon herself as a creature doomed to lose anyone or anything upon which she had set her love.

Familiarity with farming life did nothing to increase her liking for it. Rather, it prejudiced her still more against it, for its practical and unsentimental attitude towards animals began to wear the badge of cruelty. In London she had eaten with gusto the flesh of bird and beast, but then she had not been faced with the necessity of seeing or hearing them killed. Now she was required to join Charity when a pig was slaughtered, and to help catch its blood in a bowl. From the knife in the throat of a goose red ran on to the spotless feathers. Necks were wrung, guns fired, cudgels crashed on skulls. Still twitching was the food when it arrived at the kitchen.

"I like things fresh," Charity said, with satisfaction, and Rosemary, sickened with squeals and squawks of terror, found it impossible to equate the pious puritan with the Charity who could imprison poultry in diminutive coops and feed them forcibly until they were ready for death.

"How can you hurt them so?" she would demand, often in tears.

"Hurt?" Charity was genuinely surprised. "What are you talking about? Beasts are beasts. They don't feel as we do."

"Of course they do! How can you be so—" She almost said "stupid", but choked back the word, remembering belatedly that she owed respect to her uncle's wife. "You hear them cry with pain. I was taught that a Christian must be compassionate."

Charity sniffed. "You were taught a lot of frivolous nonsense. The Lord created animals to serve as food for man, and as his beasts of burden."

"How do you know? Perhaps we have invented that to serve our own convenience."

"Ah! Now you would question the will of God. Well, I'll have no such talk in my house, girl. And I'll not have you polluting the minds of my children. So watch your tongue!"

"I have a right to my opinions."

"You have no rights, only duties. Do not forget you are living on the charity of your relatives. And though you are over-nice when you are required to help prepare the food, I notice you have no such qualms when it comes to eating meat."

"I do. I have many qualms since I have seen how living creatures are made to suffer, and in the future I will eat no flesh."

"Please yourself, madam! But do not imagine that eccentric ways will exempt you from your proper tasks."

So she was compelled to continue to assist at those slaughters which caused the yard to run with blood, must handle the slimy chitterlings and the still-warm organs, and look into the staring, innocent, uncomprehending eyes. But at least she knew that she was not adding to the orgy of greed and indifference. "I am on your side," she would breathe, silently, as if in some way that could offer consolation to the poor, torn bodies.

But though her sympathies were with the animals, she feared the larger and more aggressive ones. She shrank from the livelier horses, would not cross a field occupied by a bull, and sent Charity's children into peals of laughter when they watched her trying to outstrip the wind as she was chased by a bad-tempered gander. Her faint-heartedness surprised herself, for in the busy city with its streets crowded with wagons and

carriages and hackney coaches she had been as bold
as any, threading her way between the wheels, crossing
the roads under the horses' very heads. Perhaps, she
thought, it was that here in the countryside the land
seemed to belong to the animals, and she felt herself a
trespasser.

Yet there were things she loved, and her happiest
times were when she could go off to the woods and
meadows with pencil and sketch-book to picture the
scenes which caught her eye as the fairest, and the
small, timid animals which would emerge when she
was quiet, the squirrels, the rabbits and the field-mice,
as well as the birds which were a constant delight.

She managed to make a drawing of a woodlark, and
colored it when she returned to the farm, reproducing
the faintly spotted breast, the black and reddish-yellow
back and the white line like a wreath about the head.

Stand Fast saw it and approved. "That is a woodlark. It is not bad. You should get one for yourself."

"Get one?"

"Yes. In a cage. Then you could watch it."

"I do not want one. Birds should be free."

"But you have them in the towns. Many folk have
them."

"Yes. In the towns there are not so many wild birds.
There are sparrows, of course, but—" Suddenly she
realized a truth which had never before occurred to
her. It was foolish, she knew. It was more than foolish. "Do you mean—Oh, do not tell me they catch the
wild birds and cage them and—"

Stand Fast burst out laughing. "How else do you
imagine you come by them?"

"I had not thought. How stupid! Perhaps I expected
they had been born prisoners."

"No, the boys from around here take them and sell
them. They will not let me join them yet, because I
am too young, but later I shall go. There is money to
be earned that way. They catch larks and nightingales,
and thrushes and blackbirds, but those must be taken
from the nest, else they'll never be tamed. But woodlarks, now, they will be caught this month, with clap-

nets. They are better taken in September, for they sing longer."

Rosemary placed the picture on the closet beside her bed. She had, she thought, quite well portrayed the pride and flourish of the cock-bird, but the more she looked at it, the sadder she became. How unthinking were the city dwellers! They kept live creatures for their own pleasure, and did not care that they were gaolers of unhappy captives. If she were wealthy—Ah, but she was not. Still, one did not know what might happen in the future, and she resolved that if ever she were rich she would buy all the caged birds she could find, and set them free.

But that could not help the woodlarks who would be hunted in these golden September days. Anxiety built up in her, so that she could not rest within the confines of the farm, but roamed the countryside, looking about her for signs of the birds, wishing that somehow she could warn them.

"That girl Rosemary is useless," Charity complained, to Peregrine. "She will not soil her hands with honest work, simply walks out by herself, like a mazed creature. I think she is not sound in the head."

"She will grow out of it," Peregrine said, easily.

"Grow? Grow out of it? Grow into something worse, maybe. A lot you care!"

"I care enough to do my duty by my nieces."

"Well, I've not so much fault to find with Bridget. She is a willing child, and if it wasn't for her I'd send them both packing, whatever you might say."

It was not until two weeks had passed that Rosemary came upon any bird-catchers. She was three or four miles from the farm, crossing a field towards a patch of thick woodland, when she saw five or six youths among the bushes on the edge of the woods. They were armed with nets and they made no sound, stealthily stalking their helpless prey. Approaching them she was as quiet as they, so that they neither saw nor heard her. In any case, their attention was fully occupied, for as she drew near, a bird was in a net, and the string tightly drawn.

Without hesitation she rushed forward, clapping her hands and shouting with all her power. It was sufficient to cause the disturbance she hoped. Birds rose from the bushes and the grass and the branches, uttering cries of alarm. Again and again she shouted, and the woods were in a turmoil.

The boys turned and stared at her, open-mouthed. For a moment they did not speak, then one cried out, "What you doing, you twort wench?"

"Ain't you got no sense in your noddle-box?" demanded another. "You jacked up our hunt properly."

"I intended to," Rosemary told them. "You have no right to catch wild birds."

"Crumbs! Who says so?"

"I say so."

They seemed at a loss to know what to do or say, their minds working slowly, but their anger building up. They were, she thought, the most unpresentable country boys she had seen, rough and surly, the offscourings of the villages, louts who lived by poaching and whatever game they could pick up from the common-lands.

"You had no-ought to come bellicking like that," said the first, a heavily-made boy who might well have been the ringleader. "Be off with you, fagot!"

"Not until you cease tormenting these poor birds. And release that one from the net immediately!"

They burst out laughing, and one knelt down and took the captured bird, transferring it to a basket.

Rosemary went closer to them. "I shall report you."

"Who to? We're not breaking the law. Farmers is glad to get rid of some of the pests."

"You do not think I am serious. You do not think I am determined to prevent you."

"Try!" exclaimed the youth, with a gesture of contempt.

In reply she again clapped her hands and shouted, the high, clear calls echoing defiantly through the trees.

With two strides the largest boy, who appeared also to be the eldest, had reached her and fastened a hand across her mouth. "Now squawk, crow!"

"Give her a spat!" advised one of his companions. "Teach her to come meddling!"

"I dunno," said the youth. "She's purty. I got a fancy for her."

"Then why don't you have her?"

"Maybe I will."

"Me, too," said another.

"No, you don't!" The youth glared threateningly at them. "What I finds I keeps to myself."

"Then we'll watch."

"Watch if you want to," he said, indifferently. "I don't care."

"We could hold her for you."

"I can hold her myself. She don't weigh much more than a woodlark."

Rosemary jerked her head away from his hand. "I shall scream. Someone will hear. You will be beaten. You will be put in the cage."

"Nobody'll hear. This is an elynge place and there's no houses around."

She bit and kicked and scratched so violently that he had some difficulty in getting her to the ground. The other boys made a circle, enjoying the entertainment. They amused themselves by jeering and making bets on the success or failure of their companion, and their coarse conjectures on his virility so angered him that he was more brutal than he might otherwise have been. The pillow for her head was a clump of stinging-nettles, but she was not aware of them. She continued to fight even when fighting could no longer help her, and only once did she scream. She screamed when her maiden-cord was cruelly torn, when he paused before the vital thrust, and drops of blood dripped and were lost in the rough, yellowing grass.

CHAPTER FOUR

Ah! What is pleasure, but a bubble burst?
And what is time, but as a transient stream?
And what is hope, a spark o'erwhelmed with smoke,
And what affection, but a troubled dream?

Rev. F. Skurray

Rosemary wanted to die. On her way back to the farm she stood on the bank of the Rother and yearned for the consolation of the water. One swift leap and the river would close over her head, cloaking her against shame. She was spoiled, she knew, soiled and spoiled, and it did not occur to her to offer her unwillingness as an excuse. The rabbit was unwilling for the teeth of the stoat, but his reluctance did not win him salvation. No power on earth or in heaven could restore virginity once it was lost, and a woman deflowered was of little value. She had taken her standards from the old poems and romances she had read. Knights rode forth to rescue virgins, but she had not heard of one of them who would stir a foot from the stirrup for a harlot. Harlots were left for the dragons to devour.

She let her foot slip a little way down the bank. If she lost her balance it would not be a deliberate act of taking her own life, and then perhaps she would not forfeit her immortal soul. Not that she cared much about her soul at that moment. If it burned in hell it could suffer no worse than her body had done. Every inch of her skin felt sore and bruised, but the true torment lay in the center of her being. The secret path which led upwards from between her legs was now a highway on which marched soldiers with drawn swords and muddy boots. I am so filthy, she thought, despairingly, so unutterably filthy.

It was because of Bridget that she restrained herself, not because of her mother and brothers. There was still resentment burning in her at Rebecca's ruthless separation of the family. They were in two portions now, both bereaved, and she and Bridget were alone. How could she leave the poor child who had no one else? If she did, it would be piling sin upon sin. Obviously her punishment was to endure.

And endure she did. Charity commented on her miserable looks and lack of appetite, and dosed her with some nauseating concoctions whose potency, she believed, lay in direct ratio to their disagreeable taste.

"It is a green sickness," Charity said, "and idleness is no cure. You will do well to occupy yourself with honest toil, else I shall have to send you back to that sink of iniquity you came from."

"London is not so evil," Rosemary said, heatedly, her apathy leaving her. "The countryside is more iniquitous. London people are civilized, but here they are half beasts, and they would be wiser to go on all fours."

"Hoity-toity, madam! If that is your opinion of us, I do not know why you continue to grace us with your presence."

"I do not speak of you or your family, but of the ignorant rustics."

"Oh? And when do you meet with them?"

Rosemary was silent, feeling she had already said too much, though there was within her a biting need to speak to someone of her trouble, as though the disclosure would somehow purge her shame. But who was there on the farm to understand, to sympathize, not to condemn? Certainly not her younger sister, for Bridget must look up to her, respect her, or for Bridget there would be no guiding star. Charity as confidante was right out of the question. Grandmother might be more tolerant, except, reflected Rosemary, artlessly, she was so old she must have forgotten about such things.

A fortnight after the assault on her, as Rosemary was going across Wilderness Close, a figure jumped out of the hedge, almost on top of her. She was so startled that she dropped the basket she was carrying, and when she saw that it was the boy who had attacked her she almost fainted with terror. She wanted to scream, but there was no voice in her. She wanted to run, but her legs were paralyzed.

"Where you going?" the boy asked, conversationally. He picked up the basket and handed it to her, but she was too weak to take it.

"Where you going?" he repeated.

She made a great effort, and managed to speak. "Keep away from me! If I shout they will hear me at the farm. My Uncle Peregrine is working in Broad Field. If you touch me I'll scream and they'll come, and you'll be sorry."

"You feared of me?"

"I hate you!"

"You've no call to. I fancy you."

"After what you did——" She snatched the basket from him and turned away.

"You wild faring?"

"I was. I was going to pick blackberries, but not now."

"I'll join with you. Well, what can I do to tice you?"

"Nothing. You get off our fields, and if ever I see you on them again I'll tell my uncle to take you to the magistrate."

"I'm no scaddle. I'm doing nought wrong. Just came visiting you."

Rosemary drew herself up. "I do not desire you as a visitor, and I've no wish ever to set eyes on you again."

She felt brave as she spoke, but when he lunged forward and caught her arm she was trembling and helpless once more.

"I want to pestle," he said.

"What?"

"You know."

She did know, and attempted to pull away, but his hand was clamped fast on her upper arm.

"Why's you afeared?" he asked, reasonably, as if with a genuine need to know. "I've been up your petticoat. What's done's done. Now you can pleasure yourself."

"Pleasure" she exclaimed. "I would rather kill you, or kill myself."

Her violence surprised him, so that when she gave a sudden jerk she found herself free, and took to her heels and dared not look back until she reached the gate to the yard, where she paused, gulping great breaths to ease her straining lungs. He was nowhere in sight, and she hoped she had convinced him that he was wasting his time by pestering her.

But four days later, as she went down across the water meadows with a message from Peregrine for her grandmother, the boy was standing by the bridge.

She stopped, unable to decide what to do. If he did not step aside to let her cross, she would not be able to reach Sweetwillow Shaw, and what excuse could she make for not delivering the message?

"Go away!" she commanded.

The boy did not move.

"What are you doing here?"

"Waiting for you."

"You did not know I was coming."

"I watch. I can see the yard and the door. I know when you come out."

A sensation of doom and failure assailed her. If he waited all the time, spying on her; if his mind was grotesquely set in this groove, so that nothing would deter him, then there was no escape.

"My name's Abel," he said. "What's yours?"

"I have no name that concerns you. Now stand aside! I want to cross the bridge."

He grinned. "You be melancholy brabagious."

"I will fetch the parish constable."

"Lawks! I ain't worritted 'bout the bozzler. He's my

father's brother. Tell you what, I'll wed you, if you like."

"Wed me?" She was even more shocked than at his previous proposition. That was horrifying, but this was so ridiculous and obscene that it robbed her of fear. "Me to marry with you, you foul oaf?"

"You'll come running quick enough if you've got a baby under your pinafore."

She was silent, for he had voiced the fear she had tried to push away from her. In about another week she would know, would either awaken from a part of the nightmare or would be completely submerged. Perhaps after all it did not matter what he did to her.

She went forward, but he did not move, even when they stood face to face. He stood smiling, and then put out his hand and touched her.

"You beast!" she shouted. "You evil beast!"

The bridge swayed slightly. The boy looked over his shoulder, then pushed her aside and went off, loping easily across the meadow.

Over the bridge came Dickon. "What the rabbits is going on?"

Rosemary looked away, unable to meet his eyes. "Nothing."

"That was young Abel Polsted, wasn't it? Friend of yours?"

"No!" she exclaimed, violently. "No, he is not a friend of mind. I did not even know his name."

"Sounded like you were giving him a dish of tongues. Was he pestering you?"

She began to cry, with the soft flowing tears of despair. No sobs, for sobs would have been a protest and a struggle. This was resigned hopelessness, for there was nothing she could do.

"You look a mite peaked," Dickon said. "What ails you? Has Charity been scolding?"

Rosemary shook her head.

"Reckon you miss your family. I know what it is to be lonesome. 'Tis like being a bull by himself in a meadow of fine grasses, with the cows loving and beautiful behind a great high fence."

His sympathy made her tears run faster.

"You could tell me," he suggested.

She shook her head. "I can't tell anybody."

"All right, then. But things untold can canker in you. Reckon you can look on me as your grandfather."

She lifted her head and stared at him. "My grandfather?"

"Well, I'm your grandmother's husband, so that's what it makes me, doesn't it?"

For a moment curiosity caused her to forget her troubles. "How can you jest about it? Doesn't it trouble you?"

"That Caroline should be older than me? Why should it?"

"But so much older. There are some who would consider it indecent."

"Then the dirt is in their own hearts."

"You must be a good man," she said, impulsively.

"Geemany, no! I'm a breaker of the law and a vagrant. I'd have been dancing a Newgate hornpipe if your grandmother hadn't saved me."

"I wanted to see a hanging," Rosemary confessed, "but Mother would not allow it. She said there were too many common people on such occasions, and one could catch something."

"So you see," he persisted, "no confession would make me throw up my hands and cry 'Dear Heaven!'"

"I cannot," she muttered, but she found that she could. With hesitation, with sighs, with more tears, she recounted her experience with the bird-catchers.

When she had finished he was silent, and this silence she could not bear. She must know what he thought of her. If he, even he, a self-confessed criminal, held her to be beyond redemption, then indeed she was lost.

"I am disgraced," she said. "I am ruined."

"That," he said, slowly, "is a matter for thought. You have no need for shame, for you were forced. But foolish you were. It is not safe for a maid to interfere in such matters as you did. Poachers and such are desperate men, and the Sussex Weald is wild and solitary. You could have met a highwayman and been shot. You could have met body-snatchers in the churchyard at night."

She shuddered. "Oh! Not them!"

"But you met a party of boys and were raped."

"They watched," she said, her cheeks flushing.

"Ah! They have no manners. Could you bear to wed Abel, do you think?"

"Never!"

"No, he is a sockhead, of low mind and habit. Still, if you should have a babe—"

"I shall kill myself," she cried.

"That would be still more foolish. What has an unborn baby done that it deserves to be murdered? Come to me before you do anything of a desperate kind."

"How could you help me?"

He scratched his head. "Why, I'd be flummuxed," he admitted, "but I'd think of something."

She was somewhat comforted, though she could not imagine why. Dickon was a simple man, without education, but there was a warmth and humanity about him which infused his most naïve remarks with a deeper meaning than their obvious sense. He cared what happened to people, she thought. He cared what happened to her, even though he scarcely knew her, and so when, eight days later, she knew she need no longer fear that she was with child, her first action was to go and find Dickon.

He clapped his hands, threw back his head and laughed, showing his level white teeth, pleased as a child, pleased as if she had presented him with a valuable gift.

"Now you've nothing to fear."

His joy both angered and saddened her. After all she had over-estimated him. He did not understand that a possible pregnancy had been only half her grief and dole. There was still her lost virginity, by which she had forfeited her value in the eyes of respectable young men. She had told her mother she was not interested in marriage, but lately she had begun to change her mind. A husband could be a blessing, especially should he be someone resembling her cousin Lancelot, but now Lancelot and others like him were as far above her as the sun was above the earth. That some females cheated she was well aware, concealing their blemish until the words had been spoken over them and they were safely bedded, but she did not see how a woman could so deceive a man she loved. Dickon, it seemed, was not sufficiently sensitive to realize this, so she sighed and merely said, "I still fear him."

"Why? Has he been around?"

"I do not know, but sometimes I feel he is watching me."

"Perchance you imagine it."

"Bushes rustle when I pass."

"It is the wind."

"Shadows move from behind trees."

"It is a trick of the light."

"I hope so." But she was not convinced, and she became afraid to go out alone, even to cross the fields, and would ask Bridget to accompany her, or one of Charity's children.

"You are mighty keen on company all of a sudden," Charity observed.

"The country is lonely."

"No doubt, after the stinking crowds of London, but you should be accustomed to it by now."

"Well, I am not, and I like to talk with someone."

"Then you must talk to yourself, for the children have their stent to do when they come back from school."

"You give them no time for play," Rosemary grumbled.

"Oh? And what is play, pray? It is an invention of the devil to turn God-fearing children into light-minded men and women. They are not babies that must have their kites and marbles and hobby-horses."

"Bridget can come with me."

"Bridget is occupied. She is the only sensible creature in this household, and a help to me. I depend upon her."

This was perfectly true, for shortly after the arrival of Rosemary and Bridget, Charity had dismissed two of the indoor servants, and now was left with only an old woman whom Peregrine would not allow to be turned away, for she had been with them since he was a boy. The reduction in the staff was, as Peregrine well knew, Charity's revenge on him for having saddled her with his nieces, and, as often, the victory was hers, for though she had to feed the girls she did not pay them wages. Peregrine could tell that she was gloating, in her sour, mirthless way, but he was past caring, and he did not trouble to point out that Rosemary and Bridget merited a little money for their labors. The easy way was the only way for Peregrine, these days.

Sometimes, when Rosemary thought about it, she was conscious of a feeling of guilt where her sister was concerned, for there was no denying that Bridget worked harder than she did. But, then, Bridget liked the work, whereas Rosemary did not, though she admitted to herself that it would have been more pleasant without a severe taskmistress like Charity, and with the presence of Lancelot or others of her age and tastes. Now, since her experience with Abel, and his hounding of her, her heart was less in the farm work than ever. Tasks performed around the house and dairy she undertook willingly enough, but those that necessitated going further afield she avoided whenever possible. One of these was the carrying of "levenses" to the workers, who were sometimes in the furthest fields. "It's too heavy," Rosemary would complain.

"What! Some bread and cheese and a gallon of cider? Are you grown so weak?"

"May Bridget come with me?"

"Bridget may not. And I'm growing weary of you, girl, you and your uppity ways. If there's no improvement I shall write to your mother, and a grief that will be to her, poor as she is and with your brothers to educate. I'd not be surprised if it broke her heart and caused her death, and that would be on your conscience all your days, if you have a conscience, which sometimes I doubt."

There was nothing more Rosemary could do. She had herself contemplated writing to her mother, but she realized there was justice in what Charity said. If she confessed her unhappiness she would only be adding to her mother's troubles. She was a prisoner at Hastingford, and because of her sense of confinement the farm and the surrounding countryside lost its beauty for her. Fields were patches of brown or yellow or green. Woods were bundles of leaves. And as that autumn darkened towards winter she felt as though she were shut in a cold, damp cell. Oh, for the warmth and noise and comfort of London, where night was not a harbinger of the blackness of the grave! In London the things that happened were exciting, not sinister. There were scientific inventions such as were not dreamed of in Sussex. She herself, before she left home, had seen Pall Mall lighted by the new coal-gas lamps, and it had been wonderful, brilliant, almost turning night into day. But here they had to rely on the changeable, silly old moon.

Several times during that autumn she saw Abel in the distance. Not always was he on Hastingford land, yet she could think of no other reason for his appearance than the wish to see and annoy her. She reported the matter to Dickon, chiefly for the sheer relief of mentioning it to someone, for what, after all, could he do?

"I wish you lived nearer," she said. "I wish you lived at the farm. I so seldom see you."

"No chance of that," he laughed. "Hastingford is a fine place, but for Caroline and Charity to live together would be like putting a fox in a pen with a gander."

"No, it wouldn't," Rosemary contradicted, amused. "We know which would survive, out of the fox and the goose, but who could forecast the victory, if Grandmother and Charity should take up arms? All the same, I am afraid, Dickon. I am very much afraid of that— that boy." She would not say his name, would not endow him with even that much of identity.

"What can he do?" Dickon asked. "He daresn't come close, for if I happened upon him I'd give him a good larruping. And he'd be scared to come face to face with Peregrine or any of the men on their own ground. No, he wants to rile you, and when he finds you don't care he'll get tired of hanging about and go back to his old haunts."

Rosemary tried to be convinced by what Dickon said, for to be convinced was to be re-assured. Sometimes she was sure Dickon was right, and then the relief was a weight lifted from her heart, but at other times, when she saw in the distance that slouched figure, waiting, always waiting, with a kind of indestructible patience, she was not so sure.

The closing in of the days and the approach of Christmas did not give her an added security. True, she could spend more time indoors, but when she did go out, even to cross the farm-yard, she could not help but feel the menace of the darkness, and she found herself looking back and hunching her shoulders, for fear someone might spring on her.

She and Bridget made presents for everyone, having no money with which to buy gifts from the chapman or the village store. Bridget suggested they might ask Charity for a few pence, since the money would be spent on others and not on themselves, but Rosemary had already overheard Meek requesting the same favor from her mother and being refused on the grounds that the harvest had been so bad that money was short. It was true 1809 had been a bad year, but Peregrine grew no wheat and bought only what was required for family bread, and therefore was not greatly affected. However, any excuse was sufficient for Charity to avoid paying out good coin of the realm, and Rosemary would not lower her pride to ask and be denied.

They made do with whatever materials were to hand, and certainly some of the presents were rarely seen on a farm. For Charity and Caroline there were painted paper fans; for Peregrine and Dickon Rosemary embroidered toothpick-cases, though she had never seen either of them using toothpicks. Bridget was neat with her pen, and inscribed for Stand Fast the Lord's Prayer on a circle of paper no larger than a florin, surrounding it with a circle of flowers. This, she reflected, somewhat cynically, would probably pleasure his mother more than the boy. Meek was to have a silken rose for her bonnet, made from Bridget's last town dress, now too shabby and small for her to wear. Deliverance, in Rosemary's opinion, was still a child, and so she collected wool from the hedges and made for him a lamb.

Charity, virtuously determined to do her duty, had sent a formal invitation for Caroline to spend Christmas with them, but Caroline had declined.

"Your mother!" Charity snorted, to Peregrine. "To deal with her one needs to be, not merely a Christian, but an angel."

"You do not enjoy having her here," Peregrine pointed out.

"Enjoy? Enjoyment has nothing to do with it. It is a question of duty."

"Well, no doubt she finds the journey tiring. She is growing old."

"Nonsense! We could send a wagon and bring her round by the road. You always make excuses for her. I shall see to it, anyway, that you and the girls do not creep away to her cottage on Christmas Day. And I shall bake some pies for her. She will never succeed in making me act otherwise than as a Christian."

On Christmas Eve Rosemary asked if she might take their gifts to Sweetwillow Shaw. "Since Grandmother is not coming here, and we shall be at church tomorrow morning, it is my only opportunity."

Charity agreed. "Yes, and while you are there, tell her there will be some fresh-baked pies ready this evening. She can send her man for them."

"Her man? Do you mean Dickon?"

"Who else?"

"But he is her husband. And," Rosemary added, innocently, "he is my grandfather."

"Be off with you!" Charity commanded, angrily. "And let me have no more of your sauce."

It was a bright morning and Rosemary was not much afraid of going alone. For several weeks she had not set eyes on Abel, and she was beginning to believe that Dickon was right, that the boy had tired of his vigils.

She was always glad to go to Sweetwillow Shaw, for

there was laughter in that house. Caroline chattered away, garrulous as ageing women sometimes become, but gay and lively, so that she could not help but be entertaining. Dickon too seemed pleased to see Rosemary, and he promised to walk up to Hastingford after his work was done.

There was little air of celebration at the farm. Peregrine was out, visiting his mistress in Burwash, and Charity, tired from her cooking, was short-tempered.

"No, you cannot taste the pies," she said, to Stand Fast. "They are for tomorrow. Tonight you shall have porridge. Rosemary, take a bowl and fetch some oatmeal."

The oatmeal was kept in a sack in the old barn. Rosemary did not like to go there after dark, because there were mice and rats, but she did not care to own herself afraid of small animals to which the country people paid no attention. She lighted a lantern, and carried it with the bowl across the yard. A wind had risen since the morning and clouds were scudding across the sky, making strange shapes and shadows as they alternately veiled and unveiled the moon.

Rosemary set down the lantern, opened the sack and scooped out a bowlful of the meal. She hurried, for she had heard a rustling and she was not sure whether her light would keep the furry creatures at bay.

She was about to straighten up when an arm was flung about her waist and she was jerked off her feet. She gave a cry and dropped the bowl, the oatmeal spilling on the earthen floor.

"Got you at last," said Abel.

"Let me go!"

"Not this time."

It was useless to struggle, and so she attempted to reason with him. "Listen! My aunt sent me. She is waiting to cook the porridge, and if I do not return she will send someone after me."

"Hold your maw, girl! You're pulling the wrong pig by the ear."

In the corner was a pile of straw, and towards this he dragged her. Rosemary screamed, but only once, for he immediately clapped his hand over her mouth. In any case, she thought, hopelessly, they were unlikely to hear her at the house, right across the wide yard, and with the wind beginning to make a moaning song of its own.

He threw her down and stood over her, like a thick, ungainly tree. She drew her legs up and together, realizing as she did so the futility of the gesture. Now it was going to happen again. Please God, she prayed, oh, please God, do not let it happen!

And then a voice asked, "What's going on?"

Abel swung around. "Get out!"

"It's Abel Polsted, isn't it? Yes, I can see it is. I am going to stop you pestering this young lady. I shall take you to the magistrate and you'll be whipped and put in the pillory."

"You!" Abel sneered.

"You're a danger to respectable girls."

"Respectable? She's a whore."

Rosemary struggled to her feet. Dickon was slighter than Abel, and not so tall. He was standing just inside the doorway, apparently unafraid, but she was afraid for him. Abel was as mindless as a thwarted animal. He would be utterly ruthless, with the added strength of his rage. It occurred to her that she should go for help, but she hesitated. She did not want anyone to know what had happened between her and Abel. Particularly she did not want Charity to know. Charity would never believe in the innocence of a girl from London who had lain with a country lad. By Charity, so lacking in charity, Rosemary would be doubly stigmatized.

As she wondered what to do, Abel flung himself on Dickon and they began to fight, in the awkward, wholehearted way of those who had not been trained in the art of fisticuffs. Back and forth they went across the barn, and Rosemary dared not run towards the door. It was all she could do to keep out of their way. In the dim light she could not tell where the advantage lay, and her fear was that they would knock the lantern over and set fire to the barn. She saw that Dickon's nose was bleeding and he was breathing heavily. What would happen if Abel knocked him unconscious she did not know.

Presently Dickon slipped and Abel flung himself on top of him. They rolled over and over, Abel's hands searching for Dickon's throat. With an immense effort Dickon dragged himself free. He braced his back against one of the broad upright beams, and as Abel came at him yet again he pushed with all his strength. Abel staggered back towards the wall, tried to regain his balance and failed. His head hit the wall, he slid to the ground and lay there without moving.

"My eye!" panted Dickon. "That was lucky. I didn't aim that such a light blow would knock him out."

They both went towards him. "There's blood!" Rosemary cried.

Dickon turned the boy over. At the back of his head, wedged into the skull, was a bough-spud, a heavy bill-hook used for trimming branches.

"That was hanging on the wall," Rosemary whispered. Somehow it seemed that now was the time for whispering.

"He's dead."

"It was not your fault," Rosemary said, quickly.

"I know, but it doesn't alter things, does it?"

"We must fetch the constable."

Dickon glanced up in alarm. "No!"

"But we must. There is nothing else we can do."

"Then I am lost," Dickon said, soberly.

"Oh, that is foolish. You did not murder him. You had no intention of so doing. It was an accident. He attacked you, and you defended yourself. I can bear witness to this."

Slowly he got to his feet. "Rosemary, you don't understand. Such a plea would free your fine gentlemen, but not me. I should be condemned before ever I was tried. I told you I was a law-breaker."

"But you have done nothing bad."

"I was a body-snatcher. There! Even you turn from me in disgust."

"No, I—it shocks me to think that you—Dickon, what can we do?"

"If you tell anyone, if you ever mention this to a living soul, you can watch me hang."

"No! No harm must come to you. You were protecting me. But what of the—the body?"

"I must get rid of it." He looked around. "Yes! The very thing. Which is the one place that will never be ploughed up? The floor of this barn. I will bury it here, beneath the straw, and by the time the straw is used, the ground will be firm again."

"Dickon, are you sure?"

He made a gesture of helplessness. "I may be wrong, but I know of nothing else to do. Are they expecting you back at the house?"

"Yes. I came for some oatmeal."

"Then take it and go."

"Will you need the lantern?"

"No, I dare not keep it. I can manage in the dark."

"But the—the blood?"

"Earth is kind. It soaks up blood."

Rosemary refilled the bowl. She said no more, for there seemed no more to say. At the doorway she turned to look at Dickon, but he was not looking at her. He had found a spade and was planning the work he had to do.

So she went back across the yard. The wind whined, and the clouds still teased the moon, but the shadows in the yard were fantastic as the lantern leaped and danced in Rosemary's trembling hand.

CHAPTER FIVE

Rosemarie is for remembrance
Between us daie and night;
Wishing that I may alwaies have
You present in my sight.

A Nosegaie alwaies sweet, for lovers to
send for tokens of love at Newyere's Tide,
or for fairings, as they in their minds shall
be disposed to write.

Something Philadelphia once said had always remained in Peregrine's mind. She said, "Farmers can think wise thoughts. Out there in the empty fields there is nothing to confuse them. Nothing goes by but the wind. Nothing disturbs but the birds."

At the time he had considered it a beautiful and poetic remark, raising his status, placing him on a step above that of the young bucks of her acquaintance, but now he looked back on it as a pathetic fallacy of youth. The sun had set early on his ambition to be a successful farmer and something of a gentleman. Without Philadelphia to drive him, he had too much of his father in him. The bold boy who had demanded the right to use modern methods of farming had died within the body of the mature man. Habit stiffened in him, and a reluctance to change. His marriage to Charity had not stirred him deeply, and to its disappointing outcome he quickly became resigned. Indeed, during the passage of many years his only emotional storm was the discovery that Philadelphia had been unfaithful to him and Lancelot was not his son. At first he welcomed the departure of Sylvanus and Lancelot, imagining their absence would relieve him of the constant reminder of his betrayal, but he found his loneliness greater than his anger and resentment. As the months passed, and then the years, he missed them more and more. He was no great talker, but on a farm there were always matters to debate, and he had no one with whom he could argue or agree, no one from whom he could ask the advice he would almost certainly not follow. Dickon was young and without education and experience, and, besides, Peregrine had never forgiven him for marrying Caroline. The house was full of females and children, and full of Charity's tongue, so that Peregrine spent as little time there as possible. This left only his hired men for companionship, and to them Peregrine was the master, whatever his tastes and breeding might be.

The dragging, seemingly interminable war with France was felt less at Hastingford than in most other places. As a freeholder Peregrine was not concerned with rent, and as a farmer taxes did not lie as heavily on him as on others. True, he did not make a fortune, as some with arable land were able to do, but his beasts fetched good prices, which enabled him to afford the increased cost of flour and of the few necessities his family must buy rather than produce. In place of Sylvanus and Lancelot he had to take on two more men, but, paradoxically, in this period of high costs he was able to pay low wages, chiefly because of some Berkshire magistrates who inaugurated a policy by which the wages of the laborers were supplemented from the parish, so that they might not suffer hardship from rising prices. This had the effect of keeping wages down and putting the poor-rate up. Farmers might grumble at the rates and taxes, but they were the least of the sufferers. Being no drinker, Peregrine was no gossip, and missed most of the tavern talk, but at market he could not help hearing some news and opinions, and when other farmers grumbled, he joined in with them. Times were so bad, he said, that he couldn't afford to extend or modernize, or make the improvements he'd like to have done, and his acquaintances nodded wisely and sympathized. But in his heart Peregrine was glad of the excuse. He did not want to alter anything. It would be too much trouble.

The only event during the following five years to which he attached any importance was the birth of a son. His mistress, Mary Atkinson, was a widow woman of more than thirty years, and when she announced that she was with child he was astounded rather than pleased. Bastards were not looked upon with favor, not so much from moral disapproval as from the fact that they usually became a charge on the parish. For this reason many of them were conveniently stillborn, or survived only a few hours or days.

But as Peregrine became used to the idea of being a father once again, he felt first a flicker and then a steady flame of interest.

"You're a good girl, Mary," he said, one evening, as he sat comfortably by her cottage fire.

"Oh, no, I'm not, master," she replied. "Begging your pardon, I'm a bad woman, and my shame that's been hidden and decent will be seen by all when I'm dragging a bairn around."

"You'd not do aught to harm it, would you?"

"I would at this time," she confessed, "though I'm afeared of injuring myself. But should it get to being born and opens its little eyes, I'd not have the heart to touch it."

"You mind it then, and I'll take care of you both."

Her eyes opened very wide. "You mean you want the poor creature?"

"Yes. I've a fancy for another child."

"Then have it you shall," she declared, warmly, "though I shall look to you to give it a home if I should die."

She did not die, but produced a healthy boy whom Peregrine named William, after his father. That was when he began to spend even more time in Burwash. The new son he looked upon as a kind of consolation prize from life. This was to make up for the loss of Philadelphia, the loss of Lancelot, and the three children Charity had never really permitted him to possess. Bastard or not, the boy should have a good education, he vowed, and he smiled to himself as he reflected that this was the first time he had appreciated Charity's miserliness, and that her economies, though she did not know it, would benefit his illegitimate son.

It was not to be expected that such an event would pass unnoticed in the district. Parishes whose boundaries were contiguous with each other had a close association of interests, and news traveled from one to another almost as quickly as it ran fire-swift down a village street. Peregrine's regular visits to Mary Atkinson's cottage were common knowledge and his tethered horse was quite a landmark. When, therefore, Mary was brought to bed, and later appeared as a proud mother, there was no doubt in anyone's mind as to the paternity.

Soon the information reached Charity and pierced even her indifference to her husband's actions.

"I suspected as soon as I reached the altar," she cried, "that I was marrying into a godless family, and, mercy me, how right I was! Had it not been too late I would have returned to my father's house. But I had given my promise, and my promises are not broken. Think what I have had to endure! Your first wife betrayed you. Your father was a drunkard. Your sister ran off with a Frenchman, and has never been heard of since, and never will be, in my opinion. Your mother in her dotage shames herself by marrying a boy young enough to be her grandson. And now this! You have shamed me. You have made it impossible for me to hold up my head again. I dare not show myself in the village, but must live as a hermit."

"I don't see as *you've* any call to be flustered about it. You've done no sin, and my falling from grace don't make you any less upright."

"That is no more than I expected of you," she said, bitterly. "Up to the neck in your own selfishness you are. But now she has made you look foolish, let there be an end to it."

He could scarcely believe his ears. "Made me look

foolish? Well, if getting a child is to be a fool, then the world is full of idiots."

"They will say there is something wrong with you, to go outside when you have a young wife of your own and only three children."

"Let them say, whoever they are. I'll not eat carp-pie from you or anyone else. I shall do what I can to provide for the boy."

Charity went pale. "You won't acknowledge him as yours!"

"Why not? Where the seed falls, there the plant grows."

"A woman like that! The village harlot! I guarantee her child could have any one of a dozen fathers."

"Mary Atkinson is a respectable, god-fearing woman who's had little enough of luck in her life, and I know the child is mine, which is more than I can say for the boy who was born to my wife and carries my name."

"Your name or your brother's," Charity sneered. "It comes to the same thing. The Dykes have no more principles than tom-cats."

There was no way in which her anger could empty itself, and so it turned inwards, making her even more sharp-tongued and irritable than she had been before. Nothing that anyone could do was pleasing to her, and her own children did not escape her asperity. She must be severe with them, she excused herself, for they were of Peregrine's blood as well as hers, and the depravity must be drained out of them. Now more than ever she was determined to deny them the pleasures of life. They should learn that they had been born to work and suffer, that not in this world could they look to their rewards. Religion was their hope and salvation, and in order to impress this on them she instituted long readings from the Bible both morning and evening, passages to be learned by heart, and communal prayers to keep the devil at bay. With this discipline she reckoned could be found no fault. It manifested her growth in piety, and the idea that her stringency with the children was the only way she could find of being revenged on Peregrine did not remotely occur to her.

Rosemary and Bridget also suffered from this excess of religiosity, though Charity was not able to force on them the rule of learning the Bible by heart. But passages from it they had to endure, and lengthy prayers, before so much as a morsel of breakfast appeared on the table.

"No wonder Uncle Peregrine prefers the stables," Bridget observed. "She must be a sore trial to him."

Rosemary nodded. "I am sorry for the children. Stand Fast is becoming unnaturally holy for his age, and Meek and Deliverance are so secretive they scarcely open their mouths."

"And what are we becoming?"

"We are older," Rosemary said, somberly. "I think we have already become."

Bridget sighed. "Oh, Rosemary, I am so weary of being here. Once I enjoyed the work, but it is no fun since Charity has grown even more cantankerous. It is as if we are abandoned in a place where time has stopped while the world goes on. Imagine! In four years Mother has visited us only once, and we have not been home at all. Have you written to ask whether we may return?"

"You know I have."

"I mean, once again."

"Yes, and when she replies she will say the same. We are young ladies untrained in any profession. What is there for us in London? To take a menial position would be degrading."

"And what is our work here but menial?"

"Oh, it is different on a farm, and we are a part of the family."

"I don't believe you wish to leave," Bridget said, sulkily.

Thinking about it afterwards, Rosemary wondered if her sister could be right. Perhaps her experiences, tragic and terrifying as they had been, had changed her outlook. Certainly she would never forget the horror of the night when Abel was killed. Dickon had waylaid her the following morning, to warn her that there would be inquiries when the boy's parents reported him missing.

"Perhaps they will think he has run away to join the Army," she suggested. "Many young men do."

"He may have been seen hanging around this place. They are sure to come and ask questions."

"Whatever they ask, they cannot hold us responsible."

"His companions saw what he did to you."

"Yes, but they are scarcely likely to boast of such a thing."

He hesitated. "Rosemary, I don't want that you shall get mixed up in this. There's no call that you should be—should be—"

"Implicated? But I already am. You did it to save me. Your conscience needn't trouble you, Dickon."

"It does, though. I never killed nobody before."

"You did bad things."

"Like digging up corpses? That was temptatious, and didn't hurt them none."

"Look innocent and sound innocent, and they can't accuse you of anything."

"It means lying," he said, distressed, "and lying won't hurt me, for I'm used to it. You, you're no blob-tongue, but you're good, and a lady, and I reckon it'll be lamentable hard for you."

"Do you expect me to betray you?"

"I could go away, and then you could tell the truth."

"Go away and leave Grandmother? Oh, Dickon, I am ashamed of you. How could she manage at Sweet-willow Shaw without you? No, we are together in this, and we must deny any knowledge of Abel Polsted."

Though she spoke with confidence, Rosemary was extremely nervous, both of her own and Dickon's capabilities of deception. Yet after all it was not so bad. Abel's uncle, the constable, made inquiries at all the local farms, including Hastingford, but no one apparently had seen the boy. The river was dragged, in case he might have drowned and lodged in the weeds, and local schoolchildren volunteered to search the surrounding woods. But for the most part people had only a perfunctory interest in his whereabouts. He was one of eight children, his father a poor laborer, and even the parents had to confess he was idle, boorish, and a bit of a bully. His loss was little loss to anyone, it seemed, and in a comparatively short time the search was abandoned.

For several nights Rosemary lay awake, wondering whether she had committed a real crime, or, if not a crime, then a sin, perhaps one of the seven deadly ones. With more than usual fervor she prayed, confessing that the suspense was hard to bear, and suggesting that if God contemplated striking her dead, He should do so immediately, so that she knew where she stood. Nothing happened, and after a few days she was able to rationalize the whole affair. Obviously, she concluded, it was Abel who had been struck down, as a punishment for raping an innocent girl. God had killed Abel, using Dickon as His instrument. This was such a neat solution that it put her mind completely at rest.

Whenever she saw Dickon she was conscious of the secret they shared. A look would pass between them, of complicity and reassurance and friendliness. After the danger of discovery seemed to have passed, there was almost something pleasant in this hidden alliance. Rosemary no longer felt lonely, and when she visited her grandmother, which she did fairly frequently, she had a sense of being one of the family. Had she not, after all, done her grandmother a favor by concealing the murder? Had she admitted her knowledge of it, Dickon would no longer be there. He would either be fled or—horrible!—hanged. His dependence on her for his life and safety gave her a feeling of protectiveness towards him. At Hastingford she might be an unwanted poor relation, but at Sweetwillow Shaw she was important, even though her grandmother was not aware of it. It was fun to make cryptic remarks to Dickon, which only the two of them understood, and then watch his slow smile and catch the light which flashed like a signal from his eyes.

Spring brought a restlessness and sadness, a feeling that all around her were festivities from which she had been barred. The dawn song of the birds was strident and insistent, as though the very thrushes and black-birds were mocking her for being a woman unloved and unwanted. For who had ever wanted her except a lusting peasant intent on easing himself and pro-claiming his manhood? To him she had been no more than a captured woodlark or a butterfly to be dewinged and made hideous. The clouds of March pelted across the brilliant blue sky, and Rosemary, herself blown about, was a part of the excitement and could not find one reason for being excited. Delicate leaves and stalks pushed themselves inexorably through the complaisant earth and were crowned with violets and daffodils and wallflowers, trembling in the wind with tenderness and calling from Rosemary a tenderness for she knew not what. Daisies gave themselves to the sun in utter faith, but to Rosemary it seemed she had nothing to give, and beside her to receive that gift stood a gaunt nobody.

On the farm the usual seasonal work was in full swing. There was barley being sown on Broad Field, following last year's turnips, and oats on two of the good Wivelridge fields. On Dun Bogg's Close, which was cloggy land, they harrowed in hog-peas, and the potato field was ploughed into ridges. The cattle were kept close in the yards, that they might not poach the new grass, but the hurdled sheep feasted in the water meadows, and lambs began to fall like snowflakes. There was much work with the poultry at that time, the setting of eggs and the hatching, as well as the careful feeding of the turkey poults. Charity's aim was to keep Rosemary and Bridget constantly busy in the dairy and the poultry-yards, but, as she frequently and bitterly declared, she was not endowed with eyes set all around her head, and her suspicions that the girls some-times played truant were correct.

It was on a blustery Sunday afternoon that Rose-mary walked with Dickon to Dallington Forest. He had whispered to her in church that they should meet down by the river bridge, and there she found him looking almost unnatural in his best clothes.

"Is there something important about this outing?" she asked. "Is it a special occasion?"

"Reckon every day is special when spring first shows," he answered, "but most days is working days. Caroline is resting now, and she tells me to go out and lift my eyes to Heaven, 'stead of to earth, as I must when ploughing and such."

"Where are we going?"

"To Dallington Forest to see the primroses."

"It is a long way."

"And you have strong legs."

"There are primroses here."

"Yes, and there are people here, but still travelers go to America to see the people there. You stay too close to the farm."

"There doesn't seem much reason for going further," she replied, evasively.

"You still afeared?"

"No. No, I do not think so. Why should I walk out alone, anyway? Other fields are like ours."

"That's London talk."

"Perhaps it is, but I'd not be in London on a day like this. I feel light-heeled and light-headed. I believe the wind wants me to fly. Let us run, Dickon! Let us run!"

They ran until they were breathless, then walked, then ran again, and at last came to the forest. There, once they had been received by the trees, it was a different world. Up above, in the top branches, the wind sounded like breaking waves, but at ground level all was quiet and still. Under the oaks, in the sheltered places, the hazel-buds were shooting, but the catkins still hung, each swaying slightly as if from its tiny gibbet. Over them was the majesty of the standard oaks, and under, like the embroidered rosettes of an old tapestry, were the neat and perfectly formed clusters of the primroses. Delicately green they were, carrying above them the cream-curd-colored circles of the flowers.

"Spring is so tidy," Rosemary said.

"You like tidy things?"

"I don't know. I don't know what I am or who I am. Oh, Dickon, I have lost myself."

Suddenly she was crying, and Dickon took her by the hand and led her to where a fallen tree spanned a clearing. It made a good seat, so long as they avoided the place where ants were working.

Dickon looked at her wonderingly. "You should be happy."

"Happy? Why?"

It took him a few minutes to decide. "Well, you are beautiful, and you've had education."

"Education!" she echoed, scornfully. "What is education? It means that when I look at primroses I can say, "Bring the rathe primrose that forsaken dies, The tufted crow-toe, and pale jessamine, The—" Oh, I forget the rest. Dickon, am I really beautiful?"

"I think you are."

"You think? What kind of a judge are you? Have you seen the fashionable ladies, who look as though they would melt if you touched them?"

"No, but I have seen you." He lifted her hand which lay on the sun-warmed bark of the tree. "You are not like the girls I have known. You do farm work, but your hand is small and narrow, with smooth, fine bones. It is a lady's hand."

Rosemary snatched it away. "My grandmother also is a lady."

"Yes, but her hands are old and wrinkled."

"You have no right to find fault with them," Rosemary told him, angrily.

"I don't find fault, but I must confess they're old."

"You married an old woman, knowing what you did."

"Yes, and I don't regret it. Why are you so tessy?"

She sighed, and shook her head.

"And why did you cry?"

"I have no need to tell you."

"No, you've no need to tell nobody, but it's melancholy broody you'll be, keeping it pent up."

"You wouldn't understand. I doubt if there is a man

who could understand. It's what he did, that boy. He has made me a bad woman."

"Against your will."

"Who would believe that?" she asked, with quiet desperation. "I am like other girls. I want a husband and children, but I am ruined."

"I wouldn't hold it against you."

"You?" She smiled. "You are a married man, and—"

"A country-put? You are reckoning how you would stand with those London fellows?"

"Oh, I've no taste for dandies."

"You are troubled what Lancelot would think, then?"

"Lancelot?" she asked, sharply. "Why Lancelot?"

"Oh, I dunno. Lancelot is away to Brighton and Lord knows when we'll see him again. But don't be lonesome, Rosemary. Don't be lonesome in the Spring."

"Spring is the worst time."

She felt the tears coming again, and at the same time she felt his arm circling her and pulling her head on to his shoulder. The back of his neck was burnt mahogany, but his throat was soft as a child's. He smelled warm and sweet, with a freshness of new grass touched by a faint odor of cow and horse.

"If we don't move," he said, "you'll have ants under your skirts. Come and lie on these primroses. There! Now you look right, like part of a picture."

It was all she could expect, she thought, the desire or affection, or both, of a young man like Dickon. No doubt he would be rough and hasty, like a bull, but she was so solitary, so shut away from the participation in the ritual of spring. Besides, there was within her a tightness as of a river dammed which strains to throw out its water in a wild cascade. Perhaps if she closed her eyes and thought of someone, someone like Lancelot—

She opened her eyes and sat up suddenly. "We can't! It would be wrong. There's Grandmother—"

"Caroline's a wise woman," Dickon said, soothingly. "She knows as folk are only human. She doesn't expect more than anybody can give. She leaves me free, and I'm right fond of her."

He meant every word he said, and bound up with his desire for Rosemary was his love for Caroline. Oh, yes, Caroline knew he was human, for she had made him so. She it was who had made it possible for him to love a young girl. Gratitude flowed out from him, through his lips and his finger-tips, but it was intended for Caroline rather than for this bitter, frustrated girl.

Rosemary sank back. She did not speak again, but once she laughed, and that was when the thought occurred to her that Grandmother had taught him well.

CHAPTER SIX

"We have John Dories, turbots, soles, mullets and red gurnets, jumping alive out of the sea; but as price is the true test of flavour, the Gourmands are assured that they are much dearer here than at Billingsgate. The South Down mutton is here in perfection, and floats about the dish in its own gravy upon the first cut. How it contrives to have either flesh or gravy is not for such a sheepish understanding as mine to develop, for the Downs on which it feeds are as bald as an old billiard cloth!"

A Letter from Brighton, 1803

There would be times, in years to come, when Lancelot would look back with a smile upon his romantic affair with the sea. Love at first sight, plunging in heels over head, blinded by skin-deep beauty, it was the story of any young man losing his heart, whether to a woman, to an element, or to a dream. And, whatever the object of his affection, he would find, as intimacy grew, that reality stepped in. The woman would prove to be human, the element unpredictable, and the dream temporal. The dream would fly with the morning, the woman say yea or nay, and the sea demand more from a man than either. Oh, yes, a fisherman's life was no feather-bed, and Lancelot found himself looking back on Hastingford days as upon a playtime. The land gave up her spoils to the patient tiller, but there was no manure which could persuade the sea to offer her treasures if she were unwilling. On a farm the cattle could be led or driven, but no coercion of man could force the fishes into the net. Wind and weather ashore could ruin the crops, but at sea they lay in wait to snatch a man's very life.

Yet there was not a moment of hardship or heart-break or fulfilment which Lancelot would have missed. It was engrossing and exhilarating, whether they rode out a gale, or crept back with an empty boat, or returned in triumph with great gleaming piles of dead and dying fish slithering under their feet. He had wondered, before he came here, whether the work would prove monotonous, but he found that it had its changes with the changes of season, even as the land had. Early in the year was Tucknett Fare, the plaice fishery, for which they had shares in a Tucker, a boat carrying eight men. Then came Shotnett Fare, the mackerel fishing. During the summer they fished for conger-eels from hooked lines, and Autumn until Christmas saw them engaged on Cock Fare, the herring fishery in waters near their home port. Lancelot learned a whole new vocabulary; of ranns, the divisions of a net; of a warp, which was four herrings when counting them; of a trotline and a spear-pole; of keveling, the Brighton name for the skate; of rippiers, the men who carried baskets of fish to inland towns, and many other expressions which would have sounded like foreign words to the people at home.

There were great occasions, like the night when their boat brought back more than two thousand mackerel, which sold for three pounds six shillings a hundred. So delighted was the crew that each member without exception spent the day in drinking, and were all so drunk by dark that they sank down where they were to sleep off their celebration and missed that night's fishing.

During their leisure time there was nothing the old hands liked better than to entertain Sylvanus and Lancelot with tales of fish they had caught or had almost caught, great fish, gigantic fish, always larger, those fish of yesterday, than the fish of today. It wasn't much more than twenty years agone, said one, that a gentleman bathing in the sea was chased by a tiger shark. He ran and the shark chased him so violently that it threw itself right out of the sea and on to the shore. The gentleman fetched help and a crowd of them killed the shark. "My father was one. He had a hatchet. And when they opened the fish, what d'you think they found? A man's head, just like life, except that it was soft and pappy. You wouldn't catch me bathing. I come over of a cold clam to think of taking off my clothes and going into the sea."

Life on shore was comfortable enough, for Sylvanus and Lancelot lodged at the house of an old woman in Ship Street, the widow of a fisherman, who was glad to take them for a modest rent and feed them adequately if not luxuriously. She'd have none but fisherfolk, she said, having lost her husband and two sons at sea. Nowadays, with Brighton so grand, and the Prince of Wales trailing half London behind him during the season, she could have let her rooms to the gentry and made bags of money. But land-people didn't smell right, she declared. They had a strange tang to them. No, let be how 'twill there was nothing so homely as the fine scent of herring on a man and on his clothes.

But not all of Lancelot's thoughts were fixed on boats and the sea. Working at night left the day free, except for sleep, and what young man would want to sleep his life away, when Brighton in the season was a gay raree-show, and he could see the high and the mighty and the fashionable, on whom in ordinary places he could never have set his eyes?

On August the twelfth was the Prince of Wales's birthday, and that was a day to be remembered. Ships of the Navy anchored in sight of the Pavilion, as brightly decorated as was every building on shore. A band played on the lawn in front of the Pavilion, a royal salute was fired from the ships at sea and the batteries on shore. The Prince drove in his carriage, followed by a crowd of ladies and gentlemen, to the race-course on the Downs, where he reviewed the troops. At night there were balls and illuminations and fireworks. It would have been enough to turn the head of any country lad, had he not known his place was on the outside of such company, such festivities. He could watch, but these creatures in their velvet and feathers and dia-

monds were surely half-divine, and emanated from another world than this.

There were many such occasions to offer Lancelot
free entertainment, but they did not touch his personal
life. For companionship, at play as well as at work, he
mixed with the fishermen. They were for the most part
cheerful, friendly fellows, and though they had not
been given the advantage of education, Lancelot was no
skipjack. Farmers or fishermen, all were alike to him.
There was plenty of talk about keeping to your station
in life, chiefly from the clergy and the petty squires
who would be kings of their small kingdoms, but he
didn't attach much importance to such things. Above
and below were relative terms. Be your blood of the
deepest purple, and your gold reach to the top of Black-
down, there was always someone above you, and were
you the lowest and most miserable of mankind there
would be another sunk still deeper in the bog. So he
talked and laughed and drank with whoever was beside
him, and he counted no further than the next hour, because once he had counted, and fate had discounted his
hopes. Once he might have been a wealthy gentleman,
but he had resulted in becoming a bastard, and a fisherman. He did not think he was bitter, but he knew he
now faced life with an amused cynicism.

It was not until the summer of 1812 that anything
out of the ordinary happened to him. The three years
in Brighton had passed smoothly enough for his father
and himself. They had worked hard and made themselves a living, but had been able to put little or nothing
away for savings. Sometimes they talked of paying a
visit to the farm, but there never seemed sufficient time,
though, with the fast coaches running regularly, it was
none so far away. The truth was, perhaps, that they had
no great desire to return yet into their past, it being
still too close to them. For Sylvanus there was no one
he would wish to see except his mother, and no doubt
she did well enough with her young husband. For
Lancelot, Hastingford stood for disappointment and
frustration, and for both of them the prospect of the
kind of welcome Charity would give them was not an

inducement for them to travel even the necessary twenty-seven miles or so. Here life was free and easy. It was a man's world, without ties or the obligation to mind their manners.

The Prince of Wales, now made Regent, was still a frequent visitor to the town. Some said he was less wild than formerly, but there was no lack of gaiety when he was in residence, though he apparently paid a certain attention to affairs of state, now that the poor old king was incurably insane. Certainly his fondness for Brighton persisted. In addition to his fantastic Pavilion he had purchased a number of properties, and that very year bought Marlborough House.

In public matters there had been one outstanding calamity, when on May 11th the Prime Minister, Spencer Perceval, had been assassinated. The war with France dragged on, and no one knew whether to believe the rumor that in April, on the eve of war with Russia, Napoleon had made overtures of peace with England. True or not, it came to nothing, and now half-heartedly we were fighting America once more. In the north, one heard, there were riots, with factories damaged and provisions carried away, but in the south people shrugged their shoulders. Taxes were high, and no wonder, with an interminable war for which someone had to pay, and that meant everyone. This latest budget was crippling. It made the rich less rich and the poor poorer, but what could one do? Little would be gained, in the opinion of most people, by arming themselves with guns, pick-axes, scythes and pitchforks. One item in the budget which angered Sylvanus and Lancelot was the increased duty on horses employed in husbandry. An extra three-and-six-pence! It was disgraceful, considering the country would be ruined without her agriculture. Farmers should pay no taxes at all, Lancelot declared. He was so incensed that he contemplated going to Hastingford and telling Peregrine what he thought about it. But what good would that do? Better be thankful that there were more fish in the sea than ever came out of it. With courage and industry a fisherman need not starve.

It was on a morning in July that the incident occurred which was to make so much difference to him, though it seemed slight enough at the time. He had been on the beach attending the fish auction, and was just leaving it when he heard a cry. At first he took no notice. Cries, and even screams, were common when ladies descending from the bathing-machines felt the first shock of the cold water on their sensitive skins. Like most of the fishermen, he felt a good-humored contempt for the gentry who treated the ocean as an entertainment. The fishermen knew to their cost that the sea was no pet, but a tiger, and the hordes of visitors from town who boasted themselves on intimate terms with this powerful element in whose edges they dipped were no more than ignorant children at play. However, it was good for the prosperity of the resort, and no one complained, certainly not the women who arranged with a man and a horse to conduct the machines in and out of the water at a charge at one shilling each, children sixpence. The famous Martha Gunn, a Brighton institution and on friendly relations with the Prince, was now over eighty and did not go into the water, but she still superintended the beach.

So Lancelot thought nothing of the feminine cry until he noticed an arm waving frantically, and since there was no one else within twenty yards or so, he judged the signal to be for him and went forward.

A young lady was sitting on the pebbles. She did not look at all awkward, for her muslin dress flared in an elegant circle around her, but as Lancelot drew near he saw an expression of pain on the face beneath the large straw hat.

"Come here, my man!" called a rather peremptory voice. "I have fallen and twisted my ankle, and it is devilish painful."

"How did you do that?" he asked, for something to say.

"How do you imagine I did it?" she demanded. "On a stretch of ground which has stones of all shapes and sizes, and not one firmly set in its place, it is a wonder one does not break one's neck."

Lancelot laughed. "Reckon it's your first visit to Brighton."

"What if it is? There must be a first time for everything. Previously we took our change of air at the spas. Oh, I know them all. Tunbridge Wells, Bath, Cheltenham. Once we even went as far north as Leamington. But this year the doctor advised my mother to try the seawater."

"Has she gained benefit?"

"Who can tell? We arrived only three days ago. But give me your hand, pray, and help me up, for I shall gain no benefit from sitting on these stones, which I suspect to be damp."

Lancelot offered his hand and she clutched it, but it was not sufficient support, and she would have fallen if he had not caught her with his other hand.

"Ugh!" She made a grimace. "It is worse than I thought. I cannot walk a step. I cannot bear my weight upon it. Whatever shall I do?"

"I could carry you," he suggested.

"Oh, no! No, certainly not! It would not be proper to be carried in public by a perfect stranger."

"Then I must fetch someone else. Unless," he added, wickedly, "you would care to lodge upon the beach. There are rough characters who bed on it every night."

She shuddered. "Do not even mention such a thing! Well—" she hesitated. "Since there seems to be no alternative— After all, where there is no jetty sailors do sometimes carry ladies from boats to dry land. You may carry me from the beach, but no further. I cannot be seen crossing the Steyne like a bundle of washing. La! What a scandal that would cause!"

He lifted her carefully, so carefully that he seemed clumsy, and she asked sharply, "Am I then so heavy?"

"No, mistress, you weigh no more than a handful of herring, but—" He stopped and felt himself blushing, though it was unlikely a blush would show on his sunburnt face. How could he explain his fear that were he awkward he might expose her ankles, or, even worse, her legs? But her skirt was full, and when he was satisfied that it trailed almost to the ground, he moved forward. She did not steady herself by putting her hand on his shoulders, but lay limp, one hand clutching the handle of her parasol.

"Now what shall I do?" he inquired, as he felt firm ground beneath his feet.

"Put me down."

"But you cannot stand."

"I can, on one foot, with my parasol as crutch. You may call a chair."

A strange disappointment swept over him. "I could take you home."

"Thank you, but there is no necessity."

She spoke so firmly that there was nothing for it but to find a sedan-chair and help her into it. It was the end of the episode, and in a sudden panic he found courage to ask, "Would you do me the favor of telling me your name?"

At first he thought she would refuse, but after staring fixedly at him, she said, haughtily. "It is Miss Petronella King."

He thanked her, and listened to the address she gave to the front chairman, and then she was gone and there was nothing left of her but a most pleasant smell which clung to his clothes and almost succeeded in obliterating the odor of fish.

There was no reason why he should not have told Sylvanus of the incident, but he did not. Somehow there was no opportunity until it had become such old news that it would have been foolish to revive it. Besides, to speak of it would have been to endue it with false importance. Ladies fell down and were helped to their feet, and neither they nor their helpers gave the matter a second thought.

It was strange, therefore, that a week later he should put on his best clothes and go to the address he had heard her mention. The house was an elegant one, facing the sea, of the type of accommodation rented at exorbitant prices by substantial and fashionable families in search of health, pleasure, relaxation, or husbands for their daughters.

To the maidservant who opened the door Lancelot

explained that he had come to inquire after Miss King's health.

The girl stared doubtfully at him, then asked him to enter. She was nervous when people called, because unless people were expected she was never sure of her mistress's response. Miss Petronella was what she thought of as temperamental, though in one of her own class she would have changed the word and called it ill-tempered. Still, she was fairly confident that this time she had done right. The young man was polite and ravishingly handsome, and Miss Petronella had had a dull time with her poor foot, to say nothing of her dull parents who, in the servant's opinion, had no idea of the correct procedure for mixing with the best society and ensuring that their daughter was given what the servant thought of as, with a capital letter, Opportunity.

"I will see whether my mistress is receiving," the girl said, demurely, and left Lancelot in the hall.

Through the open door of a room on the right he heard a muttered colloquy, and then a sharp word in Petronella's clear voice. "Who?"

There was further muttering, from which, rising like a peak out of mist, again Petronella's voice. "Oh, drat it!"

The maidservant came out, flustered and breathless, to show Lancelot into the room.

He expected smiles and party manners, but Petronella put on no show of gladness at seeing him, and for this he respected her, though he was not sure why. Was there really anything admirable about an irritable girl who could not be bothered to extend courtesy to one who had helped her?

"Please forgive the intrusion," he said, "but I was anxious to discover if you had recovered from your accident."

"You mean you were curious," she said, ungraciously.

He smiled. "Perhaps."

"Well, it is mending, but still it is weak."

She was lying on a sofa covered in rose-pink damask, and she wore a dress the color of blue forget-me-nots.

He thought she made a delightful picture, and he wished someone would paint her like this. Rosemary, for instance, should paint such things instead of her constant landscapes which could be surpassed at any time merely by looking out of the window.

"You do not talk much," Petronella said.

"I was looking at you."

"So I noticed. And I was fearful of having you enter, in case you might fill the room with the aroma of raw fish."

"When you first saw me I had recently returned from a trip."

"Now you appear practically human, and, thank heaven, you do not smell at all. I have not conversed with a fisherman before, but I do not imagine they speak as you do. You have an educated air."

"I am not a fisherman born."

"Ah! A gentleman who amuses himself with humble toil?"

"Not that, either. I am a farmer."

"And what is wrong with the land, that you must plough the sea?"

He laughed. "Now who has become curious? No, do not be angry, Miss King! I intended the remark as a jest, though I fear I am not witty. Nothing would give me greater pleasure than to tell you the somewhat complicated story of my life, but you would find it tedious, since you scarcely know me. To endure such confessions requires the tolerance of a friend."

This was perhaps the longest speech of its kind he had ever made, and he was pleased with it. To talk to a fashionable lady, one needed a polish he had not known he possessed, and confidence grew in him. No doubt it made a difference having a grandmother who was a lady, and now he was grateful for the time he had spent with Caroline, listening to her tales of olden days.

Petronella sighed. "I must confess I find Brighton tedious."

"Brighton?" He could not believe his ears. "Why,

there is greater entertainment here than anywhere in the world. London cannot equal it."

He made the statement with no idea as to whether it were true or not, but since he could not conceive of a town gayer than this "reigning seat of fashion," he risked the comparison.

"Why, what is there to do here?"

"There are balls and assemblies."

"For those who have escorts."

"There must be many who would be honored to accompany you."

In most men, Petronella reflected, this would have been a trite expression of gallantry, but this young fisherman said it simply because he meant it, and so it sounded as fresh as if it had not been stated before. She had never been a conventional creature, but his sincerity caused her to speak with even more frankness than usual.

"My parents are of quiet habit, and so far I have had little chance of making the acquaintance of anyone, certainly not of suitable young men."

"I am a young man," Lancelot pointed out.

"You?"

"Oh, I grant I am not of your station in life, and I should not be acceptable at the fashionable assemblies, but I trust I should not disgrace you at the races or the theater or other entertainments of that kind."

She would not say yes and she would not say no, but made her ankle an excuse to put him off for a week, during which time she consulted her parents. Her father was a brewer from the Midlands who, persuaded by her mother, had agreed to give their only daughter the chance to marry into a good-class family.

When she told them of Lancelot, her father let out a great roar. "Damme, miss! Am I well-nigh ruining myself for you to be mixed up with a fisherman or a farmer or whatever he calls himself? You came down here to find a nib and a nib you'll get."

"Can you provide me with one?" she asked, bitterly. "Are you or my mother able to arrange the right in-

troductions? Oh, I grant you have given me an education, but I can scarcely walk the Steyne advertising
myself for sale, as though I were a barrel of your ale."

"I shall look an object," Mr. King grumbled, "if I go
back with a son-in-law whose baggage is a fishing-net
and a lobster-pot."

"I do not propose to marry him," Petronella explained, with as much patience as she could muster,
"but at least if he escorts me I can mix with the company of this town, and can be seen. Or am I so plain
that nobody will notice me?"

"Fie upon you, dearie!" cried her mother. "You're
as pretty as a picture, and your father knows it. But
you don't want to leap over the hedge before you come
to the stile. The season's young yet, and we can wait."

"Wait!" snarled her father. "At twelve good guineas
a week for this house which stands on no more land
than does our privy at home? I am not the Bank of
England, whatever you may think."

"Very well," Petronella said, briskly. "I see you are
agreed with me. We must not waste time, and so I will
permit this young man to entertain me."

Lancelot required no further encouragement than
her consent. His free hours were at her disposal, and as
these were the whole of the day, he had no lack of
leisure.

"Do you never sleep, boy?" Sylvanus asked. "How
can you work all night and gallivant all day?"

"I don't need that much sleep," Lancelot replied,
easily.

"You may not *want* it," Sylvanus corrected him,
"but you *need* it. I watched you dozing as you helped
to pull in the nets. One of these days you'll be falling
into the sea in your sleep."

"Leave me alone!" Lancelot snapped. "I am a grown
man, not a babe, and you are not my wet-nurse."

"I am your father and I am concerned for you. You
earn good money most times, yet you have none, but
must borrow from me."

"Upon my soul!" Lancelot exploded. "Are you be-

come such a pinch-penny
lar or two?"

"It is a woman, is it not?

"And if it is, inquisitive
unnatural about that?"

It was no use talking to
boy was bewitched, and
sickened of it.

But Lancelot showed
took Petronella to the th
pleasure-boats. He took
Downs, and to the novel
as the jumping in sacks, and the girls racing for a new
smock, and the officers, ridden by officers, running
against octogenarians.

When these entertainments began to pall, Lancelot,
appreciating her adventurous spirit, took her to places
which ladies of fashion did not usually frequent. They
went to the Bear public-house for the baiting of a
badger, to a bull-baiting at Hove, and to cocking at the
White Lion in North Street. This last appealed to Petronella's gambling spirit. "A main of Cocks for Twenty
Guineas a Battle, and Fifty Guineas the Main; between
Gentlemen of the Isle of Wight and the Gentlemen of
Sussex." To Lancelot's surprise she did not find the
sight of blood and violence repulsive, but was enthralled, and when she discovered she could make a
wager upon the outcome, she declared she could think
of no finer entertainment.

But the season drew to an end. When the Prince
Regent had left the town it was not long before others
followed suit. Velvet gave place to linsey-woolsey, and
bands of musicians on the Steyne to draperies of
fishing-nets.

Petronella said, "My father proposes to leave within
the week."

The shock to Lancelot was great, though he should
have expected it, he knew. But with lack of sleep, with
entertainment, and with his growing passion for Petronella he felt his brain becoming befuddled. He longed

but realized it would be unfair to
e had a fondness for him or not, he
he was a complicated creature, lively,
offended. Once he had thought her mer-
now he was not sure. Of one thing only
re, that he was no fitting match for her. She
n-born, reared on the profits of industry. He
he illegitimate son of a farmer turned fisherman,
an without land or fortune. The only honest procedure would be to say goodbye, no more, goodbye as
if he, like her, had enjoyed a pleasant season, as if
heart had no part in a relationship purely social.

And this he did. He said goodbye gracefully, lightly,
and she replied in like manner. Then he went back to
his lodging and relapsed into something which resembled sleep but which gave him no refreshment. He
slept and awoke and slept again. He did not eat, scarcely spoke, and showed no inclination for work. To Sylvanus, anxiously watching, it seemed like the crumbling
of a life, like a brain overtaxed which could well sink
into imbecility.

CHAPTER SEVEN

To man how sweet is breath! Yet sweetest of all
That breath which from his native air doth fall.
Anon

On a warm day in August a post-chaise drew up outside Hastingford, but the occupants did not alight. Instead, the lady directed the coachman to open the gate —an ordinary five-barred field-gate, not at all impressive—and drive through the orchard to the front door of the house. This he did, and having helped his passengers down, he unloaded their luggage, which consisted only of two portmanteaux and a small trunk, and, having been paid, departed. The travellers, a middle-aged lady and a very young one, then opened the door and entered the house.

Hastingford had once been a "hall-house," without an upper story, and the hall had been known as the "great hall." In its beams and its long windows it still bore evidence of past importance, though now it was bare and slightly shabby. Gone were the heavy refectory table and the carved armchairs designed for the head of the family and his sons. The walls which had displayed horns and masks and other relics of the chase betrayed their lost ornaments only by nail-holes and flaking plaster.

Charity, having heard hooves and wheels and voices and a closing door, came to see what was to do, and discovered the two females gazing about them. At first she did not recognize Marthanna, judging her to be

231

foreign, for her dress was by no means such as was commonly seen in Sussex, except perhaps in Brighton, a town to which Charity never ventured, and of which she would heartily have disapproved.

"Charity!" Marthanna cried. "Do you not know me?"

"Why, you are— You must be—"

"Marthanna. Have I grown so old? Well, it is ten years, or more, is it not? This is my daughter. Mignon, greet your aunt!"

The child curtsied and said something Charity did not understand, but Marthanna stopped her. "No, no, cherie! Not in French. We are in England now, and you must practice your English, which is really quite admirable when you take pains with it."

"Yes, maman."

"Please, Charity, tell my mother I have arrived."

"She is not here."

"Not here? What has happened? Oh, God, is she dead?"

"No. She lives at Sweetwillow Shaw."

"Sweetwillow Shaw?" Marthanna was bewildered. "That ruined cottage? In heaven's name, why? Hastingford is her home. Who has deprived her of it? If she has been turned away—mon dieu, the villain will have me to contend with, whoever he or she may be.

Charity smiled, a smile so rare that it gave her the expression of a stranger. This, she felt, was a moment for which she had waited, and the news she was about to give Marthanna would make up for snubs, or fancied snubs, endured in the past.

"Your mother wished to move to Sweetwillow Shaw. She has married again."

One look at Marthanna's face, and Charity's triumph was complete. This had hurt her sister-in-law, and was as unexpected as it was unpleasant. Charity knew how devoted Marthanna had been to her father, and she suspected, not without reason, that news of her mother's death would scarcely have been more overwhelming. It was on the tip of Charity's tongue to add the information of the unnatural nature of the match, but she restrained herself. No one should say she enjoyed tormenting Marthanna. She was a Christian and would let Marthanna discover the worst for herself.

"I must go to Sweetwillow Shaw at once," Marthanna said.

"Are you not tired?" Charity asked, as graciously as she could manage.

"Not too tired to see my mother."

"Perhaps a glass of milk."

"I thank you, no," Marthanna said, but Mignon pulled at her sleeve. "Please, maman, I would like a glass of milk."

"Very well, but you must drink it quickly, for I am impatient to be on my way."

Charity fetched the drink and gave it to the child, who swallowed it eagerly and then made a wry face. "I do not like English milk. It is thin."

"It is skimmed milk," Charity told her, calmly. "That is what we drink." She turned to Marthanna. "Have you a carriage outside?"

"No. I have dismissed it. We can walk over the fields. We have sat so long that it will be refreshing to stretch our legs. Oh, I can scarcely wait to see my brothers, but my mother must come first. Ask Peregrine or Sylvanus to put my baggage in a wagon and bring it over before dark."

"Sylvanus—" Charity began, but Marthanna was already striding out of the hall, with the child half running to keep up with her.

"Ask Peregrine" Charity thought, resentfully. As if he were a porter with nothing better to do than run after her! Madam, it seemed, was ready to resume her masterful ways, imagining she could run the farm. Well, this time she would find herself mistaken, and no doubt in a few days or a few weeks she would be glad to return to wherever she came from. Airs, Charity sniffed, elegant French airs! That sort of thing, she had understood from the newspapers, had been done away with. What was the use of a revolution if it permitted females still to deck themselves in silks and feathers and bows?

Across the fields and down to the river Marthanna went, holding Mignon's hand. It was a still day, as if the season hung, poised and breathless, between summer and autumn. The air was gold and the land was gold, corn turning color, grass ripening from the yellow stalk to the purplish head of seeds. Even the green of the trees had sobered, half minded to draw back the juices and allow the leaves to flame to death. It was a golden country through which they walked, and Marthanna looked down at her daughter wondering whether the child was touched by emotion, whether the heritage of her blood revealed to her more than her youthful brain could know.

"This is a day to be remembered," Marthanna said.

It was, and more than she realized. It was a day to be remembered in history, for the *Northumberland* had weighed anchor and sailed from Torbay, carrying the ex-emperor to St. Helena, his last and bitter residence.

But to Marthanna it was the homecoming she had awaited so long. It was both sweet and sour, as most of her life had been. It was the final parting from Gerrance and the final reunion with that part of the earth to which she so irrevocably belonged that while her heart wept for Gerrance her bones throbbed as at the embrace of a lover.

She longed to convey some of this to Mignon, but even had the child been older, she doubted if she could have done so. Words were not golden. They were black and white, like print.

"This is our land," she said. "This is where we belong."

The child looked up and spoke. It was a moment to be shared. "My feet hurt," said Mignon.

At the bridge they paused. The water too was golden, opaque and torpid, heavy with summer. Marthanna suggested Mignon should remove her shoes and stockings and bathe her feet, but the child was shocked at the idea. "It would not be proper."

"Ah, wait until you have lived here a while. You will find the conventions do not matter so much. Nature's children learn to be natural. You will throw off your clothes and roll in the grass like a little horse."

"Must we live here?" Mignon asked, with distaste.

"Why, where else should we live? Where else is there?"

"There is France."

"Oh, no! In France we were prisoners. We were unhappy."

"I was not unhappy. My father was French. *I* am French."

The child began to cry, and Marthanna knelt beside her and took her in her arms. "Please, my little one! Do not distress me! This is the day when I have come home. You will be happy here, I promise you. You *must* be happy. Now dry your eyes. We do not want your grandmother to think you are a baby."

They were both subdued as they crossed the bridge and walked the path to Sweetwillow Shaw. For Marthanna a cloud had drifted across the day. So excited had she been that it did not occur to her that Mignon might feel differently. Mignon was all she had of Gerrance, all she had of their intense and perilous love. If Mignon should persist in disliking the farm, what could be done? Marthanna shuddered at the agony of choosing between her child and her home. Even the prospect of it was so unbearable that she thrust it from her resolutely. Let that be hidden away in the future.

The sight of Sweetwillow Shaw was a considerable surprise. In memory it was a ruin in which they as children had played, half fearful that it might hold ghostly or horrendous secrets. Now it was a trim cottage, sweetly white as a freshly-bleached sheet upon a line. In front were clumps of late summer flowers, asters and marguerites, michaelmas daisies and phlox, edged with mignonette. A young man, stripped to the waist, was digging a vegetable patch. As Marthanna and Mignon approached, he stopped, smiled and touched his forehead.

"Goodday, my man!" Marthanna greeted him. "Will you be good enough to take me to your mistress?"

"Yes, ma'am!" Suddenly he realized his nakedness, and could not remedy it, for his shirt was inside the house. Uncertainly he murmured, "Excuse me!" and opened the door of the cottage for them to enter.

During the years of her exile Marthanna had sometimes visualized her meeting with her mother, and from the distance of an enemy country she had endowed the reunion with a sentimental flavor. She would, she had thought, fling herself into her mother's arms. They would both weep the easy tears of relief from stress. Affection would flame afresh between them, the stronger for its frozen interval. But now she found herself regarding her mother almost with embarrassment, and it required an effort to bend forward and plant a dutiful kiss upon her cheek.

"Well," Caroline said, cheerfully, "so you have come home. And who is the child?"

"My daughter Mignon."

"Upon my soul!" Caroline exclaimed. "Another grandchild! What a surprise! I must say I did not think you capable of such an accomplishment, you and your sickly Frenchman. Come here, girl! No, closer! Let me touch you." She took the child's hands and pulled her on to her knee, patting her cheeks and running her fingers through her hair. "Why, it is a pretty little thing. Min—Min-non. No, I cannot get my tongue round those foreign words. I shall call you Minnie. And how old are you, Minnie?"

"I am nine years, Madame."

"You must call me Grandmama. Now I am nine times a grandmother, but Charity will not permit her children to visit me, for fear I might contaminate them with what she calls the inborn wickedness of the Dykes."

Marthanna was not listening. She was thinking, almost jealously, that her mother was like a child distracted by a new toy. Why did the old so dote upon their grandchildren? Was it perhaps that they rejoiced to see their line secured by yet another generation? Did they feel that in their descendants lay the only immortality on which they could safely count? If this were so, it was a poor reward for the act of living, to enjoy their future through the eyes of a horde of strangers who had never known them.

"Get down, Mignon!" she commanded, sharply. "You will tire your grandmother." The child obeyed her. "Now go outside and talk to the young man. We have private matters to discuss."

Caroline looked sideways at her. "I hope you will not be malicious, like Charity. I demand the right to see my grandchildren, only nowadays I seem to have no rights."

"Now, Mother, you know me better than that. Mignon may visit you whenever you wish. But it is ten years since I saw you. I crave your attention and your news."

"There is plenty of news," Caroline allowed, "and most of it bad."

"Yes, indeed. Mother, Gerrance is dead."

"Ah! I am not surprised. He was not of the flesh to make old bones."

"Is that all the sympathy you can express?"

"It is your grief, not mine, child. If I had allowed sorrow to conquer me I should have been dead long ago. I have suffered, you have suffered, and Minnie will suffer. That is life, and there is nothing we can do to change it."

"An easy philosophy," Marthanna said, with some bitterness.

"Maybe, but not easy to attain. I pray you may, by the time you are my age."

"Charity says you have married again."

"I have."

It was on the tip of Marthanna's tongue to reproach her mother, to remind her of Will's devotion and long illness, but she restrained herself. She and Caroline were not made of the same stuff. She could never fill Gerrance's place with another man, but many widows re-married. It was no sin. So she steeled herself to accept with politeness some farmer, rough, ageing, uneducated, undoubtedly poor, for a man of substance would have taken her to his own establishment, not lived with her in a cottage on her son's land.

"I look forward to meeting him," she said, as graciously as possible.

"You have."

"I beg your pardon?"

"Dickon. You saw him digging in the garden. He brought you to me."

"That boy?"

"Yes, that boy. He is without money or schooling. He is not a gentleman. He was reared among criminals and the lowest class of person. But I needed someone to care for me, and he cares."

Marthanna burst out laughing. "Oh, mother! I might have guessed you would do something truly outrageous."

"Outrageous, do you call it? Do you not mean indecent, lunatic, irreligious and unforgiveable? That is how Charity would describe it."

"No, Mother, I do not mean that." Suddenly Marthanna was at ease. "Strangely, I am relieved. I cannot understand why. Perhaps it is because I winced from the thought of someone in Father's place. But this boy, this Dickon, can offer no comparison with Father."

"There is no sense in comparing one man with another," Caroline said, briskly, "or one woman with another, either. One does not compare sugar with butter."

"All my life," Marthanna confessed. "I have been surprised by you. Often I have been angry and hostile, but in the end I have to acknowledge a certain unexpected good sense in what you do. Once I felt you were becoming old and forgetful, but now . . . You are bright and lively. You have scarcely aged these past ten years."

Caroline smiled slyly. "Some witches swear by the virtue of living with a young man."

Marthanna laughed. "You talk of witches in this enlightened age? Now indeed I know I am in Sussex once more. My one regret," she added, soberly, "is that you should need a young man to care for you. You have two sons."

"Yes, and a daughter-in-law. You would not believe a family could be so shattered and scattered by one Christian young woman who cannot open her mouth without uttering a prayer."

"Tell me!" Marthanna urged. And Caroline told her all that had happened during her absence. She told of her own dethronement and removal to Sweetwillow Shaw, of the tragedy of Rebecca's family and the coming of Rosemary and Bridget, of the discontent of Sylvanus and Lancelot and their departure for Brighton.

"Five years," she said. "It is five years since they went, and not one visit have they paid."

"They should have come to see you," Marthanna said, angrily. "It was their duty."

"Duty? What is duty? It is an action performed unwillingly which gives no pleasure to anyone. No, I do not blame them. Charity drove them away, and Charity keeps them from me. She has robbed Peregrine of ambition and made of him a sour, unsociable man. He is no longer a good husband, father or son, and certainly he is not a good farmer."

Marthanna sighed. "So much has changed."

"Yes, but you are home, and in Minnie Hastingford has gained another child."

"Oh, Mother! You speak as if Hastingford were alive, with a soul."

"It is, and it has. But what will you do, child?"

"Why, I shall go to Wivelridge, of course. Don't tell me something has happened to Wivelridge!"

"No, it is as you left it. Dickon tells me that wind and rain have broken some of the glass in your grand hot-house."

"That is a small matter. We have carried only a few necessities with us, but in a week or two the stage-wagon will arrive with our luggage. Oh, you cannot imagine the beautiful things I have brought from Gerrance's home! French furniture, statues, delicate china,

silken sheets. Wivelridge will be almost as elegant as
the Prince Regent's Pavilion in Brighton. Until then,
may we remain here with you?"

Caroline got to her feet. Now there was something
to occupy her. Glad day! she thought. And then she
fixed her attention on pillows and blankets, and her
stock of tea and jellies and coffee-berries.

That evening Charity waited eagerly for Peregrine to
return to the house, which was an unusual state of affairs. Ordinarily she was scarcely aware of either his
presence or absence, and he counted as little more than
a clock which indicated meal-times. But now she had
news for him, and she prayed, yes, actually prayed de-
voutly that he had not met Marthanna or heard of her
arrival from some other source. News was as rare as
strawberries in November, especially the kind of news
which did not get into the newspapers, and she guarded
jealously her right to impart it. If any of the children
had given their father information Charity considered
lay within her preserves, he or she would have been
severely beaten.

Darkness fell, and another two hours passed before
Peregrine came home. By this time Charity's pleasurable anticipation had turned to anger, and when Peregrine entered the room she gave one sniff and then
attacked.

"So! You have become a drunkard as well as a
whoremonger! Is there no end to the catalogue of your
sins? No, do not deny it! The Lord has been pleased to
furnish my nose with as keen a sense as I could reasonably ask, and sometimes keener than I would wish.
You have been drinking."

"Yes, my dear," Peregrine agreed, without a flicker
of shame.

Confession and honesty should have softened her;
instead, they made her more furious. "Fie upon you!
Have you no decency, that you would acknowledge it
openly, boast of it? I declare, you fall lower every day.
How can I keep it from my little ones, the kind of man
their father is? No doubt you have been with that harlot, and you have been tippling together."

"Peace, woman!" Peregrine growled. "You've a tongue as long as Lewes race-course. I've been these past few hours in the King's Arms at Rotherfield, but with no woman. I've been drinking with a man, and when you hear the reason you'll not be calling me over. You'll be singing hymns."

"What do you mean?" Charity asked, coldly. She was not deeply interested, for she suspected him to be excusing himself.

"Mr. Jonathan Carswell," Peregrine said, slowly, as if he wished to imprint the name on his memory. "I have been with Mr. Jonathan Carswell. He has come a long way, from Lancashire in the north, where he has a cotton-mill. He is a wealthy man."

"And what has that to do with us? Riches are a weapon of the devil."

"He's right eager to buy the farm."

Charity's mouth opened, but no words came. Her legs were suddenly weak, so that she was forced to sit hurriedly upon the nearest chair. "The farm?" she stuttered, at last. "What would he want with the farm?"

Peregrine shook his head. "Times I wonder what anyone would want with a farm. Seems these tradesmen have a hunger to be squires. Mr. Carswell says they are all around the south, buying up farms."

"How can they farm in the south and tend their factories in the north?"

"With money you can do anything," Peregrine said, with what was for him, nowadays, unusual aggressiveness. "There's managers and tenants. Mr. Carswell says he must make himself a landowner, for he's a fancy to become a Member of Parliament."

"You refused, of course."

"No." Peregrine hesitated, and wondered why he did so. Was he become so weak that he dared not tell her? Had she, the sharp young woman of Kent, finally vanquished him, taken from him the last vestiges of his manhood? Deliberately he spoke loudly. "No, I didn't refuse."

Charity prepared to launch into a tirade, but stopped herself in time. This required thinking about. After all, there might be no cause for blaming Peregrine.

"He would buy the farm? All of it?"

"All of it. Hastingford, Wivelridge, Sweetwillow Shaw and the whole of the land. He would pay me twenty thousand pounds."

For several minutes Charity was silent. What did Hastingford mean to her? It meant hard work and the animosity of those around her. It meant Caroline at Sweetwillow Shaw, smugly smiling like a cat with a saucer of cream. It would mean Marthanna at Wivelridge, acting the great lady and rearing a wanton little French offspring. It would mean Sylvanus and Lancelot returning when they had had a sickening of Brighton, and Peregrine perhaps would suffer a change of heart and leave the farm to his wife's adulterously-begotten son. There was danger at Hastingford, whichever way one looked. Why, if they left the place she would be able to rid herself of Rosemary and Bridget.

"Do not think the money has influence upon me," she told her husband, severely. "Money brings evil in its train, and I doubt you are fit to be trusted with such a sum. But I would welcome it for the sake of the children. Their schoolmaster tells me they have intelligence above the average. With education they can go far in any profession. It is the children who must be considered."

"Yes," Peregrine thought. "It is the children. It is young William, who is worth a dozen of scrawny Charity's brood. With this money I can provide for William and his mother. They will be safe."

He looked at Charity, and Charity returned his gaze with confidence and rectitude. They were agreed, they who so seldom could agree on anything. Their desires might be different, and their motives, but on this matter they were agreed.

Peregrine nodded. "Very well," he said, "I will accept Mr. Carswell's offer."

CHAPTER EIGHT

Now, musing o'er the changing scene,
Farmers behind the tavern-screen
Collect; — with elbow idly press'd
On hob, reclines the corner's guest,
Reading the news, to mark again
The bankrupt lists, or price of grain.
Clare's Shepherd's Calendar

It had seemed an easy way out, to sell the farm, and
Charity's acceptance of the proposition—no, more than
that, her approval, made it the easier. Peregrine would
be free of the responsibility of ensuring that the farm
was run at a profit, a responsibility doubly onerous
since Sylvanus had left him with only the assistance of
hired hands who had no care for the stock or the crops
beyond the wages they received. The peace celebrations
were sixteen months past, and now the people wondered just what they had been celebrating. Last year
the plentiful harvest had ruined many farmers. This
year they were protected, but gained small benefit.
Taxes were high, food dear, wages low and hours long.
Half a million soldiers and sailors were demobilized,
with little prospect of finding employment. Britain
might be called "The Savior of Europe," but her urgent task was to save herself. In many counties tenant
farmers were giving up their leases, and rents dropped
sharply. With this trouble and unrest all over the country Peregrine saw nothing unpatriotic or traitorous in
selling out at a favorable price.

Reasoning upon the matter in this manner he could

not understand why he felt so miserable. A man was at liberty to do as he pleased with his property, yet his conscience troubled him. It was as if he had betrayed and reduced to nothing the early struggles of his parents. Vaguely he could remember his mother's anguish when his father took to smuggling, in order to feed and clothe them. Less vaguely he remembered his mother's strength and unconquerable optimism when she bought the farm and drove his diffident father to become a successful farmer in spite of himself. With a flash of pride Peregrine remembered the part he had played in this. Oh, then he had been a bold youth, a real cockolorum who fancied himself a gentleman and insisted that he, and not gentle Will, could best choose and employ the laborers. Well, he had not been wrong. His father had relied too much on tavern-teaching, and it had required almost an earthquake to jolt him from old, safe ways. But now, ah, now! Peregrine sighed. It was history repeating itself. He, like his father, was opposed to change, for change had changed its face since his boyhood. Then it had the appearance of adventure. Now it was spiked with disaster. Better to sell and sit back with a quiet mind. The difficulty lay in announcing his decision to his mother and Marthanna. From day to day he put it off, having sworn Charity to secrecy, and before he breathed a word to anyone he took a trip to Lewes to see a lawyer and instruct him to prepare the contract.

No sooner had he done this than a new burden was placed upon him—"foisted" was how he described it to himself, and then was shocked at his own insensibility. What was the matter with him, that the welfare of his kind did not count beside his convenience? Had his heart frozen to all natural feeling? Had his misfortunes squeezed him dry of compassion? Or was this a condition common to middle age? Did the sap sink into the roots when youth was past, never to rise again?

The reason for his soul-searching was the homecoming of Sylvanus and Lancelot. They arrived in the carrier's cart, two work-roughened, unimpressive fishermen, with no more possessions than when they left. It was as if the five years of their absence had added up to nothing. Yet it was not this alone which troubled Peregrine. Chiefly he was shocked by Lancelot's appearance. Gone was the sturdy glowing boy, and in his place was a drawn, haggard, pallid-faced man.

"Has he been ill?" Peregrine asked Sylvanus.

Sylvanus shrugged his shoulders. "You could explain it in such a way. It is an illness of the spirit which scourges the body. He does not speak of it, but I'm not blind. Reckon he's had a bit of muslin and she's deserted him. I waited a while, to see if he'd get over it, but he grows no better. So I thought maybe the memories in Brighton pierced too deeply, and I brought him home. There's healing here, or a chance of it. Besides, I'm wondrous wishful to do my bout on the farm. I've had sufficient fishes' eyes staring at me to last the rest of my life."

Almost Peregrine said, "There will soon be no farm for you to work," but his courage was not equal to it, and he excused himself by reflecting that it was only right and proper his mother should be told first.

"More lodgers!" Charity fumed. "Am I never to be more than a scullery-maid?"

"It will not be for long," Peregrine said, to placate her.

"Oh? How long? Has the contract been signed? Is the money paid?"

"Not yet. These things take time. Besides, Michaelmas is almost upon us, so he cannot have possession until Lady-day. I have to dispose of my stock."

"Another six months."

"It will soon pass."

"Have you broken the news to your mother?"

"I intend to."

"When? Come now, when? Would you put it off until you must load her belongings on to a cart and make a gypsy of her and of her co-habiter? Oh, what a coward you are!"

Peregrine went away without answering back, for he realized there was some justice in Charity's remarks. He had been postponing his interview with his mother, because he knew full well it would be the cruellest task he had ever undertaken, and the most difficult. But it could not be avoided for ever, and so one evening, after milking, he walked heavy-footed across the fields to Sweetwillow Shaw.

September was half gone, and the drought which had held in most parts of the country showed no signs of breaking. Ponds were dry, grass brown and sparse, and the earth was honeycombed with cracks broader than a man's thumb. Already the cattle were having their feed supplemented with hay, and many farmers had been forced to take a part of their herd to market, to sell for whatever amount it would fetch. It had not been necessary for Peregrine to do this, for before the end of the winter all of his stock would have gone, and therefore shortage of fodder would not matter. But though men might be anxious, nature was not troubled by the dryness. The brave yellow of dandelion and ragwort still shone out, blackberries hung from the hedges, and ripe hazel-nuts hid behind their leaves. Thrushes took up the tale where they had left it at the end of spring, and wood-pigeons chuckled in content. It was the fruitful month, sunburnt and thirsty though it might be.

Peregrine went down into the sunset, a fiery furnace which threw out every color every painter had ever put upon canvas. Crimson flared to burn away to pink, and then fade tenderly to primrose and green and blue, as though a great note of music blared across the universe, to stretch and vibrate to the merest whisper. It was a display beyond human ingenuity, a sight to lift the heart, but Peregrine scarcely noticed it. His eyes were on the ground, and his only moment of pleasure was when he reached the river, shrunken but still creeping between its banks. We are fortunate, he thought, for not many farms could produce this amount of water at present. And then he remembered it no longer mattered whether they were fortunate or not.

When he reached Sweetwillow Shaw the light was beginning to go. On the windowsill beside the door stood his mother's weather-glass, a leech in a jar of water, the mouth of the jar covered with a rag. The leech, he noticed, lay curled at the bottom, a sure sign of fine weather. He could have wished to find it crawled to the top, which would have meant rain very shortly, but that was more than he could hope for. All the other signs were against it.

Realizing he was deliberately wasting time by poring over the jar, he lifted the latch and walked into the cottage. Caroline and Dickon were at supper.

"Why, Peregrine!" Caroline cried, gladly. "This is a pleasant surprise! Will you join us at food?"

"No, thank you, Mother. I am not hungry."

"Ah, but you must! This is a ham from one of our pigs, and a better one I never tasted. Dickon has a way with animals. He merely has to hold out his hand and they eat till they are fit to burst. Come, now! Dickon, draw up a chair!"

There was nothing for it but to take part in the meal. If he did not, Caroline would fuss and question and think he ailed. It was an effort to eat, with his errand sticking like a lump in his throat, but at least, he thought grimly, a plate of ham and a wedge of cheese would delay it. He was reminded of his childhood, when having committed what he considered to be a major crime, he had awaited discovery in fear and trembling, and had prayed that God might strike him dead before the hour of reckoning.

When the meal was over he was sorely tempted to talk of small matters, local gossip, and allowed his mother to consider this a purely social call. But that would solve nothing. Time was the fiddler who called the tune, and, come what may, the tune must be played.

"Mother—" he said at last.

She glanced at him, surprised, for she had been in the middle of a sentence to which it was apparent he had not been listening.

"Mother, I have had an offer for the farm."

She frowned, not understanding. "An offer? What do you mean?"

"There is a man who wants to buy it."

"To buy Hastingford?" She bristled with anger. "I hope you well roasted him for his impertinence."

"I—I have accepted his offer."

"You?" She stared at him. "You have— What have you done? Are you mad?"

"My mind's made up."

She started to speak, then stopped and pressed her hand to her breast. Her eyes closed and her head fell forward. She appeared to have difficulty in breathing.

"Crumbs!" Dickon cried, jumping to his feet. "What are you at?" He put his arm round Caroline's shoulders and pressed her head against him. "Can you not hold your peace awhile? Are you aiming to kill her?"

"I tried to break it gently," Peregrine protested, excusing himself, "but I'm not one to be bumbling about a thing. I got to say what I mean."

Caroline opened her eyes. "Dickon, fetch me a bottle of my cherry brandy. I need it to refresh my heart, and Peregrine needs it to loosen his tongue, for what he says has a rusty tone, with more squeak than purpose." She held up her hand as Peregrine made to speak again. "No! Say nothing until we have glasses in our hands and comfort in our stomachs. That's right, Dickon, pour it, and pour good measures, for I reckon we shall have a use for strong spirit."

"It's unaccountable difficult," Peregrine grumbled, "to put it in a nice way."

"That is not necessary, son. I am not nice by nature, and all I ask of you is the truth. It seems you were tempted by the Devil, as Our Lord was tempted on the high mountain and by this I mean no disrespect. Such temptation comes to every man at one time or another. He is promised all the treasures of the world, all the power and glory, and the Devil asks nothing in return but the man's soul. Is your soul so unimportant, Peregrine?"

"Reckon it is. Reckon I'm less than a shadow on the grass, and when I'm gone the shadow won't be missed."

"Then let me put it another way. The Devil asks not for your soul, but for the farm. Now is there enough money in the world to put beside the value of Hastingford?"

"It wasn't the Devil," Peregrine said, in an aggrieved tone. "It was Mr. Carswell, and he's a decent man. He offered twenty thousand pounds, and that's as much as Hastingford is worth."

"To you, perhaps, but not to me. If you brought me the biggest Sussex wagon ever built, piled high with the largest diamonds and rubies and emeralds in the world, and asked for my farm, I'd tip the wagon into the Rother."

"But it's no longer your farm, Mother."

"So it seems. It also seems you would wantonly undo the work of two generations, and the hopes of the third. What of your children?"

"Charity says they're clever. She wants them to be something better than farmers."

"What is there better than a farmer?"

"I don't know."

"No, you don't know. You would make us all homeless, your widowed sister Marthanna, your orphaned nieces, your brother, your dead wife's son, and me. What of us?"

"Well, what of me?" Peregrine demanded. "Have I had an easy time? Philadelphia cuckolded me with my brother. Sylvanus went off and took the boy, and left me alone to work the farm as best I could. Charity is a scold, and I'm a slave to every freak of the weather, working from dawn to dusk and earning little more than a pittance. Have I had an easy time?"

"It's more than any mortal should ask, an easy time. You make your own destiny. Was it something lacking in you, that Philadelphia should love your brother? And you were not forced to marry Charity. You made a bad choice, that was all. As for the farm, are you bankrupt?"

"No, of course not!"

"Then perhaps you should look to your methods. Husbandry is an art, like everything else."

"I'm too old to change."

"You are fifty-four."

"That's middling old, and it's no sin to sell property and live in prosperity."

Caroline could no longer sit still. She got up and paced the room. "Peregrine, the law may say the farm is yours, but you have no moral right to dispose of it in this manner, and still less right to render your relatives homeless. Do they mean nothing to you? Do I, your mother, mean nothing? Can you so pitilessly break my heart?"

"Hearts don't break," Peregrine said, bluntly. "They're like leather. They get toughened and weathered."

Caroline looked at him, and was silent for a few minutes. Then she asked, quietly, "So you mean to go on with this?"

And Peregrine answered, "Yes," and without another word stood up and went from the cottage.

Caroline looked at Dickon. "It is the end," she said.

Dickon shook his head, perplexed. "What d'you mean, it's the end?"

"I don't know. Perhaps I mean it's the end of a dream, the end of all I've tried to do, and so it makes a mockery of what went before. There have been other times when everything could have ended—when Will had his money stolen on the way back from Gretna Green, when he was in danger of being apprehended for smuggling, when Hal was killed, when Will died and I found myself no longer mistress of my house, but somehow those other times, bitter and terrifying though they were, there was a light burning ahead. But now I can see no light. I can see only the darkness, and that is nothing to see."

She went to bed, though she did not sleep, and in the morning she made no attempt to rise.

Dickon waited until mid-day, and then he walked up the hill to Wivelridge, to find Marthanna.

"It's your mother, miss," he said. "She's took to her bed."

Marthanna smiled. "You mustn't call me miss. You must call me Marthanna. After all, we are—" She stopped and burst out laughing. "How foolish relationships can sound! I was about to call you my step-father. But what is wrong with Mother? Is she ill?"

"Not exactly."

"Does she feel the heat? We shall all be better when the rain comes."

"No, 'tis not the drythe troubling her, but I'm feared for her. I think her heart is breaking."

"Dickon! What do you mean?"

He told her, and as he spoke her looks grew blacker, until she could scarcely contain herself.

"Peregrine!" she exploded, when Dickon had finished. "My brother! He said those things? I can barely believe it."

"It's God's truth," Dickon told her, earnestly, "and Caroline will witness that it is. Come to her, miss—I mean Marthanna. She's no longer a young girl, and she's not laid up for a single day since we were married. I don't like to see her lying there. It's no more than one leap from the bed to the churchyard."

Angry and anxious though she was, Marthanna could not help but be touched by his concern for her mother. He was a good young man, she thought, one for whom an old woman could be thankful, even though convention might sneer and snigger at such a union.

She went to Caroline and attempted to reassure her, which was not easy, for Caroline lay with stony face and scarcely opened her mouth. Gone was the warm vitality which had so pleased and impressed Marthanna when she first saw her mother after ten years' absence. Now she looked her age. "Why, she is an old woman," Marthanna thought, with a pang, and doubted whether Caroline would live to see Hastingford pass into other hands, whether she would even want to live. "She has given up," Marthanna thought, "she has turned her face to the wall."

That night she went to seek Peregrine, and found him in the old barn, with one of the laborers, contemplating a pile of straw in one corner.

"Not good enough to be used for litter, even," Peregrine was saying. "The way the grass has baked up, the cattle'll be eating their bedding before winter's over, and glad of it."

Noticing Marthanna, he nodded and she went over. "May I talk with you for a few minutes?"

"Here?"

"Yes, and privately."

The man bade them good evening and went away, but Marthanna seemed loth to begin. She wandered from side to side of the barn, touching the upright beams, fingering the disused horse-brasses which hung from hardened, unoiled straps.

"Do you remember when we played here, Peregrine? It was a magic, fearsome place, and we believed it to be haunted by ghosts. I jumped half out of my skin when something white flashed, but it was only the owl that nested in the rafters."

Peregrine merely grunted, and Marthanna continued, "It has seen life, this old barn. Generations of children must have played in it."

"If you've come to talk about barns and children," Peregrine interrupted, "I'll be getting back to sup, for I've had a hard day."

"I wanted to talk about the child you were, about the time you swore you would be master, and persuaded Mother to allow you to engage the servants, and got round Father to change his old ways."

"Well, why not?" Peregrine demanded. "He was behind the times."

"As you are behind the times now."

"These are bad times."

"All new times are bad times if you haven't the stomach for them."

"I've done my best," Peregrine declared, angrily. "Once I was a brash youngster, without experience."

"But you had courage. I cannot believe people utterly change. I believe you must have some remnants of that courage left."

"Courage!" Peregrine snarled. "Courage! Oh! yes, I know about courage, and it's all right in battle, when you've nothing worse to fear than a musket-ball in your guts. But farming! Farming is a slavery that finally beats a man into the ground."

"Does it rob him of humanity, as well as of ambition?"

"You've been talking to Mother, but I'll not be boffled by you, butter my wig if I will!"

"Mother has taken to her bed. If you sell the farm it will kill her."

"If you reckon that'll stop me, you're mistaken. I've been a dutiful son and it won't be on my conscience, whatever happens to her."

"You're a hard man, Peregrine, but I wouldn't have held you in such low esteem as to be a mere money-grabber."

"I've seen little enough of money in my time. Money turns into stock and seed and fodder before you can as much as put it in your pocket."

"Is that not what it is for, to buy things? Or do you wish to keep it in bags and play yourself the music of the clink of gold?"

"I've plenty to do with it."

"Have you?" Marthanna asked, innocently. "Then you must have acquired accomplishments and tastes of which I was unaware. Perhaps you have a yearning to be a dandy, to wear the Cumberland corset, the Brummel tie, and swing a quizzing glass on a gold chain. Or perhaps you have become addicted to cards, and would go to London and join the gaming clubs. Certainly you cannot require the money for Charity, she being concerned always with cheese-parings and candle-ends. Ah, but I forgot. Possibly you need the money for your new son, for whom you betrayed Charity, just as Sylvanus betrayed you."

"Devil take you!" Peregrine roared. "Will you tie a knot in your tongue! Otherwise I'll do it for you, sister or not sister, woman or no woman."

"You can," Marthanna said, scornfully. "Yes, you can. You still have sufficient manhood to thrash a female and to break your mother's heart. But I tell you this, Peregrine Dyke, if you do what you threaten to do, I will let it be known. I will advertise it so widely that decent men will turn aside and vomit as they pass you."

"I've no care what people think."

"That is apparent. And who is he, this future owner of Hastingford, that for him you would renounce your birthright? What hold has he over you?"

"Mr. Carswell? Why, none! I scarcely know him. He's nought but a customer."

"So if another came and offered more, say twenty-one thousand pounds, you would accept?"

Peregrine shrugged his shoulders. "Why not? But this is haggling talk. Mr. Carswell is the one as wants to buy."

"Not the only one. I am another. I will buy the farm from you."

He stared at her. "You? You're making game of me. Or else you should be put in a mad jacket."

"No, Peregrine, I mean it. Gerrance was not a poor man in his own country, and I was able to realize the value of the greater part of his estate, though not until the war had finished. My money now is safely in the Bank of England. When I have paid you I shall have little left, but that will be no grief to me. My grief would be if I could not spend the rest of my life on Hastingford land and let my bones lie happily beneath this soil."

"I couldn't do it," Peregrine grumbled. "To sell to my sister? 'Twouldn't be proper."

"Think!" she urged. "It will suit both of us. You can take Charity and the children away, and Mother can return to the house to live. Sylvanus and Lancelot will run the farm. Oh, it is an excellent idea."

"You're a managing woman, and I don't like it."

"Would you rather make us all homeless?"

"It would be no hardship, you being a wealthy woman. You could provide a roof for the lot."

"Ah, the roof I want is Wivelridge, and for the rest of the family the other two houses. You will do it, Peregrine, for if you refuse I will fight you, and if there is any justice in this country I will tear Hastingford from your hands."

She went towards the door, and in the lamplight her shadow was large and threatening, like that of a giantess.

CHAPTER NINE

Our honest friends in Parliament
   Are looking vastly sad;
Our farmers say with one consent
   It's all immensely bad;
There was a time for borrowing,
   But now it's time to pay;
A budget is a serious thing;
   So take the sword away.
             Winthrop M. Praed.

When blood turned bad, it turned worse between those of the same blood, Peregrine found. Never before had the family ties been so strained, not even when he had learned that Lancelot was not his son. That had been a sore blow, but it had not caused a complete estrangement between the brothers, for a dead woman stood sentinel, and both Peregrine and Sylvanus sensed the indecency of wrangling over the dust of the departed. There had been quarrels in the past, and hard words spoken, as when Caroline had married the boy Dickon, but nothing had been as strong as this tug-of-war, with Marthanna fierce and ruthless on the other end of the rope. The fact that she had been his favorite sister, and that he had always respected her, made Peregrine the more obstinate.

Strangely, the affair brought him closer to Charity than he had been for years. It supplied them with a subject for conversation which they mutually thought enthralling, which they could discuss tirelessly, and on which Charity was in complete accord with her husband.

"Never!" she declared, not once but a hundred times. "I would never let her have the farm. A woman who married a foreigner, and an enemy at that! She has no right to the money, anyway. It is not good money. It is French, and stained with blood of our brave soldiers. How could you look your neighbors in the face, with their sons wearing the Waterloo Medal, and you knowing that you were living on the money belonging to their murderers?"

Peregrine did not attempt to decipher the meaning of this rather confused question. It was enough that Charity was indignant, and that she was on his side.

"She has offered a thousand more than Mr. Carswell," he reminded her.

"I do not care if she has offered ten thousand more," Charity declared, not quite truthfully. It gave her a pang to think of even one thousand pounds thrown away. What miracles of saving could she not accomplish with so much money! But the thought of Caroline back at Hastingford gave her a still sharper pang. Caroline would fill the house with strong drink and servants and all kinds of fal-lals. She would disport herself most unbecomingly with that young savage who had married her for some unknown, but certainly evil, reason. Charity had kept the house clean, both spiritually and materially, and she did not intend to have it contaminated.

"I suppose it'd be a sensible solution," Peregrine said, grudgingly, for the pleasure of having her contradict him.

"Sensible!" Charity exclaimed. "It is as mad as most of the things the Dykes do. With your sister Marthanna in charge, and Sylvanus saying yea, yea to her, and never a nay, they would be bankrupt inside of a year. No, Peregrine, you would be doing them a great disfavor even to consider the idea. Marthanna would come crying poverty and asking for her money back. Besides, you have given your word to Mr. Carswell, and you cannot break your word."

"That's true," Peregrine agreed, relieved.

"And the sooner the matter is settled, the better."

"Marthanna will be lamentable swolk."

"Are you afraid of a woman's temper?"

"They say Mother has taken to her bed."

"She is a cunning one," Charity told him, "and will stop at nothing to get her way. Are you ready to believe her heart will stop beating because she puts her hand on it? Do not be so simple! She is as strong as the oxen that pull your plough."

"I hope so," Peregrine said, earnestly.

"You must prove you are master of your own land."

Peregrine frowned. "But soon I shall have no land. What shall we do, then? Where shall we live?"

"Have no fear! I have decided. There is no need for you to trouble yourself. We shall go to Tunbridge. Perhaps to the Wells. They have built many elegant houses there now. After all, it is my home, and it has become fashionable."

Peregrine stared at her. "Since when have you run after fashion? I disremember that you ever cared for the baubles of this world. You were concerned with the next one."

"And so I am, but I must not consider myself. I must consider our children. Stand Fast is a clever boy. You have not been sufficiently aware of his talents, but his schoolmaster speaks highly of him. I intend he shall go to Oxford University."

"University! That's no place for a farmer's son."

"You will not be a farmer. You will be a gentleman of a modest but reliable fortune, and so we must keep a suitable establishment, that our son may bring his friends and patrons to visit us."

" 'Twill be unaccountable strange," Peregrine said, slowly, "having nothing to do all day. How will I pass the time?"

"Oh, you will find ways with which to occupy yourself."

He hoped she was right, though he himself could think of no ways, and often in the midst of one of his many tasks he would stop and scratch his head and ask himself, "Now what would I be doing if I was not doing this?"

But the handing over of the farm still seemed a long way ahead, and so he did not worry over much. He had not seen Marthanna since their conversation in the barn, but after a week he received a letter from her lawyer setting forth her offer in official terms. It was a document which required a reply, but he put it on one side, not knowing what to say to it, or how to say it. Silence would be best, he reckoned, for silence would express his sentiments adequately.

Some ten days later the postboy arrived with a communication from Peregrine's own lawyer in Lewes, requesting his presence. The contract between him and Mr. Carswell was now prepared, and required his signature.

It was a special day. Charity said it was, and she made him put on his best clothes, and had his horse smartly groomed to carry him to Lewes.

Peregrine realized his heart should be light, but he could not shake off a feeling of oppression. The responsibility of what he was doing weighed him down. How could a man be certain he was right? By what authority did conscience dictate its terms? Charity would say it was by the authority of God, but who could guarantee the source of the message? Whence came it? From Heaven or Hell? From God or the Devil?

He rode out grandly, with Charity waving him godspeed like any bride. He rode down the path between the apple-trees where once he and Philadelphia had caressed with the sickle of the moon cutting between the branches. But he did not remember that. It was too long ago.

To open and shut the gate there was no need to dismount. His horse knew the way as well as he did, and in the lane he turned right for the two miles at the end of which it would meet the main Lewes road.

The drought had at last broken, and the thirsty earth had drunk the rain for two nights and a day. This morning it breathed forth its gratitude. The sun shone, but the blades of grass still glistened wetly, and leaves had hollowed themselves to form miniature lakes. From pools at the side of the road rose a steaming mist, and from dark woodland shadows issued a scent like that of a newly-created world, a scent surpassing that of the five-days' camel ride through the rose-gardens of Gulistan in Persia.

Peregrine breathed deeply, and in his own body he seemed to feel the stirring of the earth on his land. In the water meadows the grass would already be thrusting, though unseen, and in the drier fields the invisible streams would be flowing. In Dun Bogg's Close, where Hal was killed, the cracks would be healing, and in Broad Field, and Bush Meadow and Cow-Hill Field and the Whinny.

Without fully realising what he had done he found he had turned his horse. Back he rode to the farm, but he did not go in. He continued along the lane, taking the long way around to Wivelridge, where he dismounted and knocked formally on the door, thus dissociating himself from any intimate connection with Marthanna.

The room in which she received him was strange and foreign and grand. He disapproved of everything about it, and put on an angry expression to show his disapproval.

"Peregrine!" She held out her hand, but he flicked his boot with the whip he carried, and turned away churlishly. "I have been expecting you," she went on. "You did not reply to the communication you received."

"No. There was no need. I have decided not to sell to you."

Her face set sternly. She could be as stubborn as he. She would fight him until she dropped exhausted. "I see. You would sell to your industrialist from the north."

"I was on my way to Lewes, to sign the contract."

Suddenly he threw the whip carelessly on to a chair and strode to the window. This was a view he rarely saw. It was the other side of the picture, the reverse of the mirror. From here also the fields dropped down to the Rother, and then rose again, but those were topped by Hastingford, the oldest building on the land, the parent house. Beautiful it looked in the autumn sunshine, clean and austere in line, rose-red in brick and tile. From this angle, the rear of the house, its roof swept low, like a hat pulled rakishly over twinkling eyes. Something rose in Peregrine's throat as he looked, a lump that made speech difficult. Marthanna did not hurry him. She stood waiting, and presently he spoke.

"I will not sell to Mr. Carswell," he said, violently, "I will not sell to anyone. Devil take it! Devil take the money! What use is money to me? I've not got the habit of dealing with money. And what does money do? You can't put it in the ground and grow it. You can't milk it. It's as dead as a thrown horseshoe."

Her eyes lit up and she went towards him with outstretched arms, but he kept his shoulder towards her, pretending not to notice. "It's nothing you said. That carried no weight with me. And it's nothing Charity said. I won't be druv. No, that I won't."

"Then what made you change your mind?"

"Dunno. Reckon it was the idea of being without land. Take my land away from me, and what am I? I'm like a fly on a window-pane, and a fly on a window-pane just doesn't get nowhere."

"I'm so glad!" she whispered. "Oh, Peregrine, I'm so very glad!"

"You've no call to be. You've lost the farm."

"Oh, Peregrine, what a silly boy you are! I've lost nothing, and I've gained everything. You don't have to own a thing in order to possess it. The only way I could lose the farm would be to be turned out into a cold and empty world. If I lived in a stall in one of your cow-houses I would still own the farm, in the only way anyone can own anything."

"That don't make sense to me."

"Ah, but it is sense. How do you own the farm? You see it, but so do I. You bend down and pick up a handful of earth. I can do the same. You work all day until your shoulders ache and your feet drag and your back gets a little more bowed. And what are you doing? You are running back and forth, waiting upon the land, ministering to it, feeding it cleaning it. Is that ownership? No, that is the work of a servant, of being owned. And when we are both dead we shall be equal, neither of us owning so much as a blade of grass."

"All the same, I'll stay. I'll not be a puppet in Charity's grand house. You'll not change my mind, so you'll have to be reconciled to losing the farm."

Marthanna sighed. "Have you not understood a word I've said? I don't *want* the farm, in the way you think. But can you manage? I mean, can you make it pay?"

"I always have, haven't I?"

"You haven't always had so many to provide for. There's Charity and your children and Rosemary and Bridget, and now Sylvanus and Lancelot are back. That is putting a fair burden on the farm, especially since you have given thirty acres to Mother."

"Not given. Lent."

"Very well, you have lent them to her, but that means thirty acres less for your own production."

"I'll manage."

"Prices are rising all the time. So are taxes. I believe we have hard days ahead of us. It is always the next generation that pays for this generation's war. Are you content to farm as you have done these past fifteen or twenty years?"

"I'll have to, shan't I? Changes cost money."

"If you had money, would you make improvements?"

"I might," Peregrine allowed, cautiously.

"I see. You might. Well, this is what I wish to say to you. I cannot buy the farm because you are not selling, and I am in favor of such a decision. But at the same time I have revealed that I am a woman of some substance. Is it not ridiculous, therefore, that I should be inhabiting this house rent free?"

"You always did, after you married."

"Yes, but then my husband was a poor refugee, and I relied upon the generosity of my family. Now—Peregrine, will you sell me Wivelridge and one acre of garden for five thousand pounds?"

"I dunno. I don't want no favors from you."

"Oh, what a suspicious man you are!"

"Suspicious?"

"Yes, that someone might offer you the insult of helping you. You do not need this house, but I do. It is my home and I wish to secure it, that no one may take it from me. Five thousand pounds would be of inestimable value to the farm. You could cull your herd, introduce new blood, breed from the best. You could buy new machinery. Peregrine, a farm is a business. Make it a profitable one."

Had the proposition come from anyone else, Peregrine would have leapt on it, but he resented the fact that Marthanna had suggested it. She had always been a manager, he remembered, from the days when she had read to their father from agricultural treatises. The trait was inherited from their mother, he supposed, but it did not cause him to be any the more approving of women who usurped the province of men. A woman should be pliant and malleable, as Philadelphia had been, and as Charity was, once you discounted her unfortunate tongue.

So he went no further than to promise to think over the matter, though he knew what his answer would be. Who could refuse such a sum for a house which had never brought him a penny, and which he himself would never need to use? Land was good, and his mother had been right to purchase the two smaller farms, but dwellings on those lands were no more than so many ant-hills. Besides, there was William to be considered. Cattle he would certainly buy, and perhaps some machinery, but a portion of the money would most definitely be put aside for William's education and for setting him up in a respectable profession. In no way should he be allowed to be inferior to Charity's children. Were Stand Fast to go to Oxford University, then William should be given an equal chance.

It was with a slight embarrassment that he bade Marthanna farewell, for he had been viewing her with anger and resentment, as though she were an enemy, and he was not able suddenly to reorientate his mind to a state of friendliness. Let her realize she was a female, and a widowed one at that. On the farm she had no rights, and what favors she received were by the grace of her brother. If he permitted her to purchase Wivelridge it would be for her benefit, that she might not suffer the indignity of living on his charity, like a pauper.

Marthanna, on the other hand, was not in the least embarrassed. She was overflowing with high spirits, for she considered she had brought off a highly successful coup. She had saved the farm, secured the beautiful house for herself and her daughter, and at the same time had financed her ineffectual brother in a manner which would not hurt his pride.

"Before you go home," she advised him, "call upon Mother. You should not delay giving her your news."

He lifted his eyebrows. "My news?" It was as if he had already forgotten that he had been within an ace of selling the farm.

"Yes. Your news." Her face stiffened into lines of severity. "She is ill because she believes she is to be turned from her home."

He felt like a small boy who had been reprimanded. What a shrew she was becoming, this sister of his! Women were all alike, it seemed. Maids were sweet and soft as custard, but loosen their girdles and you loosened their tongues.

"Reckon it's none so urgent that I have to break my neck," he grumbled, but all the same he turned his horse down the field in front of Wivelridge and across the bridge to Sweetwillow Shaw.

As he rode he began to plan, and the depression of the past weeks lifted from him. Things were not so bad after all, and life, though it was a funny business, could be worse. Now he would not have to worry where the next penny was coming from. Lancelot was looking slightly less peaked, and would soon be fit for a full day's work. With Sylvanus working as well, it would mean he could dismiss two of his laborers. What other situations they would find in these hard times he did not know, but that was not his concern, and they could always go on the parish. The advantage of employing relatives was that one did not have to pay them much, and if they should complain—Well, they had their keep, didn't they? And he, the boss, took no wages for himself. Why should they expect to be better off than he was?

So in good spirits he came to Sweetwillow Shaw. Caroline was still in bed, and he went straight up to her room. She lay with uncombed hair, and her face looked pinched and gray. The sight of her somewhat alarmed him, but he did not let this show.

"I'm not selling the farm," he said, without preamble. "Everything will go on the same as before."

"Ah! Then I shall not be forced to take to woolgathering."

"Don't be foolish, Mother!" He was angry, for woolgathering—plucking sheep wool from fences and the thorns of hedges—was one of the most beggarly of employments, done by only the poorest of old women.

"I know I am foolish," she whispered. "Kiss me, son, that I may show my gratitude."

But when he had departed she rose and dressed herself, and put on a cap of real lace, and went downstairs, and said to Dickon, "Boy, if you could dance I would ask you to perform a jig with me this day."

CHAPTER TEN

Love sees what no eye sees: love hears what no ear
hears; and what never rose in the heart of man, love
prepares for its object.

Lavater

In the year of Waterloo, which was how many people spoke of 1815, that battle being a kind of touch-
stone for assessing other events, Rosemary and Bridget
had been seven years at Hastingford. During that time
they had visited their mother only once, in the winter
of 1814, towards the end of January, and had been
held prisoners in the metropolis, by the extraordinary
weather which blocked most of the roads out of London. For a week, from the last day of the month, the
Thames was completely frozen over, and the tradesmen took full advantage of this. Booths were set up
for the sale of souvenirs. There were swings, dancing,
and games of skittles. Sheep were roasted, gin and
beer sold, and any number of books and toys which
had hastily been labelled "Bought on the Thames".
Printing presses were erected, and commemorative
sheets containing anything from the Lord's Prayer
to doggerel verse were actually printed on the ice.

Arthur and Edward were proud to take their sisters to join in the revelry, and Rebecca remarked
with satisfaction that the girls could not have visited
at a better time, as if, Rosemary thought, she had arranged the frost especially for them.

266

It was certainly gay enough to divert two young women who had been country mice for so long. There were shops filled with tempting things, but though Rosemary and Bridget had been given money by Caroline they bought little for themselves, because their mother and the boys appeared to need so much, and because with anything left over they felt they should take presents to their relations in Sussex. The noise of the traffic, unused as they were to it, made their heads ache. Not only was there a continual stream of carriages and hackney coaches, but wagons and wheelbarrows and carts made a hideous din on the cobbles. Beggars there were in plenty, some so crippled as to be nauseating, and other more sinister characters who stared and sometimes followed the girls. Rebecca warned them against venturing out alone after dark, and they were ready enough to heed her warning.

They had formed in their minds a picture of their mother's shop, a little vague, perhaps, though they saw it as a neat, homely place, with shining windows displaying goods in the most impeccable taste. The reality was so sadly disappointing as to be shocking. The shop was situated in a street off Seven Dials, and was so dark and dismal that its wares could scarcely be seen, though this was little loss, Rosemary considered, for it sold second-hand clothes, which in truth might have been third or fourth hand, worn-down boots and shoes, and the cheaper type of groceries.

Running her hand through a sack of sugar, Rosemary said, in disgust, "I declare, there is sand in this sugar."

She expected an indignant denial, but Rebecca merely sighed and said, "For what they can afford around here, people are fortunate to get sugar in their sand."

Rosemary said no more, for it was true. On every side were courts and lanes of the greatest squalor, and to see a child with a pair of shoes to its feet was a rarity.

"Mother, why did you not take a shop in a respectable quarter?"

Rebecca shrugged her shoulders. "Is it not obvious? To acquire such shops costs a considerable amount of money, and I needed every penny for your brothers' education."

"But a decent shop would surely bring greater profit than this."

"Yes, in time. How could I pay school fees when building up such a business?"

It was unanswerable, and Rebecca went on, more gently, "That was why I did not wish you to come here, though I longed to see you both. From year to year I put off inviting you, hoping . . . Oh, I do not know what I hoped. But the boys are almost grown up. Soon they will have excellent careers, and then they will look after me. Oh, yes, they will not neglect their mother, so you need have no fears on my account. Go back to Hastingford, my dears, and be thankful. In the country life is gracious, and clean."

They were glad enough to leave, though on the morning before their departure Rosemary climbed to the dome of St. Pauls, and saw the different face of London. From there the river was bright and shining, its shipping like so many gay toys. On one hand was the noble pile of Westminster Abbey, and on the other the impressive column of the Monument. The chimneys were like the turrets of palaces; the church spires reached adventurously towards Heaven. The trees of the Inns of Court were like scraps of the countryside carried and dropped by some celestial bird, as were the gardens of the distant squares. It was all so different from Seven Dials that Rosemary could scarcely believe one could walk from that place to the places she saw beneath her. It was a matter of money, she supposed. In London beauty must be bought. In Sussex it was free. She could hardly wait for the moment when she and Bridget would mount the coach, though being dutiful daughters they should, she knew, be sad at leaving their mother. And so they were. They both cried, and Rebecca cried, but by the time they reached Kennington Turnpike they had dried their eyes and were all smiles, enjoying the journey and childishly eager for its end.

At Hastingford everyone declared the change of air had done them good, which made them laugh, for who could possibly benefit from substituting London air for the pure atmosphere of the countryside?

"It is like breathing ashes," Rosemary said, "like breathing the effluvia of thousands of fires, for the smoke comes out of the chimneys and settles in the valleys between the buildings. It has the smell of old soot, and is composed of whatever rubbish is burnt."

"Then it must be the change, if not the air," they said.

Rosemary smiled, and did not argue. She thought she knew the reason for the healthy bloom, at least in her case. It was not the going away which had effected the change, but the return. She had seen her mother and brothers, and the way in which they lived, and though she grieved for them yet she could not help but be thankful for her own environment. Now she would have no regrets for London, no sensation of being buried in the country and having life pass her by. The city was all very well for the monied classes, but for the poor it was hopelessness and squalor.

So she settled down to life on the farm with greater zest and contentment than she had previously known. Often the work was monotonous; frequently Charity was irritable; but nothing prevented the impact of spring, which came with such a shock of novelty that it might never have happened before. Numbed fingers became warm and supple, the blood hurried in the veins, and frozen faces thawed into smiles. Rosemary found herself singing as she worked, and her secret meetings with Dickon took on the colour of festivity. At first he had been merely a fellow-conspirator, someone with whom she shared the awful knowledge of murder and a portion of the guilt. Then as the fact lost its sharpness and they were able to begin to excuse themselves, he was a sympathetic companion, comforting her. Their copulation had been almost casual, a part of that comfort, but it came to be a habit, indulged in dark corners, usually hasty with the fear of discovery. Despite Dickon's reassurances concerning her grandmother, Rosemary had felt uneasy. To picture so old a woman partaking of what should be essentially a youthful feast was grotesque, yet after all Caroline was a woman, and Rosemary could not quite reject the idea that she was a thief, robbing her grandmother of what was rightfully hers. Frequently she contemplated telling Dickon that their surreptitious love-making must cease, but she did not manage to put her intention into words.

When she returned from London all was different. It no longer mattered that she shared her lover with her grandmother. Now she really wanted him for herself. Life as it surrounded her mother and brothers was brutal and horrid; therefore it followed that for Rosemary it must be pleasant. Youth was brief and must be enjoyed. Dirt and poverty were to be avoided, and how better to avoid them than by taking joy in the enjoyable? And what more enjoyable than the embraces of a lusty young man? That she did not love Dickon Rosemary well knew. He was ignorant and lowly bred. His conversation was commonplace. But she lusted for his body and the exquisite pleasure he could give her, lifting her for a few moments high above human misery. Their brief encounters became insufficient for her, and she would lie in bed, hot and sleepless, picturing him with her grandmother, and would bite her nails in longing and frustration.

"Now spring has come," she said, "we must have longer together. We must go to the fields and the woods, spend whole nights there."

"I can't leave Caroline at night," Dickon objected. "She'd miss me. And what if she was taken ill?"

"In the daytime, then. There are many quiet places where we'd never be seen."

"It's not easy to get away."

"Surely you can make an excuse," Rosemary urged,

impatiently. "She cannot keep you a prisoner. You must have some freedom."

"We've managed."

"And is that enough for you, fumbling beneath my skirt, straining to finish as if we were animals? But perhaps you no longer want me?"

"I do want you."

"Then do as I suggest. I will tell you what to say to her."

Dickon was not reluctant. Though he was simple and not prone to investigating his own feelings, he realized that his fondness for Rosemary went deeply. Had he not married Caroline, Rosemary was the girl he would have chosen. To possess her was delicious, but to have installed her in his home and stocked her with babies would to him have been heaven on earth. He did not delude himself that she loved him in any so whole-hearted a way, for he was humble. Also he did not waste time or energy in bemoaning his matrimonial bonds, for he had taken on these willingly, and still believed it was worth being thus saved from a life of crime and vagrancy. Dickon was a realist. All the same, he could not have enough of Rosemary, and if she could advise him how to arrange it . . . Why, his flesh throbbed at the very thought of long hours on the springiness of beech leaves, or hidden in a jungle of grass, or bedded in a scented wilderness of hay.

So when the weather was fine they laid their plans, and knew a heightening of passion in the freedom of time and space, when they could take off their clothes and feast their eyes and fingers, exploring the exciting body they had never really known.

Dickon found his tongue loosening, and said, bravely, "I love you, Rosemary."

At this she laughed and pressed closer. Oh, it was good to be loved!

He waited, but she said nothing, and at last he was driven to ask, "Do you love me?"

"Yes, oh, yes! Of course I do!" She was not sure that she spoke the truth, but she could not bear to hurt him. He was beautiful and devoted and satisfying. Perhaps she truly did love him. Who knew what love was, and how could it be recognized?

She began to consider the future. Bridget was being courted by the son of a neighboring farmer. Soon they would get married, in the proper and conventional way. Rosemary found herself envying her sister. What would happen to her when Bridget had gone? She would have no companion, no one with whom to exchange confidences. Come to that, what would happen to her and Dickon when summer was over? She was sure neither of them would be content with furtive caresses beneath a wagon or in the shadow of a cow. That was in the past. Sometimes she caught herself thinking of her grandmother's age. Old people had to die sometime. And then she would be shocked at herself, or would tell herself that she ought to be shocked.

But August started a train of events which overshadowed even her preoccupation with the facilities of making love. There was first the homecoming of Marthanna and Mignon. This did not affect Rosemary to any great extent, though it added richness to life. Now at Wivelridge were people of culture and intelligence, cosmopolitans with experience beyond the confines of an island which for years had been cut off from its nearest neighbor. For middle-class country-dwellers access to an educated society was not easy. True, the gentry and the nobility were well-read, well-traveled, but their houses, set in extensive parks, were to most of the population as distant as if they had been built upon the moon. Rosemary became a frequent and welcome visitor to Wivelridge, and in her Aunt Marthanna found a friend and an ally. She could talk to her of everything and everyone, except of Dickon. Together they could laugh over Charity's peculiar ways, and so transform those ways into a joke rather than a burden. Marthanna lent Rosemary books; Mignon played to her on the square piano made by Sebastian Erard, which they had brought with them from France. It was the opening of windows on to new vistas, and Rosemary found herself with less and less to say to Dickon, though physically she still needed him as she needed light and air.

When Peregrine contemplated selling the farm, Rosemary was in a fine panic. What would happen to her? Where could she go? Back to her mother? Heaven forbid! It was all very well for Bridget. Her future was assured. In Sussex she could live, in Sussex she could die. Desperately Rosemary flew to Marthanna, and Marthanna reassured her, Marthanna the sensible, Marthanna the strong.

"My dear child, do you imagine that I could bear to leave Wivelridge? It is the center of my being, the very core of my life, for here Gerrance and I knew the kind of happiness which is granted to few human beings. Of course it could not last. I understood that from the beginning, but, you see, it has given this house a kind of glory which will shine from it for as long as I live. I think it was the yearning to return which enabled me to endure those years of imprisonment in France, and Gerrance's death. Be patient, Rosemary! I shall somehow solve the problem. Hastingford will not be sold."

And it was not. But before the matter was finally arranged came the third event, and for Rosemary this caused the others to diminish and almost disappear from sight.

She was not present when Sylvanus and Lancelot arrived in the carrier's cart, but she saw Sylvanus at the evening meal. Lancelot was tired, Sylvanus said, and had gone to bed. Had they come for a visit, Rosemary asked, or were they planning to stay? Sylvanus shrugged his shoulders. He was loth to foretell the future, he said. Who could count on anything in this life? But he, for his part, was ready to forswear fish for ever, except as manure.

Rosemary was pleased they had returned. It was a comfortable feeling to have her relations around, especially those like Aunt Marthanna and Lancelot, who were interesting people. Lancelot had proved a good companion when she first arrived, lonely and disconsolate, and though she did not expect to depend on him now as she had done then, she looked forward to renewing her friendship with him.

It was the following morning when she came upon him. She had been in the dairy, churning, and the butter, made from sour cream, had taken forty minutes to come. Her shoulders ached with the effort, and she had been glad to leave Bridget to salt and wash the butter. The air was fresh with autumn, but she was hot from her efforts and she decided to cool herself before entering the house. She walked across the yard, and as she went she saw Lancelot leaning on the gate of Dun Bogg's Close.

"Hello!" she called, and he turned.

Time had clouded her memory of him, which in any case was not very clear. He had been a fresh-faced young man, handsome, almost too handsome for a man, in her opinion. In London she had seen many pretty boys. Most of them were fops and dandies. So chiefly she remembered Lancelot's violet eyes, and apart from that he was a vague friendliness.

Now his appearance shocked her. Older he would certainly be. No doubt she herself had matured in five years. But he had changed more than she would have thought possible. He was thin, almost haggard, and on his face were lines which spoke of suffering. His lips which so easily had smiled were thinner and straighter, and the set of his jaw was sharp and defiant. But even more striking than these material features was, to her, his expression, vague and brooding, the look of a creature both lost and vulnerable. All this she had seen even before she reached him, and instantaneously it awakened in her an emotion never before aroused, the ancient, innate, female mother-love. In her relationship with Dickon there had been nothing maternal. Dickon was a healthy, uncomplicated young animal, sufficient to himself and his environment, able to give as generously as he would receive. But Lancelot—ah, what care he needed, what tenderness! In some way life had hurt him. His soul was bleeding. Rosemary became aware that her arms were aching, not only from the churn but from the yearning to put them around Lancelot and draw him close, with his head dropped upon her shoulder. At the moment there was nothing carnal in her desire. It was all gentleness. And at that moment Dickon ceased to exist for her.

"Rosemary!" Lancelot cried. "It is Rosemary, isn't it?"

"Is it so difficult to recognize me?"

"Not really, but girls change. They are invariably geese which become swans."

"You are not very flattering," she laughed.

"Ah, but I do not need to be. There is something nature does to young ladies. At one moment they are plump, solid little girls, and at the next they are goddesses. It is a trick to bewilder men."

"You have changed too."

"I don't doubt it. You should try being a fisherman for five years. It is, now that I look back on it, a purgatorial existence, for it is not natural to work at night and sleep in the day-time. At least, for men it is not. We leave that to the badgers and the foxes and the owls."

She listened, entranced by the magic of his voice, and her heart denied the truth of what he was saying. It was not fishing which had etched those lines on his face. It was something else, and what it was she intended to discover.

Sylvanus and Lancelot adjusted easily to their former position on the farm, and Peregrine dismissed two of the hired men. Soon it seemed as if they had never been away, except that Sylvanus no longer urged Peregrine to make alterations and improvements. It was as if his second absence from Hastingford had finally squeezed him of whatever restlessness or discontent or ambition remained. Now he could take the farm as it was, acknowledge that times were hard and Peregrine both stubborn and parsimonious, and could inhabit the fullness of his small world from day to day, admitting that he had gone further and fared worse.

Peregrine sold Wivelridge to Marthanna, and cautiously invested in another score of heifers and fifty Southdown lambs. But the major portion of the money he deposited in the Old Bank at Lewes. This he did to ensure the future of his son William, and also to provide for that rainy day which Charity had persuaded him might well come.

Lancelot was not concerned with improvements or policies. He worked hard and well, and worked long hours, because physical toil numbed thought and feeling, and because he, like his father, had come to learn that solace seeped through the hands and the feet from the soil, and in the eyes of the beasts was an understanding which required no words. A tired man slept soundly and ate heartily, and so gradually his cheeks filled out, and he no more bore the appearance of one who had been touched by the fingers of death. When he needed companionship, which was not often, he found that Rosemary was always near, and so without realizing it he came to have some dependence on her, and had she suddenly vanished would have missed her.

That Christmas was the most festive for years. Charity would have made little of it, as usual, but Marthanna overrode her objections.

"This is my first Christmas at home. We must celebrate it in an appropriate manner."

Charity turned down her mouth. "Christmas customs smack of popery."

"Yes, and many are pagan also. But that does not make us the less Christian. Tradition belongs to a country, not to a sect. Besides, my mother is growing old. We do not know how much longer she will be with us. We will all celebrate the season at Hastingford."

"At Hastingford!" Charity turned pale. "Oh, that would never do! I could not afford the expense, and the labor would kill me."

"Dear sister-in-law," Marthanna said, sweetly, "it will not cost you one penny, that I promise you. And as for hard work, there are Rosemary and Bridget, as well as Mignon and myself. You may, if you wish, put your feet up like a lady, and you will not be missed."

So vigorous and dominating was Marthanna that Charity found her objections being swept aside almost before she could formulate them. Also there was the question of money. If the whole affair should really cost her nothing, why, then, she would stand to profit, for even to entertain her own family would not be as cheap as she could wish. So she gave way, and Marthanna found herself with a free hand to devise such a festival as she hoped would never be forgotten.

The somewhat bare hall of Hastingford was decked with ivy and laurel and bay, and candles of a very large size were made, that night should be nearly as bright as day. The yule-log lay drying in the hearth, and a score or more of beasts and birds were fattened and doomed to die. From the kitchens drifted a smell of spices and herbs, and Caroline stripped her cupboards of their wines and brandies. "For," she said, "if Charity had her way we should be toasting the Nativity in pump-water, and that's not the manner of religious or of human observance."

Marthanna invited Rebecca and the boys to join them for the holy-day, and, when Rebecca declined, sent to London a large hamper of seasonal foods.

"I cannot understand your mother," she complained, to Rosemary. "This is a time for families to be together. Does she no longer care for us?"

But Rosemary understood the pride which would not allow her mother to confess she could not afford the coachfare, or clothes which would not disgrace her. If Marthanna were told, she would gladly provide the wherewithal, Rosemary knew, but she also knew that her mother would be more offended than pleased by such a gesture.

Early on Christmas Day Marthanna sent her carriage and pair of fine gray horses down the lane to Sweetwillow Shaw to fetch her mother and Dickon, and then the four of them drove over to Hastingford, the horses decorated with knots and bows, and ribbons streaming from the coachman's whip.

It was a day such as the Dykes had not known for many years. Everyone ate and drank a great deal, and Peregrine, who now was unused to strong liquor, felt constrained to make a speech which, though somewhat incoherent, seemed to be a sentimental recollection of the old days. Caroline cried softly into a lace handkerchief, remembering other Christmases which on looking back appeared to be nothing but jubilees of laughter and joy. Why had they been so happy, she wondered, and why was it only after they were long departed that she could savor their quality?

When the remains of the dinner had been removed the children played games—drop-glove and fox and geese and the poor woman of Babylon—games of immemorial antiquity, passed down through the generations by word of mouth, and they found it amusing to initiate the sophisticated little French girl into those things they had known from their cradle. The adults took out dice and greasy, little-used packs of cards and tried to remember the rules of whist or cribbage or ombre. Bridget went off to visit her sweetheart's parents, and Lancelot and Rosemary were left looking at one another.

"Shall we go for a walk?" he suggested at last. "It will soon be dark."

They went through the orchard and into the lane, the fields being knee-deep in mud.

"It will soon be dark," Rosemary said, echoing Lancelot's words. "We can't go too far."

"No, but it's good to breathe the air, isn't it?"

"You're not happy indoors, are you?"

"Reckon not. What's a roof for, anyway, but to keep out the rain? And what is there to do indoors but eat or sleep?"

"Aunt Marthanna and Mignon find much to occupy themselves."

"Oh, needlework and such. That's for women."

"Books and music are not exclusively for women."

"Ah! Well, once I had a fancy for reading books,

but these five years past I've led a rough life. I'm no learned gentleman."

"I think you have intelligence," Rosemary said, somewhat stiffly.

"You may. There are some who don't." He sounded so angry that Rosemary did not care to pursue the subject.

Instead, she said, "I suppose we should join the card-playing."

"Because we are grown up? Maybe we're too old for nursery games, but Grandmother and aunts and uncles still look upon us as children."

"We are the odd ones," Rosemary said. "Everyone else in the family is so much older or so much younger."

"I am five years older than you."

"That is nothing."

They were silent for twenty or thirty paces, while Rosemary cast around for something to say. She longed desperately to establish friendship and easy intimacy with Lancelot, but it was more difficult now than when she had first known him. He had become reserved, almost secretive, and sometimes she despaired of breaking through the armor he had built around himself. Perhaps the only way was to be bold, to ask questions. She shrank from behaving in a manner which might appear unmaidenly, but she was making no progress with him, and ahead she could see nothing but a dreary future in which they would drift further apart and become strangers.

"Are you lonely?" she asked.

He shrugged. "Who isn't?"

"We are surrounded by relatives."

"You can be loneliest in a crowd."

"I know. I'm lonely too."

"You?"

"Why not?"

He turned and looked at her curiously. "You are a pretty girl. Why don't you marry?"

"Who is there?"

"Bridget has found someone."

"It is easy for her. I mean——" She broke off. "What happened in Brighton, Lancelot?"

"You've heard all about it. We worked as fishermen."

"Yes, but—Why did you come home?"

"Because we were tired of working as fishermen."

He spoke lightly, and suddenly it was too much, too great an effort to make. She felt the tears coming, and went and leaned on the top bar of a gate, keeping her face from him.

"What is it?" he asked. "What is the matter? Have I said something to upset you?"

She shook her head and turned towards him, groping, so that there was nothing for it but to put his arm around her, and she clung to him, sobbing.

"Oh, Lancelot, I'm so unhappy."

"Poor lass!" He smoothed her hair. Fine hair it was, fair and silky, lying close to her head. She was a Ball, he thought, not a true Dyke, for all she was his cousin. "Why are you unhappy?"

"Because you are."

This surprised him. "Well, I'll be jiggered! That's an unaccountable strange reason. You shouldn't be bothering your head about other folks' troubles. Anyway," he added, as an afterthought, "there's nought wrong with me."

"Yes, there is! There is!" she declared, passionately. "You've been hurt, and I want to heal you." She lifted her face towards him, straining her neck upwards. He was taller than she, and so he had to bend down a little, which he did, somewhat embarrassed, and planted a kiss on her forehead.

"A woman has hurt you," she insisted. "Yes, she has. I know it. I am not a fool. A man looks only as sad as you when a woman has betrayed him."

Lancelot burst out laughing. "I have seen men look monstrous sad when they had lost all their money."

"Do not make fun of me, I beg you!"

"I did not intend to," he said, serious. "You are kind and good, and I am grateful for your sympathy."

"It was a woman, was it not?"

"I don't want to talk about it."

"I could kill her!" Rosemary cried. "Lancelot, are you fond of me?"

"Yes, very fond."

"I love you."

He looked startled and dropped his arms. "Rosemary, you should not say it."

"I know. It is not womanly, but I don't care. I am twenty-three and you are twenty-seven. We are not children. In fact, I am almost an old maid. No, do not shake your head. I am, but it does not trouble me. I would rather be a spinster than wed one I did not love."

"There is time," he said, lamely.

"But I love you, so how can I marry someone else?"

"If I went away——"

"Away!" she exclaimed, dismayed. "Would you run away once more? It would make no difference to me, and where would you go? Back to Brighton?"

He shuddered. "No!"

"We belong to the farm. It is our life. We are both lonely. Lancelot, let us marry! I can bear it that you do not love me, so long as you are kind. I will be a comfort to you. That is what a wife is intended to be, is it not?"

She looked small and frail as she stood there, a fairy-like creature, but brave, brave enough to defy convention. She no more resembled the fashionable vivacious Petronella than a wood-anemone resembled a garden rose, and he was glad. His feeling for Petronella was like a growth inside of him, which could not be cut out without causing his death. He was not sure that the feeling could be described by any one word, such as love. It was an obsession of which he could not rid himself, a flash of lightning which had seared him and burnt out his power of responding to anything but itself. He had never so much as kissed her, but had she taken him she would, he knew, have possessed him utterly. A comfort? No, that was what Petronella would never have been.

He took Rosemary's face between his hands. It was small and pale and oval, and when he kissed her lips they were cold.

"I am sure," he said, "that you will be a great comfort to me."

CHAPTER ELEVEN

My love a kind of dream was grown,
A foolish, but a pleasant one;
From which I'm wakened now; but, oh!
Prisoners to die are wakened so.
Abraham Cowley

The news of the betrothal of Rosemary and Lancelot was received with such calmness by the family that Rosemary felt its reception as something of an insult.

"Are you not pleased?" she asked Marthanna, and Marthanna replied, "Naturally, my dear. It is most fitting."

"Is that all you have to say?"

"What else would you have me say?"

Rosemary was at a loss to explain. "Well, I do not know. It is a cold word—fitting. It is as if it were convenience and not love."

Marthanna laughed. "Ah, you would have me leap in the air and clap my hands. But that I must leave to you and Lancelot. I am truly happy that you are happy. Is not that sufficient?"

It should have been, but somehow to Rosemary it was not. She would have liked people to be astounded at the wonder of the thing, and envious of her incredible good fortune at having Lancelot as her promised husband. There was only one Lancelot in the world, and she was the woman who was to be his wife. Was not that a miracle in itself?

"You should be excited," she said to Bridget, severely.

"Why? I do not love Lancelot. I love Benjamin and I am to marry him."

"Yes, and I am excited for you. I am excited for everyone who loves a man. There is nothing so wonderful, so glorious, as to be married."

"It is natural," Bridget said, practically.

"To me it is amazing," Rosemary said, dreamily, "but to you and the rest of the family, even Charity, it is as if our announcement were expected."

"No doubt it was. You are not very young, either of you, and whom could you marry else? We meet few young men. If I had not fancied Benjamin," she added, frankly, "I might well have been an old maid, for all I am three years younger than you."

Rosemary realized that Bridget spoke commonsense, yet still she was put out. Her relations were guilty of insensitivity, she thought. Perhaps it came from dealing so much with animals and so little with people of sentiment.

But from Dickon there was an explosion violent enough to convince her that he at least was not without feeling.

"Marry Lancelot? You don't mean it."

"I do. I love him. I'm sorry, Dickon, but I can't help it."

"Why, geemany, who can help it, then? Are you nought but a kite, that you must lie with one man and cast sheepseyes at another?"

"Dickon, we could never be anything but friends."

"Friends do you call it? Friends, what we've been?"

"You are my grandmother's husband."

"Ah!" he cried, bitterly, "A lot you thought of that when you was lusting after me."

"Every woman wants to be married."

"For you I killed."

"Hush! We must forget that."

"It's in the barn, plain for anyone with a spade, what I did for you. I was good enough for you then, but soon as he comes home, him that didn't send you so much as a word these five years past—"

"We scarcely knew one another when he went away."

"Made up for it now, haven't you? You've not been slow with the knowing."

"Don't you want me to be happy, Dickon?"

"I don't know that I do," he said, slowly, "if so be it that it's someone else you're happy with."

"If you love me—"

"I said so, didn't I? And you said so. Was you lying?"

"No. Not then. I didn't know what love was."

"And now you do? But what about him? You're not such a lumping pennyworth."

"What do you mean?"

"Blame ye! You know what I mean. Maiden you wasn't when I had you, and less maiden you are now, less by all those times you've lain with me. What will he say when he finds the poor bargain he's got?"

Suddenly she was stricken with fear. It had not occurred to her that Dickon might constitute a danger. Indeed, she had scarcely considered him from the moment Lancelot arrived. He was a part of the past, friendly, useful, sympathetic, but no longer important, and because she had not needed him, she had not stopped to consider whether he might still need her. But now she saw him as a menace to her happiness, and she was ready to both hate and fear him.

"You would not tell Lancelot?"

He glanced at her pityingly. "There's no need for any telling. Reckon he's man enough to know if he's taking a virgin."

Crowding on fear came a new fear. How could she have been so stupid as not to have thought of it? It must have been love which put it out of her mind, she decided. It must have been love which made her feel as if no man had ever touched her before.

"Perhaps he will not notice," she ventured, hopefully.

Dickon laughed. She loathed him for that laugh,

which was coarse and cruel. "Not notice? He'd as soon mistake an old cow for a maiden heifer."

Rosemary turned on him, beating at him with her fists. "Stop it! Stop it! You are a foul and filthy beast. You are a murderer and a robber of grave-yards. I do not wish ever to speak to you again. Because of your jealousy you have tried to spoil my happiness. But you will not succeed. I shall explain to Lancelot that I was raped by the bird-catchers, and he will be sorry for me and love me even more. I shall not mention you, and you will not dare to breathe a word of —of what we did together. If you do, my grandmother will turn you out, and you will have no home. If you do, I shall take them to the barn and show them what lies buried there."

He looked at her, sadly and speculatively. "Don't know which you're best at, loving or hating. But there's no need to lie sleepless on account of me. I wouldn't tell Lancelot what you are. I love you, and I don't know how I can abear seeing you tied to another man."

"Thank you!" She touched his arm, and then snatched her hand away, thinking he might mistake her gesture for an expression of affection. With Dickon, she knew, love was a matter of physical closeness, of flesh speaking to flesh, of the silent words of the hands and the lips, of the unspoken promise of the genitals. He would not understand she was now so divorced from any but Lancelot that she could not grant to anyone else even the favor of her finger-tips.

He sighed deeply, accepting the fact of his loss but unreconciled to it.

"Reckon he should be unaccountable grateful at getting you."

"You do me too much honor," she said, formally. "I am the one to be grateful. He is an exceptional man."

Dickon nodded. Who was he to disagree with her, she who was so much cleverer than he? "He's proud, though. You'd best tell him."

"Tell him?"

"Yes. That you've mislaid your virginity. A man prefers to hear such things before he marries, not to learn afterwards. He'd feel cheated."

"Of course! Certainly I shall tell him."

And it was her genuine intention to do so, but somehow the opportunity did not occur, the right moment never quite arrived. Not often were they alone together. A farmer's long hours were chiefly spent in the fields, while the women were occupied in the house and the dairy and the yards. True there was bad weather during the first two months of the year, when field-work came to a standstill, but then there was hedge-laying and tree-felling to be done, and when Lancelot was in the barns or stables or cow-houses he was generally in the company of one or two of the other men. Rosemary did suggest to him that they might take a walk together, but he looked so astonished that she blushed, feeling as though she had made an improper advance.

"I've been on my feet all day," he said, "and I'm middling weary. Besides, it's cold and dark outside. It's the chimney corner I've a fancy for this night."

"I see you so rarely."

He laughed, pulling her hair teasingly. "I'm across the table from you at every meal. Isn't that enough?"

"I could never see you enough."

"Ah! You shame me."

"How? How do I shame you? Tell me!"

"You are so sweet, so good. I'm not worthy of you. But, then, what man could be?"

This was her chance. Now she should tell him that she did not deserve his opinion of her. He placed her too highly. To him she was the fair sun-ripened apple on the topmost branch, while she knew that in reality she lay windfallen and maggoty in the grass. But would it not be cruel so to disillusion him? He had been sufficiently hurt, and her heart went out to him in love and sympathy so that she wanted to protect him even from herself. Besides, this was not the time or the place for telling him, here in the hall at Hastingford, and standing by the hearth, and, as if to justify her objections, at that moment Charity walked in.

She waited for him to ask her to name the day for their wedding. For two months she waited, until one wild March morning she could bear it no longer and went to find him. Lancelot was not really alone. He was following Sylvanus with a pair of light harrows, covering the clover-seed as Sylvanus drilled. Rosemary, was almost blown across the field, feeling herself scarcely heavier than the clouds which were so elongated and twisted by the wind that they appeared to writhe like agonized worms.

"Lancelot!" Rosemary called, but he did not hear her until she had drawn level with him.

"Lancelot!"

He looked startled. "Is anything wrong?"

"Does anything have to be wrong when I come to see you?" There was a tinge of bitterness in her voice, of which even she was not conscious. "Spring is on the way. Can you not feel it?"

"I can feel a deal of roughness and buffeting. If it's spring, then she's trying to blow the buds off the trees, so it's as well they're not shooting yet, otherwise the leaves would be scorched. This wind comes straight from the sea. Can't you taste the salt on your tongue?"

"No. No, I don't think so."

"Ah, you've not learnt the savor of the sea, as I have. I know it like a wine-drinker knows the vintage of the grapes. There's the taste of the sea in anger, and the taste of her when she's lying half-asleep under the moon."

He spoke dreamily, and Rosemary was suddenly jealous. "You talk as if you wish you were a fisherman again."

"A man always wishes to be what he's not. This salt, now, it comes from Brighton, blown in a spray over the Downs and settling on our land. Look at those gulls! There's no bird more brave and free. They're free of the land and the sea and the air. Have you ever wished to be a bird?"

"No," Rosemary said, resentfully. "I prefer to be a woman."

Lancelot laughed and would have turned back to his work, but she caught at his sleeve. "I've come to ask you something."

"Yes? What is it?"

"Well, in truth I have come to ask you why you have not asked me something."

"That sounds wondrous tied up, like a knot in a pig's tail."

"It is quite simple really. You have not asked me to name the day for our wedding."

"Well, I must have forgot. But since you have remembered—"

"That is not the point," she said, severely. "It is the man's place to ask, and it is not the woman's place to remind him. You embarrass me."

He put his arm around her shoulders and squeezed her. "My sweet child, I would not wish to do that. I am obviously a person of low breeding, a common farmer. As in Brighton—"

He stopped, and she prompted him. "As in Brighton?"

He shrugged his shoulders. "Oh, it is nothing, merely that in Brighton I could not expect to mix with the gentry. In such a town one learns more of the gulf between the classes than on a farm."

"So I must remind you that we should fix a day for our wedding."

"Yes."

He was silent, as though he had disposed of the matter, and she was forced to say, gently, almost timidly, "Well, I have reminded you."

"And which month would you recommend?"

Which month? She almost cried out in disappointment. Now, her heart cried, now and now and now. "As soon as you would wish," she said, and was shamed at her own eagerness.

"Then shall we decide for June?"

"June?" Oh, God! June was three months away. "Why June?"

"It's the month young ladies are reputed to favor. It's the season of roses and nightingales. But if you cannot be ready by then—"

"I shall be ready," she interrupted, hastily. "Yes, let us say June."

Charity somewhat ungraciously provided a bridal chamber, a small, dark room at the side of the house, inadequately furnished and with no view.

"I would have wished something larger," Rosemary faltered.

"Beggars cannot be choosers," Charity told her, briskly. "With Sylvanus and the servants, and with my children growing up, so that Meek cannot in decency share a bedchamber with her brothers, Hastingford is crowded to its extremities. Houses cannot stretch beyond their walls. However," she added, astonished at her own magnanimity, "after Bridget is married you may remove to your old room, if you prefer it."

Rosemary nodded. "I thank you, but Bridget does not propose to marry until next year."

"Very wise, too. Not like some, who seem to be in an unconscionable hurry. Hasty weddings cause wagging tongues."

Rosemary was tempted to answer hotly and sharply, but she had learned that little or nothing could be gained by crossing swords with Charity. Charity was impregnable, being drowned in her own rectitude. Besides which, Rosemary and Lancelot must continue to share the family home, and so nothing would be gained by quarrelling with its female ruler.

Marthanna it was who helped prepare for the marriage, Marthanna who, with characteristic generosity, provided linen for the bed and a wardrobe for Rosemary.

"I cannot permit it," Rosemary protested. "You give me too much."

"You are my niece, and I am not a poor woman. I am merely doing what your mother would wish to do."

"I love you, Aunt Marthanna, but I have my pride."

"Lud!" Marthanna smiled. "We cannot deprive you of that, can we? So, if it will salve your precious pride, shall we re-make some of my old dresses? As you can see, having been transformed by marriage into a frivolous Frenchwoman, I have presses full of clothes I shall never wear. Living in the country they would last me another two hundred years."

To this arrangement Rosemary consented, though she could not help but see that her aunt chose those garments which patently had scarcely or never been worn.

"We shall have the wedding-dinner here at Wivelridge, and I shall throw open the conservatory, which is commodious, though of course a poor, bare place compared with its condition when Gerrance cared for it."

"I think it is very grand," Rosemary said. "It has a foreign look."

Marthanna sighed. "You should have seen it! There were orange and lemon trees, gigantic ferns, grapes ready to drop into your mouth, melons caught in nets like strange fishes, and a banana tree that could hardly be restrained. But what am I doing, dreaming of the past, when we should be planning your future? Your mother and brothers will stay with me, naturally. I wish them to remain several weeks. They deserve an adequate rest from those filthy London fumes."

"I am not sure Mother will leave the shop for so long," Rosemary said, doubtfully. "And there is my brothers' schooling."

"Leave that to me. I shall send your mother a gown, mantelet and hat, and in case her pride is as prickly as yours, I shall swear it is an outfit I have worn until I tired of it and it became downright shabby."

"Aunt Marthanna, you are terrible!"

"No, merely self-indulgent. It seems that as a comfortably-endowed widow I am of little use to the world. Indeed, what is there in life for a woman who has lost her husband? If I lived in London I could gamble and gossip, but those things have little appeal for me. Anything I can do to add to your happiness at this moment when you are about to set out on your greatest adventure is to me a pleasure and a luxury. Now we must decide what you are to wear."

It was Marthanna who actually decided, but Rosemary was only too glad for her to do so. Rosemary would not have cared had she been married in an old corn-sack.

For a country wedding, said Marthanna, correctness lay in simplicity. Rosemary should have a flowered muslin dress, falling straight to the ground with a frill on the bottom, banded close under the breasts with narrow black ribbons. On her head she would wear a small poke bonnet, and to add a touch of true elegance Marthanna would trim it with a cluster of ostrich feathers she had purchased in Paris.

"They are the color of Belle Hélène roses, and are most divinely curled. Come, I will show them to you."

Dutifully Rosemary admired them, and was suitably grateful, and then Marthanna sat back and regarded her with some perplexity. "You are too amenable, my dear. You agree with everything I propose. It would be easier if sometimes you objected."

"How can I have objections, dear aunt?" Rosemary asked. "Your taste is perfect."

"Young girls like to have their own way, especially where a wedding is concerned."

Rosemary shook her head. "These outward trappings are pleasant, but unimportant. Nothing matters except Lancelot."

"You love him very much, do you not?"

"I would not marry him unless I did."

"Oh, youth! Idealistic, incurably hopeful. Be strong, Rosemary. Love as much as you will, but be strong as well. Women need strength."

"I'll remember, Aunt Marthanna."

"Yes. Remember. Now have you no particular desire connected with this wedding? Is there nothing you want for yourself?"

Rosemary smiled. "Yes, please! I would like the date of the wedding to be announced in the *Sussex Weekly Advertiser*."

"Why, what a strange request! And what a strange girl you are to make such a request! Of course it shall be done. It is a simple matter. But why do you wish it?"

Rosemary thought, and then she said, "Because I would like to see it in print. When it is in print I shall feel it is really going to happen."

That was her prevailing emotion during those weeks of preparation, the feeling that her marriage with Lancelot was too good to be true, was more than she could ask of mortal life which was supposed to be a mingling of sweet and sour. To be Lancelot's wife would be all sweet, and what right had she to expect fate to be so prejudiced in her favor? She went about her work with a kind of feverish intensity, and a dozen times she asked Lancelot, "Are you happy? Are you really happy?"

His replies were varied. "Of course!" or "Wouldn't I be an ungrateful devil if I weren't?" Or, "Foolish girl to put such a question!" And once, in despair at quieting her restless heart, "What is happiness?"

This last she could not answer. It should have been easy, for if she did not know happiness now, when could she hope to make its acquaintance? But an inborn concern for truth whispered that the edges of her present joy were gnawed by anxiety.

The passing of each day was a relief, for it shortened the time in which something could happen to rob her of her heart's desire, and when no more than four days remained before the wedding, the final burden of her apprehension seemed to roll from her, and all was light and longing and anticipation.

She was staying at Wivelridge for the last few days before the ceremony, but her desire to see Lancelot was so great that she made an excuse to go to Hastingford to put the finishing touches to the bridal chamber.

Over the Rother she went, and climbed the hilly

fields, but she was not aware that her feet touched the ground. They seemed rather to skim the top of the grasses without bending the stalks, just as the air nourished her lungs without her having to gulp it down, and sweet scents insinuated themselves, not requiring anything so earthy as a sniff. It was like being dead, she thought, dreamily; like being a spirit cognizant of all beauty direct instead of by the passage of the senses. It was an ordinary June day, yet it was individual and unique. A sun shone, plants grew, birds sang. The panting and yearning of spring was over. Nature had settled down to the fulfillment of the marriage-bed.

Thinking of marriage-beds she resolved scrupulously to go to her room and Lancelot's before seeking him out. Already it was as perfect as she could make it, the floor bees-waxed, the window diamond-bright, the sheets lavender-strewn, but she was content to take another peep at it, to endow it in advance with an ecstasy she expected it to witness.

Through the yard door of Hastingford she went, and into the hall to the staircase. It was dim after the sunlight of the open air and she almost missed the figure standing quietly there. But the figure saw her, and asked, "Will you tell me where I may find Lancelot Dyke?"

She answered without thinking, "Oh, he will be taking the thistles from the wheat, or sowing turnips, or busy with one of a dozen other tasks. Who can say where a farmer may be found? But from the yard one can see most of the land. Shall I take you there?"

"Please!"

Before she had left the hall curiosity pricked her, and once they reached full daylight and she could take a sideways glance at the visitor curiosity was reinforced by apprehension. The visitor was a young woman, and unlike any Rosemary had come across in Sussex. Indeed she made Rosemary feel positively rustic. Instead of Rosemary's lightly frizzed curls, this girl's hair, so dark as to appear black, lay straight and heavy about her shoulders. Her eyes were large and shadowed, her voice deep, and from her low-cut gown to the broad-brimmed hat which dangled carelessly from her hand, everything about her bespoke the fashionable young lady.

Rosemary, perplexed, asked, "Have you come for the wedding?"

The girl did not answer directly, but said, "I read of the wedding, in the Lewes newspaper."

"You know Lancelot?" There was no reply to this, and Rosemary added, almost defiantly, "I am the bride."

Some instinct shrieked out that she should send this visitor on her way, should pretend that Lancelot was not to be found, had gone to market, anything. But inexplicably she could not do this. As if in a nightmare, when one walks inevitably to doom, she led the way across the fields and did not stop until they were within a few feet of Lancelot.

"She has come to see you," Rosemary said, but the other two did not hear her.

Lancelot cried, "Petronella!"

The girl looked at him. "I read of your wedding."

"Yes."

"I had to come. I could not allow it to happen."

Lancelot rubbed his hands across his eyes. "I must be dreaming."

"You thought me so shallow," the girl said, violently. "You went away. You gave me no chance. Did you imagine that a dandy in wide pantaloons, pinched in with stays, peering over the top of a collar, smelling like a civet cat and lisping out of a mouth with a velvet patch at the corner would be a substitute for a real man?"

Lancelot's body leaned forward as if it would of its own accord annihilate the distance between them. With an effort he drew himself back. "It is not my affair, the kind of man you prefer. I am promised."

With one accord they turned and looked at Rosemary.

"She would not wish it," Petronella said. "She would not wish it, now that she knows."

"There is nothing to know," Lancelot declared, strongly. "There was nothing between us."

"Nothing that showed, perhaps. But there are things which are not said, things which are not done, and they bind the most tightly."

Rosemary watched Lancelot. This, she knew now, was what she had always feared. This was the menace of the passing hours, the threat which could have been averted had it delayed by four more days. But she had wanted the announcement of the wedding to appear. She, the fool, was her own murderer. Before her eyes she saw the fatal miracle performed, saw Lancelot coming to life, saw the real Lancelot resuscitated, and knew that Lancelot her betrothed had been a man of straw, empty, spellbound. But to be sure, she asked, "Do you love her?"

"How do I know?" Lancelot demanded, angrily. "Who can tell? Perhaps I hate her."

Rosemary shook her head. "That would be the same, as far as we are concerned. She is right, of course. I would not wish it, not now."

She turned but over her shoulder remembered her manners. "Thank you, Lancelot, for being so—polite."

Down to the bottom of the valley she went, and her feet were so heavy that it was as though she walked in treacle. There was no hurt yet; at least, none that she was aware of, and she did not intend to wait for the pain to begin.

Half-way across the bridge was the middle of the river, not yet summer-depleted of its water, deep enough. By sitting on the planks she could slide under the rail. Her feet dangled over the space between bridge and Rother. The sun was hot on her legs, the same sun, but never again the same. In a few moments it would be over. Thank God, it would be over!

She pushed herself forward, but before her hands and buttocks had parted company with the bridge, an arm was flung about her waist and she was dragged back.

For an instant she imagined a miracle. Could time turn tail, an event be rubbed out?

Then Dickon's voice spoke. "You'll have to make do with me now," he said.

Part Three

CHAPTER ONE

When a prince is born they are told to rejoice, and they rejoice — that is, they make bonfires, they get drunk, they ring bells, they give their apprentices holidays, and are loyally delighted, in due form. When a king dies they are told to be sorry, and they are sorry: — that is, they put on black, they look as grave as they can, they crowd to the exhibition of lying in state, they shut up their shops on the day of the funeral, lament that the best monarch that ever has been is called to heaven; and run directly away to shout at the coronation of the best king that ever will be.

The Black Dwarf, 1820

The tolling of the bells which marked the death of George the Third were unheard by Caroline, for it was a cold January day, too cold to open the windows, too cold for an old lady to do anything but crouch over the fire and draw her shawl close about her shoulders and sip her cup of tea, which beverage she persisted in taking, despite Charity's repeated warnings that it was a pernicious draught and expensive, to boot.

"Do you not realize, mother-in-law, that you are wasting fivepence a day on a noxious liquid containing no nourishment whatever?"

"I enjoy it," Caroline replied, smacking her lips.

"What is wrong with sage? You know what they say. 'Why do men die, whilst sage in gardens grow?' Then there is balm. John Hussey, of Sydenham in

Kent, took balm tea with honey for fifty years, and he lived to be one hundred and sixteen."

" 'Twas his birthplace, not his tea," Caroline said, maliciously. "Those foreigners from Kent live for ever. You can't get rid of 'em. When a Sussex man marries a Kentish woman he's got her for life. For his life, that is."

"Mother-in-law, why do you continue to look upon Kent as a foreign country? In your time, perhaps, folk did not travel far, but now we move around, and Kent is merely over the way."

Caroline laughed. She had lost most of her teeth, and her laughter was as toothlessly merry as a baby's.

"Daughter-in-law, why do you continue to lecture me on the evils of tea and coffee and other beverages? You began it as soon as you entered my house. How long ago is that? Twenty years? It becomes monotonous."

"But none the less true. I have been reading Sir John Sinclair's Code of Health and Longevity."

"And do you desire to live long?"

"As long as the Lord ordains."

"Then you might as well let the Lord decide whether tea is good or bad for you, for if you are intended to live long, then live long you will."

Caroline was not sure whether a long life was a benefit or a liability. Much of hers had been pleasant; all of it had been interesting, yet, being a kind of patchwork, as lives were, extra years meant extra sorrow as well as extra joy. Certainly she would not wish to die today, and perhaps not tomorrow either, but there were times when her seventy-seven years lay like a burden on her. Naturally she did not expect to escape the growing frailty of her flesh, and was able to bear the ills of age with cheerfulness. It was the burden on the mind which often daunted her. There was so much to remember, and sorrow recalled still had the power to stab as freshly as on its birthday. Regret, too, was not lacking, and the guilt of the done and the undone. Only a fool, she thought, could pretend that memory, like a hen pecking corn, picked out none but the sunny hours.

Today, however, took her back sixty years, and she had no fault to find with the lumber her mind turned up. She had been sitting in the window then, listening to the bells which proclaimed the new king. Full and sweet and musical they had been, those Blackheath bells, not like village ones, though she doubted if she could have heard even those now, for she had become somewhat deaf, yet not so deaf as people thought, for she was continually begging them not to shout at her. Still, she could not complain, if she compared her fate with that of the late king. Poor old king! Deaf, blind and witless. What a comment on the futility of state and majesty! His only happiness, they said, if such a word could be used with regard to him, was in praying and singing hymns and playing on his harpsichord, whenever his brain was clear enough for such occupation. Now, after sixty years a king—though no king for the past eleven —he had been released. Eighty-two he was, and Caroline only five years younger. That other time, when she had listened to those other bells, he had been a young man of twenty-two and she a girl of seventeen almost ready to embark on that long journey which had started with a ride to Gretna Green. Ah, well! A lot of water had run into the Rother and out to sea since then.

That evening Peregrine came to see her. It was his habit now to visit her two or three times a week and sit for an hour or so. Usually she would make him a meal, and then they would settle themselves by the fire, Caroline in the middle, with Peregrine on one side of her, and Dickon on the other. She enjoyed these cosy conversations, and Peregrine did also. The company of his mother was preferable to that of his wife, especially as he went to Burwash to see his mistress less frequently since the boy had gone away to school. He had placed William at a private school in Tunbridge Wells, under the care of a man with considerable scholastic qualifications. The cost was more than he could easily afford, but he had determined to keep to his decision made when he contemplated selling the farm, that William should receive a good education and, if he showed any talent for learning, should graduate from school to a university.

Caroline asked first, as she always did, "How is William doing?"

This pleased Peregrine and put him in a good humor. "He is doing well," he would reply, and sometimes he would draw forth a piece of paper, saying, "I have heard from him. He has written me a letter. See how his characters have improved."

And Caroline would take her spectacles and put them on and study with eagerness the childish scrawl.

But on that particular evening they did not talk much of William, for it seemed only fitting that they should pay the respect of loyal subjects to a dead king.

"So the poor old man has gone," Peregrine said.

Caroline nodded. "A merciful release, I should say. Think you it will make much difference to the country?"

Peregrine shrugged. "Not a deal. We've had the son for nigh on ten years. He's fifty-seven now, and a man doesn't change at that age."

"Kings and parliaments," Caroline said, philosophically, "they make a lot of noise, but they move little earth."

"You wouldn't believe that if you'd a farm to run."

"Dickon and I manage nicely."

"Yes, the two of you on a small patch, and I'm nought but a minnow, compared with the big farmers. You should hear what they say. This country is doomed, because agriculture is doomed, and without agriculture we can't live. We're crippled by taxes, and threatened by the men we employ. It's nothing but rioting and destruction. Mark my words, there's a revolution brewing."

"In England?" Caroline cackled. "You must have a swarm of bees under your hair."

"Ah! You can make light of it. That's the trouble. People don't see danger coming until it's too late. Anyway, Cobbett's returned from America. They say his house burnt down and that decided him. Maybe he'll be able to bang some sense into the heads of the bang-straws."

"Indeed?" Caroline murmured, politely. "And who is Cobbett?"

Peregrine stared at her, as shocked as though she had denied her Savior. "William Cobbett? You've not heard of him? I declare you're as ignorant as a wean-year-beast. William Cobbett is a man as says what he thinks, and he loves England. He's on our side."

"Whose side? Yours? Or those gowks that are making such a felelou that we're on the way to revolution?"

"Both. He's on the side of all those that till the ground, and he aims to get justice. They shut him in Newgate, but that didn't silence him. I take his paper regularly. It's called the *Political Register*."

"You? A reader?" Caroline jeered, goodnaturedly.

"Well, a man must do something when he's growing older."

"Ah, he turns from fornication to confabulation. Men were ever talkers, and that great looby who spends half his time in Brighton is no exception."

"Mother!" Peregrine exclaimed. "You've no call to say such things."

"Why not? Will he cut off my head? I've yet to see the king who will lift a finger to make a woman's lot easier. Maybe one day we'll have a queen, for a change."

"But the Queen's away to Italy."

"I'm not meaning poor Caroline. I'm speaking of a little princess in Kensington Palace. You may have politics on the end of your tongue, my son, but history's made of other things than politics."

Mostly Dickon listened while they talked, and sometimes he did not bother to listen, but paid attention to the long, slow thoughts which passed through his mind. He knew himself to be a humble, ignorant creature compared with the Dykes, and he had never ceased to feel gratitude at being permitted to partake of their life as one of the family. Indeed, as he drew towards middle age he appreciated them still more. Tiresome and obstinate Caroline might sometimes be, yet he never lost patience with her. She was both his wife and his mistress, in the sense of being his employer, and he held that he owed her obedience as well as devotion.

For pleasure, for which he sometimes felt the need, he had Rosemary. From the moment when he prevented her from drowning herself in the Rother she had become his especial responsibility and possession. The reason for this he could not have expressed in words, but he had the feeling that their lives were bound together in such a way that they could not be disentangled.

From the moment Petronella arrived it had seemed to Dickon, as well as to the others, that for Lancelot no one else existed. More, it seemed as though nothing existed, as though he could no longer see the farm, or the preparations for his wedding, or the expression on the faces of those around him. Rosemary went to the small dark room, the aborted bridal chamber, locked herself in and would not open for anyone, would not even reply when people spoke to her through the door, anxiously, persuasively or commandingly. They were afraid of what she might do to herself, but Dickon said they need have no fears on that account. She had attempted to throw herself into the river, he told them, and he did not believe that even the most stricken could twice look death in the face in so short a time.

He was right. On the third day she re-appeared, Petronella and Lancelot having by then left Hastingford. She was stony-faced and tearless, and responded sharply and ungraciously to any words of sympathy.

"Leave me alone!" she exclaimed. "That is all I want, to be left alone."

There was nothing for it but to do as she wished, unapproachable as she was, and only Dickon intruded on her sorrow.

To him at first she said the same. "Leave me alone!" But he ignored this.

"I've a right," he said. "I've a right to do what I like with you, because I saved you. Your life is mine."

"What kind of barbarous superstition is that?" she demanded.

"I don't know. It's true, though. But for me you'd be in your grave."

"But!" she mocked. "Have you never heard, 'But me no buts?' I can give you many examples of the buts which change our lives. But for our stables which gave you the idea of stealing a horse, you would not have married my grandmother and would not have met me. But for that harlot from Brighton I would now be a happy bride. Do what you wish with my life. It's of little value to me."

"I want to make you happy."

"Then what a hopeless task you have set yourself! Can you not understand that for me everything has been destroyed? As well as my happiness my pride has gone. I am the laughing-stock of the neighborhood."

"Oh, no!"

"Oh, yes! What is more shaming than for a girl to be deserted just before her wedding? I see the pity in Aunt Marthanna's eyes and in Bridget's, and I want to spit on them. I see the evil, righteous triumph in Charity's eyes, and I want to kill her."

"What do you see in my eyes? Come, look at me! What d'you see?"

"I don't know. Friendliness, I suppose."

"Love, you mean."

"Then don't waste it, Dickon. I shall never let you touch me again. After Lancelot there will be no one."

But her resolve lasted only until her grief and shock had lessened. Lancelot had been her unfulfilled passion. Dickon's love-making was a habit even before Lancelot returned, and so to that habit she went back, for comfort and for the abating of her body's hunger.

Lancelot wrote occasionally to Sylvanus, and Sylvanus passed on the news, brief and scanty though it was. He and Petronella were married, he said, and he was learning the brewery trade from his father-in-law. Conditions in the Midlands and the North were bad. In Manchester people were being convicted and imprisoned for making public the truth of the slaughter at St. Peter's Fields. But no doubt they had all heard of the incident known as Peterloo, where the soldiers were called out and killed eleven people and injured about four hundred. In Birmingham there was great distress, and many small manufacturers had been reduced to beggary. Everyone was crying out for reform, and demanding why we should be so enormously taxed. It appeared, Lancelot said, that for all the complaining of the landworkers people in the country were living in a kind of paradise compared with those in the manufacturing areas. However, he finished, he himself had no fault to find with his circumstances, and he bade his father present his best respects to all at the three houses.

"Best respects!" Sylvanus growled. "Our Lancelot has become quite the gentleman. Why could he not send his love?"

Rosemary listened to Sylvanus's recounting of Lancelot's news, but never asked to read the letters herself. At first she felt that to touch the paper Lancelot's hands had touched would be too painful, would bring him too close to her; and later she refrained for reasons which were almost the exact opposite. Lancelot was too far away, had been for too long the property of another woman. By now he could be contaminated, sullied by her ownership, would no longer be the Lancelot Rosemary had known. Her grief and hurt healed satisfactorily, and the scar opened to discharge its bitterness only occasionally. She had become hard, she knew, less sympathetic and affectionate, and side by side with her rejection of self-pity went the conviction that life had cheated her.

Bridget married her farmer and by now was the mother of two children. Rosemary visited them frequently, and maintained the illusion of sisterly love, but beneath the surface she harbored envy and jealousy. Bridget had married beneath her, Rosemary told herself, and the children were already showing signs of becoming coarse peasants. When they ailed, Rosemary ascribed it to the primitive environment. When they were robust, she shuddered at their rough manners and country speech.

There was no culture around her, Rosemary held, except at Wivelridge, and for some time she lived in hope that her Aunt Marthanna would invite her to live with her, but, friendly though she was, Marthanna reserved her home for herself and Mignon, and Rosemary continued at Hastingford, in the same small room which was to have been her bridal chamber, sharing Dickon with her grandmother and watching Charity's children grow up.

She could not deny that Stand Fast, Meek and Deliverance had received a good education. Peculiar though the Quaker school might be, it was rich in learning. No fault could be found with their behavior. They were quiet, respectful and agreeable. Rosemary thought them colorless, which was almost the only criticism she could make, and even that was not a true evaluation, for their reticence was such that she could not really judge them.

Peregrine enlisted the boys for farm work as soon as they left school, to Charity's annoyance, for she had visualized them as taking up superior professions.

"What else can they do?" Peregrine demanded.

"Many things," she raged. "Have they studied history and languages and theology merely to plough fields and rake dung?"

"They don't complain."

"No. They are good boys, and obedient."

"Dee is bright, and good with his hands, but Stan's forever got his head in the clouds. Wanders round in a dream, he does."

"Peregrine, I have asked you not to shorten their names."

"Then you shouldn't have loaded them with such a melancholy mouthful."

Charity sighed. "They are wasted in this work. Stand Fast should be a preacher."

"Ay, he's always quoting Scripture, if that's what you mean. Fegs! I'm main flummoxed sometimes, having everlasting texts flung at my head. But I'm not complaining. He saves me the wages of a man, and Dee does the same."

To Charity it was as if her soul were being torn in half. She was ambitious for her sons, and yet the economy of having them work for their father could not be overlooked. In these hard times of high taxation the family business, whether it were a farm or a factory, was the one with the greatest measure of security. And not only was it the saving in wages. It was the saving in fodder, the gleaning of the last ear of corn, the squeezing of the last drop of milk. Hired hands had no vested interest in their employer's prosperity, but sons had, and she hoped she had reared hers to lay up treasure on earth as well as in Heaven.

To salve her conscience and unify her desires, she prayed, and in due course believed she had received an answer to her prayers.

"I was wrong," she said to Peregrine.

This rare admission was sufficient to make him prick up his ears. "Oh?"

"Yes. I wanted worldly success for the boys, and to attain this they would have been forced to go away, to a large city, to London, no doubt."

"Well, naturally you can't be learnt to be a fine gentleman at Hastingford."

She ignored this. "In London they would have been subject to many temptations. They are young. They might have fallen."

Peregrine chuckled. "You don't go to London to live like a monk."

"This is no matter for levity, Peregrine. I am horrified when I reflect that I might have been responsible for putting their immortal souls in danger."

"Ah, that would be something to horrify anybody," Peregrine said, keeping his face straight.

"So they shall stay here. It is pleasant to have them at home, is it not, two fine young men?"

"It is," Peregrine agreed, and was amused and somewhat gratified that after all these years he and Charity should discover a point on which they could agree.

Charity said no prayers for Meek. For Meek, being a girl, there was a routine into which she could easily slide, a rut ready for the wheels of her days. Yet Meek, female and compliant, was to precipitate a crisis that, could she have foreseen it, would have kept Charity upon her knees until she had rubbed away the skin.

CHAPTER TWO

It is not good to speake evill of all whom we know
bad; it is worse to judge evill of any who may prove
good. To speake ill, upon knowledge, shews a want of
charity; to speake ill, upon suspicion, shews a want of
honesty.

A. Warwick

Between Charity's three children was, almost from
birth, a close relationship which resembled a secret
society, so binding was it. With only a year between
Stand Fast and Meek, and two years between Meek
and Deliverance, they grew up in a world of their
own, a world of three, complete, requiring no more
contact with others than was necessary. In their feeling for each other was not only love and loyalty,
but also a sense of need which forged the strongest
link. That they were outsiders they knew instinctive-
ly. They were their mother's children, and everyone
else could be classed as "the others," even their father.

"Why are we different?" Meek asked once.

"You are no different," Charity assured her, se-
verely. "We are all sinners, but salvation is possible.
There are only two kinds of people, those who do
God's will, and those who do not."

To Meek this was incomprehensible, but when she
discussed it with Stand Fast he understood perfectly,
for he had listened carefully to the conversation of
the grown-ups and he knew they preferred their own

will to God's. His cousins Rosemary and Bridget were forever considering what they wanted for themselves, and the farm workers and the dairymaids were even worse; their desires were not merely selfish, they were actually inspired by the Devil. When he heard his mother and father quarrelling, he realized it was because his mother was for God and his father was for himself. To all three children their mother was clearly God's lieutenant. She spoke with the voice of God, demanded from them what God demanded, and punished like God. Their respect for her was equal to their respect for God, but neither Charity nor God earned their love. Love was too soft for the God of Charity's religion which, though it had come indirectly from the Quakers, had none of their peacefulness and tolerance. It was a religion of Charity's own brand, tailored by her to fit her nature.

At school the children were happy, but were self-sufficient enough to need no intimate friends. Each day they attended the establishment, learned their lessons, and then returned to their own environment, secure in their threefold unity. But despite their affinity they were as dissimilar as any three human beings. Stand Fast, the eldest, appeared to have partaken of the lion's share of his mother's nature. He was the conformist, the orthodox believer, who sucked up religion with his milk and was en route for Heaven before he was out of his swaddling clothes. Truly Charity had said he was fitted to be a preacher. Scripture lodged in his brain with no trouble at all. He recited psalms as effortlessly as other children recite nursery rhymes, and before he was twelve years old he had become a species of walking Bible.

Deliverance was, by Stand Fast's standards, a poor mundane creature. He loved the concrete parts of the world, though in a harmless, sinless way. Practical handiwork gave him supreme pleasure, and when he was still a boy he was able to do a variety of jobs in carpentry, leatherwork, building, thatching and smithing with a skill that many an older man would have envied. Yet such was his humility that he held himself to be vastly inferior to his brother and tried, though vainly, to emulate Stand Fast in his uncompromising attitude towards everything which was not scripturally permitted.

Meek, being feminine, was all her brothers were not, and though she admired them she did not attempt to imitate them. Of the three she was the only one with whom love was paramount, and she even succeeded in painting with a pale tint of love the picture of God presented to her by her mother. At an early age she was susceptible to cruelty, and was hurt and revolted by the casual and insensitive treatment of animals by many farmers and farmhands. But because she was a practical realist she could not weep over a caged bird, as Rosemary had done. That beasts must be used by men and slaughtered for food, she could accept. What she could not tolerate was that they should suffer sickness and careless handling. She was no more than eight years old when her mother found her in the poultry yard wringing the neck of a newly-hatched chicken.

"What are you doing, you wicked girl? Have you no heart, no conscience? I declare, you are more vicious than a boy. Such things we can expect from men, who are born to destroy. But women are held to be the gentler sex. Really, I am ashamed of you."

Meek looked down at the limp body lying across her hand, so small, too small to suffer. "It was crippled," she said. "It's leg was twisted and it's head all awry."

"That is no excuse. What of the one behind you?"

"It was born blind."

"You little monster! Should I have murdered you, if you had been born blind?"

Meek thought about this. "It would have been best, perhaps."

"Oh, what shall I do with you?" Charity demanded, exasperated. "You are incorrigible. Well, you shall have no dinner today. And, remember, God sees all. He will punish you."

Twice punished, Meek thought, a little resentfully,

once by her mother and once by God. She did not see why her mother should call in God as a collaborator; her punishments were adequate, heaven knew.

But whatever the opinion of her elders, Meek's conscience was clear. To care for the animals was as natural to her as breathing. If she could help them, help them she would. If not, she was ruthless in securing for them oblivion from pain. For the most part her efforts went unnoticed, but as she grew up and became more ambitious, it was inevitable that sooner or later she would be discovered.

At her school there was an excellent library, and from this she picked several veterinary books and studied them. Cows and sheep and horses were subject to a number of diseases, and whereas in the past she had watched helplessly, now she was determined to make an attempt to cure them. It was not easy to find the courage to declare her intention. The men would laugh, and her father would scoff, even if he were not downright angry. In secret she could practice on the poultry, but the larger and more valuable animals were carefully watched, and would not fail to be treated after a fashion.

Her opportunity occurred when one of the laborers thoughtlessly turned the cows into a meadow of rich green clover. Before Peregrine discovered the mistake the cattle had eaten greedily and were suffering from the disease known as hoven or hoving. Their stomachs became terribly distended and filled with wind, and as the effects were often fatal, Peregrine was like to lose a great deal of money.

Cursing and calling for everyone to help, he caused the animals to be driven violently about and dosed with salt and water. This relieved some, but there were others whose condition seemed obstinate, and one of these he stabbed with a penknife. A great deal of wind came out, but Peregrine was not pleased.

"Reckon I went too far and pierced the guts," he grumbled. "The beast'll get inflammation and die. Well, the way it was it maybe wouldn't have lived anyhow."

Meek flew to find Deliverance. "Could you make something for me, very quickly?"

"Something like what?"

"Like a snake six feet long, of wire twisted round a tube, and then the tube taken out and the wire covered with leather."

"Steady!" he begged. "Stop stitch while I put a needle in! You go too fast. How soon do you need this device?"

"At once. Please, Deliverance! If you cannot make it, half the cattle are like to die."

He managed, even finding a piece of brass piping to connect to the tube, and Meek ran with it to her father.

Peregrine stared. "What is this?"

"It's to save the cows. You put it down the throat to the stomach and it releases the wind."

"Butter my wig if I will!" Peregrine exclaimed, angrily. "You had no-ought to interfere, a wean of a girl like you."

"Please, father!" She was almost in tears. "Try it at least! It can do no harm. It is the remedy of Doctor Monro, who is a professor of anatomy in Edinburgh."

Dazed and incredulous, he consented to make the experiment, and discovered that it worked. "Mazed I am," he admitted, "and I tell you to your head I was unaccountable disbelieving. But work it did."

He looked at his daughter as though suddenly she had begun to exist, as for him she had, and there blossomed swiftly between them a certain fondness. Not entirely could Peregrine approve of Meek's outlook on life. She had been reared too thoroughly in Charity's tradition, and was liable to spout texts as more frivolous young women would spout acrostics and conundrums. Also he considered her devotion to her brothers unhealthy and maudlin. But her knowledge of and skill with animals he whole-heartedly admired, and it became his habit to have her accompany him when he inspected his stock. She missed nothing, he found. The smallest evidence of neglect or unhygienic practices could not be hidden from her, and she had an eye for pending disease before ever it manifested itself to him. She became the terror of the hired men, and was not popular with them despite her gentle ways and charming appearance. Peregrine did not cease to wonder at her efficiency. She was so tiny, scarcely more than a child in figure, with close curls about her head, and delicate hands and feet. It was a sight worth watching, he thought, to see her standing upon a stool, the better to reach her patient, casually opening the mouth of a bull, to thrust a bolus down his throat as far as her arm would reach.

Under her ministrations the cattle flourished, and, as was the habit in country places, there was a deal of comment on the matter.

"That lass o' Farmer Dyke's is acting all unwomanly," declared neighbors and villagers. " 'Tis not nice for a girl to be pushing her hand up the arse of an ox. The strange thing is that Farmer allows it. She must've bewitched him."

"Ay," agreed those who listened, "and bewitched the cattle too she has, for they are as plump and sleek as if old Moses had brung them manna from the wilderness."

They used the word lightly at first, but gradually it became imbued with its true meaning. "Bewitched," they said and looked thoughtful, gazing at their own skinny cows.

In the taverns the men began to talk. It was easier there, over their pots of ale, with no wives to embarrass them in case the conversation should become somewhat coarse.

"Good doers they are, every one of them. I passed by Hastingford only yesterday—by chance, mind you, purely by chance."

The others nodded, grinning behind their pipes.

"A sweeter herd of beasts you never did see. The bags of even the heifers was sweeping the daisies, and the bull with 'em, why, his pizzle went right out of sight, maybe down a rabbit-hole."

They laughed heartily, but there was a kind of sullenness behind their mirth. They had known Peregrine

Dyke for more years than they could count, and they didn't reckon he had shown any especial talent as a farmer. What had happened, then? How had conditions changed?

A small shrivelled farmer took his pipe out of his mouth. "My lot's ailing. Manna, you say? I could be giving 'em manna, the price they cost me in fodder. But it makes no difference. In one end and out the other, with nothing sticking between the ribs. Still, that's the way it goes."

"What d'you mean?" they asked him. "That's the way it goes? What's the way?"

"Why, the fatter his get, the leaner'll get ours."

"How does that come about?"

"You never heard?" He sounded scornful. "When there's work like that going on, somebody's got to pay. Bewitched." He repeated the word, accenting the second syllable. "Be*witch*ed."

The rest stirred uneasily, not knowing how to take such talk. It was not the jolly, harmless ribaldry they usually indulged in at an inn, yet there was something novel and exciting about it.

One man sniggered. "This is eighteen-twenty-two, not sixteen-twenty-two. We're above such superstition."

"Above superstition, maybe, but will your cows be above ground much longer? Think on it!"

They thought, and presently it didn't seem so foolish, what they were thinking. It even became possible to speak of it.

"My grandmother remembered a cobbler at Bristol who died of a cat-bite on the finger. He called a woman a witch and she sent the cat, or perhaps she came herself."

"I heard tell of an old woman in Buckinghamshire, no more'n fifty years ago who was accused of bewitching her neighbor's spinning-wheel. She was weighed against the Bible, but she outweighed it, so she was let off."

"Fifty years! You've no call to go back that far. My sister married a Huntingdon man and lives in Great Paxton. Fourteen years ago there was a great to-do about a woman said to have bewitched three young girls. Mother of eight she was, but that made no difference. Two nights following, the villagers dragged her out and beat her and tore her arms with pins. They'd have ducked her next evening, but she took refuge with the parson, the Reverend Nicholson. He was mightily blamed for harboring her."

"In Scotland," said a man, staring at his beer, "they used to throw dry malt and a handful of salt on top of the mash, to keep the witches from it."

They all laughed then. "Now we can tell the landlord what's wrong with his ale."

But the wizened little farmer did not wish the conversation to tail off. "You've no need," he said, "to be shamed of believing in the black art."

These scraps of information were reported in several homes that night, for it increased a man's stature when he could say to his wife that drinking did not lead to a gloating on lechery, as she imagined, but was often accompanied by serious discourse. What, after all, was more serious than witchcraft, even though it was considered somewhat old-fashioned? Country people were not concerned overmuch with the mode. They knew townsfolk were forever running round after newfangled ideas, and frequently awoke to discover they were chasing their own tails. They also knew that many of the ideas of their ancestors were as true and as efficacious as ever they had been, the earth itself being old and obstructive to fashion. What, therefore, was so absurd about the practice of witchcraft?

The wives made little comment, but they talked among themselves in low voices, and gradually they began to put two and two together. On some of their farms had broken out the contagious distemper among the cattle, but the Dyke herd flourished as though it enjoyed the especial protection of the saints.

"Or of somebody else," muttered the women, darkly.

But it was not only among the livestock that happenings were strange. Sarah Barley and Kitty Riddling, strong young women, both miscarried within a week.

Susannah Prescot, who had since childhood been afflicted in her mind, became subject to fits of violent energy, when she sang and danced for hours at a time, as if to the music of a whole orchestra of fiddles, until she dropped exhausted.

But even more impressive was the evidence of Powell Snell, the village shoemaker, who declared there were times recently when he could not make his wax, for the ingredients would neither melt nor mix. When pressed as to the exact moment of these times, he confessed, reluctantly, that they came about when Charity Dyke's young daughter passed the door.

The villagers clicked their tongues and said he must be mistaken. The Dykes were prosperous and respected farmers. Yet they recollected that the girl had for the past few months been seen constantly among her father's cattle, which was not where a half-grown woman would be expected to be.

Some of them consulted their grandparents, who might remember the old charms, and began to carry a hare's foot in their pockets, or sent a child to the coast in the carrier's cart to search the beach for stones with holes in them that might be tied to the keys of house or barn.

"We must keep her out," they said, "whoever she is. Times are bad enough without having a mischief-worker amongst us."

There was no doubt times were bad. They had been bad for many a year. In fact, you could question any farm laborer, even the oldest, and he would not be able to tell you when times had not been bad. War or peace seemed to make little difference. The only variety was when occasionally the discontent, working like yeast within the community, bubbled up and spilled over.

Naturally the Corn Bills had been discussed endlessly, until even the most fluent tavern orator could find nothing new to say about them, but Mr. Cobbett's visit to Sussex in January had given a fillip to agricultural politics, and feelings sunk in apathy ran high once more. Though few of them had set eyes on Wil-

liam Cobbett, all were able to quote him from hear-
say.

"He says no Corn Bill can do good to anybody."

"Yes, and he says prices will go lower and stay
lower."

"He says the English plowman is a pauper."

"Well, so he is. So are we all."

Nick Freston, the farmer who had first broached
the subject of witchery, stood up. He was a man of
some small education, able to read and understand
what he read, yet singularly unsuccessful in whatever
work he undertook, and for that reason he harbored
a grievance against all who were more prosperous
than himself.

"The plowman a pauper? Yes, indeed! And I
can tell you Mr. Cobbett's exact words. He said, 'Shall
he never see an end to this state of things? Shall he
never have the due reward of his labor? Shall unspar-
ing taxation never cease to make him a miserable de-
jected being, a creature famishing in the midst of abun-
dance?'"

The men gave a faint cheer. "He's right."

"Ah, he's a good man, but he don't tell us what
to do about it."

They looked questioningly at Nick, who was still
standing, his face flushed, a sense of power infusing his
spare carcase. "No, he won't tell you that. He is hoping
to become a member of Parliament and get laws
passed."

"Laws? What good will laws do us?"

"By the time they're passed, us'll be in our graves.
Maybe our grandchildren'll benefit, or maybe not."

"Ah, you're too humble," Nick said. "It's useless
talking to you."

"No, it ain't. Tell us! Tell us what to do!"

Nick had no idea what to say to them. What
redress was there for their ills? What redress for his?
None, as far as he knew. They were unfortunate men,
as he was, born beneath an evil star. Long ago he had
given up the fight for success, had become resigned to
being an undernourished creature whose revenge on

society could consist only of bitter thoughts and viru-
lent speeches made in the silence of his own mind.
Yet he was unwilling to relinquish this little authority his words had given him. These men, his cronies,
were looking up to him, waiting, some with their mouths
open, for wisdom to drop from his lips. What he decided, they would do. It was an exhilarating moment,
and if he failed to take advantage of it, it would be of
a pattern with the rest of his life. He must tell them
something, no matter what.

"Take an example," he said. "There's Peregrine
Dyke. Nothing wrong with *his* cattle. *He's* no pauper.
Of course we like Peregrine. He's our friend. But
why should he do so well, when we do so ill?"

"He's no friend of mine," growled one of the men.
"Turned me away last week he did, and Isaac the
same, though we've been with him these five years.
Doesn't need so many hands, he says, 'cos his two
boys is old enough to work."

"And his daughter too," Nick reminded them. "If
you can call it work."

This brought a laugh, which was what Nick wanted.
Men who laughed could be swayed, could be enticed
to action, because when heads rang with laughter there
was no room for fear or caution.

"Peregrine Dyke should be made to see his danger,"
he said.

"Where's *his* danger?" someone asked.

"Ah! That's a good question. His danger is that he
himself is bewitched, and so he can't see the peril of
being different from his neighbors. It's not good to
have fat cattle while others are lean. It's not good to
have a full belly while others are empty. We, now,
we're peace-loving people, but there's some places
where they'd be after Peregrine's blood. Look what
happened three years agone, in Manchester. Peterloo, they called it, after Waterloo, for a battle it was.
Look what happened seven years ago, in the year of
peace! Rioting about the Corn Bill, uprising of the
sailors in the northern ports, disturbances and fight-

ing by the miners in the Midland counties. I tell you, we don't know the terrible things that happen in other parts. But here we're good Christians."

He paused, and his companions were silent, feeling deflated and somehow disappointed. That talk about riots gave a man strength, for it showed him that he was not the only one to suffer, that somewhere were others in the same position, others, moreover, who had actually taken steps to remedy their ills. Yes, it put heart in a man to think of it, but then Nick had spoilt the picture by reminding them they were peaceful and Christian. Secretly they were not sure that they were, but who would care to confess to such a thing?

"So there's nothing we can do," one muttered, at last.

"I didn't say that. Nothing violent should we do, but it's our duty to help our neighbors, and Peregrine must be saved."

"How?"

Nick thought quickly. He saw himself marching at the head of an army of men. It was no new vision. Throughout the long war with France he had identified himself with Napoleon Bonaparte. Nick was a small man, but so was Napoleon, and that he somehow took for a sign, though he had not been able to see how he might transform his dream into reality. Now, however—

"We must go to Peregrine," he said, "in a nice and tidy manner, and demand that the witch ceases her spells. His daughter must be restrained, and then our fortunes will change. Remember, there is only a certain amount of good luck in the air, and a certain amount of bad. If his beasts are not so fat, ours will be fatter."

"Maybe he'll take me and Isaac back," said Peregrine's former employee, hopefully.

Nick could not follow this line of reasoning, but the enthusiasm of his friends was his chief concern, and anything which would foster this was valuable.

For another week they talked, and then Nick, fear-

ing the bad humors would expend themselves in mere
talk, a kind of diarrhea of words, decided to goad them
into action.

"She's reaching out now," he told them, "reaching
out to do us active harm. It's no longer enough for
her to benefit her own. She wants to destroy us. That's
ever the way with witches. Wait too long and you'll all
be ruined. Take heed of what's come to me."

He had their full attention. Eyes were on him,
ears pricked. Even mugs stayed, untasted, on the board
or in mid-air. "She put the evil eye on one of my bul-
locks. Dropped down dead it did. Like a stone."

Actually the animal had died of a fever, but he saw
no harm in the addition of a pinch of the salt of
drama. In no way, he considered, was he tampering
with the truth. Without doubt someone had sent the
fever.

So one evening as the sun was beginning to set, a
column of men marched solemnly up the lane to
Hastingford. They were not the army of Nick's dreams,
but they were the nearest he would ever come to it—
thirty-seven farm laborers and small-holders. They
were armed with bill-hooks and beetles and doleaxes
and hay-knives. Not, Nick impressed on them, that
they would think of using weapons. They had no quarrel
with Peregrine Dyke. It was simply that men marched
better with something in their hands, and courage
came with the solid grasp of a handle in the fist. Nick
himself supported a pitchfork, whose length and
threatening spikes seemed to ratify his position of
leader.

They found Peregrine in the yard adjoining the cow-
houses. Meek was with him, which was nothing strange
at that time, but to the inflamed imaginations of the
men it was evidence of her guilt.

"Why, Nick!" Peregrine exclaimed. "What's to do?
And the rest of you! Is it a celebration? Have I forgotten one of our holy-days?"

For a moment Nick's boldness deserted him; for a
brief instant he saw his pretense for what it was, and

then the man behind him nudged him in the back and he knew he must sustain the part he had created for himself.

"We've come to talk to you."

"Talk away, then, for I'm nigh famished for my supper, and I reckon you're the same."

"You're lucky, Peregrine Dyke," Nick said, soberly. "There's supper for you, but for some of us there'll be little or none."

"Oh? And why is that?"

"Times are bad."

"Oh, is that all? Well, times are bad for most of us."

"Not for you."

"I'm not starving, if that's what you mean, but I'm no lordling, neither. Have you ever seen me flaunting a purse of gold?"

"Your beasts are fat."

Peregrine grinned. "Why not? They've a good doctor." And he jerked his head towards Meek, who stood just behind him.

"That is exactly what we mean," Nick said, grimly.

"Ah! You want her to treat your beasts. Well, she's little time to spare."

"No, we want her to cease treating *your* beasts. We want to put an end to her tricks."

Peregrine looked bewildered. "Tricks? What idiot talk is this?"

"No idiot talk. We accuse your daughter of being a witch."

Peregrine laughed, and his laughter was like tinder to their spark. "A witch? What jest is this? My dear friends, if I did not know the date I would mark this as All Fools Day."

"You yourself are misled," Nick said, earnestly. "Sometimes fathers dote, but where witchcraft is concerned they can be hoodwinked."

"Oh, go home!" Peregrine urged. "I am weary of this foolishness."

"Not without the girl," shouted a voice from the back.

"Not without—What are you saying?"

"We must take her." "Yes, hand her over." "Do not imagine you can protect her."

The voices came thick and fast. They were gaining in confidence. One, more strident than the others, shouted, "You know what we want—the good old-fashioned ordeal of sink or swim."

"Now, listen!" Peregrine was angry at last. "If it pleases your mood you may make a mock of me, but leave my daughter alone. She is a good girl and I will not have her pestered. Meek, go to your mother!"

"No!" Two of the men ran round behind her.

Peregrine's fists clenched and his face flushed. This was an insult; it was insupportable. What had happened to these ordinary people, these villagers? What devil had got into them? Most of them he had known since they were children together. Separately he could have talked to them, made them see reason, but all together, in a crowd, they had changed. Their faces had become the faces of strangers, and were reddened by the ruddy light of the setting sun, so that they were like the masks of devils from hell.

"Let us have no more of this nonsense!" he roared.

"The girl!" the anonymous voices insisted. "We must have the girl."

Peregrine turned to her, and as he did so the two men caught her arms and hustled her forward. Peregrine lunged towards them, and his movement released the pent-up violence. The man at the back wanted to be at the front. They wanted their part in the taking of the witch. She was so young, so small and delicate. Compared with her their wives were milk-cows and draught-mares, and they hated her for it. No honest farm-woman had the right to sway and tremble like meadowsweet upon the stalk. She was a witch.

They pushed and pressed, close upon each other, sweating and grunting. Nick felt himself stumbling, losing his balance. In front of him was Peregrine, big and threatening. He could have flung his arms about Peregrine, laughing, retracting, making light of the incident. But in his hand was the pitchfork, his protection. He raised it, and as he was pushed forward, it went with him. He thrust, and suddenly Peregrine was not in his way.

He stopped, and the other men did the same. Those holding Meek dropped their hands. A silence fell on them. The sun went out.

Peregrine lay on the ground. The pitchfork seemed to be growing from his heart, and from its roots washed a tide of blood, drowning and concealing the murderous spikes.

CHAPTER THREE

O, may we all for death prepare!
What has he left? And who's his heir?
Jonathan Swift

If in life Peregrine had been somewhat lacking in
color, in death he flared up to an iridescent glow, and
the manner of his death lent him heroic stature. He
was a martyr, it appeared, a saintly example of those
British yeoman farmers who had fought for their
freedom and held it against the Romans, the feudal
barons and the conquering Normans. They could not
be intimidated by a dictatorial monarchy, a suppres-
sive hierarchy, or a disorderly rabble. Peregrine had
stood his ground and had been mown down. It was
courageous, tragic, and an apt comment on the unruly
times in which he lived.

When the coroner had been informed of the happening, a jury was summoned and the coroner and
the jurors, all more than twelve years of age, went to
Hastingford to view the body.

The inquest presented no especial difficulties, for
Nick Freston made no attempt to deny his culpa-
bility, though he declared earnestly that the sad affair was an accident. He had borne no malice against
Peregrine Dyke; had, indeed, liked him as a man and
admired him as a farmer. His concern, and the concern of those who went with him, was for the farmer's
daughter, who had been behaving in a way prejudicial
to the welfare of her neighbors. A strange feature of

the inquest was the behavior of the witnesses. Those who had marched with Nick had little good to say of him, and swore solemnly that their motive in going along with him had been to ensure that no violence was done: whereas Peregrine's relations were confident there had been no quarrel between him and Nick Freston and were prepared to accept that Nick's attack was launched on impulse and was not the result of premeditation.

The verdict was manslaughter. Nick was sent for trial and was sentenced to transportion for seven years.

Naturally the inquest aroused a fever of interest and excitement in the district. Nothing had equalled the sensation since Napoleon's threatened invasion, and the local inns did a roaring trade, for where else could one hear the latest news and exchange theories and hazard speculation? But the funeral which followed the inquest was an even greater occasion. If Peregrine had been royalty, they said, he could have had scarcely more mourners, and those certainly would not have been so sincere. Farms were deserted that day, livestock left to fend for themselves, and milk cows were forced to endure their swelling udders for an extra hour or two. The coffin was placed on a newly-painted wagon strewn with flowers and rosemary and other sweet herbs, and drawn by a team of oxen groomed down to the polish on their hooves and up to the flowing black crape on their horns.

Slowly they went, a long procession which grew longer as at every lane and side-turning it was joined by fresh mourners, and at last they came to Mayfield, where Peregrine was laid beside his father, with, beyond, his first wife and his little brother Hal. The company then repaired to the Royal Oak where the men ate heartily and drank copiously, while the women discreetly hid their grief in a separate room.

And there was grief in plenty. Caroline appeared far more stricken than she had been at Will's death, and was at pains to explain the reason to anyone who was prepared to listen.

"Poor Will was dead in everything but the fact for

many years. I had grown accustomed to his absence. One must, must one not? Sudden death, however, that is wellnigh insupportable. It is a thunderbolt. No wonder we pray in the Litany to be delivered from sudden death."

"That is for the sake of our souls," Charity told her, severely, "not to soften the blow for our relatives."

"I don't care what the reason is. Sudden death is a terrible thing. I still cannot believe it. It is a nightmare. It has not happened. Peregrine! My first-born! Oh, my little boy! To be cut down so young!"

"He was sixty-one," Charity said, automatically and wearily.

"That is still young." Caroline took out her third handkerchief. The other two were soaked and she could not remember whether she had brought a fourth. It was the proper procedure, she knew, to cry at a funeral, but that was not why she was doing it. The tears flowed, and continued to flow, and she could not stop them. They gushed like a spring stream through cresses and grasses. It was as if she were crying for all the world, for all the heartache ever endured by women, for the loss of lovers and for the small white bodies of dead children and for fruit turned moldy in the womb.

"Lancelot should have come," she wept. "I need Lancelot."

"It is a long way from the Midlands," Marthanna consoled her, "and Lancelot is a man of business now. He did not have time to arrange his affairs. But are you not pleased that Rebecca has come?"

"How could I be pleased about anything this day? If I were pleased I would be a heartless wretch. Besides, Rebecca is a woman. You know my sons were the light of my life."

"Well, you have two of your grandsons with you."

"I do not look upon Stand Fast and Deliverance as my grandsons."

"Mother!" Marthanna was genuinely shocked. "How

can you speak like that! They are Peregrine's very flesh."

"And Charity's. Have you noticed how dry her eyes are? I do not think one tear has oozed out. That woman feels nothing."

"Now you are being unfair. Grief is not measured by tears. When Gerrance died I did not weep. There was nothing left to weep about. Besides, Charity has her religion. Complete obedience to God is a powerful staff."

"Rebecca should have brought the little boys with her."

"They are grown men now. You forget how time passes."

"I forget nothing," Caroline insisted. "All day I have felt the birth-pangs Peregrine caused me. I thought he would tear me in half."

"Now it is over."

Caroline shook her head. "It is not over. Nothing is ever over."

Sitting in that room, with the soft murmur of women's voices about her, it seemed to her that Peregrine's life had somehow telescoped, so that there was practically no space between his birth and his death. It was as easy to picture him as a baby as it was to picture him as a man. Indeed, she saw his youth more clearly. Death had wiped out his middle age. He no longer stooped; he no longer frowned. Caroline wanted him back, but now nothing would have contented her but the beauty of his early years.

Meek was not at the funeral. She lay in bed, too weak and feverish to rise. It was the shock, they said, of seeing her father killed before her very eyes, but to her this was not all. She suffered also from a biting guilt which gave her no peace. If it were not for her, she reasoned, her father would still be alive. He had given his life for her, and this was something she neither wanted nor deserved. She should have foreseen what was about to happen, and flung herself forward. Or when the men held her arms she should have cried out, "I will come with you," and then they would have let her father alone. She had been slow and stupid, she was convinced, and the knowledge was agony. She could not eat or sleep, but must lie there, re-living those few moments, changing them in her imagination and praying vainly, "Let me go back! Let it not have happened!" That so brief a period should have results immovably fixed in the very façade of eternity seemed unendurable to her. That she had been accused of possessing supernatural powers did not trouble her at all. People who believed in witches were stupid, and stupidity was of no account. The powers she used were of science, and she intended to go on using them. But, oh, if only she had been quicker to defend herself, and, through herself, her father! They were friends, she and this man she had scarcely known, newly-found friends, and now she had lost him.

At first she had feared her mother's anger, feared her mother would hold her responsible for her father's death, but Charity, unpredictably, had made no comment on this aspect of the tragedy, had apparently not even considered it. Her anger was reserved for the brutal villagers and, in some strange way, for Peregrine himself. Everything happened according to God's will, and if Peregrine had been subservient to God's will he would have been saved. God was a god of punishment, as well as of reward, and Charity knew —who better?—that for years Peregrine had been tempting Providence. Was it right to deny a wife the seed of his body and then scatter it on harlots? It was true Charity knew of only one illegitimate son he had begotten, but one known, she thought, darkly, could mean a dozen of which she was ignorant. The crowds could mourn him, and that was right and fitting, but she and God knew he had met his just deserts. "God will not be mocked," she said to herself, and went dry-eyed to her husband's funeral, which was not all that difficult, for God was a massive ally.

The women walked or were driven home while the men still celebrated Peregrine's release from this vale of tears. Those women who were near to him were exhausted by the ordeal of the funeral, and those who were not near found the outing tedious when the drama had degenerated into a mere gossip. They remembered the tasks which had been piling up during the day, and they excused themselves, uttering that most platitudinous of platitudes—"Life must go on."

The Dykes did not doubt that life must go on. They expected it to go on, and in the same unchanging way, and were therefore surprised to the point of being astounded when a lawyer rode over from Lewes. He was the same lawyer Peregrine had retained when he proposed selling the farm, and now he announced that he carried with him Peregrine's Will, and desired to read it in the presence of the family.

"A will," Charity exclaimed. "He never spoke of making a will."

"That is nothing uncommon," said the lawyer. "A man's bequests are between him and his Maker, and oft-times he is shy of speaking of the matter."

"And you wish to read it now?"

"If it pleases you."

Charity was thrown into a flutter. "The men are in the fields and the women in the dairy or Heaven knows where."

"If you could send for them—"

"I suppose I must. Ah! Rosemary! There you are! Go at once and find the boys and your Uncle Sylvanus. Tell them to send a message to Wivelridge and another to Sweetwillow Shaw. We require the presence of the family immediately. Your Uncle Peregrine has left a will." This last sentence she pronounced in tones of deep gloom, as though Peregrine had committed a rather nasty crime.

She then turned to the lawyer. "All this must take some time. Perhaps while you wait you will do us the honor of eating with us."

The lawyer beamed. "There is nothing I would prefer to do. Country fare is a fine treat, and I don't doubt you will provide a repast fit for a king, or, if not a king, a king's counsellor, who, from my humble standing in the law, wears almost the look of royalty."

This deepened Charity's gloom, and she led the way into the kitchen, reflecting that those who expected farm hospitality must conform to farm custom.

Two hours passed before the family was assembled, and by that time the lawyer's expression was slightly less benign. The meal had by no means been the feast he had anticipated. Indeed, it had been plain to the point of stinginess. Salt pork and coarse bread, followed by skimmed milk cheese were not comforting to the stomach, especially when accompanied by a herb drink which had not known the beneficent touch of yeast. He found himself hoping, somewhat uncharitably, that there would be certain disappointed faces when the will was read.

The family sat round the long table in the hall, with the lawyer at the head, and when he took out his papers and cleared his throat there was an awed silence, for this was an occasion never before experienced by Peregrine's relatives.

" 'In the name of God, Amen. I, Peregrine Dyke of Hastingford in the county of Sussex, being in good health of body and of sound and disposing mind, memory and understanding (thanks be given to Almighty God for the same). But considering the uncertainty of this mortal life, and being desirous to settle my Worldly Estate so as to avoid all unhappy disputes and differences that might otherwise arise about the same after my Decease do hereby make and ordain this to be my last Will and Testament in manner and form following.' "

As they listened they told themselves that it was Peregrine speaking. This solemn document was Peregrine's message from beyond the grave. This was his voice. But somehow they could not believe it, for never had he expressed himself in such a way.

" 'First and Principally I desire Almighty God my Heavenly Father to receive my Soul through the Merits of Jesus Christ my Savior and Redeemer and my Body I resign to the Earth to be therein decently Interred.' "

"That must have been the only time he gave a

thought to them," Charity reflected, cynically. "A pity he did not consider his soul when he went a-whoring."

The attention of the family eased and relaxed. After all, this was not Peregrine. It was legal talk.

" 'As for the Worldly Estate which it has pleased Almighty God to bless me with and bestow upon me I give and bestow thereof as followeth.' "

Ah! Backs straightened, drooping eyelids flew open. This was the meat hidden in the pie-crust.

" 'Imprimus I give and bestow to my natural son William, the child of Mary Atkinson, all those monies which are deposited with the Old Bank at Lewes, amounting to the sum of Four Thousand Six Hundred and Eighty-seven Pounds, Eleven Shillings and Five-pence, on the condition that hereafter he takes and is known by the name of William Dyke.' "

Charity sprang to her feet. "I will not have it! He was mad. He was seduced by the Devil. What of my children? What of his legitimate offspring?"

"Mistress, be seated! You are interrupting," the law-yer told her, severely.

" 'That part of my Estate which comprises farm lands, Buildings and Houses I dispose of in the fol-lowing manner that justice may be done and that there be no bad blood between any who are kin to me. Item, to my mother I give and bestow the house known as Sweetwillow Shaw and the thirty acres I allocated for her use. This to be her Freehold unconditionally, that she may will it where she pleaseth. Item, I give and bestow unto my brother Sylvanus and unto my sons Stand Fast and Deliverance each seventy acres or there-abouts, being equal portions of the remaining land. The Farm Buildings they may divide among themselves as is most convenient. Item, I give and bestow unto my wife Charity the residue of my Estate comprising the house known as Hastingford and all that therein is. In return I do enjoin that she shall at all times and in all circumstances give and provide hospitality to any Kinsfolk of mine, however distant, that might be in need of it.' "

The remaining and closing sentences of the Will

were not listened to or heard, but as this was a frequent occurrence the lawyer was not unduly put out. Resignedly he went on reading, right to the last word, and then took himself off. His departure troubled none, and some did not even notice he had gone.

"This is intolerable," Charity declared. "He has insulted me, his wife who has borne him three children and worked like a slave for more than twenty years. What does he consider me, a servant who shall tend any itinerant and vagrant Dyke who cares to place his dusty feet under my board? Has he no more respect for me?"

"I doubt if his present thoughts are of you in any way," Caroline said, drily. "He will be reunited with his father and dear Hal and Gerrance and Richard and the poor darling children who perished in the fire. Should he have attention to spare, he will no doubt be making the acquaintance of the angels. I understand that no particular sex is attributed to the angels, but to me there is something feminine about them. What man would give adequate care to those beautiful white wings?"

"Pagan!" Charity hissed. "That is what you are, mother-in-law, a pagan! Peregrine has humiliated me, to punish me for his own infamy. What can I do with Hastingford? What use is a house? Can I eat the floors, make a meal from the roof-tiles?"

"You are forgetting your sons," Sylvanus reminded her, "and forgetting me. Shall we not live here as before? Would your sons see you want? Will you not have all you require of our produce?"

"When Will died, I had nothing," Caroline put in. "I depended upon the charity of my sons. Had I had my wits about me, or had Will been a man of the world, he would not have died intestate, and I would not have lost the farm on which I spent all the money I possessed. But now Peregrine has righted the wrong, and I am grateful to him. My homestead, my small-holding, are my own, and I shall be able therefore to provide for dear Dickon."

"He has rescued me," Sylvanus said. "I am no

longer a pauper. I have land to farm, and never need I catch another fish."

"All this talk about land!" Charity raged. "You have forgotten the main item. The money from Wivelridge. What has he done with that? Left it to his bastard!"

"Do not fret!" Sylvanus attempted to soothe her. "You have one consolation. William Dyke can never inherit Hastingford. I think Peregrine has acted with fairness and shown good sense."

"I do not agree," Marthanna said.

It was the first time she had spoken since the lawyer departed, and they all turned to stare at her.

"You? How can it affect you?"

"It does not affect me, but I consider Peregrine has done the farm a disservice."

"How can that be?" Caroline demanded.

"Oh, mother, how can you ask? Are you grown so old that you have forgotten the part you played? After you bought Hastingford you purchased the other two farms, and so formed an estate which was not large, but neither was it mean. Two hundred and fifty acres of respectable farmland, that is a property in which a family can take pride. We Dykes had become yeoman farmers. We could hold up our heads. But what is it now? It is split asunder. Each of you is a man of small property, of small account."

Sylvanus leaned across the table and took her hand. "Do not fret, sister!"

"I could weep. I could weep more bitter tears for Hastingford than for Peregrine."

"It is not broken up. As a family we still own it entire."

"Think you it will remain that way?" she asked, scornfully. "So many owners, so many schemes. So many farmers, so many methods. What will it be in a hundred years? Thank God I shall not be here to know!"

"You started it," Charity told her, crossly. "You bought Wivelridge."

"A house and an acre. That is a matter of no importance. Farms are not houses and cottages. They are land and the pattern formed from the land. A field is not an isolated body, despite its hedges. It depends upon its neighbors, upon the slope of the land, the drainage of water, the woods which may keep from it the sun or the rain or the blast of the wind."

Charity sniffed. "You talk like a farmer. Did they teach you those things in France?"

"No, sister-in-law, I learnt them of necessity, before you were born."

"Well!" Sylvanus sighed, but it was a sigh of satisfaction, not regret. "I do not know whether it shows sufficient respect to my brother, but I for one would like to walk around the land, with a view to apportioning it. And the same with the buildings and the live and dead stock. The sooner I know what is mine, the sooner I can get to work."

"Do not hurry!" Marthanna urged. "What is gained by such haste? You might decide to continue to work the farm as before, all together."

"No!" To her surprise the refusal came immediately and from all three of the heirs.

"Why not? What have you to gain from this violent surgery? Are you so avaricious for ownership that you fear brother or uncle or nephew might squeeze a drop of milk from a cow which could be yours?"

"It is my father's wish." Stand Fast spoke reproachfully. "Would you have us go against that?"

"Have a care!" Caroline warned. "I reckon you should engage a surveyor or a valuer, or even a magistrate, to see that shares are fair."

Stand Fast turned on her angrily. "Grandmother, you make a wicked insinuation. Do you imagine my brother or I would cheat? That we would take more than we are entitled to? Remember, 'Wherein thou judgest another, thou condemnest thyself.' We are the servants of the Lord, and we are not greedy of filthy lucre. An honest, God-fearing man needs no lawyer to persuade him to act honorably."

"All right, lad, all right! But I recollect well how

your father and uncle fought over their playthings. Men are made to fight."

"Not Christian men."

"Then I have known few Christian men, for when there is a bargain to be struck they take on the qualities of the brutes—the cunning of the fox, the rapacity of the wolf and the stink of the skunk. Come, Dickon, see me home, for so much high-mindedness wearies me."

The company broke up, Caroline, Dickon and Marthanna to drive away, Charity to return to her household tasks, and Sylvanus, Stand Fast and Deliverance to wander off together, drawn irresistibly to measure and weigh up the merits and demerits of various fields, to assess the value of the cattle and the convenience of various buildings. They did not speak much, for they were seeing the farm with new eyes, as though it were a strange and unknown place.

Rosemary went to her room and sat alone. Privately she still called it the bridal chamber, not sentimentally but with a bitter, twisted irony. No one had mentioned her, or recognized that Peregrine's Will had left her no better off. True, Meek had not been mentioned either, but Meek was a part of the family, secure with her brothers. Bridget and Lancelot had not been left anything, but they were both married. Only herself, Rosemary reflected, was actually worse off than before. Now the house belonged indisputably to Charity. She could take everything away, even this—this bridal chamber!

Rosemary stared in the mirror set on a dim wall. Thirty years old, she was, landless and loveless. Loveless except for Dickon. To hell with Dickon! She raised her fists, and but for a lingering superstition would have smashed the surface of the cruel, revealing glass.

CHAPTER FOUR

What is this world with London in its lap?
   Mogg's map.
The Thames that ebbs and flows in its broad channel?
   A tidy kennel!
The bridges stretching from its banks?
   Stone planks.
Oh, me! Hence could I read an admonition
   To mad Ambition!

Thomas Hood

It had been expected that Mignon would return from her French school for the Christmas of eighteen-twenty-four, but she did not arrive until the second week in January, being reluctant to leave Paris before the celebrations of the "jour de l'an." On that day she not only gave and received presents, but visited the exhibition of Sèvres China and also the Rue de Lombards where the wholesale confectioners had made their special sweetmeats for New Year's Day. These were contrived with an ingenuity not to be found elsewhere. There were sugar containers in almost every conceivable form—saucepans, hats, musical instruments, books, boots and shoes, lobsters, bunches of carrots, and scores of other conceits, all stuffed with bon-bons. A number of these she purchased for her English relatives, and having spent a few days packing them and her extensive wardrobe, at last boarded one of the new steam packets at Dieppe.

The England she reached was enjoying a spell of

exceptionally mild weather. Nestling blackbirds had been found in hedges, ripe strawberries in gardens, bees already looking for sources of honey, and snowdrops, crocuses and anemones bursting into flower. But this promise of spring was nothing compared with the conservatory at Wivelridge, which Marthanna had once more stocked with delicate plants and shrubs and heated to an almost tropical temperature.

Mignon looked round with approval. "It is beautiful, maman. Winter has been vanquished."

"This is how it was when your father lived here," Marthanna said, with satisfaction. "I had it repaired and restocked in honor of your homecoming."

"Thank you. It makes me happy."

"Does nothing else make you happy?" Marthanna asked, playfully.

"Of course! To see you, maman. But," she confessed, "I did not wish to return to England."

"Darling, it is your home."

"I know."

"You wanted to finish your education in France, and I was willing, but—Mignon, this house will be a small piece of France for you. We have your father's treasures, and I have imported a French maid. You shall have all the pleasures and amusements any girl could ask for. We are not poor people. You will be happy, my child. I swear you will!"

"My relations are peasants," Mignon declared, scornfully.

"How can you say such a thing? They are farmers."

"Farmers are peasants."

"Not in England."

"That is what I mean. In England we have to mix with them."

"Not exclusively. We must be polite, of course."

"Of course! I am always polite."

"But we shall also make the acquaintance of other classes. I have thought about it," Marthanna said, dreamily, "and I have planned for you. There are a number of good families in the neighborhood. Why should we not entertain them? The house is sufficiently large. I have servants, and I can engage more."

Mignon clapped her hands. "Oh, maman, how good you are!" Then her face fell. "Think you they will come? Your father was a farmer."

"And yours was an aristocrat of the old French empire. Have no fear! They will swarm over the place."

Mignon cheered up at once. "At least we have such things as orange-trees, which I am sure are rare in Sussex. We will give balls and fetes, and we will spend the season in London and go to the plays and to concerts."

"Now you are more like an excited child than a sophisticated young lady."

Mignon straightened her face and smoothed down her dress. "I am seventeen, a woman of the world."

"Not quite the whole world."

"Paris *is* the world," Mignon insisted. "May we visit it when I need new clothes? I could not bear the dreadful garments which are made in England. And, maman, please buy me a horse of my own, an expensive, elegant one! I wish to hunt the foxes and the hares. That is what the aristocrats do in England, is it not?"

"All in good time, my dear! Our first entertainment, I think, should be a small dinner-party for the Dykes."

"Oh, must it?"

"Yes, tradition decrees that relatives come first, and a lady never flouts tradition. Besides, you have those charming gifts for them."

"Oh, very well!"

After all, Marthanna thought, with relief, it would not be so difficult to manage the child. A certain diplomacy would be required, but that was to be expected. Mignon was a product of two races, of two strata of society. It would not be entirely easy for her to settle down in either one. It had been a sacrifice to send the child so far away, and Marthanna had gambled upon the outcome, but now it seemed that her prayers might be answered and her fears unfounded. Mignon was all she had of Gerrance, and therefore all she had in the world. She had owed it to him, she felt, to give his daughter the best education of his world, that she might take her place among the people to whom by birth she belonged. For a long time Marthanna had wrestled with her conscience. Should she have remained in France, raised Mignon in her father's country? But the pull of Hastingford had been too strong, and so she had compromised by sending the girl back to finish her education. Only time would tell whether she had done right, but she realized that the next few years would be the critical ones, and she vowed that she would spare nothing, neither time, energy nor money in giving Mignon the kind of life to which she was entitled.

The family dinner was a somewhat somber affair. Everyone wore their best clothes, which sat almost as uneasily upon them as did their best manners. The exception was Caroline, who could play the great lady as well as anyone, and who now saw herself as the matriarch of a noble and powerful tribe, an attitude affectionately condoned by all except Charity.

"Really," Charity grumbled, "Mother-in-law becomes more senile and peculiar each day. I know she is over eighty and must be expected to grow a little childish, but her fancies are positively ridiculous. She behaves as if she were royalty."

Royal was how Caroline felt when she sat at Marthanna's magnificent dining-table, a masterpiece in mahogany decorated with inlaid motifs of amboyna, tulipwood and ebony. She was proud of Marthanna and of Mignon, and caught herself regretting that her parents were not alive, forgetting that by now they would be well over a hundred years old. Her father would be compelled to change his mind, she thought, virtuously, for Will had by no means dragged her down. She, rather, had raised the family up. She had children and grandchildren of culture and education. Indeed, in Mignon she had a modish young lady who had only to lift a finger to land a title.

The food at the party was excellent, beginning with

Milton oysters, now in their prime, made into a pie with layers of sweetbreads between. These were followed by farced woodcocks, stuffed with bacon and shallots; and just as the heartily-eating farmers were beginning to feel apprehensive of satisfying themselves with this delicate fare they were reassured by the appearance of a twenty-pound aitchbone of beef, a roast forequarter of veal, and a haunch of mutton from the Romney Marsh, tasty with the salt particles which had settled into the moist ground. After this course they were not overmuch concerned with the Parisian custard baked with apples, and masked with apricot marmalade, or the whipped jellies and the sago pudding, and they merely toyed with the dessert of Portugal grapes, oranges, pears and walnuts.

To accompany the feast were choice French wines which Marthanna especially imported for her use. Charity and her children would not touch these alcoholic beverages, and Charity even looked with suspicion on the food. Who could tell what was in it, she wondered? Such a hodge-podge was it that no single ingredient tasted of itself, and for all she knew it could be riddled with poison, or strong liquor, which was almost worse.

On such an occasion it would have been the custom of the Dykes to play parlor games, or indulge in mild gambling with the cards, but not at Wivelridge. There they removed themselves to the withdrawing-room, where Mignon entertained them with songs and a performance on the pianoforte, and Marthanna encouraged them to make conversation. But the conversation was inclined to languish, for the men, replete, kept dozing off, and there was a general relief when Sylvanus bravely excused them all, on the grounds of early rising.

That was the last of the family parties to take place at Wivelridge. A welcome there was for each and every individual member, but gradually the gulf between the houses widened, as though the valley had been flooded with some element which could not be crossed.

"They are not our kind," Sylvanus said, to Rosemary.

"What do you mean, not our kind?" she demanded. "Aunt Marthanna is your sister. According to my mother she was your favorite sister. Mother used to feel quite out of it, she said, with Aunt Marthanna so strong and clever, and everyone depending on her, and Grandfather worshipping her."

"And so he should. Father had little book-learning, but Marthanna was a fine reader, with much understanding. He reckoned that the things she told him saved the farm."

A pang of jealousy shot through Rosemary. "It is wrong that there should be favorites in families," she said, harshly. "Mother told us that the only time she felt important was when she married Father. It was her triumph, to be wed before her elder sister. She reckoned Aunt Marthanna would have been an old maid if she had not befriended and hidden the Frenchman."

Sylvanus laughed. "Oho! There's sisterly love for you! I tell you, many a man would have been proud to call Marthanna wife, but most were afeared of her. She was far above them, like a statue standing on a pillar. I'm wondrous fond of her still, but I don't aim to visit with her too often, for she moves in high circles now, and I've no wish to be sent round to the kitchen door with the tallyman."

"You are as good as any of them," Rosemary protested, hotly. "It is all the fault of that stuck-up Mignon with her French airs. I do declare she must have laid a spell on Aunt Marthanna, for Aunt Marthanna can deny her nothing."

It was true that Wivelridge had risen in the world, and could now be included among the manors and genteel houses of the neighborhood. Marthanna's refined ways and her lavish hospitality, allied to the novelty of Mignon's piquant mingling of the French and English cultures, had caused them to be accepted by the best families in the neighborhood. At any time the visitor to Wivelridge might run into a Shelley, a de la Warr, a Pelham or an Ashburnham.

Mignon, to do her justice, was not impressed by names, and enjoyed good company without counting wealth or consulting genealogies. Money was, to her, merely a means to pleasure, and she did not spare her mother's any more than she would have spared her own or that of anyone else. One of her first actions on returning home was to persuade her mother to buy her a horse for hunting, a highly-bred pure white mare of sixteen hands called Skyscraper, and during the remainder of that season she was to be seen at almost every meet, accompanied by one gentleman or another in a scarlet coat and white corduroy breeches. A neat and fearless rider, at no time did she disgrace herself, and there was rivalry among the young men to be seen beside the "French mademoiselle" on the ghostly horse.

In the evenings there were balls in plenty, held either at the local houses or in the Town houses of Lewes, where many of the gentry spent their winters. Against such a background Mignon shone as brightly as she did galloping in her riding-habit across the bare fields and through the leafless woods.

"You are happy?" Marthanna would ask, pleadingly, and Mignon would nod her head. "There are more amusements in England than I expected to find, and the men are not so stupid as I thought."

But when the hunting season was over, and her friends and acquaintances began to drift away from the country, Mignon became restless.

"There is nothing happening now, maman. It is dull."

"Dull!" Marthanna exclaimed. "It is the most beautiful time of the year. Where would you wish to be in Spring but in Sussex?"

"In London. Soon we shall be isolated. There will be no one left."

"There will be the Dykes," Marthanna said, somewhat grimly.

"Oh, farmers! They have chosen to bury themselves

in the country for the sake of their livelihood, but I am no farmer."

Marthanna sighed. "Very well. I will prepare for us to go."

"Oh, no, maman! Do not trouble yourself! I know you have no love for the metropolis, and I have had invitations to stay at a dozen houses—most respectable residences, I assure you. I will show you the letters and you will see that I shall be most adequately escorted and chaperoned."

The invitations did indeed come from impeccable sources, and so Mignon went alone, and Marthanna stayed in the house which suddenly seemed far too large for her, and empty in spite of the servants, and of a deathly quietness.

Spring and summer passed slowly at Wivelridge, and Marthanna found the weather once more becoming important in the unchanging rhythm of her days. The winter, though mild, had been one of the wettest in memory, and continued so until March. This caused an alarming amount of sheep-rot, to the dismay of Stand Fast, who for his share of the livestock had chosen exclusively to take sheep, as being less continuous trouble than cows. Now he was forced to kill those animals which had not already died, and could not even sell them, their flesh being unfit for consumption. Charity, unwilling as ever to waste anything edible, cooked three meals of mutton for her family and did not desist until Marthanna, hearing of it as one heard all gossip in the country, walked over to Hastingford and rated her severely.

"What are you trying to do, woman? Kill off the rest of the Dykes? Do you not know the flesh is tainted? I heard of a kennel of dogs fed on diseased mutton. They fattened at first, then suddenly went off and wasted and died. Have sense, Charity! If you are too poor to feed your family, starve them! But do not poison them!"

Charity took Marthanna's advice, though with poor grace, and for weeks went around muttering darkly about idle women with too much money, and fingers being poked into pies by those who had no pies of their own.

Easter brought clear, open weather, and July and August saw a spell of dry hot days such as had not been known for a number of years.

Mignon did not return during the whole of that summer, but from time to time she wrote to her mother, and when Marthanna suggested she must be finding the heat in London extremely enervating. Mignon replied that she found it delightful, was bursting with health, and had never been happier.

By the end of August Marthanna was becoming impatient and somewhat annoyed, and sent a peremptory note commanding rather than requesting Mignon to come home. Mignon replied that she could not possibly travel until the end of the first week in September, as Monday the fifth was Bartholomew Fair which could on no account be missed, so there was nothing for it but to await the young lady's pleasure. Marthanna had the indoor servants busy sweeping and polishing, and the gardeners and handymen laying on fresh coats of paint until the house gleamed like a jewel-box. There would be little time for cleaning and renovations after Mignon arrived, Marthanna judged, for doubtless they would be embarked on another season of entertainment and gaiety.

She found herself trembling with nervousness when she heard the carriage approaching. She had sent it to Lewes to pick Mignon up from the coach. It had been gone no more than two hours, but to her it was as if days had passed. What she feared she did not know. Was it that Mignon might after all have delayed her homecoming? That she might be sullen and angry at being called back? Or that a summer in London might have changed the child, stripped the bloom from her, robbed her of innocence?

One look at Mignon dispersed the fears. She was glowing with health, her eyes were bright, her mouth smiling, and as she leapt from the carriage into her mother's arms she was bubbling over with high spirits.

"Oh, maman! How glad I am to see you! I cannot imagine how I could so long abide it without your company. And the country is so beautiful. It is like a picture by Constable. All the way from Lewes I could scarcely contain myself for wanting to jump out and put a necklace of flowers over the heads of the charming cows."

"Then you did not like London?"

"Oh, I adored it. Every moment was an education to me. I do assure you that the memories of my darling Paris have wellnigh faded."

Marthanna glanced with perplexity at the luggage piled on the carriage. "Are there not more trunks than when you set out on your journey?"

"One or two," Mignon agreed, carelessly.

"I hope you have not been extravagant."

"Oh, la! Could I avoid it? In London the most delectable things are waved under your eyes. Only a woman of stone could resist them. I spent the money you kindly gave me, and am also slightly in debt. But the tradesmen were most kind and were willing to let me have the goods, for which I promised you would pay. Shall we now go inside, maman? There is so much I must tell you."

Marthanna could only stare at the girl as they sipped tea in the thin French porcelain cups. A goose Mignon had never been, but a swan she now certainly was. From an attractive child she had blossomed into a beautiful young woman with a confident and easy manner and indubitably with plenty to say.

"Such a fair as Bartholomew's has surely never been! One might have spent a week there and not viewed everything. I do not speak of the stalls which sold articles of trifling value, but of the shows. There were twenty-three of them, and they contained some of the marvels of the universe. Only a penny to enter each, and entertainment fit for a king. There was Miss Hipson, who is twelve years of age and weighs more than sixteen stone. There was the Somerset girl who is six feet nine inches tall, and Mr. Thomas Day thirty-five inches in height. As for the animals, I have seen lions and tigers and laughing hyenas and—would you believe it!—an elephant!"

Marthanna scarcely heard what she was saying. "London has done more for you than Paris."

"I was so weary," Mignon said, dreamily, "that I could have slept upon my feet, but I would not have missed one moment of it. There was Greenwich Fair at Easter, which had a pleasant country air and where I saw a bàlloon, and Deptford Fair at the end of May, but neither could compare with Bartholomew."

Marthanna blinked. "Are you still talking of fairs?"

"Yes, maman."

"But they are vulgar occasions, designed for the populace. What of the opera, the playhouse, the balls?"

"I attended some," Mignon said, evasively. For the first time she hesitated, then continued, with a certain defiance, "Medford is partial to fairs."

"Who is Medford?"

"Mr. Spring is a barrister," Mignon said, with dignity.

"Ah! One of your beaux."

Mignon sprang to her feet, almost knocking over the precious china. "No. Not one! *The* one. Oh, maman, I love him very much, and he is so poor. That is why we visited the fairs, where one may enjoy so much for a penny. No, do not frown, maman! He is a gentleman, of good family, but has spent all the money his father can afford. Life is a sore trial to a young barrister. He must wait for briefs, and who will give him a brief when he has not proved himself? He must keep up appearances, dress well, drive around in a post-chaise, eat venison, and live like a pauper when he is not observed. I could weep for him."

"And I could weep for you," Marthanna said, drily. "A season in London, at great expense, and the only beau you can find is a penniless lawyer!"

"You would have me marry for money?" Mignon inquired, with a shocked expression. "Oh, maman, I had imagined you to have higher ideals."

"And I hope you imagined correctly. But there is

a deal of difference between making a mercenary match and being entirely without resources. You have not been bred to poverty."

Mignon gave a small sigh of satisfaction and moved delicately across to sit on the arm of her mother's chair. "You are wonderful, maman, and I admire you immensely for your good sense. Poverty would bore me, I am sure, for there would be simply nothing to do. Every occupation and entertainment costs money. Even misers must eat, and Medford is no miser."

Marthanna nodded and laid her hand on the girl's arm. "You too have good sense, my dear, and I am happy you do not allow your heart to overrule your head. You will soon forget this young man."

"Forget him? Never!"

"Then wait until he has made his way in the world."

"Oh, no, maman! I have found a more pleasing solution to our problem. I advised him to marry an heiress who would support him during his struggles. I told him, maman, that you would give me a dowry of twenty thousand pounds."

CHAPTER FIVE

Boldly I preach, hate a cross, hate a surplice,
  Mitres, copes and rochets;
Come hear me pray nine times a day,
  And fill your heads with crochets.
Richard, Bishop Corbet

The division of the farm had been made without conflict, argument or rancor, and with no need for arbitration, though Peregrine's lawyer had insisted on drawing up deeds for the new status, that possible future law-suits might be avoided. When they surveyed the land and discussed their preferences Sylvanus had been wary. Knowing well Charity's stinginess which was in itself a kind of greed, he had expected from her sons a virtuous grasping of their rights, and was therefore agreeably surprised to find the desires of the three of them so different that they dovetailed instead of overlapping.

Stand Fast, who expressed his wishes first, said that apart from a team of oxen and a couple of horses, he would prefer his share of the livestock in the form of sheep.

"There is no beast which more becomes a servant of God," he said, sententiously. " 'Thus saith the Lord of hosts, I took thee from the sheep-cote, from following the sheep, to be ruler over my people, over Israel.' "

Sylvanus laughed. "You're welcome to the sheep, lad, but I doubt they'll lead you to rule over anything except themselves."

Stand Fast frowned at this levity. "They will leave me more time for the Lord's work."

"Ah! Well, don't let a good shepherd hear you say that. Sheep need care if they're to prosper."

"I acknowledge only one Good Shepherd," Stand Fast said, stiffly.

For his acreage he took some of the drier meadows, and arable ground on which he might grow their fodder, such as clover and burnet, turnips and cabbages. Chief of the buildings he chose the large old barn, with a share of stables, wagon-sheds and store-rooms.

Deliverance was, in Sylvanus's eyes, even more accommodating. He liked, he said, to do a little of everything, and so he would be mightily obliged if he could have those sheep his brother could spare, a few cows, a good horse, a hundred or so of mixed poultry, a dry room for his carpenter's shop, and all the tools he could find, saving those essentials required by the others.

Sylvanus therefore found himself possessed of a fine herd of cattle, and among his other land the rich water-meadows in the valley. At first his pleasure was marred by a strong sense of guilt. These boys were practically untried farmers. Should he not have warned them that they were taking the portion of the mouse against his lion's feast? The Sussex Weald had never been a choice district for sheep. On the level fields and under the orchard trees of Kent they did well enough. On the Downs they reached their true magnificence, thanks to their improvement during the life-time's work of John Ellman of Glynde, and to the health of the well-drained chalk hills. Southdown sheep were indeed the pride of Sussex. But back on the clay they were exposed to many dangers, as Stand Fast found later when they contracted the rot.

For a long time Sylvanus sat in conference with his conscience, and in the end did nothing. People were suspicious of advice, he had found, and if he insisted on exchanging a part of his herd for a part of Stand Fast's flock, why, more than likely Stand Fast would oppose him, imagining there must be more profit in sheep, else why should his uncle desire them? Your godly man, Sylvanus thought, wryly, was all too prone to see himself in glorious isolation among the angels, and everyone else in league with the devil.

So Sylvanus for the first time in his life had cattle and land of his own, and gloried in his inheritance, sparing no time or labor in his efforts to maintain, improve and increase them. One day, he vowed, the Hastingford herd should be famous. The choicest red roast beef of England should be from the red Sussex cattle of the Weald. Now at last, he felt, at late last, fate had relented and was rewarding him with a happiness he had not looked to find this side of Heaven. Twice exiled from the land he loved, it had taken him back, given itself to him completely. What more could he ask, except perhaps to have had Lancelot with him? On a farm a son was a symbol of the future. He was tomorrow, like the sapling oak and the sprouting wheat. How could the half-baked boy prefer brewing to plowing?

The loss of a flock from sheep-rot would have spelled ruin to many men, but Stand Fast accepted it calmly.

"It is the will of God," he said. "I can do nothing about it. 'Thus saith the Lord of hosts, As I thought to punish you, when your fathers provoked me to wrath.'"

Charity glanced at him with less approval than was her habit. "You can scarcely blame your father for the rot which started after his death."

"God sent the wet, mild winter," Stand Fast explained, patiently, "which caused the rot. But do you not understand, that was merely a sign? We know the sins of the fathers are visited upon the children, and to this I submit. My father lusted after strange women, and therefore his flock, which is now mine, has been destroyed. This is justice. Can you not understand it, mother?"

Charity was not sure that she could. "Well, now you will have to buy fresh beasts, and where is the money coming from, I should like to know?"

"The Lord will provide," Stand Fast said, solemnly, and added, "Would you oblige me with a loan?"

Charity spun around to stare at him. "I? And where would I find such money?"

"You are of a saving disposition."

"Yes. By my providence I saved your father much expense, but he did not pay me on account of this. When have you ever seen me with gold or silver in my hand? No, if you want sight of the real coin of this realm you will have to go to them that have it, to Wivel-ridge, to your Aunt Marthanna."

Stand Fast was horrified. "To that Babylon? To that sink of iniquity? Never. There are terrible tales told about the place. I shudder to think of it, staining our land. They are arrayed in purple and scarlet, Aunt Marthanna and her foreign daughter who sits upon a scarlet-colored beast."

"White," Charity said, practically, "not scarlet."

"Their money would be tainted," Stand Fast declared. "I shall go and pray."

He prayed long and often. His mother could not blame him for that, but his punctiliousness in religious observance did cause her somewhat to relax her own devotions. It was foolish, she thought, not without a touch of cynicism, for the both of them to harry the Lord so incessantly. She could not deny he was a credit to her upbringing, yet the setting of his mind on higher things seemed to have stultified his human feelings. Affection had been replaced by rectitude, sympathy by condescension. Deliverance was different. He was all eyes and ears and hands, enjoying the things which manifested themselves to his senses and apparently ignoring the invisible world. His simplicity and humility were so obvious that he had the reputation of not being very bright.

"He is a good workman," people said. "He can turn his hand to anything, but apart from that—"

They did not know how to finish their assessment of his character. Since when had tolerance, modesty and generosity been the mark of a smart fellow?

Deliverance was delighted with his inheritance, but he did not take it seriously. To him it was a boy's plaything. He would stand in a field and say, "This is mine!" then race to the farthest hedge to test the distance, and look back in wonder at the dwarfed hedge on the other side. Such a large patch of earth, he thought, for one man. The hedges themselves were fascinating, and he would forget the time, wasting an hour or two, while he traced the interweaving of quickthorn and honeysuckle, bramble and briar.

Yet he was industrious enough. He could shoe a horse or an ox, work leather and make a harness, fashion almost anything in wood, including wheels, ladders and whole wagons. At thatching he was deft, and he could turn out a basket or a trug with the best. In addition to these crafts he was always ready to help with unskilled work, such as carting and portering, digging a grave or a well. His neighbors came to depend on him. "Go to young Dyke," they said. "He's a handy man and he's cheap."

Stand Fast disapproved of his ways, and the two brothers began to grow apart.

"Why do you allow everyone to take advantage of you?" Stand Fast demanded, angrily. "The laborer is worthy of his hire, and you allow yourself to be cheated."

"Ah, well," Deliverance replied, easily, "I'll not starve while there's work to be done, and work there always will be, this world being the way it is."

"You are wasting the education our mother gave us."

"What of you?" Deliverance asked. "After all you are a farmer."

"I have land, but I am not merely a farmer. I am a servant of God, preparing to preach His word. I do not perform the tasks others consider beneath them. I do not clean out privies."

Even Sylvanus felt himself obliged to remind Deliverance of his responsibilities.

"What do you plan to do with your land, lad?"

Deliverance stared at him, perplexed and round-eyed.

"Why should I do anything with it? 'Tis a pretty piece of land, and has grass in plenty for my few beasts."

Sylvanus sighed and reflected that what people said was right. The boy must be thick-headed. "The land is your livelihood."

"No," Deliverance contradicted him. "No, uncle. My hands are my livelihood, and the strength of my back and my legs. I make all the money I need."

"Then maybe you'd care to pass over the land to someone who would cultivate it."

But this Deliverance would not consider. His land was his and he loved it. Land, he thought, had a right to its own ways, and he for his part would not think the less of it even if it grew thistles as high as Mayfield steeple.

Sylvanus was discouraged but not beaten. These two boys, he reckoned, would never make farmers. Whether it was their queer education or the fanatic teaching of their mother, they were not cast in Peregrine's mold. One day, he vowed, he would get their land, and Hastingford would be whole again, as Marthanna wished. He did not consider that this desire rendered him avaricious. He already possessed more than he had reckoned to own, but it hurt a good farmer to watch good land going to seed. The longer land deteriorated, the longer its reclamation. If it began to look shabby now, what would it be like in ten years?

Stand Fast had no intention of neglecting his portion of the farm. He was merely held up for lack of money, and so far the Lord had not answered his prayers for funds. The wise plan, therefore, was to carry on the Lord's work, and to this end he had conceived the idea of converting the old barn into a chapel. To him it seemed a heaven-sent inspiration, and now while he waited in sheepless leisure was the fitting time to advance his project.

"It is a fine building, with noble proportions," he said, "fit to be the temple of the Lord. See the girth of the beams that support it! They are the heart of the oak, set deep in the earth, and they will endure. This is where the word of the Lord will be heard."

Meek dared to question his plan. "It sounds wonderful, Stand Fast, but is it necessary? After all, the word of the Lord is already heard in the churches of Rotherbrook, Mayfield, and a score of other villages around, and our population is not extremely large."

Stand Fast gazed at her reproachfully. That his sister should throw cold, or even luke-warm, water on his holy scheme!

"Yes, the word is heard, but not *my* word. You know as well as I do that the priests have corrupted, distorted and debased the true word. I am filled with the spirit of God, and what I teach will be His message whispered in my ear."

The news ran around the district almost before Stand Fast had voiced it. There was a little wind, it seemed, which blew only when there was gossip to be disseminated.

"That boy of Charity Dyke's," they said, not naming him. There had always been a certain reluctance to speak the names of the three children. Such names were ridiculous, the local people felt, were not even truly respectable. Quakers there had been in the past, and evilly persecuted they had been, poor souls! Some had emigrated with William Penn, but those who remained had long been absorbed into the community and had graced their children with good Christian names. In these modern, progressive days there was no reason to burden a child with a name which might have come out of *The Pilgrim's Progress*.

So they said, "That boy of Charity Dyke's is building a church."

Those who heard would not believe it. "He can't. 'Twouldn't be allowed. The churches was all built long ago."

"A chapel, then."

"Ah!" That was different. To most of them a chapel was inferior, a kind of make-believe, something which could be erected by a man. Churches were not in the same category. They were God-sent, attained by prayer and miracle, accomplishments of the saints, who, like Dunstan, performed such deeds as putting a shoulder to the edifice and pushing it into place.

Therefore, curious but not impressed, everyone asked, "And what would he be wanting a chapel for?"

Caroline was amused when she heard of Stand Fast's activities, though she could not help being somewhat put out as well. "What does he think he is doing? This is a farm, not a monastery. And where will he get his congregation? Reckon he'll find himself preaching to rows of cows and sheep, with roosting birds dropping blessings on his head. Talk, talk! That is all Master Stand Fast is useful for. He should pay less attention to the organ which is between his ears, and more to that which is between his legs. But they always were bumbling great sockheads, were Charity's boys. Peregrine should have known better. Marrying a foreigner from Tunbridge! I wonder what he's doing to that barn? If it weren't for my rheumatics I'd walk up and see."

"I'll go," Dickon offered, eagerly, "and come back and tell you."

Caroline nodded. "That's right, boy. You do that. You're a good boy. No woman could have a better son."

Often now she forgot Dickon was her husband, and more than ever since Peregrine's death had come to look upon him as her son. Dickon never contradicted her. Husband or son, it made no difference to him. She was his dear mistress who had given him comfort and security, and whose last days must be made as easy and happy as possible. Rosemary complained because she saw less of him, but Dickon took no notice. Caroline was his first concern.

"You are her lap-dog or her slave," Rosemary said, spitefully. "You run after her day and night, and sometimes, if she remembers, she throws you a bone. You've no life of your own."

"You can't say that," Dickon objected. "It's a fair and proper life, and I've my duty to her."

"What of me?"

"I give you what you want."

"What *I* want? Isn't it what *you* want?"

"I like you, Rosemary. You know that."

"Then show it. How long is it since you've lain with me?"

"I've not counted the days."

"Days? More likely months. And then you could scarcely attend to what you were doing, for wanting to get back to her."

"I can't stay away at nights. Her limbs grow stiff, and if she has the need to piss I must help her out of bed."

"Oh, you make me sick! You talk of what she has done for you, but what of the debt you owe me? If I had not kept silent you would have hanged for murder."

Dickon's mind worked more slowly than Rosemary's, and before he could frame a reply she had gone. He remembered this conversation as he walked up to the old barn at Hastingford. Had Rosemary's silence really saved him? He had thought at the time that he had attacked Abel Polsted in order to save her. What else could he have done? Stood and watched her being raped? Also he had imagined the boy's death to be an accident. When he lashed out, pushing Abel across the barn, there had been no murder in his heart, only the male instinct to fight and to protect. The rest had been bad luck, and Rosemary had agreed in this. But now she threatened him, and Dickon was bewildered and not as confident as he had been. He remembered, as he had not done for ages, the days of his youth when he had been one of the underprivileged, one of those whose every action is suspect, one of those who could reach the gibbet by merely laying hands on a loaf of bread or a shoe-buckle, one of those who could be whipped for setting a foot in the wrong parish.

He was apprehensive as he approached the barn, but he did not hesitate. He, more urgently than Caroline, needed to know what was going on.

Stand Fast had already done some work on his proposed chapel, with the help of Deliverance who made a large, unpaid and uncomplaining contribution. Deliverance it was who had replaced a number of tiles on the roof, matching the new lovingly with the old ones, and keeping painstakingly to the ancient, elaborate design. He it was who had nailed the loose weatherboards and put sound ones in place of those which were rotten. Together they had given the outside a coat of creosote, no small task considering the size of the barn, and now they were starting on the interior. In front was a pile of rubbish they had thrown out, the accumulated lumber of generations.

Dickon went in and greeted them. "Are you wanting some help?"

Stand Fast nodded. "A labor of love is pleasing in the sight of the Lord. Carry out some of this straw and burn it. It is too old and bug-ridden even for cattle-litter."

Dickon did this, and when he returned the floor was swept clean. "It looks strange," he said, "I never saw it like this."

Deliverance was in the corner, staring at something. "Come here!" he said, to Stand Fast.

Stand Fast walked over. "What is it?"

"The rest of the floor is trodden hard, but this looks as if it has been dug."

"It's where the straw was, and hasn't been walked on, that's all."

"No, there's a well-marked edge, and the earth inside it is soft and crumbling."

Dickon was cold. He felt as if his heart had turned to ice, but he forced himself to go and look at the place. " 'Tis nothing," he said, "some hens have been scratching." His voice sounded hollow and unnatural to him.

Deliverance shook his head and plunged his hand into the earth. "Hens wouldn't loosen it this far down. Stand Fast, pass me a shovel."

Dickon tried to think of something else to say, but there were no words. He wanted to walk away, but his body had become fixed to that spot. He wanted not to see, wanted to close his eyes, but his eyelids might have been glued open. He had to watch as Deliverance removed the soil and came—oh, how shallow and inadequate had been the grave!—came upon a skeleton.

With amazement and horror they lifted it out. The bough-spud was still in the back of the skull.

Dickon felt faint and sick. The two young men were talking, but he could hear them only as though from a vast distance. They were wondering whose was the body, and how it had got there, and how long it had been buried. They did not question Dickon, and why should they, he wondered. They could not connect it with him. All he needed to do was to deny knowledge of it, be as mystified as they were, talk naturally about it. If only the muscles of his jaw were not so stiff!

A voice spoke from behind him. "What have you found?" And Rosemary came forward.

"Don't look!" Deliverance warned her. "It's no sight for a lady."

"Why not?" Stand Fast demanded. "It is what we must all come to. It is a lesson we should learn. 'Our bones are dried, and our hope is lost.' I would like to hang this from a beam when I preach."

Deliverance was shocked. "It would not be reverent."

"I am not so weak," Rosemary said, scornfully, "that I would swoon at such a sight. I can tell you who it is —who it was."

Dickon put out his hand as if to stop her, but she did not see it.

"It was Abel Polsted, and Dickon killed him."

In the silence the sounds of the countryside flowed in with the sunlight through the open doors. And then a shadow fell across the floor.

Slowly Rosemary turned, and she was aware of the identity behind that shadow before ever her eyes told her the news, before her mouth could form the name. It was Lancelot!

CHAPTER SIX

Though sure it's the best way to die,
O! the devil a better a-livin'!
For when the gallows is high
Your journey is shorter to heaven.

The Night Before Larry Was Stretched

Loyalty was more than a word to Marthanna. It was an act of keeping faith with those to whom you owed your being, your safety and your prosperity. Once it had led along a clear, straight road, a highway without shadows, which she had walked without doubts. She was a loyal to the King and his government, for they were the protectors of the people of England. She was loyal to her family, as a matter of course; and later this loyalty extended to Hastingford the place, because to her it held together the family as a group, was nurse and cradle, symbol of security. But later, with a husband of enemy nationality, her loyalties became confused, and there was nothing to guide her but her love.

The peace with France had been the lifting of a great burden from her, though it had posed the problem of the rearing and education of Mignon. That was a bitter tug-of-war, and the solution of residing in England and sending Mignon to school in France had not entirely satisfied her conscience. It was all the more pleasing, therefore, when Mignon on her return settled down happily to the English way of life. Marthanna was prepared to spare no expense to please the girl. What was the use of money if it could not smooth the path of the daughter who owing to her mixed parentage and the unsettled state of Europe had suffered too much of variety and too little of security?

But now when Marthanna looked to giving her conscience and principles a well-earned rest, here was Mignon putting them to work again.

"Twenty thousand pounds!" she exclaimed. "That is a dowry for a princess."

"You are a wealthy woman."

"No, child. I was never wealthy, only well-off, and that is vastly different. We have been home little more than a year, and already my fortune is shrinking alarmingly. You are a young girl, and you have a right to mix with society, but last winter's entertaining, and your season in London—I am sorry, darling, I have nothing like twenty thousand pounds. Remember, I paid your Uncle Peregrine five thousand for this house."

Mignon shrugged her shoulders. "Then I suppose I shall have to be content with less."

Anger flickered in Marthanna at the blind selfishness of the young. "I would have wished you could have found a suitor who loved you for yourself rather than your fortune."

"He does!" Mignon exclaimed. "Medford does, and you are a horrid creature, maman, to suggest anything different. Medford suggested no dowry. He was all humility, apologizing for declaring his love, confessing he had no means wherewith to support me. I tell you, he is a romantic young man, prepared to wait ten years, or to live with me in rapturous poverty. It is I who am not prepared to wait, nor am I accustomed to live as a pauper. I want a dowry, Maman. *I* am asking for it."

"Then we must see what we can manage," Marthanna conceded. "In the meantime I would like to meet your beau. Will you invite him to stay with us?"

But before Medford Spring arrived, there had broken the scandal of the skeleton in the barn. Dickon was in Lewes prison, awaiting trial, and Caroline was in a state of desperate despair.

Marthanna fetched her to Wivelridge, against her will.

"I have my own home. Do you think a grand house and a fleet of servants will console me?"

"You cannot remain alone, Mother. You cannot care for yourself."

"No, and they have robbed me of my dear companion. What have I done that they should so persecute an old woman? What crime have I committed?"

"You have committed no crime. It is Dickon who has done wrong."

"That he has not!" Caroline declared, stoutly. "He has told me of the circumstances, and I believe him. He is a good boy. He does not lie to me." She was silent for a few minutes, staring into the distance, then she said, abruptly, "They will hang him, of course!"

"Now, Mother—"

"It is no use pretending. He has a bad record. You do not know how bad, but I do. He was a thief and a vagrant, and, what is worse, he was a resurrectionist, a body-snatcher. He does not stand a chance." She began to cry softly. "It will be the death of me. I no longer have reason for living. No one wants an old woman."

"You are wrong. I want you. We all want you."

"Except Rosemary," Caroline said, slyly. "She fancied him, you know. Oh, yes! I may be old, but I am not blind and I am not silly. She was only waiting for me to die. Now for some reason she has turned against him, the little bitch! She will give the evidence that will hang him."

"If we could persuade her—"

"Persuade her!" Caroline cried, scornfully. "Have you not heard, 'Heaven has no rage like love to hatred turned?' That was written by William Congreve. You see, I have not forgot my genteel education."

"There must be something we can do."

"There is," Caroline replied, promptly. "We must obtain for him the best barrister in the country for his defence. The rich are more easily acquitted than the poor, I say, which is but commonsense. The rich live

longer, for they have the cleverest doctors, and the rich
become richer, for they have wise brokers. To be poor
is to have every hazard multiplied a hundredfold, and
who should know better than I?"

"You are an old cynic," Marthanna said, to lighten
the conversation.

But Caroline would not be put off. "Marthanna, you
are my daughter, and from whom can a mother ask
favors, if not from her own child? You are a woman of
substance. Lend me the money that I may buy help for
Dickon."

Marthanna sighed. "Oh, Mother! This is a bad time
to ask such a thing. I would if I—"

"You would? You mean you will. Yes, surely that
is what you mean!"

"Listen, Mother! I would not refuse you anything. I
would give you the clothes from my back, the hair
from my head. But Mignon loves a poor man, and
needs every penny for her dowry."

Caroline stared at her. "Daughter, what are you saying? You are talking of tablelinen and bedlinen, of
gowns and frills, of silver and porcelain. I am speaking
of the life of a man."

"She is my only child. She has a right to marry."

"And Dickon, I suppose, has the right to kick his
heels in the empty air."

"Mother, I am sorry."

"Where else can I turn? Charity and her children
have little or nothing, Sylvanus has little, Rebecca,
from what we hear, has lived as a pauper for years,
and now Lancelot has returned, leaving, in his pride,
not only his wife but her money as well. You see? The
Dykes have their meadows and their cows, but I
could wish I had not changed my money into land.
Were it in my pocket I could save my unfortunate
man."

"If only I could help!" Marthanna murmured.

"When you speak of poverty," Caroline went on, ignoring Marthanna's remarks, "you speak as a woman of
wealth, in a relative way. Look at your damask-cov-
ered chairs and inlaid tables! Look at your statues

and the pictures on your wall! Sell those, and Dickon could have the most soft-tongued barrister in England to plead for him."

"Sell them? How could I sell them? When Mignon brought her friends here, she would be shamed."

"It is I who am shamed," Caroline said, looking at her steadily, "I am ashamed of you." And Marthanna felt compelled to turn away her eyes.

The preparations for the visit of Medford Spring were no less elaborate than the previous winter's programme had been. Dinner-parties were arranged, and the date fixed for a grand ball. This was to be held in the large drawing-room which led to the tropical conservatory. On that occasion the glass doors between the two would be opened out, and Marthanna reflected with satisfaction, as she had done before, that though there were many greater houses in the neighborhood she did not know of one in which the guests could dance beneath orange and banana trees. They had been known to pick the fruit, which angered her exceedingly, but since the depredations were doubtless made by young people, and since for Mignon's sake the presence of young people was essential, Marthanna must needs resign herself to any damage done.

For outdoor sports at that time of the year there was cub-hunting and woodcock-shooting. Mignon, who had practiced and become a reasonably good shot, persuaded her mother to buy a couple of Sussex spaniels, these having a wonderfully good nose for the scent.

Caroline remained at Wivelridge, but kept to her own rooms, for which Marthanna was thankful. It was bad enough to ride on the see-saw of her conscience—feeling at one moment a murderess and at another a dutiful mother—without the added discomfort of Caroline's accusing eyes. She had made no mention to Mignon of Caroline's request for money. Why spoil the child's pleasure by bestowing on her a sense of guilt? Marthanna was prepared to endure the guilt for both of them, and she made her position bearable by reminding herself that the day of reckoning was still a fair way off. Dickon would not come up for trial until the Lent Assizes, and anything could happen by then, even a miracle.

At Hastingford there was a deal of controversy concerning Dickon's crime and arrest, and feelings ran high, but, strangely, the allies did not consist of Charity's family against the rest. Charity approved of Rosemary's confession, and a belated friendliness developed between the two of them.

"Why did you shield him for so long?" Charity demanded.

"Out of a mistaken kindness," Rosemary said, demurely. "I knew it would mean a sentence of death for him, and I shrank from being responsible."

"But what quarrel had he with Abel Polsted?"

Rosemary dropped her eyes modestly. "It appears that both had a fancy for me."

Charity glanced at her. Sakes! It was not easy to imagine men killing one another over such a woman. Dried-up she was, a disappointed spinster with a sour expression and lips like red thread. Still, it all happened quite a while ago, when Rosemary was a pleasant-faced girl and had not been jilted.

"I hope you did not encourage them," Charity said, severely.

"You know I would not."

"Ah, well," Charity went on, briskly, "all we can do is to pray for the vicious, low-down, good-for-nothing wretch. He'll be hanged for sure, and that is a fate too merciful for such as he. How your grandmother could have been so foolish as to take such a viper to her bosom I shall never understand. But, then, she was always a headstrong, contrary woman."

Stand Fast continued converting the barn into a chapel, and looked upon the finding of Abel Polsted's body as a sign of approval from the Lord.

"Had I not cleansed the old barn we should not have brought a murderer to justice," he said, piously. "I was led to do it, and I am favored in the sight of God. My plans will prosper."

Deliverance made no comment on Dickon's misfortune, and was secretly sorry that he had discovered the makeshift grave. A crime so old that the evidence was reduced to bones had somehow lost its evil meaning, and it was difficult to believe that Dickon, so simple and so gentle, could deliberately have taken the life of a fellow-creature.

Meek, belying her name in her indignation, openly defended Dickon, and attempted time and again to persuade Rosemary to change her mind.

"What have you against Dickon?"

"He is a murderer."

"How can you be sure?"

"I saw him do it."

"What! And you told no one? You did not speak of it at the time?"

"I was afraid."

"What did you fear?"

"That Dickon would harm me."

Meek laughed. "Now I know that you invent fantasies. Dickon would scarcely close his fist on a moth, though it laid its eggs on his Sunday woollen jacket. I have worked with him, tending the animals. He is a man who does not care to give pain."

"Men are transformed by lust."

"Did he then lust after you?"

"Why should he not? Would it be so outlandish a thing?"

"I did not say so."

"No, but there was a smile upon your face, a mocking smile, as if I were a monster no man could desire."

"Rosemary, I was not smiling."

"Oh, yes, you were! You make fun of me, all of you, because I am thirty-three years old, and unmarried. I will not speak any more on this subject. I will save it for the Assizes, where I will stand up and testify upon my sacred oath that two men hungered for my body, and murder was done."

Meek reported this conversation to Sylvanus.

"It is no use. I cannot awaken in her any sense of

mercy. She is concerned only with the charms she exercised, which, she declares, were the motive for the crime."

"Then Dickon will die," Sylvanus said. "Either she retracts at the trial, or there is no hope for him."

Deeply troubled though he was, Sylvanus harbored another emotion—joy at Lancelot's return.

"Boy, this is what I did not dare to hope for. Were I my nephew Stand Fast I would have kept up a continual patter of prayer. Well, sinner though I am, perhaps sometimes I did pray, adding of course a codicil that the Lord's will and your happiness must come first. When Peregrine left me this portion of the farm, my first thought was, 'Ah, now I have an inheritance to leave my son, my natural son.' And then I remembered that my son, my natural son, was a wealthy man brewing beer for us poor farmers to drink."

Lancelot grinned. "One can get monstrous sickened of the smell of brewing. The smell of good cowdung is a treat beside it, and it's a perfume I don't weary of. You'll see me shunning ale now in the preference of the Frenchified wines."

"Ah, lad, it's good to have you with me, and we'll not want for a comfortable livelihood. But tell me, seriously, are you home to stay, or is this a visit, a whim?"

"I am home to stay, Father."

"And what of—I do not wish to pry—but what of your wife?"

Lancelot hesitated, then replied, "Shall we say that sometimes the most violent fevers rage for the shortest time?"

"Ay, and we'll say no more. I only wish for happier conditions on the farm, and I'd be right merry if poor Dickon were not in such a stew."

"Yes, and if our relations were not ready to tear out each other's hearts on account of him."

It was true there was anything but harmony at Hastingford, and a few weeks later, with Christmas approaching, the storm broke. It was like a vat with the yeast too lively, Lancelot thought, that works and works until it overflows.

Charity had been tetchy ever since Lancelot returned, and she considered she had a genuine grievance. Peregrine had divided the farm, taking from her sons a portion of what she held to be their rightful inheritance, but he had in no way divided the household. Her work and responsibility were not lessened. Rather, they were increased, for she must be hostess to all relatives, even though they tilled land which did not benefit her or her offspring. Rosemary had been foisted on her at no invitation of hers. Her brother-in-law she lodged and fed, cleaning after him and washing his clothes as though she had been his wife, and now without a by-your-leave his son had descended on them.

She glanced at Lancelot's plate, which had emptied in a remarkably short time. "It seems that brewing strong liquor sharpens the appetite. Or were you half starved in those pagan parts?"

"Neither," Lancelot answered, laughing. "We ate well. Yet I would say it is farming that sharpens the appetite. Brewers are far from healthy. They have a florid look, and are often stout, but this may mean they suffer from a congestion of the veins. They do not live to a great age, though tillers of the soil may do, if they have sufficient nourishment, which many do not."

"Do you infer that here you lack food?" Charity demanded, heatedly.

"I said no such thing."

"But it was your insinuation. I am not your slave, Lancelot Dyke, and I did not request you to take up residence in Hastingford. I have two sons for whom I toil, and this is my duty as their mother."

"It is Lancelot's home," Sylvanus put in.

"I do not consider it so. Peregrine willed the house to me."

"On condition it should be open to his relatives."

"Peregrine was besotted," Charity said, recklessly. "He was led away from sense and decency by his lusts. Why else should he leave a fortune to his bastard?"

Suddenly Meek burst into tears and beat the table with her fists. "Be quiet, be quiet! Cease your brawling and think on what you are saying before further ugly words pass your lips! Do you begrudge food, mother? Are you dissatisfied, Lancelot? Then remember the rough fare Dickon must endure! Would you deny a home to Uncle Sylvanus and Lancelot, Mother? Well, we may now be a large family, but we have such space as would seem a continent to Dickon in his cell. Does a brewer live a short life? I tell you it is a month of Sundays compared with what Dickon can expect."

"Have you finished your outburst, girl?" Charity asked, coldly. "I declare, I don't know what has come over you lately. I had thought your rebellious spirit would be quelled when you were responsible for your father's death."

"I was not!" Meek cried. "Indeed I was not! It was the evil minds of those who suspicioned me. Mother, how can you be so cruel!"

"Sometimes," Charity said, slowly, "I wonder if there was truth in what they said."

Meek gave a cry and ran from the room.

"You are a hard woman, Charity," Sylvanus said.

"I did not ask your opinion, brother-in-law, any more than I asked Peregrine to bring me here. He pestered me to marry him, and my parents urged me. A good, prosperous farmer, they said. What more could any girl ask? But had I known the evil ways of the family, the black hearts and sinful doings, I would have chosen rather to be in my grave."

"You were always uncharitable," Lancelot told her. "You hated me when you thought me Peregrine's son, and when you found I was not, you hated him for being cuckolded. Oh, you are a cantankerous woman!"

"Do not speak so of my mother!" Stand Fast commanded.

"I will speak as I feel. It is time truth was told, instead of being allowed to fester within."

"You shall not belittle my mother."

"No? And what will you do, preacher? Will you fight me and betray your religion? Or will you swallow my words? What? Are you silent? Have you no text for the occasion?"

Sylvanus looked at the faces around the table. They did not make a pretty picture. Charity's was distorted with anger, Rosemary's with a sly and bitter pleasure, Stand Fast's with outraged virtue. Deliverance looked sad and confused, and Lancelot was a man who must at last spew up past unkindness and injustice.

Into the momentary silence Sylvanus let fall what he hoped was a suggestion of sanity.

"If we cannot live together," he said, "it is better we should live apart."

CHAPTER SEVEN

In good days of yore they ne'er troubled their heads
In settling of jointures, or making of deeds;
But Adam and Eve, when they first entered course,
E'en took one another for better or worse.

Unknown

Sylvanus went to Marthanna. He went to her, remembering that she had been his sanctuary, that she had been the keeper of his letter from his beloved Philadelphia, telling him that Lancelot was his son. He remembered also that from the beginning she had put the welfare of Hastingford before the mere mortal desires of its inhabitants. She had been, as it were, the genie of the place, guarding it, and seeing it as the composite hive of the family rather than the living quarters of one or another of its members.

Yet he went with less confidence than heretofore, for he believed her personality had suffered a change. In the past she had been single-hearted, a woman concerned with the future rather than the present, a woman for whom the coming generations rested more in the heart than in the womb. But now, he thought, she was bedazzled by the beauty of material possessions, and he doubted if her sight were as clear as once it had been. Yet go to her he must, for not more than once or twice in a lifetime was there a person to whom one could speak as to oneself.

Not at all did he relish a visit to Wivelridge, for in

these days the place was become strange and forbidding. On all sides were servants, both outdoor and indoor, and in no way did they bear the homeliness of farm laborers in round-frocks, for these underlings were as proud as overlords in their wigs and liveries. Sylvanus, in fact, did not dare to apply to the massive front doors, but went around to the back like any tradesman. Fortunately one or two of the older servants knew him by sight, and conducted him to his sister.

Marthanna went towards him with outstretched hands. "Sylvanus! I see you all too seldom these days."

He could think of no reply but lamely to say, "We are at Hastingford if you care to come."

"You know I care. But time is not my friend. I am much occupied."

"With your fashionable acquaintances."

"Oh, come, now, Sylvanus, it is not like you to be bitter."

"I am sorry. Circumstances have made me so."

"Surely not! You are above circumstances. You do not change. Sylvanus, promise me you do not change! On whom can we depend, at our ages, if not on those we knew when we were young?"

"I thought to find you different," Sylvanus confessed.

"Because I lived in France? Because I was able to realize a part of Gerrance's fortune? Oh, brother, you know me better than that? You knew Gerrance. You trusted him. Remember, I am his widow."

"Your way of life—"

"Has changed. Yes. But not by my choice. It is for the sake of Mignon. How can I deny anything to the daughter of the man I loved?"

"It is Mother," Sylvanus said, speaking with difficulty: "Dickon is her husband."

"I know. The family considers my money should defend him, rather than providing my daughter with a dowry. This is a matter of principle, almost a problem of philosophy. I cannot pretend to defend my action. I can only follow my heart."

"I would not presume to judge you," Sylvanus assured her, "and I have not come to debate the matter. The family is by no means unanimous in its opinion. It is split asunder, and this is the news I bring you."

Marthanna laughed. "That is no news. Dykes are no longer true Dykes. They are hybrids, and the right hand does not agree with the left."

"Ah, but now it is not so simple. Families can be divided against themselves. Meek defends Dickon, and quarrels with her mother."

"So? The little Meek!"

"Rosemary is bitterly vindictive, and has formed an alliance with Charity."

"Why are you telling me this? It is merely family politics."

"I tell you because Hastingford is to be split."

"What do you mean?"

"The simple truth as I say it. The builders are to come and convert Hastingford into two houses."

"What!" Marthanna stiffened, then stood up and began to pace the room. "It is nonsense you talk. It would not be permitted."

"Everyone is agreed."

"Two houses, you say? Two cottages, rather! How can such sacrilege be achieved?"

"By interior walls as barriers, and by exterior doors as outlets."

"It will ruin the house."

"Isn't that better than breaking bread in anger and argument?"

"Who will care for you and Lancelot?"

"Ah, that is strange. Meek will come with us, and Rosemary will stay with Charity and the boys."

"The poor house!" Marthanna mourned. Suddenly she straightened. "Take care our mother does not hear of this."

"I will not tell her."

"And warn others. Such news would kill her. Poor soul, she has sore trouble, such as a woman of her age should not suffer. To have her house defiled could be the end."

Sylvanus was bewildered and confused. Someone,

he reasoned, painfully, had placed the values of human benefits in a wrong order. It might be himself, but this he doubted.

"Marthanna, I love Hastingford as much as you do. Perhaps I love it more dearly. Perhaps I love it more than any other member of the family has done, for I have been an exile."

"So has Lancelot."

"Yes, but of his own choice. I absented myself because I was guilty of the sin of adultery with my brother's wife, and when I returned I was a deserter sheltering an enemy prisoner. You remember the weary years when I posed as a laborer, not daring to call myself Dyke, not daring to lay claim to my own son. What do you think those years did? They rivetted to me the love of the place with nails which can never be withdrawn. And then, those five years I spent in Brighton, undertaken for Lancelot's sake and because I still could not lift a clod of clay and say, 'This is mine!' What were they but exile? Now a part of the land is mine, and I ask no more of earth or heaven. Yet, to my mind, not the house of Hastingford nor all its land can count beside the life of one man."

"What are you trying to say?"

"That Mother will die from Dickon's death, not from the erection of a few bricks, the knocking of a hole in the wall."

"Are you blaming me?"

"Yes, I fear I am. Mignon will not die from lack of a dowry."

"There are worse things than death."

"Not that I have found."

They looked at each other, closely, sadly, and then without another word Sylvanus turned and went away.

Marthanna sighed and shook her head, but within ten minutes the visit of her brother had passed from her mind. There were so many urgent matters to consider, and if she intended to make a success of her entertaining, she must attend to a hundred matters, for these, down to the smallest details, could not safely be left to the servants.

Medford Spring was now their guest, and would remain with them until after Christmas. Marthanna had tentatively suggested this period of time, adding that she would in no way hold it against him if his commitments precluded so protracted a stay.

Medford laughed. "Gladly will I take advantage of your hospitality, madam. As for commitments, there is a saying that a lawyer is an odd sort of fruit—first rotten—then green—and then ripe. At present I have too little of work and too much of leisure, and even if it were not for your delightful company and the joy of being with Mignon, I vow I would stick like a limpet for the benefit of three good meals a day." He glanced at Marthanna's shocked face and said, quickly, "I was but jesting. I do eat, if only neck of mutton."

Marthanna could not deny he was a charming young man, gay, intelligent and sympathetic, presentable in every way, and had she not known of his circumstances she would have judged him an excellent match for her daughter.

"Are you certain you love him?" she asked Mignon.

"Yes, maman. Have I not told you so?"

"Well, I know the sentiments are not easily controlled by the young, but I could have wished you to set your heart upon another."

Mignon pouted. "You would have me marry for money."

"Not unless love went with it. You will find no stronger advocate for love than I am. It was your father's love, not his money, which made me a rich woman. I am anxious only about your dowry. Our way of living is somewhat extravagant."

"Then we must spend less," Mignon said, artlessly.

"Oh, darling, how can we? We entertain the gentry and the nobility. You hunt and shoot with them. We accept their invitations, and this we could not do unless we were willing to fulfil our obligations. To economize would mean living like farmers, like our relations."

Mignon shuddered. "That would be horrid and dreary."

"So, you see, I can but do my best. I may be able to settle two thousand pounds on you."

Mignon's eyes widened. "No more?"

"It will enable you to live in a reasonable style until Medford has established himself. Remember, the ball we are to give will be a considerable expense, but I know you look forward to it, and it is my plan to announce your engagement on that night."

Mignon brightened, and threw her arms about her mother. "Dear, sweet parent, that will be divine! Let us think of some amusing fancies and inventions. I would wish it to be an occasion renowned throughout Sussex."

This was over-ambitious, Marthanna felt, but all the same she was prepared to strain her finances to the uttermost to please Mignon and make of it a memorable evening.

The date of the ball was fixed for Thursday, the ninth of December, so that it might not impinge upon the Christmas celebrations, and almost a hundred invitations were dispatched. Marthanna engaged an orchestra of six players, and the banquet preceding the dancing was to be so lavish that Medford declared the dancers would surely weigh heavily enough to sink through the floor into the cellar and finish their quadrille on top of the barrels. From Brighton was to be sent a cart of turbot, whiting, halibut, oysters and lobsters, all carefully packed in ice. Poultry and butcher's meat presented no problem, since Sylvanus would slaughter and hang a prime bullock, Stand Fast would furnish a couple of sheep, and Deliverance had promised capons, pullets, geese and turkeys. There would be custards and pies galore, and Marthanna had earmarked so many of her choicest French wines that she feared she would be drinking water during the greater part of eighteen-twenty-six.

"You are fortunate," Medford said to Mignon, "to possess a family farm. Nothing is more wholesome than country fare. When may we take a walk to Hastingford to meet your relatives?"

Several times he asked this question, but always Mignon was hasty with excuses. "There is no time. This evening Lord Abergavenny has asked us to Eridge Castle, and tomorrow we go to Buxted Place." Or, "I am tired, and there is cub-hunting in the morning." Or, "See those clouds! Soon the rain will pour. Let us not trouble ourselves. Besides, farmers are exceedingly dull."

When she spoke of this to her mother she was almost in tears. "Medford has expressed a desire to meet the rest of the family. What can I do? I have used every pretext to put him off, but now I am at my wit's end."

"Would it not be better to take him and introduce him?"

"Oh, maman, how can you talk in that way? It would shame me if he were to meet the Dykes. Imagine! Aunt Charity would snap like a crocodile, Stand Fast would pray over us, and Lancelot and Uncle Sylvanus would look as rough and unkempt as their own laborers, if they had any, which I doubt. Did you know, maman, that once one of the new servants turned Uncle Sylvanus away, imagining him to be a vagrant?"

"No, I did not know. But I do know it is vulgar to be ashamed of friends or relations because of the clothes they wear."

"Of course! And I am not ashamed, for myself. But townspeople are different. They do not understand. Besides, that is not the worst. Would not anyone feel shame for a grandmother who marries a boy, and him a murderer into the bargain?"

"It will be necessary for Medford to learn the truth at some time or another."

"Yes, but later. After we are married." Mignon spoke confidently, hopefully believing, Marthanna thought, with pity, that marriage of itself would be the panacea for all sorrow, all shame, all inequality.

There was, however, one thing which had not occurred to Mignon, and this, Marthanna realized, she must be told. "You do understand, do you not, child, that the Dykes must be invited to our ball?"

Had she suggested including a pack of malefactors ripe for the gallows, Mignon could not have looked more horrified. "The Dykes? Here? Mixing with the Nevills and the Shelleys and the Ashburnhams? I vow, maman, you must be deranged."

"Do not speak to me in that manner!" Marthanna said, coldly. "You are an ignorant girl, and you were reared in difficult times, but I trust there is sufficient Dyke and Gildridge blood in your veins to forge a bond between you and them. They are the only family you possess, and without a family the world is a lonely place."

"You cannot care for them. You visit them seldom."

"I have never neglected your grandmother, and none could be dearer to me than your Uncle Sylvanus and Lancelot. It is true I do not go often to Hastingford, but that is because your Uncle Peregrine married an outsider who refused to become a part of the family but curdled everything with which she mixed. There was a time when I was at Hastingford as often as at Wivelridge."

Mignon was scarcely listening. "Perhaps they will not accept. I am sure Aunt Charity does not possess a ball-dress, and she considers dancing sinful."

"That is true, but I think we can rely on Sylvanus and Lancelot. There, do not make a moue! You can depend on their knowing the proper habit for a gentleman on such an occasion. They will not appear in smocks and gaiters."

Mignon was not so sure, but she had learned how far she could go in an argument with her mother, and now she had reached the point beyond which Marthanna would not budge.

As the important day approached there was so much to be done that infrequently Mignon's assistance was necessary, and so for an hour or two Medford was left to his own devices. It was on one such afternoon that he decided to walk down to the river and, having done so, there seemed no reason why he should not cross it and climb the hill towards Hastingford. A watery sun had struggled through the clouds, its first penetration for days, and from the stuggy ground which squelched beneath every footstep rose a fresh, rich smell of soil.

In one of the higher and drier meadows he came upon Sylvanus who was taking in the cattle, having given them a couple of hours' airing and the treat of a few mouthfuls of grass.

Medford greeted him formally and went past, then hesitated and turned back. "Forgive me, sir, but is this your field?"

"It is."

"Then I must make my apologies for the trespass, yet I am not an utter stranger. I am a guest at Wivelridge. My name is Medford Spring."

Sylvanus's face remained set, not relaxing into a smile. "Ah! Well, I'm Sylvanus Dyke. Marthanna is my sister."

Medford beamed with pleasure. "I am honored, sir. I have wished to meet you."

"But they took care that you didn't, huh?"

Medford frowned. "I do not understand."

"No matter. I reckon you're Mignon's beau."

"That is true."

"Why didn't she bring you herself?"

"She is much occupied preparing for the ball."

"Ay, that ball! Women get bees in their hair, and they go buzz-buzz until the poor souls are not capable of a sensible thought. Marthanna would hold that ball come wind, come weather, come earthquake, come flood."

"It is to celebrate our betrothal," Medford said, defensively, "and I feel that has the merit of some importance."

"Oh, yes! The successful conclusion of a piece of business is a matter for celebration. The world must be told."

"I should scarcely describe our betrothal as a piece of business." Medford spoke stiffly, because he was angry and did not wish to be rude.

Sylvanus knew he should have stopped there. It was none of his business really, and none of this lad's either, yet both were unavoidably involved in the moral issue. Besides, he too was angry, angry with Marthanna who by money had been seduced from her integrity.

"Maybe that emperor who fiddled while Rome burned didn't think it was his business either."

"I do not understand to what you refer, sir."

"I refer to my poor, deluded sister who considers herself compelled to buy a husband for her daughter."

"Buy a husband? Why—why, how dare you! If you speak of Mignon, I will not have her insulted. She is beautiful and talented and good. I know a score of men who would be honored should she deign to give them her hand. I am favored far more highly than I deserve to be."

"Yet you do not refuse her dowry."

"Why should I? It is the custom."

"The custom, yes, just as it is the custom for some men to hang with a broken neck from a hempen rope."

Medford stared. "This is something I do not know."

"Then I will tell you," Sylvanus said, with relish, and tell him he did, the whole sorry story from beginning to end.

That night at Wivelridge was a quiet one. There were no visitors, and Marthanna, Mignon and Medford dined alone. Afterwards, in the drawing-room, Marthanna yawned frequently, and protested, between yawns, apologetically, that she was mighty weary and must retire early.

"Who would have thought it would require so much toil, to give a ball? And there is still much to be done. The flowers I am forcing in the hothouse are still only in bud, and I wish to arrange them thickly around the platform on which the orchestra will play. I think it a pretty conceit, for the music to arise, as it were, from a bed of daffodils, crocuses and snowdrops."

"It will be a great occasion," Medford said, "and an expensive one."

"We do not speak of money," Marthanna reminded him, gently.

"Not in company, but I am almost one of the family, am I not?"

"Of course you are, my dear boy. To me you will be

a son. Had my husband lived, I might have borne a son."

"I do not yet feel like your son. I know so little of your family. Your mother lives in this house, yet she does not eat with us."

"She is old, and she is a temporary guest, not a member of the household."

"Perhaps she grieves too much to eat in public."

"Grieves?"

"Yes, for her husband who is in jail and like to hang."

Marthanna sprang to her feet. "To whom have you been talking?"

"To one of the family."

"Oh, it is too bad! I trusted you, Medford."

"Trusted me?" He stood up and faced her. "Oh, no, madam, you did not trust me. You did not trust me sufficiently to be honest with me. You accepted me as a future son-in-law, and did not warn me that I would be connected with a murderer."

Mignon burst into tears and ran to him. "Medford, take no notice of what they say! We will ignore them. We will go away. We shall live in London, and never, never return to Sussex. They are no concern of ours. Who will believe that respectable people like ourselves could be even distantly related to such rogues? My father was a gentleman, Medford. Forget the Dykes, as I will."

He took her by the shoulders and held her away from him, gazing earnestly at her. "Do you realize what you are saying, Mignon?"

"Of course I do! Medford, I love you."

"What of the dowry?"

"Why, it is not so much as I hoped, but it will suffice."

"What if I tell you I would not touch one penny of it?"

"But you must! We must. We cannot manage without it."

"It is possible to be poor."

"Possible, but terrible. Oh, Medford, you must be out

of your mind. You don't mean it. You need this money for your profession."

"Not to buy pretty gowns for you?"

"That too, but—"

"Mignon, that money is blood-money, Judas-money. You cannot hide such things from me now. The Dykes have property but nothing else. What they require is immediate gold and silver."

"Dickon is a murderer," Marthanna said, harshly.

"You cannot tell, madam, and I cannot tell. The verdict is not known before the trial. But this I will tell you, poor, inexperienced barrister as I am. Dickon in his circumstances has little chance unless he is ably defended. The money intended for Mignon's dowry must be used to help your family, otherwise both you and Mignon will have no peace. A damaged conscience does not mend like a broken leg."

Marthanna sank into a chair and covered her eyes with her hand. "What have you done to us, Medford Spring?" she asked, brokenly. "Well, it is for Mignon to decide."

"Me? Oh, no, maman! I am too young. I do not understand these things. I want only to be happy."

"Not too young," Medford said, sternly. "Not too young if you consider yourself fit to be a wife. Now, decide! Will you come away with me, tomorrow, at first light? We will go to London, get married."

Mignon shrugged herself free from his hands. "Oh, Medford, what a foolish idea! How could we? How could we miss the ball?"

"There will be no ball."

"No ball? Well, of course there will be a ball! It is all arranged. I am simply living for it. Maman, tell him not to be stupid!"

"If there is a ball," Medford said, sternly, "there will be no betrothal announcement, for I shall not be present."

Mignon began to cry in earnest. "Oh, you cruel wretch! I thought you loved me, but if you love me you cannot hurt me so. Say you are joking. Promise me it is no more than a wicked jest!"

"Decide, Mignon!"

She did not reply, but flung herself on a satin-covered chaise-longue, sobbing frenziedly.

"I think you have your answer," Marthanna told him.

He nodded. "I loved a child, imagining her to be a woman, but how spoiled a child she was—that I did not know."

He turned and went out of the room, his steps so noiseless on the thick carpet that they did not hear him go.

CHAPTER EIGHT

Let ladies of fashion the best jointures wed,
And prudently take the best bidders to bed;
Such signing and sealing's no part of our bliss,
We settle our hearts, and we seal with a kiss.
Garrick

When Stand Fast had completed the chapel to his liking, he held services there. He found no need to install pews, but only two benches, for his congregation did not consist of more than his mother, his sister and his brother, and not always those three. What he preferred was to go there on a stormy evening, with no light but that of an agitated candle, and worship God alone. He would sing hymns, and read from the Bible, and pray for those for whom he considered his prayers were required, and these included almost everyone he knew, and a number of people with whom he was not acquainted, including politicians, Roman Catholics and the more conventional prayees, such as gamblers, lechers and whores. He had even been heard to say that he was not afraid to pray for the Pope himself.

After his devotions were finished he would return to the house, entering it through one of the new doorways. Once or twice he had mistaken the door and burst in on Sylvanus, Lancelot and Meek, but this was a mistake most of the family had made. In time they would learn to which half of Hastingford they belonged. It would not be true to say that the division of the house had made them happier, for there was not one of them who did not feel to some extent deprived, but at least there were less opinions from which they could differ, less people with whom they could quarrel.

At Wivelridge conditions were more difficult because of the necessity for keeping up appearances. A heart-broken girl could not weep in front of the servants; a harassed and tormented woman could not lose her temper and raise her voice. Everything must be smooth and silken on the surface. That was one of the penalties of prosperity.

In spite of Medford's defection the ball had been held, for it was too late to cancel it. As Marthanna pointed out to Mignon, the guests did not know the reason for the celebration and would not be expecting to be informed of an engagement to marry. Mignon had only to smile, and no reputation would be sullied to the smallest degree.

But everyone had seen her with Medford, Mignon pointed out. He had been her only escort for weeks.

Marthanna laughed, not that she felt like laughing, but somehow Mignon must be reassured. "Foolish child! What is an escort more or less? They expect a beautiful young girl to have ardent suitors pleading for her company. It is best, if you would save your pride, to collect as many men as you can, and have them treading on your tail."

"I don't want many men. I don't want any except Medford."

"Darling, lift up the corners of your mouth, or you will look as sour as your cousin Rosemary. I see your eyes are again red. Were you crying in bed?"

"There is nowhere else I can cry."

Marthanna sighed. "Who will explain to me the working of the minds of the young?" She did not think that she had forgotten her own youth, but that the youth of the present generation was altogether more complicated and less innocent. "You did not want Medford without money, yet now you grieve as though you had been robbed. Remember, it was your own decision not to marry him."

Tears came into Mignon's eyes. "That merely makes it worse. I simply cannot face all those people."

"I have told you, they will suspect nothing."

"The family knows. Medford went and talked to them. He must have told them we were to marry, or they would not have confided in him."

"Then I shall ask the family not to come to the ball." And this she did. "I know you would not wish to embarrass little Mignon."

"Little Mignon is a fool," Charity said, bluntly, "like all those fashionable young ladies. They are puffed up with vanity, and fear neither God nor the Devil. Who does your daughter think she is, to turn down the offer of an honest man? Mark my words, she will end up as an old maid. But have no fear, we do not desire to toady to the so-called gentry. We are simple people and, what is more, we do not owe a half-farthing to a living soul."

Marthanna went back to Mignon. "All is well. No Dyke will be present at the ball. You can hold up your head, and you can even be thankful that I do not have to provide your dowry. Now I can pay my debts."

Mignon stared at her, dismayed. "My dowry? You would use my dowry for that?"

"It is no longer your dowry, child, and debts must be paid."

"But if Medford had accepted, what of your debts then?"

"I do not know. In all honesty I do not know. I tried not to think of it, for always I have put you first. Perhaps I would have sold Wivelridge, or your father's beautiful heirlooms. Don't ask me!"

"But Medford refused the money in order that it might be spent on Dickon's defense."

"Dickon? Why, what is Dickon to you?"

"Nothing. But you don't understand. It is because of Dickon I lost Medford. Medford renounced the dowry intending it should be used for Dickon. Anything else would be dishonest." She started to cry.

"Hush!" Marthanna hissed. "In a few moments the

servants will be in with the tea-kettle and to draw the curtains."

"I don't care. I shall stare at the fire. They will not notice."

"Oh, what an unreasonable girl you are! Do you want to leave Wivelridge and live in a pokey little house to which we dare not invite your friends?"

"No, but you must do as Medford asks."

It was impossible to discuss the matter logically, Marthanna decided. Mignon was in an emotional state and could see nothing clearly, otherwise she would realize that both their lives could not be ruined for the sake of a ne'er-do-well, a self-confessed murderer who, even with the most expensive advocate in the world, was more than likely to be convicted and executed.

Sylvanus, when he heard that Medford had departed, pleaded once more with Marthanna to help Dickon, but to no effect.

"The money is already pledged," she said, flatly, "to pay my debts. Our mode of living has rendered me well-nigh ruined."

"More fool you!" Sylvanus exclaimed, and turned away in a huff, for it seemed to him that Marthanna was a changed woman, a woman who had lost all sense of proportion from doting on her daughter.

As a last resort he visited neighboring farmers and the villagers of Mayfield, Rotherbrook, Heathfield, and Wadhurst, and even went as far abroad as Burwash, begging donations for Dickon.

"We want him to have a fair trial," he explained, "as you would want a fair trial for anyone belonging to you. But who can depend on the law?"

"What will money do?" the people asked, for they could not be expected to give money away without knowing how it would be used.

"Why, we can hire a clever barrister to defend him."

"That's only another name for a lawyer," they said, "and, in your own words, who can depend on the law?"

"But this one will be on Dickon's side, because we'll pay him to be."

They shook their heads. "Don't you believe it! You know what we calls them long trailing brambles. Lawyers, we calls 'em, 'cos once they take hold of you, you can't get free."

The schoolmaster went so far as to quote, with relish, a verse he had read.

> " 'Two lawyers, when a knotty case was o'er,
> Shook hands, and were as good friends as before.
> "Zounds!" says the losing client, "how comes yaw
> To be such good friends, who were such foes just naw?"
> "Thou fool," says one, "we lawyers though so keen
> Like shears, ne'er cut ourselves, but—what's between." ' "

Sylvanus smiled, from politeness, though he did not feel like smiling, for it wasn't everyone who refused to donate apologetically, or on account of their disbelief in the efficacy of advocates. Some were distressingly blunt, and sent Sylvanus packing with derision and abuse.

"What the pest has got into you, asking us to help a murderer escape his right deserts? There's folks around here has lost their lives doing most harmless things, like smuggling and poaching. And we'd not condemn a hungry man that stole a loaf of bread. But that Dickon is no-good truck and a foreign varmint. Where's he come from, afore he got around your mother?"

One or two of Sylvanus's acquaintances were even threatening. "You should watch your family, else the Dykes will come to a bad end. Murder and witchcraft are unaccountable nasty things. Then there's queer goings-on in your old barn. Those that have passed Hastingford at night have seen flickering lights and great black shadows. Maybe somebody is calling up *him*."

Angry and empty-handed, Sylvanus went home. "Ignorant, foul-mouthed and evil-minded, that's what they are!" he raged, to Lancelot. "After accusing Meek of being a witch, and Stand Fast of being in league with the Devil, how can they credit the innocence of Dickon?"

"Do you believe in it?"

"Yes. Don't you?"

"I think I do," Lancelot said, slowly. "He is at heart a gentle man. I feel it was an accident, or else he was unjustly provoked. Whichever it was, we must see he is given a fair chance. But how? How?"

It was a question to which they could find no answer, and as winter drew to a close, the matter became urgent. The robins mated, and the female ceased to sing. Stand Fast discontinued his devotions in the barn. Having obtained some sheep on credit he learned that at this season they were even more demanding than cows, and he must pray without folded hands, for hands were needed to help deliver the lambs. The hedgehog awoke to the first pangs of hunger, and the celandine went on display to shame the primrose with its brazen gold. Deliverance was begged, coaxed and wheedled into working twelve and fourteen hours a day, fashioning this and that, repairing one thing and another which farmers had forgotten and neglected during the dead and frozen months. Daisies and bees arrived together, and soon it would be time for the Lent Assizes.

During January and February there had been such quietude at Wivelridge that Marthanna felt it might well have been a nunnery. She would have gone on entertaining bravely had not Mignon violently opposed this. She would see no one, Mignon declared. She would not hunt, and sold her beloved and spectacular Skyscraper.

"I at least am determined to practice economy," she said, harshly, and Marthanna, feeling herself rebuked, dismissed half the servants. How, in any case, could there be sufficient work for them, with no more than three women to tend?

Now Caroline ate and sat with them, but they were mournful company, all three. Caroline was sunk in a lethargic melancholy, speaking little, and Mignon was scarcely more voluble. Sometimes Marthanna felt like crying out to them, "Take it! Take all! Take Wivelridge and with it whatever money is left, and do what you will with them!" But she was restrained by a stubborn belief in her own commonsense. Was she not the steady one of the family? Had she not advised her father and helped to save the farm? Had she not sheltered Sylvanus and Gerrance when they were fugitives? They had owed their lives to her resourcefulness and composure. Why, therefore, should she be wrong now? Would it not be foolish to gamble the meager remains of her fortune in an attempt to save a man who was probably guilty; an attempt, moreover, which, were he guilty or innocent, was more than likely to fail?

She longed for, yet dreaded, the day of the trial. What its effect would have on her mother she dared not think. Yet almost anything would be better than this static time, dreary and hopeless as it was. Change was itself a season, as necessary to humans as the transient months were to plants and animals.

Yet the change which took place was one she had not foreseen. One morning she awoke early which, being farm-bred, had been her habit, but which habit she had lost during her years in France. Now, with her troubled mind, sleep was hard to come by, and every dawn was a relief. This particular day was a gift from spring, with a southerly wind and the sun coming up in a splendor of pink clouds drawn out like the veils of an oriental princess. For half an hour or so she walked on the terrace, then went to Mignon's room to see whether she had awakened.

Mignon's room was empty, the bed smooth, with coverlet drawn up, and in the center of it the whiteness of a folded letter. It was quite brief.

"Dearest Maman,
I have gone to Medford, because I have discovered he is of more value than dresses and horses and jewelry, so with him I shall be rich. Also he will take away my guilt, for I shall persuade him to defend Dickon

without payment. Medford is not yet famous, but I
believe in him. He is clever. Please do not disown me,
as Grandmama's parents disowned her. As you told
me, without a family the world is a lonely place, and
I love you.

Yours ever,

Mignon"

Marthanna took the note to Caroline and read it to
her. When she had finished she did not say anything,
and Caroline looked askance at her. What would the
girl do, Caroline wondered, thinking, as always, of
Marthanna as a girl. Would she fall into hysterics?
Would she rant and rave? Weep like a fountain? Wear
reddened eyes as a badge of her grief? One never knew,
with these doting mothers.

But to her surprise Marthanna did none of those
things. She was smiling, and she had the look of a woman from whom a great burden had fallen. Before three
hours were past she was on her way to Hastingford to
spread her news, which she did in a blithe manner,
as though a piece of good fortune had befallen her.

Meek said, "I am sorry, Aunt Marthanna. It was
cruel of Mignon, for you have been a worthy mother."

Marthanna brushed this aside. "No, no! I do not
blame her. I am proud of her. The girl has shown spirit
and, more, she has shown she is not mercenary. Naturally I shall miss her, but—"

The "but" hung in the air, finishing the sentence
Marthanna could not complete, for it entailed too much
and yet too little. Some things could not be said, even
to near kin, things like love of a place being as obses-
sive as love of a daughter. The prospect of having to
sell Wivelridge in order to provide a dowry for Mignon
had been a nightmare from which she had awakened
to find her world still around her, solid and unspoilt.
So relieved was she that she could have wept, not for
the loss of Mignon but for the recovery of her birthplace, and on her way to the farmhouse she had
stopped in the edge of a field where the corn showed
small and green, and had sunk on to her knees and

taken up a handful of soil, running it through her fingers as if it had been gold-dust.

Lancelot suggested, "Now you will have money to spare for Dickon, will you not?"

Marthanna turned on him, angry because she was alarmed, like an animal scenting danger when it had imagined itself safe. "Money? I have no money. I have only debts. Would you see me in Newgate?"

"It is no use," Sylvanus said, later. "Either she cannot or she will not."

Lancelot told himself it was none of his business. He told himself this while he worked, and while he ate and took what little leisure was available. Dickon was his grandmother's husband, her creature, plaything of her whim. He was no Dyke, to merit the loyalty and sacrifice of the family. It was a pity, Lancelot thought, that Dykes showed so poor a judgement in marriage, that they should include a Frenchman, a Puritan, a vagrant and—himself having made no wiser a choice—an heiress. Yet his reasoning brought him no comfort. To label a person this or that did not render him or her the less a human being, and a vagrant could die as painfully and undeservedly as could a king.

Once his mind was made up he did not hesitate. To his father he disclosed his intention, and then prepared to leave.

The evening before the start of his journey he helped Sylvanus deliver a cow of a stillborn calf, and was in the cowhouse making her comfortable when he became aware that someone had walked in.

"Who is it?" he asked, for it was dusk and little light filtered through the small windows.

"Rosemary," a voice replied.

He was surprised. Since his return she had exchanged few words with him, and he realized she still bore him ill will for having jilted and deserted her. For this he did not blame her. He was the blameworthy one, and if she could not find it possible to forgive him—why, she acted only as many another woman would have done. Sometimes, looking at her tight lips and cold eyes, he would congratulate himself on

what he had escaped, and then would remember guilti-
ly that he had helped to paint that bitterness on her
face.

"Are you seeking my father?" he asked.

"No. I met him outside. He told me you are leaving
tomorrow."

"That is true."

"So you could not stay away from her. So you must
return like a whipped dog, tail between your legs. Oh,
how I despise you, Lancelot Dyke!"

"You have a right to do that. I treated you badly."

"Save your humility! It does not ring true. Yes, you
treated me shamefully, and made of me a laughing-
stock, but that was not the worst. The worst was to
come back here after she had tired of you, to creep
out from between her legs and show yourself in these
parts again."

"This is my home."

"It should not be. You waived all claim to it when
you went off with that harlot."

"She was no harlot. She was a virgin."

"What! A virgin? I guarantee she deceived you.
How many are virgins among those modish wenches?"

"I do not know. I married only one of them."

"And now she wants you back. She crooks her
finger and you crawl to her."

"She does not know I am going."

For a moment Rosemary was silent, as though his
words had shaken the patterned trail of her anger.
"So? It is you, then, who cannot keep away. Oh, what
a scent these women must exude, who can fetch a
man from two or three hundred miles away! Well, do
not return again, I pray you. Go! Leave us in peace!"

"I fear that is what I must do," Lancelot said, sadly.
He walked over to the window, where the dying light
fell upon him. "This time I cannot wanton with her. I
must say goodbye to Hastingford."

Rosemary went towards him. "You do not have the
look of an eager lover." She spoke jeeringly, but beneath her harsh tones was a deep concern.

"I do not go as an eager lover. Surely, Rosemary, you know me better than that! Between us, between Petronella and me, was a searing flame. It burnt us. It could not be denied. There are some passions which burn in such a way, and God help those in whom the fire is kindled! We are taught that Hell, not Heaven, is the place of fire, and I believe it."

"I envy the victims of that fire, not pity them."

"You would feel pity if you had known it. Those flames die down and leave a bed of ashes."

"As yours did?"

"Yes."

"And hers?"

"I do not know, but I think the fire touched only her body. With me it scorched my soul."

"Then do not go back! Stay, Lancelot! Please, I beg of you, stay! Oh, do not look alarmed! I will ask nothing from you. All that is over, and with you I believe it never really began. But to have you here, to see you sometimes, casually, walking across the yard or in the fields, that brings something to life in me. Even to walk about the house, knowing you are working on the farm causes me to break into song. It is your coming and going which kills me. Please, Lancelot! You need not think of me. Forget I am here. Ignore me! But stay at Hastingford, which you love, and I'll be content loving the land, because you love it."

"You do not understand," he said, gently. "I go back as a supplicant, to ask her for the money she can so easily spare. It is to save Dickon."

"Dickon!" she exclaimed, dismayed. "You would do this for him?"

"Yes, wouldn't you?"

"No, I would not. But since that is your reason, get the money and return."

"That is impossible. Am I to treat my wife as a purse into which I can dip? Besides, she would not agree. For the sake of her pride she will demand that I remain with her. For Dickon's life I sell my freedom. That is fair, is it not?"

She was silent again, this time for so long that it seemed she had no more to say, and he made to leave the cowhouse. But Rosemary blocked his way.

"Is this the truth? Do you swear it is the truth? If Dickon did not need your help, would you go?"

"Upon my soul!" he laughed. "For what do you take me? I came home, didn't I? And home I reckoned to stay."

"Then swear you will stay, Lancelot! Swear by everything that is holy! Swear by God and Our Savior and the Blessed Virgin and the Holy Ghost!"

"I will, if I must, but I assure you my word is enough."

"Then I can free Dickon, by the evidence I can give at his trial."

"You?"

"Oh, yes! I was not the pale, cool, innocent maid you thought me. I was raped by Abel Polsted, and Dickon had no intention of killing him, but fought him to protect me. Dickon has been my lover these many years. You see? I am not unwanted. Men have lusted after me."

"You will say this in Court? You promise?"

"Yes, yes!" she agreed, impatiently. "But I shall not do it for Dickon. I shall do it for you. Now let me see the contempt in your eyes! Oh, it is too dark."

"There is no contempt in my eyes."

"What is there, then? Not love. It is pity?"

"It is faith in your courage, no more."

"Courage? No courage will be needed. I shall rejoice in my confession. They can no longer call me withered old maid, for men have entered me." Her voice rose to a shout of triumph, then sank almost to a whisper. "But let me see you sometimes, Lancelot. Let me hear your voice."

CHAPTER NINE

Life is but thought: so think I will
That Youth and I are house-mates still.
Samuel Taylor Coleridge

On a spring morning Caroline sat in the window of her parlor. She was alone, as she wanted to be, though Marthanna had made a great to-do about leaving her. It seemed that at eighty-three one was pushed back willy-nilly into childhood.

"If you should fall, Mother, and not be able to raise yourself." "If a spark from the fire should light upon the rug." "If you should be taken ill."

What they meant, Caroline thought, practically, was that she might die there, by herself. Yet how could death find her more mercifully than sitting in her armchair looking across the valley towards Hastingford? Death was a lonely business, anyway, not like birth, which was a partnership.

All the same, she did not want to die just now. She was back in Sweetwillow Shaw, and in a few hours Dickon would be with her. Soon, when she could accumulate sufficient energy, she would rise from her chair and go to the kitchen and prepare a meal for him, but just a little longer she wanted to sit and savor the particular taste of being home and free from gnawing anxiety.

It was not right, she argued, angrily and silently, that misfortune should fall on the old. They should be released from it, as a prisoner is at last released from his cell. Those long weeks at Wivelridge would have been unbearable, had she not known from experience that everything which must be borne was bearable. Hope for Dickon's life had flickered and almost gone out, until the day Lancelot had come and told her that Rosemary would at the trial give evidence which would almost certainly exonerate Dickon. And so it had been. Dear Lancelot! He was of the very essence of the best of the Gildridges and Dykes. If only he had a son!

In the weeds of the neglected garden two male blackbirds were quarrelling over a wisp of straw, which to them would be a part of the foundations or the walls or the decorations of their home. Men and birds, they were all alike. They saw themselves as travellers, but when they fought and died, it was for some part of the earth to which they laid claim—a cottage or a castle or a kingdom. Earth was the cloak of mortals, the earth of a farm or the earth of a grave.

Tomorrow she would set Dickon digging, else there would be no tender peas to melt in their mouths, no marigolds or sunflowers to imitate ambitiously the blazing disc in the sky and entertain kindly the fragile eye which could not endure the straight sight of the sun. In the hedgerows there would be violets, more precious than primroses because more sparse. Why had she not gone out to pluck them every spring, she wondered, idly. Perhaps she would have done, had she known the time would come when her back would be too stiff to stoop, her knees too stiff to bend, and her eyes not sharp enough to espy the shy amethyst hiding behind every available leaf and blade of grass. But she had always been too busy, and she had never really believed she would grow old. Who did? Old age was for others, not for oneself. She was not even sure that she believed it now. This person in the chair might be Caroline Dyke, but she was only a part of Caroline Dyke. There were other Caroline Dykes, hundreds of them, making love, giving birth, racing down the meadows with the wind in their hair.

In a few days it would be Easter, the day when the sun danced for love of the Son of God. It seemed to be dancing now as, still low enough in the season to strike slantwise, it caught the glass of the upper windows of Hastingford. Oh, what a noble house that was! From here she could take pleasure in its proportions, as she could not do when she had lived there. Never would she cease to congratulate herself on having so wisely chosen a home. For generations, for centuries, it would endure, unchanged, unspoilt. She did not know it had been divided, for they had been careful not to tell her, and the two doors were on the other side, facing the road, looking away from Sweetwillow Shaw.

So engrossed was she with the day and the sight of the scene she loved that her intention to make a meal for Dickon faded right out of her mind. She watched, and meditated, and perhaps dozed a little, and the hours went by.

She was only roused when a figure passed the window and Dickon opend the door. Startled, overwhelmed, astonished with happiness, she struggled to her feet and called a name. What name it was she did not know. It could have been Will or Hal or Lancelot, but it did not matter, for to her at that moment Dickon was all of these, was all she asked from life.

For years a bestselling author in England, ... readership today is worldwide. Now one of the ... and best-loved writers of romantic fiction, her spellbinding novels are memorable stories of love, tragedy and courage.

☐	A GRAND MAN	2233	$1.50
☐	THE INVISIBLE CORD	2350	$1.75
☐	THE LORD AND MARY ANN	2432	$1.50
☐	THE MALLON LOT	6323	$1.50
☐	THE DWELLING PLACE	7246	$1.25
☐	FEATHERS IN THE FIRE	7289	$1.25
☐	OUR KATE	7599	$1.25
☐	THE MALLEN STREAK	7806	$1.50
☐	THE GLASS VIRGIN	7962	$1.25
☐	PURE AS THE LILY	8079	$1.25
☐	THE FIFTEEN STREETS	8174	$1.25
☐	THE MALLEN GIRL	8406	$1.50
☐	KATE HANNIGAN	8646	$1.25
☐	FENWICK HOUSES	8656	$1.25
☐	KATIE MULHOLLAND	10078	$1.50

Buy them at your local bookstore or use this handy coupon for ordering:

...ok Catalog

It lists over a thousand money-saving bestsellers originally priced from $3.75 to $15.00 —bestsellers that are yours now for as little as 60¢ to $2.95!

The catalog gives you a great opportunity to build your own private library at huge savings!

So don't delay any longer—send us your name and address and 25¢ (to help defray postage and handling costs).